Reviewers say . . .

This novel is clearly written with a keen understanding of the culture of the 19th century Pennsylvania German farmers and residents, and the Civil War buff will appreciate the attention to historical detail. For those readers who enjoy historical fiction, *The Unfinished Work* has broad appeal for both men and women, and it has an excellent storyline that holds the reader's attention.
> Scott L. Mingus, Sr., Civil War historian and author

For one who has studied this campaign and is as familiar with the "ground" as I am, I found myself envisioning the places and events as they unfolded in Meredith's fabulously-written narrative. I loved this book and the story!
> J.D. Petruzzi, Civil War historian and author

My roots and life are in Hanover and I thoroughly enjoyed the book. It addresses the slavery issue in a way that William Faulkner and Thomas Wolfe would have admired. This book is not a dime novel: it's literature and history.
> Henry McLin, Borough Councilman, Hanover, PA

I loved the book. It isn't often that I get to say that. I'm glad that you didn't sugarcoat the ending or other parts of the novel. I think it's necessary to describe the toll of war on society. Yet the love story gives the novel a lighter tone.
> Jess Krout, *The Evening Sun*, Hanover, PA

Frank has a firm grasp of the events surrounding Hanover, Hunterstown, and the East Cavalry Field fight at Gettysburg. But what struck me most was the development of the fictional characters. Buy this book, you will surely be as enthralled as I was.
> Michael Noirot, BattlefieldPortraits.com, St. Louis MO

By making his fictional characters interact with the likes of JEB Stuart and George Custer, the author gives a history lesson in an effortless and entertaining way.
> Jessica James, Civil War author, Gettysburg, PA

There is a fine line to be walked when blending historical facts and storytelling. Frank Meredith is to be congratulated on both counts. His heart-warming account of the characters, along with the telling of a 'little known' cavalry clash in Hunterstown that was critical to the outcome of the Gettysburg Campaign, is truly amazing. Excellent subject matter for a movie! Future generations will thank you. Hunterstown does!
> Laurie Harding, President, Hunterstown Historical Society

The Unfinished Work

For Nancy —
You are truly an angel and
a blessing!

 *Eph 3:14-21*

Frank Meredith

EMERALD
BOOK CO.

Published by Emerald Book Company
Austin, TX
www.emeraldbookcompany.com

Distributed by Emerald Book Company

For ordering information or special discounts for bulk purchases, please contact Emerald Book Company at PO Box 91869, Austin, TX 78709, 512.891.6100.

Design and composition by Frank Meredith
Cover design by Greenleaf Book Group LLC
Edited by Dianne E. Dusman

Publisher's Cataloging-In-Publication Data
(Prepared by The Donohue Group, Inc.)

Meredith, Frank.
   The unfinished work / Frank Meredith. -- 2nd ed.

      p. : ill., maps ; cm.

   Includes bibliographical references.
   ISBN: 978-1-934572-45-0

1. United States--History--Civil War, 1861-1865--Fiction. 2. Gettysburg, Battle of, Gettysburg, Pa., 1863--Fiction. 3. Hanover, Battle of, Hanover, York County, Pa., 1863--Fiction. 4. Historical fiction. I. Title.

PS3613.E74 U54 2010
813.6   2010922786

Part of the Tree Neutral™ program, which offsets the number of trees consumed in the production and printing of this book by taking proactive steps, such as planting trees in direct proportion to the number of trees used: www.treeneutral.com

TreeNeutral

First edition published 2009
Savannah Books, Schoharie, NY

Printed in the United States of America on acid-free paper

10 11 12 13 14   10 9 8 7 6 5 4 3 2 1

Second Edition

*For the One who inspires my creativity
and nourishes my soul*

Foreword

In one sense, this book has been more than forty years in the making. As a nine-year-old boy, I witnessed the 100th Anniversary reenactment of the Battle of Hanover in June of 1963. Swarms of cavalrymen charged through Center Square, their pistols and carbines sounding like cannon fire in the confined space. Clouds of sulfurous smoke billowed around the "dead" and "wounded" men littering the streets. Years later I learned the full import of this first battle on Union soil.

Great care was taken to faithfully portray these historical events. Since my two fictional families interact with historical people, I have included an appendix to clarify what is fact and what is fiction in this account. You will also find some additional historical notes that did not make it into the narrative. (I recommend reading the appendix last.)

Through all my years of education, I had been taught that slave-abusing Southerners were the "bad guys," while Northerners were heroes for wanting to free the Negroes and maintain the Union. No one made clear to us that "sovereign states" believed they had *legally* seceded. Or that only 6% of Southerners even owned slaves. Nearly half of all white Southern men served in the Confederate Army at some point during the war, yet two-thirds of them never owned slaves (or even lived with someone who did). So why did they risk their lives? And were Northerners as pure in motive as depicted in our history books? Did they assist the emancipated slaves and welcome them into their communities following the war? Many of the events in this book deal with those questions.

For a title, I looked first to Abraham Lincoln's "Gettysburg Address." Many phrases from this great speech have become well known, yet as familiar as I was with these words, I found the phrase "the unfinished work" particularly striking. Perhaps the greatest "what if" in American history is this: how would life in America have been different if the Founding Fathers had outlawed slavery at the start?

While researching this book, I was very surprised to learn of the great cavalry battle that took place outside Gettysburg on July 3, 1863, on what has become known as East Cavalry Field. I had driven past that location numerous times over the years and, like millions of visitors to the Gettysburg Battlefield, I had never heard of this critical event. Overshadowed in history by the simultaneous Pickett's Charge, this heroic story deserves to be well known. I hope this book will not only help with that effort, but also serve as a lasting tribute to the men and women who have sacrificed so much for freedom and equality: humankind's unfinished work.

Frank Meredith, Schoharie, NY
May 6, 2009

Maps

{JH} – Maps by John Heiser used by permission of Eric J. Wittenberg and
       J. David Petruzzi

{LC} – Library of Congress, Geography and Maps Division

{SS} – Courtesy of Steven Stanley, cartographer

{YH} – From the collection of the York County Heritage Trust of York, PA
Full credits appear on page 323.

Photographs and Illustrations

{AC} – Author's personal collection

{AP} – With the artist's permission

{GD} – Courtesy of GettysburgDaily.com

{HW} – Harper's Weekly in author's personal collection

{LC} – Library of Congress, Prints and Photographs Division

{PH} – A Photographic History of the Civil War, Volume 4

{PS} – Courtesy of Barbara Huston, Poist Studio, Hanover, PA

{SL} – Smithsonian Libraries

Full credits appear on pages 322-23.

"The historian will tell you what happened. The novelist will tell you what it felt like."

E.L. Doctorow

Time, June 26, 2006

Part One: Days of Decision

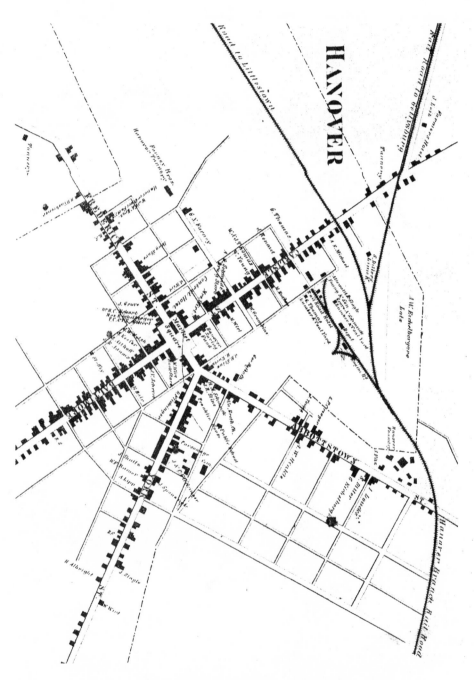

Hanover, Pennsylvania, 1860 – Population 1,632

Market Shed and Central Hotel (1863)

One of the earliest photographs in Hanover (1845)

Saturday, June 27, 1863

-1-

Was it the sizzle or the smell that woke him? Savoring the aroma of hickory-smoked bacon, Jake Becker sat up and stretched. He could tell by the dull light filtering through the curtains that they were in for another cloudy day, but at least the rain had finally stopped. From down in the kitchen came the sound of a spatula scraping against a skillet. He figured that must be Myrtle, making flapjacks with the blueberries they'd picked yesterday. His stomach rumbled.

From the bottom of the stairs Pa's voice boomed, "Your sister says breakfast is almost ready!"

Jake flung back the light quilt and swung his feet onto the floor. He went to the dresser and exchanged his nightshirt for a work shirt, then pulled on his trousers, socks, and boots. As he turned his attention to making up the bed, his blue eyes fixed on the swirling browns and oranges and yellows on the cover of the book lying next to his crumpled pillow. Gilt letters on the book's leather binding read, *Life at the South*, *W.L.G. Smith, 1852*. Jake picked up the tome and thumbed to the title page: Life at the South. 'Uncle Tom's Cabin' As It Is. Real 'Life Of The Lowly.'

"If only more folks read the whole truth of it, maybe we never would've had this awful war," Jake muttered. Sighing, he slid the book back into its place on the shelf mounted above the headboard, right between Oliver Wendell Holmes' *The Autocrat of the Breakfast Table* and the latest Beadle's dime novel, *No. 53, Hates and Loves*.

Jake adjusted the mattress atop the ropes, fluffed the pillow, and smoothed the quilt, careful to align the blue and white diamond pattern as his mother had taught him. He stepped back to survey his work.

Satisfied with a job well done, Jake dashed down the stairs, went out to the privy, hurried to the rain barrel at the corner of the house to wash his hands and face, ran wet fingers through his wavy brown hair, and then joined his father and sister, seated at either end of the kitchen table.

A platter of flapjacks, plump with blueberries, took pride of place in the middle of the table. On the other platter lay a dozen strips of bacon and eight eggs, sunny-side up. Myrtle reached for the breadbasket and pulled back the red-and-white checkered cloth, revealing a loaf of marbled rye bread. "I got this special for you at market yesterday, Jake."

"My favorite! Thanks, Sis!" But as their eyes met, Jake's grin turned to a frown. Was that sadness on Myrtle's face?

She put her hand over Jake's. "Sam talked to some militiamen who rode through town at daybreak. They said the Confederates have taken Gettysburg without a fight and are probably on their way east! Papa and Sam agreed that it would be best if I leave today for Uncle Benjamin's."

Jake's heart sank. Myrtle had become his favorite sister. Eight years earlier, when she was twelve and he was ten, their younger sister Hope had died of consumption, followed by their mother a fortnight later. Their elder siblings, Grace and Faith, had already married and left home; so, bonded by grief, Myrtle and Jake set aside their childish rivalries and became best friends.

Myrtle brushed away a tear and cleared her throat. "Lancaster should be safe from the Rebels, especially if the bridge is destroyed before they get there." She leaned forward, her voice resolute. "I know Sam will get me to safety in time."

Samuel Forney was a good man. He'd been Jake's cohort in mischief in their youth, but they hadn't spent much time together in the years following grammar school. Now Sam worked up the road on his family's farm, while Jake worked with Pa in his carriage and wagon business. Sam would soon become Jake's brother-in-law. Myrtle had often joked, "I must marry before my twenty-first birthday. I don't want to be called an old maid!" Jake winced. The wedding date was less than three months away. Must she now leave even sooner?

Pa shuffled his chair closer to the table, and said grimly, "There is talk the Rebels are advancing on York. We need to get your sister to safety before the bridge over the Susquehanna is put to the torch."

Anger welled up within Jake, and not only because the war was about to separate him from his beloved sister. The use of the word "Rebels" irritated him. He had seen the Union Army in action during the opening battle of the war two years ago, when he and his father delivered a new carriage and hay wagon to the Biglers in Manassas, Virginia. Thankfully, the Northern invaders had been repulsed and sent back to Washington City in full rout, but not before they had profaned the beautiful Virginia farmlands with thousands of dead and wounded men. Mr. Bigler had prevailed upon Jake's father to take the new carriage back to Hanover, along with Mrs. Bigler and their two teen-aged daughters, so that the women might wait out the conflict with their Pennsylvania relatives.

On the way north, Jake had sometimes ridden in the back of the carriage next to Eliza, the elder of the two daughters. Eliza's brown eyes seemed to shimmer in the summer sunlight. As the carriage made its way over the rutted roads, Jake's heart raced at the sight of her radiant smile and the way their bodies jostled together. Long before they reached the Mason-Dixon Line, he was thoroughly smitten . . .

"Let us pray." Pa's voice sounded tight.

Hoping it would not be for the last time, the three joined hands. Lost in private thoughts and fears, they ate the repast in silence.

2

Jake brought Myrtle's valise down to the parlor, then went to the kitchen to help her finish the dishes. "I'll wash, Sis."

She smiled and handed him the dishrag.

He fished in the basin for a cup. Taking careful aim, he plunged the cloth to the bottom of the glass and sent a spout of soapy water in Myrtle's direction. As intended, it only splashed her bare forearm. She squealed and jumped back a step.

"I figured I owed you one more shot," Jake said with a smirk.

She rolled the damp towel with a flourish and thwacked him soundly on the rump. "Like Papa says, 'Don't start what you can't finish!'" Her eyes gleamed like a cat stalking a bird.

Jake scooped some water into the cup and countered with another of their father's axioms. "But did you 'count the cost' before you acted?" Feinting and laughing, the adversaries circled the kitchen,

Pa called from the front hallway, "Are you ready, Myrtle? Grace and the girls are here." His voice faded as he went outside to greet his daughter and granddaughters.

Myrtle's face clouded and her mouth formed a tiny "o." A sob racked her slender frame.

Jake slipped the towel from her hands, put it on the table with the cup, and gave her a hug. "Everything will turn out all right, Sissy," he said softly. She seemed to relax at the sound of his childhood name for her. "You'll have a nice visit and then be home in no time. Why, I bet with all those women around it'll take weeks before you even miss us men folk." He stepped back and studied her expression. Her bittersweet smile awakened so many sad memories. He hadn't felt such a crush of impending loss since Mama and Hope fell ill.

Myrtle took a deep breath and sighed, then swiped at a strand of hair curling around her nose. Jake reached over and tucked the wayward tress behind her ear.

"Thanks, Jakie."

A little girl's voice screeched from the front hallway. "Where's Aunt Myrtle?"

Three little girls rushed into the kitchen, shouting, "Where's Myrtle the turtle! Myrtle the turtle!" Jake nimbly dodged the sudden onslaught of outstretched arms and flopping pigtails.

"Turtle, am I? Well, Susie, is it a turtle or a bunny that moves this quick?" Myrtle's wiggling fingers dashed from one niece's armpit to another's belly to another's side until one by one, each giggling girl managed to choke out in surrender: "Myrtle, Queen of the Bunnies!"

Pa appeared in the doorway, his face nearly as gray as his temples. "Your valise is in the wagon, Myrtle. Sam is outside waiting for you. I put our five hens in the cage with Grace's, since chickens won't last long here if an army comes through. I suppose Jake and I will have the rooster for Sunday dinner." He wiped a tear from the corner of his eye. "It's time to go. You need to meet up with Faith in Spring Forge."

"One more minute, Papa, I'm not done with the dishes yet." Myrtle disengaged herself from the rambunctious girls and picked up the towel.

Grace called over her father's shoulder. "Come, girls. Let's wait outside while Aunt Myrtle says goodbye to Papaw and Uncle Jake."

Seeming to sense the adults' anxiety, the girls obeyed without a fuss. The clatter of little shoes receded down the hallway.

A few moments later, Jake handed the last fork to Myrtle. She dried it, slid it into the drawer with the others, and hung the towel on the hook next to the window. She turned to face her father and brother.

"All finished." Her smile looked brave, but then the corners of her mouth curled downward.

Pa gave her a long hug and kissed her tenderly on the forehead. "I love you, baby girl. God bless you, precious lamb."

"I love you, Papa."

Jake joined them in a lingering hug and, with that, the trio headed for the door.

-3-

It was nearly 7:30 AM by the time Jake and his father walked the hundred yards down Frederick Street to the building site, where three men were already hard at work digging the foundation for the new Methodist Church. Delayed by rain the last several days, the men hoped to make up some of the lost time before tending to their regular vocations.

Harvey Stremmel, a gnarled, sun-darkened farmer, looked up from the knee-deep trench. "I'm sorry, David, did the sound of our shovels awaken you?"

The blacksmith, Peter Frank, added, "Summer solstice was a week ago, so the days are getting shorter now, you know."

Klaus Pfeiffer huffed, "Ya, alt man vinter ist on his vay. Ve better yetzt hurry before dee shnow comes."

David gave a dismissive wave. "We thought you'd be finished by now, but little wonder you're not, what with all the gabbing going on." He turned to Jake and lowered his tone as if he didn't want the others to overhear. "I guess these squawky old hens will need our help if this foundation is ever to get finished."

As if taking offense, Peter flung his hat to the ground and lunged from the trench, lumbering like an escaped bull. "Care to call me a hen to my—"

The banter died beneath the rumble and creak of a heavily laden oxcart approaching from the west. Atop the cargo sat an upside-down rocking chair, framing the vehicle's driver: a haggard-looking woman of indeterminate age. She squinted at the men from beneath her wide-brimmed hat. Shadows clung to the lines etched in her face. As the cart drew nearer, one hand slipped beneath the shawl covering her lap. Her eyes grew wary. Her scowl was enough to curdle milk at ten paces.

Jake saw the tip of a pistol barrel poking from underneath the shawl. Hastening to ease the apparent refugee's fears, he doffed his hat and bowed with a flourish. "Good morning, ma'am. Have you any news from Littlestown or Gettysburg?"

Her voice croaked with the dust of too many miles on the road. "Johnny Reb is on his way. I seen a flock of 'em stealing horses da udder side of Littlestown yedderday night. This danged world's all upside down, so you fellers better save your fighting for da Rebs." As the cart passed, she turned and yelled over her shoulder, "And best hope dat ain't your own graves you're digging." Her cackle sent a shiver up Jake's spine.

The ox never broke stride as the cart groaned and rattled its way toward the center of town a few blocks away. A scrawny hound poked its head over the back of the cart and loosed a melancholy howl. Jake wanted to throw the poor beast a bit of his lunch, but the cart bounced over some ruts in the crossroad and the dog retreated from view.

"We best get to work," Pa said tersely.

Jake recognized his father's tone: *While we still can.*

Jake welcomed the labor. Working up a good sweat often helped him put his thoughts in order, and he had a lot to think about today.

Over the next few hours, Jake's mind drifted from fond memories of times spent with Myrtle to dreams of his future with Eliza Bigler. But all too soon he found himself wrestling with the problems brought on by the war. He wondered about the accusation the woman on the oxcart had made about Rebels stealing horses. He didn't think Confederate troops stole from or abused their neighbors when the fighting was in Virginia, but would they steal from their enemies? And would Union men defile their own countryside now that the war had moved north? Just how safe was any civilian? The rumor mill ground out many stories of thievery and worse: unspeakable outrages against women and girls. Even if only a few of the tales were true, what about the atrocities Union soldiers had committed in Virginia and points south these past two years? Did that justify retaliation? Were such acts part and parcel of war? How many stories were merely exaggerations or outright lies?

Jake remembered the shocking full-page illustration in *Harper's Weekly* the month after the battle at Manassas. The caption had read, "The Rebels bayoneting our wounded on the Battlefield at Bull Run." That was a damnable lie! He had been there! He and his father had helped move the horribly maimed men from both armies and then helped bury the dead. There were no reports or evidence of atrocities by either side. Jake clenched his jaw. As a result of that magazine drawing, how many young men had gone off to war thinking to rid the earth of monsters that would do such things? What if that picture gave a false sense of justification to Union soldiers bent on revenge, soldiers who really did act as depicted in the magazine and thus killed their prisoners? Would not *Harper's Weekly* bear some measure of responsibility for the resultant deaths?

Rebels Bayoneting Our Wounded on the Battlefield at Bull Run

Standing to stretch his aching back, Jake gazed at the steely gray sky. He thanked God for the mercy of an unseasonably cool and cloudy day on which to dig and prayed there would be no rain to torment Myrtle and the rest of their kin as they traveled.

Images of his sisters fleeing before a pursuing army flashed through Jake's mind. Would they make it across the Susquehanna before the bridge was destroyed, or would they become trapped between the river and a horde of men driven by hate and lust?

He remembered the soldiers' faces he had seen in Manassas that hot summer day two years ago, the ones frozen in death. Some grimaced in agony, or was it fury? Others looked surprised, as if shocked the Reaper had come for them so soon. Then there was the Smiling Man: the one sprawled as if for a mid-day nap. His face had looked so relaxed, so peaceful, so oblivious to the carnage and the stench. His smile looked as if he dreamt of home and family. The Smiling Man haunted Jake's dreams. That sleeping face . . . so innocent . . . so free of malevolence . . . yet so very dead. Never again to kiss his wife . . . or play with his children . . . or laugh with his friends.

How many tens of thousands of men had died in the two years since? What was worth so high a price?

The shovel caught on a tree root thicker than his thumb. Jake gritted his teeth, put his foot on the top edge of the shovel's blade, and drove the tool into the root with all his might, consciously venting his fury. The root gave way with a snap.

"Dat tree ist alretty dead, young man," Klaus said.

Jerked back to the present by Klaus' comment, Jake shook off his angry thoughts.

Harvey leaned on his shovel. "Hey Peter, I thought I told you to make sure you pulled up all the roots when you took out that stump."

The smith grunted and stabbed with his shovel at a tangle of vine-like roots hindering his progress. "These must be from the stump David and Jake pulled."

Jake grinned. "Yep, we left the nastiest roots just for you."

Out of the corner of his eye, he noticed some movement across the street, followed by the uniquely musical sound of young women in conversation. Someone spoke of going to Schmidt's apothecary. Jake snapped to attention as he recognized the loudest voice. Eliza!

Eliza Bigler, her younger sister Kat, and their older cousin Lydia strolled arm-in-arm up the street. He knew they had planned to be at the Lutheran Church this morning, but now they appeared to be taking a circuitous route toward the Center Square. Jake smiled. He felt certain Eliza had brought them out of their way so she could see him. He caught her eye and she treated him to a dazzling smile. As the girls turned toward the center of town, Eliza glanced over her shoulder for one last look, then gave a little wave before turning back around.

Peter tapped Jake's shoulder and whispered loudly, "What do you see, boy? Did you catch a scent? Good dog! Go get 'em, boy. Fetch 'em back here. That's a good dog!"

Harvey picked up on the cue. "If that love-sick pup can dig as well as he can hunt, we'll be done by nightfall!"

Jake returned to work with a flurry of digging.

"He looks like a starving dog in search of his last bone," Peter said.

Klaus nudged Pa. "Dat tall girl vas Gufernor Bigler's niece, no?"

"Senator Bigler," Pa corrected, though both were former offices now.

Jake heard Harvey mutter, "Copperhead," but the word died when Jake turned to face the source of the epithet. Harvey went back to work, his shovel clanging against another root.

Peter scratched his chin. "You know, I have a pickaxe back at my shop that would be perfect for severing those roots . . ." His voice trailed off as if lost in thought, then he put on a tone of mock sincerity. "Maybe someone should go and get it."

Klaus pulled a kerchief from his pocket and, as if exhausted, made a show of wiping his brow. "I vill go. Yust tell me vere you keep it."

"No, I'll go," Harvey and David said at the same time.

Peter scratched his head. "Well, if you're going to argue about it, I guess Jake will have to go."

Jake shrugged as if ambivalent about the idea, but he could barely contain his excitement. Might he manage to see Eliza while he ran the errand? He looked across the fields that filled the angle between the church lot and southbound Baltimore Street, where Peter Frank's smithy stood a few blocks from the Square. The wheat and hay were already waist-high. Not only that, but all the rain during the past week was sure to have made the fields a morass. He would have to go through the center of town to get to the blacksmith shop, and Schmidt's apothecary, Eliza's destination, anchored one corner of the Square. Jake tried to sound dejected. "All right, I guess I'll go." He stepped out of the trench, laid his shovel on the ground, and started on his way.

Peter called, "Would you like to know where the pickaxe is, or are you going to spend the rest of the morning looking?"

Harvey chuckled. "I bet he'd like to spend the rest of the morning looking, but it wouldn't be at some old pickaxe."

"Better he looks now before she turns into an old battleaxe, right?" Peter added.

Jake cocked his head and frowned. He couldn't imagine an old, ugly Eliza.

"You'll find the axe hanging on the wall to the left of the bellows," Peter said.

Jake waved his thanks and headed for town. In the distance, he spotted Eliza and her escorts just reaching the Square. He hurried after them, calculating how much time he might take away from his mission in order to stop by the apothecary.

Dogging him down the street was the specter of Eliza as an old woman—looking very much like the crone on the oxcart.

-4-

The clock on the tower of St. Matthew's Church chimed half past the hour of ten as Eliza, Kat, and Lydia drew even with the Central Hotel. Now that the entire Square was in view, Eliza noticed a cluster of anxious-looking men staring north out Carlisle Street. Several women huddled quietly over by Carver's store. On the opposite side of the Square, Broadway stood empty. Eliza looked south, down the eerily vacant Baltimore Street. Her heart quickened.

"Girls, you must get to safety! The Rebels are on the way," a man's voice said gruffly.

Eliza spun to face the speaker. She began to relax at the sight of her pastor, Rev. Alleman, but then tensed when she saw the anxiety in his eyes. What had happened in the fifteen minutes since she had last seen

him at the church? Rumors of approaching Confederate soldiers had
flown through town for days, but this was the first time she had seen
empty streets and alarmed citizens.

Rev. Alleman took a deep breath as if to steady his nerves. "A farmer
just rode in to town shouting that the Confederates are coming. They're
already in McSherryville."

Lydia gasped. "Only two miles away!"

Eliza and Kat exchanged bemused looks. Eliza could barely contain
her excitement. "How many of them are coming?" *Enough to end this
dreadful war so we can finally go back home to Virginia?*

"I don't know," Rev. Alleman said. "Come back to the church with
me, girls; you will be safe there. We'll make more bandages, and we can
pray they will not be needed here."

Eliza had no intention of missing this opportunity to get firsthand
news from the brave men of the Confederacy. She loved her relatives in
Pennsylvania, but she desperately missed her home in Manassas,
Virginia. Besides, sharing a room with her sister and cousin had become
so very tedious. She flashed her sweetest smile, the one that always
worked on men. "We are on our way to the apothecary, Reverend. Aunt
Ida needs us to get more medicine for her—condition." There were some
things a young lady never mentioned in public, especially to her pastor.
Eliza put on the demeanor and tone her mother used when she wanted to
seem polite, but was unwilling to have anyone's way but her own.
"Perhaps it would be best if we got the medicine while we can. If some
'Southern visitors' indeed arrive, we shall await their departure at the
apothecary."

Without waiting for a response, Eliza gave the pastor a small curtsey
and headed for Schmidt's. Lydia and Kat followed in her wake.

-5-

Jake reached the edge of the Square just as Eliza and the other girls left
Rev. Alleman's side. The pastor turned and scanned the marketplace, a
look of consternation on his face. Jake followed the pastor's eyes to the
small crowd at the head of Carlisle Street.

The cluster of men retreated a few steps. An eerie hush filled the air.
Somewhere a door slammed, and dozens of pigeons and sparrows took
flight from the trees and rooftops.

Jake hurried to join the men. At six feet tall, he was easily able to
see over the heads in front of him. Two mounted soldiers wearing gray
uniforms walked their horses down Carlisle Street. Two officers and a
man in civilian clothes followed about a hundred yards back. Not far
behind them came rank upon rank of Confederate cavalrymen, four
abreast. Rifles at the ready, the soldiers scanned the rooftops, windows,
and alleyways as they proceeded.

Carlisle Street, viewing north (c. 1870)

Jake turned to search for Eliza and saw her standing on the cobbled pavement in front of the apothecary. Kat and Lydia huddled beside her.

The first pair of soldiers entered the Square. The crowd slowly gave way, backing up against the Market Shed. Rev. Zieber, pastor of the Reformed Church and head of the Committee of Safety, stepped out to confront the apparent leader of the intruders.

The soldier looked surprised to see so many men. "Where do all these people come from?"

"From the town of Hanover and its immediate vicinity," Rev. Zieber said, using his preacher's voice.

"Are there any Yankee soldiers in town?"

No one answered.

The soldier surveyed the crowd of men, as if seeking his answer in their faces. "So you Yankees are not all in the army, I see."

"No, we are not," Rev. Zieber replied. "But we are beginning to find out what real war is, and I suppose we will soon all join the Union Army."

"The devil you say!"

The second pair of soldiers arrived. Jake's eyes were drawn to the large man with the ruddy complexion, whose insignia and bearing revealed his authority.

The officer rose up in his saddle and announced, "I am Colonel Elijah White, 35th Virginia Battalion. We mean you folks no harm. Although my soldiers wear uniforms of faded gray, we are gentlemen. We are fighting for a cause we believe to be right. We intend to patronize the businesses of your fair town, and then we shall be on our way."

Jake's heart skipped a beat. Patronize the businesses? He edged away from the crowd. He wanted to rush over to protect Eliza, but realized that might not be such a good idea. The first few ranks of cavalrymen had arrived. A running man might be viewed as a threat. At the very least, the soldiers were unlikely to ignore someone in such a hurry to leave. Better to walk away calmly and hope for the best.

Eliza's face beamed like a beacon. Jake ambled toward her as if out for a Sunday stroll, but with each step his anxiety rose. Surely, any moment now a horseman would fire a warning shot or gallop up and block his path. Sweat beaded on Jake's brow.

When he was only a few yards from the apothecary, the clatter of horses' hooves filled the air behind him. Jake kept walking, his eyes fixed on Eliza's. If he was to die, he wanted his last view to be of his beloved's sweet face.

Eliza's eyes grew wide.

Jake's heart pounded.

Kat and Lydia shrunk behind Eliza.

Jake's spine braced for an assault.

The horses shuffled to a stop behind him.

Jake reached Eliza's side. Finally, he dared to turn and look. Several cavalrymen dismounted and stood guard at the end of the street. The Square teemed with mounted men in gray.

Broadway and Center Square, viewing west (c. 1870)
Schmidt's Apothecary is on the right.

-6-

At the sound of a woman's cry, David stopped shoveling and turned to see what was the matter. His neighbor, Mrs. Mary Winebrenner, hurried from the Square. "The Rebels are here! The Rebels are here!"

David dropped his shovel, scrambled from the trench, and ran to her side. His mind raced, *I've got to get back to the house to protect Myrtle! Oh, that's right. Thank God, she's already gone. But is Jake safe?*

Mary fanned her face and gasped for breath. "A whole army . . . of Rebel riders . . . coming down . . . Carlisle Street."

David stared over her head toward the Square. Two gray-clad cavalrymen appeared in the center of town.

"Dear Lord," Mary moaned. She hoisted her skirt above her ankles and dashed down the block to her house.

"I vill get mein musket unt be right back," Klaus said gruffly.

David cleared his throat. "No time for that, Klaus. You can use Jake's gun. Let's go to my house." He knew all about Klaus' musket, a 1742 vintage Brown Bess his grandfather had used when he was a Prussian mercenary fighting for the British in the Revolution. The weapon hung over Klaus' mantel, part of his proud German heritage. David couldn't help wondering when it had last been fired. He didn't think he'd want to be standing nearby the next time it went off.

Harvey sounded the voice of reason. "Wait a minute, let's think about this. Look how many Rebs there are."

The incoming cavalry swarmed the Square like ants on a sugar cube. Some of the soldiers pulled a wagon across the road next to Grove's store. Several others pointed their rifles down Frederick Street.

"You're right," David said. "Best we go protect our own homes. If Union troops are coming, there will be a battle. Maybe these men are just a troop of raiders. In any case, we're no match for them."

Peter nodded his agreement and took off through the fields for the smithy. Harvey and Klaus exchanged grim looks with David and then went their separate ways. David stood in a quandary. Should he try to find his son? Jake might already be at the smithy, if he had gone directly there. But knowing Jake, it was more likely he had gotten caught up in the events unfolding in town. Maybe he had already met up with the girls. Either way, there was little David could do for his son at the moment. He decided to go home and keep an eye on the horses.

At the sight of the empty house, his heart sank. Were his daughters far enough away to remain safe? They should be meeting up with Faith about now. He prayed they might manage to stay ahead of the Confederate cavalry. Perhaps this incursion in Hanover might provide the time needed for his precious daughters to make it to safety.

Remembering the horses, David went around to the small field behind the carriage shop and whistled for the two chestnut Morgans. He grabbed a bucket of grain and coaxed Streak and Skipper into the storage room behind the shop. Fortunately, as the rumors of approaching troops had grown more urgent, he had practiced this maneuver several times. The horses tolerated the close quarters, especially since their master had replaced some of the shelves with a makeshift feed trough. The room would not escape a thorough search; but David hoped any raiders, Confederate or Union, would not expect to find livestock in a workshop and would move on to a more likely target.

With the horses as safe as possible in the storeroom, David entered the workshop. He sat at his bench and let his eyes wander: a carriage frame rested on blocks in the middle of the room; four beautifully painted wheels, white with blue and gold trim, hung on the wall; a piece of partially carved scrollwork protruded from the vise on Jake's bench.

They had been working together on Myrtle's wedding present, a finely crafted carriage, such as David had made for each of his other daughters' weddings. But this carriage was even more special. At Jake's request, David had allowed his son to take the lead in executing the final design. It would mark the completion of his informal apprenticeship.

Now what would become of the wedding plans? With the war on their doorsteps, should they postpone the ceremony?

Anger stirred in David's soul. *It's not right! Hasn't there been enough killing already? There must be a better way!* He stalked outside, slamming the door behind him. After a deep breath to calm himself, he headed for the Reformed Church. Maybe Rev. Zieber, President of the Safety Committee, would go with him, and they could request a meeting with the Confederate commander. Perhaps they could persuade the Rebels to listen to reason, to abandon the war, and return home to their families. After all, didn't men on both sides want the same thing? To raise their families in peace and safety. To grow old spoiling a multitude of adoring grandchildren. Why invite death so far from home? He thought of how their families worried for them, just as he did for his own.

It was a long shot, of course, but David wondered if anyone had ever tried such an approach. He didn't feel optimistic about his chances for success, but it was the only constructive thing he could think to do.

-7-

Eliza gasped at the sight of two Confederate cavalrymen in the Square. Now there were four! Her delight grew as dozens more followed. What did it mean? Would there be a fight? Or had her fantasies come true: were they here to rescue her? Could she finally go back to Virginia? Kat tugged at her elbow, but Eliza couldn't take her eyes off the men who had come to take her home. Four of the horsemen trotted in her direction. She shook off her sister's hand and took a step forward, smiling for all she was worth.

The men stopped at the head of the street, dismounted, and tied their horses to a rail. Rifles in hand, the soldiers spread out across the road, blocking access to the Square. Eliza smiled encouragingly. Which man would be her rescuer?

"Eliza, I'm so glad you're safe!"

Eliza blinked. It took her a moment to realize it was Jake who had spoken. When had he gotten here?

The grin dissipated from Jake's face. "Come on, let's get inside. The soldiers are planning to buy some supplies."

Her euphoria evaporated as reality set in. *Of course, no one sent the army for me. What a silly goose I am! Amazing what homesickness does to a body.* Eliza swallowed her disappointment and took Jake's proffered arm. Once inside the apothecary, she took a deep breath. The heady aroma of herbs and medicines steadied her. Kat and Lydia hurried to the far corner of the store.

A flurry of shouts came from out on Broadway. Jake moved to block the door, so Eliza went to the window. Joseph Dellone and several other men stood arguing in front of the apothecary. Two of the men exchanged shoves. "We will *not* surrender the town!"

Eliza's hand flew to her cheek. "Oh dear, I think there may be fisticuffs!"

Kat eagerly peeked around Eliza's shoulder. "Who?"

A half dozen Confederates strode into view and the scuffle quickly ended, but not before one last epithet rang out. "Copperhead!"

Kat giggled. "Copperhead? Is that the worst he could come up with?"

Lydia arched an eyebrow at her cousin. "It's more than just calling him a snake. Don't you know? 'Copperhead' is what they call people who say, 'The Union as it was, the Constitution as it is, and the Negroes where they are.'"

"I've heard Uncle William say that, but I thought he was against slavery," Kat replied.

Bitterness shrouded Lydia's answer. "He is, but he didn't think banning it in the new states was worth breaking up the Union or going to war over. That's why he was voted out of the Senate."

"Girls, you had better come behind the counter with me," Mr. Schmidt said nervously. The citizens on the street had dispersed, and now one of the soldiers headed for the apothecary.

Kat and Lydia moved behind the counter, but Eliza went to stand next to Jake in front of a nearly empty shelf. The door opened and a lanky young Confederate soldier entered. Tufts of light brown hair hung over his ears. His hat bore a shiny brass pin.

An officer! Eliza's heart fluttered and she smiled coyly.

The man doffed his hat and bowed, first to Eliza, then to Kat and Lydia. "Good morning, ladies."

He crossed to the counter and directed his attention to the druggist. As he spoke, his Southern twang was low and soothing, as if he were lulling a baby to sleep. "I would like to purchase a toothache remedy, sir."

Mr. Schmidt pulled a quart-sized ceramic jug from the shelf behind him and prepared to pour some of the medication through a funnel and into a small brown bottle.

The soldier held up his hand. "That's fine as 'tis. I'm sure y'all'd have an easier time getting more of it than I'd, so I'll just buy that whole jug. Now, what is there for—excuse my language, ladies—the dysentery?"

The druggist put a second jug on the counter. "Will there be anything else, sir?" His voice sounded polite, but his face betrayed his dismay.

"Y'all have any whiskey?"

Mr. Schmidt sniffed. "I don't sell that."

The soldier's blue eyes twinkled. "Didn't ask if you did. I just asked if you had some. I will gladly pay you for it, sir." He winked at Eliza. "I assure y'all, it is strictly for medicinal purposes."

Mr. Schmidt nodded and went into the back room.

Eliza dismissed propriety and gave in to the rush of curiosity. "Where are you from, sir?"

The soldier smiled warmly, then snapped to attention. "Captain Frank Myers, 35th Battalion, Virginia Cavalry."

Eliza's knees felt weak. *A captain!* She leaned on Jake for support. Was this what it felt like to have the vapors? "Virginia . . ."

Jake whispered in her ear, "Are you all right?"

She recovered her composure and gazed into the captain's inviting blue eyes. "Were you at Manassas?"

"No, miss, but my home is in Leesburg, not far from there."

A wave of warmth welled up within her. She wanted to hug him, to feel a piece of Virginia. She smiled prettily. "Manassas is my home. I miss it so. I do hope you and your men will soon clear the way for our return."

Captain Myers' eyes filled with kindness. "We shall surely do our best, Miss—?"

Mr. Schmidt returned and clunked a little brown jug of whiskey onto the counter. "Now, is that all?"

The captain reached into his pocket, pulled out a roll of greenbacks, and laid two fresh-looking five-dollar bills on the counter. "This oughta cover it. And I know they're gen-u-ine," he grinned slyly, "cuz I made 'em myself just this morning!"

No one laughed. Nonplussed, Myers tucked the rest of his money into one pocket and forced the small jug of whiskey into the other. "Can you'ns direct me to the nearest blacksmith?"

"I'll show you the way!" Eliza quickly offered. Kat and Lydia stared at her, but she ignored them.

Jake stepped in front of Eliza. "I'm on my way to the blacksmith shop, sir. Let me take you there."

Mr. Schmidt cleared his throat and added, "No lady should be on the streets while the Reb—, uh, army is here."

Eliza wanted to stomp her foot and protest, but she decided it would not make a good impression on her fellow Virginian. She picked up the medicine jugs from the counter and gave her sweetest smile. "Allow me to assist you with your things, Captain Myers." Without waiting for a reply she started for the door.

Jake hustled to open the door and followed Eliza outside. A cavalry mount stood tethered in front of the store.

Myers took the jugs from Eliza and stowed them in his saddlebag. Then he reached for her hand and kissed it.

It was as if her fantasy had come true. Like an actress in a melodrama, Eliza started to swoon. Would the captain catch her in his arms and carry her away to Virginia?

Instead, Jake's voice boomed, "You leave her be, sir!"

Eliza's heart stirred at the fury in Jake's tone. Were the two young men about to fight over her?

Anger flashed in Myers' eyes, then vanished as he released Eliza's hand and stepped back. "No offense, miss. I merely wished to show my appreciation for your kindness." He turned and nodded to Jake. "I meant you no disrespect, sir. You are indeed fortunate to have such a fine lady."

Jake tugged at Eliza's arm. "Please go back inside and wait. I'll take him to the smithy and then come back to see you all safely home."

Mr. Schmidt came out onto the pavement and gestured toward the door. "Come along, Miss Eliza."

She went without another word, but her heart danced. She knew that look in the captain's eye. He wanted her. She couldn't wait to write about it in her diary.

-8-

Jake escorted Eliza to the door, his emotions in turmoil. Had his beloved flirted with that man? Encouraged his affections?

The demon of Jealousy shouted, "Yes!"

The voice of Reason gently reminded him of Eliza's friendly, outgoing nature, one of her most endearing qualities.

Jealousy taunted, "She wanted that man to kiss her, right in front of you!"

Insecurity added, "She doesn't love you at all!"

Jake's stomach knotted.

Before passing inside, Eliza turned to face him, flashing that smile he loved so much. He searched her eyes, wondering. She leaned up and brushed his cheek with her lips. His spine tingled; his cheek and his doubts cooled after the moist touch of her lips.

"Thank you, Jake. I'll be waiting for you."

His heart leapt at the promise in her voice and the look in those incredible brown eyes. He loved her more than ever.

Jealousy and Insecurity retreated to the dark corners of his mind.

Then she was gone. The door clicked shut behind her. Mr. Schmidt threw the bolt and pulled down the shade.

"You're a lucky man," Myers said.

Yes, I am. Reassured, Jake stepped to the corner of the wooden walkway. He pointed past the Confederates guarding the Square. "Peter Frank's smithy is out Baltimore Street. Or," he turned and gestured behind Myers to the street a short block away, "we can go out York Street and cut across, but that's a little bit longer."

Myers nodded toward the Square. "Shorter is better."

The men walked in silence with Myers' dappled gray stallion trailing behind them. As they passed through the Square, the horse whinnied as if greeting the small herd of cavalry mounts. Jake stifled a smile, wishing Myrtle were there so he could wonder aloud if the steed was bragging to his friends that he was on his way to get new shoes. Myrtle always laughed at his jokes. How he missed her, and she had only been gone for a few hours.

They passed several Confederates on Baltimore Street, their arms filled with such things as food, blankets, jackets, boots, shoes, and—for some unfathomable reason—a mantel clock. Jake shook his head. Did the cavalryman have so many urgent appointments he needed a timepiece on his saddle? Jake scanned the shop windows and perked up his ears but didn't see or hear any evidence of abuse, other than a merchant grumbling about worthless Confederate money.

The offending soldier replied, "You can always use it for privy paper like we do."

Jake glanced at Myers to gauge his reaction to the comment. There was none.

Nearing the smithy, Jake was surprised to see Peter Frank standing outside, his beefy arms folded and a glare on his face. A smattering of burrs clung to his pants. Mud clods caked his boots.

The captain called, "Are you the smith? My horse needs to be shod."

Peter didn't budge. "I ain't working today on account it's a holiday. The Johnnies are in town."

Jake's jaw dropped. What would the officer do in the face of this insolence?

Myers glared and very deliberately laid his hand on his pistol.

In spite of the tenseness of the situation, Jake couldn't help imagining the captain drawling, "Not even for my friend, Mr. Colt?"

Sure enough, the gesture was all the persuasion Peter needed. He reluctantly went inside and fanned the bellows.

The horse only needed two shoes. Jake marveled at Peter's skill and speed. The officer paid two greenbacks, thanked the smith, and mounted up. He nodded to Jake. "Take good care of that little lady of yours."

"I assure you, sir, I shall." *And all the better once you fellows are gone.*

The officer gave Jake a salute, then reined his horse around and cantered up the street to rejoin his comrades.

Even though Jake sympathized when the Virginians defended their own lands, he didn't like having the Confederate Army "visit" Hanover. He especially didn't like the way Eliza had fawned over the captain.

Jake knew all too well that Mrs. Bigler thought his station too low for him to make a suitable match for her daughter, but what if he were to join a Virginia regiment? Perhaps if he distinguished himself in battle, he, too, could become an officer. He had heard about the high casualty rate among officers, meaning there was a constant need for more. Maybe that would serve as a stepping-stone to some post-war position that would make him worthy of the Biglers' acceptance.

But what about the family carriage business? Jake remembered his excitement when Pa had accepted him as an apprentice. Pa counted on him to take over the business some day. And then there was Myrtle's unfinished carriage. How could he leave now?

Perhaps this Confederate invasion into Union territory would finally bring the war to its resolution. Many folks around town simply wanted the war to end, union or no union. Besides, hadn't things already gone too far to hope for reconciliation?

A commotion arose in the center of town. Evidently, the cavalry was mounting up. Jake went into the smithy and found Peter banking the coals. "Do you know where my father is? I need to let him know I told Eliza I would escort her back to the Wertzes'."

"We decided we should each return home, so I expect you'll find him at your house. When the Rebs finally leave, let me know if you fellows decide to do any more digging."

Jake dashed out the back door, then stopped. If he slogged through the fields, he would look a mess when he got back to Eliza. He went around to the street, looked toward the Square, and saw what appeared to be the last of the Confederates mounting up. The rumble of cavalry on the move echoed from over on York Street.

Now that the way would be clear, Jake jogged for home through the center of town. The rain-soaked ground in the Square, churned by several hundred hooves, looked ready for planting. He slowed to pick his way through the many piles of dung surrounding the Market Shed, then rounded the corner of Eckert's Concert Hall onto Frederick Street.

His father nearly bowled him over.

-9-

David oomphed from the contact, and then sighed with relief at finding his son safe. But what was that expression on his face? "What's the matter, Jacob?"

Jake looked surprised to hear his formal name. His answer spilled like water from a millrace. "Oh, I'm so glad I found you, Pa! I was with Eliza and the others over at Schmidt's when the cavalry was here, and one of their officers came into the apothecary and bought some things—paid with greenbacks, believe it or not—and then he wanted someone to show him to the nearest blacksmith's, and Eliza wanted to be the one to take him. I did not like the way that soldier looked at her, no sir! So I said no, I should be the one, since I was going there anyway, and then I promised Eliza that I would come back to Schmidt's to see her and Kat and Lydia safely home."

David smiled wistfully. Such unbridled devotion brought back memories of his own youth and his wonderful wife, Rose, gone to be with the Lord eight years and eight days ago. His heart ached. His family knew all too well the agony of an untimely demise due to disease; he asked God to spare them the horror of a brutal death in war.

Jake pointed his thumb over his shoulder toward Schmidt's. "Is that all right, Pa? The army went out York Street. Can I go now?"

David clasped his son's shoulder. Overwhelmed with emotion, he added a quick hug. Blinking back a tear as he stepped back, David said, "Yes, of course. Want some company?"

"Sure!" Jake beamed. "And then we can talk some more on the way home."

As they re-entered the Square, David rubbed his nose in the vain attempt to drive away the lingering stench of hard-ridden horses and unwashed soldiers. In front of the Market Shed, a throng of agitated townsfolk surrounded Rev. Alleman. Everyone spoke at once.

". . . tried to get into the safe . . ."

". . . stinkin' Confederate money . . ."

". . . broke into my store and helped themselves . . ."

". . . took my clock! Then he . . ."

". . . shot at me when I rode away."

That last comment seemed to be the topper. The griping immediately ceased, and all heads turned to the speaker, Abdiel Gitt. David and Jake stopped to listen.

Abdiel hitched up his pants. A touch of the dramatic entered his voice. "Malcolm Warner and I were minding our own business, riding on home, see, when a pack of Johnnies rode up behind us and ordered us to stop. Well, I heard what them fellows do to folks, so I looked at Malcolm and he looked at me, and then we took off riding up the alley 'tween

Wintrode's Hotel and Young's warehouse. Danged if those rascals didn't fire at us!"

He hooked his thumbs in his pants pockets and rocked on his heels. "We crossed the Commons behind the warehouse and headed for the Abbottstown Pike. The Rebels musta run up against the cut by the railroad switch there. That's the last I saw of them. I holed up at Malcolm's, then come back here soon as we heard they left town."

David arched one eyebrow and looked knowingly at Jake. It wouldn't be the first time Abdiel had stretched a tale to his liking. Judging by the murmurs in the crowd, others thought likewise.

"It's true, I saw it," said William Stall. All eyes turned to the man in the white shirt with rolled-up sleeves. "I was with Danny Trone in the telegraph office. There were about a dozen Rebels. After they gave up the chase, three or four of them came to the loading platform and tried to break into the office. Good thing Danny and I had already hid the telegraph equipment. We ran out the front door. There was a sentry guarding the Pike by the time we got there, so I hid in the foundry. I don't know where Danny went."

A voice from the crowd added, "I heard them asking for the telegrapher."

"Anybody seen Danny?" a worried voice asked.

Noticing Jake's anxious look, David nodded toward the apothecary and they continued on their way. Once out of the crowd's earshot, David muttered, "Sounds like we might not be able to get a telegram from your sisters today."

But Jake looked too preoccupied to respond. David followed his son's eyes.

Eliza Bigler stood at the corner by Schmidt's. One hand held onto a post, her arm posed in a graceful curve. She stood at an angle with her generous bust line in silhouette. Her brown eyes sparkled and her lips parted in a generous smile as Jake drew nearer.

David stifled a groan. What chance did his son have against such a formidably beautiful creature?

-10-

As they walked past the Reformed Church on Abbottstown Road, Jake offered Eliza his arm. She exchanged grins with Kat and Lydia, then slipped her arm into his.

Jake luxuriated in the warmth of Eliza's touch. His mind flashed back to the afternoon of her seventeenth birthday when she had led him out to her uncle's barn and asked for her very first kiss. It was his first kiss, too, but he hadn't known whether he should tell her. Myrtle later assured him that Eliza would probably like to know that fact, but he never got up the courage to tell her.

**Abbottstown Road and the Reformed Church,
viewing southwest toward Broadway (c. 1870)**

He remembered the way she had stroked his arms as he reached to hug her. The sensation of her warm lips on his. Her body pressed—

Eliza tightened her grip on his arm and shook it gently, breaking the reverie. "Tell me what happened at the blacksmith's."

Jake caught himself just as he was about to imitate Abdiel Gitt's dramatic story-telling tone. Thinking better of it, he took a deep breath and answered in his usual voice. "When we got there, Mr. Frank was standing outside. He told the captain that his shop was closed on account of it being a holiday since the Confederates had come to town. Then the captain put his hand on his pistol, as if to say, 'Would you open up for my friend, Mr. Colt?'" Hoping for a laugh, Jake paused; but Eliza's face looked blank, waiting for the story to continue. Kat snickered, then glanced away when Eliza shot her a glare.

Shaking off his disappointment, Jake said, "So Mr. Frank took care of the horse, and the captain went on his way."

Eliza smiled demurely. "Did Captain Myers ask about me?"

Jake's heart felt as if it were caught in the grip of a vise.

In an innocent tone Eliza explained, "I was just curious, since we are both from Virginia. You know how people like to inquire as to one's relations. Often times we meet a stranger, only to discover he is a friend of our cousin or uncle. The world can seem so small, can't it?" She leaned her head against Jake's shoulder for a moment, then, for the second time that day, touched her lips to his cheek.

His heart sprang free, but he decided he had to know the intent of Eliza's questions. "Tell me, Eliza, what did you think of Captain Myers?"

"Oh, he certainly was dashing!" She paused, and the girlish excitement faded from her voice. "I truly admire any man who risks his life to free our beautiful Virginia from those horrid Yankee invaders."

Jake gulped. Hoping his father would not overhear, he leaned closer and lowered his voice. "What would you think if I joined up? With a Virginia regiment?"

"Would you? Could you? How?" Eliza whispered eagerly.

He motioned with his eyes toward his father, walking behind them.

She quickened the pace, leaving Jake's father several feet farther back. As though responding to some form of silent female communication, Kat and Lydia drifted toward the side of the road. Eliza put her head back against Jake's shoulder.

He couldn't breathe. He longed to hold her in his arms, look into her eyes, and ask her to marry him. But he knew he couldn't. Not with the war going on. Not until he had made something of himself. He had to enlist.

"Eliza, do you remember my friend Herb Shriver? You know, from Union Mills?"

She nodded.

The softness of her cheek against his shoulder made his heart race. He took a deep breath to steady his voice before he spoke. "He has two brothers in the Confederate Army. One of them is in the 1st Virginia Cavalry. Herb wants to join up, only his mother hasn't let him because he's their youngest. But maybe he can go if we enlist together."

"What does your father think about that?"

"We haven't discussed it." Jake felt her grip slacken. He dared not disappoint her! "But after what happened today, I plan to talk with him about it tonight."

Eliza gasped, lifted her head, and squeezed his arm, tight. Her eyes had a faraway look. "Will you carry my portrait? And a lock of my hair?"

"Of course! It will be my honor!" *And I will write to you every day. Will you write to me? I will make you proud, my love. And then when this war is all over, I will come ask you to marry me. We will be so—*

Pa's voice rang out. "Jake! Isn't this the way to the Wertzes'?" He pointed down the road to the right.

In his rapture, Jake had led Eliza right past the turn for her uncle's house. Grinning with bemusement, Kat and Lydia stood arm-in-arm at the crossroad.

"Yes, Pa. Sorry."

The three girls linked arms and chattered incessantly the rest of the way. Jake soaked up the sound of Eliza's voice, hoping to recall it at will in the days to come. He prayed he would not need to be apart from her for long. He refused to consider the possibility that he might never return.

-11-

Aunt Ida insisted the men stay for lunch. David and Jake went outside to wash up, while the girls helped prepare the table.

Kat followed Eliza into the pantry and whispered, "I heard you and Jake talking about him joining the Confederate Army. And you asked him to carry your picture and hair. And you kissed him!"

Eliza spun, her face inches from Kat's. "Why you little—"

Kat backed up against the shelves. "I'm gonna tell Mama! I saw your face. You were smiling. You *liked* it!"

Eliza pinched her sister's arm. "You keep your mouth shut, you brat!"

Tears welled up in Kat's eyes. "You leave me alone, or I'll also tell her what you did in the barn with Eddie Rohrbaugh. No—I'll tell Jake!"

"You sneak! I didn't do anything wrong. I was just saying goodbye before Eddie left for the war."

Aunt Ida called from the dining room, "Eliza, would you get me down off the shelf the silver salt and pepper shakers? They're behind the brown pitcher."

Eliza smirked at her aunt's quaint Pennsylvania Dutch way of saying things, then answered in a singsong voice. "Yes, auntie."

Her whisper turned venomous. "Keep your mouth shut, Kathleen Anne, or I'll tell Mama about your flirting with the boys after church last week. And in the graveyard, no less."

Kat scoffed. "We were just putting the altar flowers on some of the graves, like Rev. Alleman asked us to."

Eliza fumed. She had to assure her sister's silence and she didn't have much time. Was that part of the little rat's plan? "What do you want from me?" Her eyes narrowed. "You want my locket, don't you?"

Kat shook her head. "I want to be included."

Aunt Ida's voice drew nearer. "Eliza? Can't you find them?"

"Yes, ma'am. I'll be right there. Kat was just asking me something."

Footsteps on the porch signaled the return of Jake and his father.

Eliza hissed at her sister, "Included? In what?"

A tear rolled down Kat's cheek. "When you and Lydia talk, you never let me be a part of it. You always send me away. I'm not a little girl any more."

It was true. Why hadn't she noticed before? Her little sister was no longer a tomboy, and she filled out Eliza's hand-me-down dress rather nicely for a girl of only—was it fifteen? Yes, fifteen. Eliza had forgotten her sister was getting older, too.

Kat's voice trembled. "Well? What are you staring at?"

"You. You're . . . pretty." Eliza just couldn't quite bring herself to say the word "beautiful." Kat looked well on the way to a measure of beauty that might someday surpass her own. And those green eyes!

From the kitchen came the sounds of Aunt Ida playing mother hen. "David. Jacob. Please come in and make yourselves to home. Henry's on his way to York with a load of hay, so he et himself already. Irene Bigler is taking lunch at her brother George's."

Eliza looked into Kat's pleading eyes and softened. "All right. We'll include you in our secret talks."

Kat gave her a quick hug.

Lydia poked her head into the pantry. "What are you two waiting for? Come on!"

Eliza grabbed the salt and pepper shakers, and then she and Kat joined everyone in the kitchen.

Aunt Ida pointed to the row of pegs next to the door. "Gentlemen, you may hang your hats there."

Jake's father nodded toward the bootjack on the floor underneath the pegs. "We should clean our boots, we've been digging the new church foundation."

"You needn't *butz* your boots. This is a farm. We all work here."

Eliza flinched, suspecting there was more than a little sarcasm in the words, "We all work here." Slaves did the farm work back home in Virginia, surely no one expected her to work here, especially since she was a guest! The fact that Kat liked getting dirty was irrelevant.

Aunt Ida ushered the men to their seats at the dining room table, David at the head and Jake on the right; then took her place at the end nearest the kitchen. The girls settled into the chairs opposite Jake.

A platter with three kinds of meat and two kinds of cheese nestled amidst crocks of butter and apple butter, a cutting board with a loaf of Lydia's oat bread, a bowl of *smierkase*, a plate of Kat's devilled eggs, a dish of Aunt Ida's pepper slaw, and a bowl of huckleberries Lydia and Kat had picked early that morning.

Aunt Ida unfolded her napkin and spread it on her lap. "David, would you ask us the blessing?"

The lengthy blessing included a request for the safety of all of their loved ones in such hazardous times. Eliza's eyes wandered during the prayer, coming to rest on the sideboard. A pie peeked from beneath a linen napkin. She hoped it was strawberry rhubarb, her favorite.

Over lunch, the three girls took turns telling Aunt Ida about the morning's events in town. Eliza took care to hide the excitement she had felt as she told of her encounter with Captain Myers.

Finished with the main meal, Aunt Ida asked the girls to clear the table while she served dessert. Eliza gathered up some dishes and was on her way back from the kitchen when Kat squealed, "Blueberry pie, my favorite!"

"Mine too!" Jake echoed.

Not to be outdone, Eliza chimed, "I guess that makes three of us."

Aunt Ida cut the pie into six large pieces. "Don't hold back, I made another one for when Henry returns."

Despite a chorus of protests about being too full, the pie disappeared in short order, though Kat ate the last half of Eliza's piece.

Aunt Ida motioned toward the next room. "Would you care for some coffee in the parlor?"

David sighed. "That is very kind of you to offer, but I must get back to the shop and let the horses out. I hid them in the storage room so no one would steal them."

She nodded sagely. "Well done. I know Henry will be disappointed he missed seeing you. He just loves that hay wagon you made. Now he can haul as much in two loads as his other wagon carries in three. And it must be nice having your son in the business with you."

"Yes, ma'am, it surely is."

Aunt Ida turned to Jake. "Your mother would be very proud of the young man you have become. You come back and visit us any time. We would all be glad of your company."

"Especially Eliza!" Kat quipped.

Eliza rolled her eyes.

Jake cleared his throat, but still his voice quavered. "Mrs. Wertz, may I call on Eliza tomorrow afternoon?"

Eliza caught her sister's smug grin. The grin vanished just before Aunt Ida glanced in her nieces' direction.

"I cannot give permission in Mrs. Bigler's place, but you may surely come to visit us *all* tomorrow afternoon. We always enjoy a hymn-sing after Sunday dinner. Eliza plays the spinet quite well. Do you like to sing, Jacob?"

"Yes, ma'am, I do." He smiled adoringly at Eliza.

Eliza felt her face redden. She imagined Jake sitting next to her on the piano bench as she played, his hip pressed against hers. The room grew silent. Everyone stared at her. Eliza blinked, then realized her Aunt had spoken. "I'm sorry, Auntie, what did you say?"

Kat stifled a snicker with her napkin.

Aunt Ida over-enunciated, "Would you like it if Jacob came to sing with us tomorrow?"

Eliza bristled at her aunt's tone, but accepted the offense as a rebuke for her inattention. "Yes, ma'am, that would be very nice." She gave Jake her sweetest smile and was pleased to see him blush.

"Well then, we'll look for you around the four o'clock hour, Jacob."

"Thank you, Mrs. Wertz. Four o'clock it is."

Kat and Lydia cleared the dessert dishes while Eliza and her aunt escorted the men onto the porch. Once outside, Jake reached for Eliza's hand, bowed over it, and kissed it. Though the gesture lacked the captain's deftness, the tingle in her spine and the warmth in her belly more than made up for it.

He gazed deep into her eyes. "Until tomorrow, Miss Eliza."

"Yes . . . tomorrow." Her voice sounded far away.

Jake and his father thanked their hostess, then went on their way.

Aunt Ida sighed. "Eliza, I'm going to tell you something my mother once told me, and I hope you never forget it. 'If you want to know the quality of a man's character, look at the quality of his work.' That Jacob Becker will make some lucky girl a fine husband some day."

Eliza folded her arms and leaned against the porch post. "Yes, ma'am, he will." *Perhaps I shall marry him some day.* She turned and went into the house. *But Mother knows a lot of families around Washington City. Who knows what may happen when this wretched war finally ends?*

-12-

They were halfway to town before Pa broke the silence. "So, my young man has his first social engagement."

"Yup, guess I do." Jake scuffed at a rock in the road and sent it skipping into the underbrush.

"Eliza *is* quite a beauty."

Jake wondered about the tone of his father's voice. "Don't you approve?"

"Well, let's just say I have my concerns. The more important question is, does her mother approve?"

"Mrs. Wertz sure seems to." Jake chuckled.

His father's voice took on a gentle tone. "You didn't ask to call on Lydia, you asked to see Eliza, and we both know her mother intends for her to marry a society fellow after the war."

"But Pa, we love each other, and we have ever since we met two years ago. I'll be nineteen in August. You married Mama when you were nineteen."

"There was no war then."

Was this a good time to broach the subject of joining the army? Jake longed to get it all out in the open, but what were the right words to say? Pa would certainly be less than pleased. Would he give his blessing anyway? Jake sagged under the weight of the dilemma. He had to enlist; but would he go, could he go, without his father's blessing? He had told Eliza he would discuss enlistment tonight. If he followed through with that plan, then he could tell her the results when he called tomorrow.

"Can we talk about this later, Pa? I want to do some more thinking on it."

"Good idea." Pa patted Jake on the back.

Jake imagined carrying Eliza's portrait and lock of hair in the pocket over his heart. He daydreamed of leading the charge that drove away the

Yankee invaders, once and for all. He pictured the joy on Eliza's face when he returned to take her home to Virginia.

Virginia. He hadn't thought about that.

What about Hanover? He had always assumed he would live in Hanover. Would Eliza be happy living so far away from her family? She rarely spoke of her father or little brother and, if she did, it was never in glowing terms. She treated Kat as a pest more often than not, and she didn't seem to be particularly close to her mother. Eliza was very popular in town, especially among the girls at the Lutheran Church. Would she join the Methodist Church with him, or should he become a Lutheran? He didn't mind either way. And, of course, there was the carriage business. He had promised his father he would continue in the family trade.

The solution seemed obvious. He would marry Eliza and they would live in the house with Pa. Surely, Pa wouldn't object to that. Who would want to live in such a big house all alone?

The church tower chimed three as Jake and Pa reached Broadway. A small cluster of people gossiped on the porch of the apothecary. The Square looked busier than usual. Jake noticed the horse dung had already been cleared, which reminded him of his trip to the blacksmith.

"Oh, Mr. Frank said to let him know if you want to do some more work on the foundation today."

"I have to check on the horses, and then I want to work on Myrtle's carriage before supper, as we'd planned," Pa replied.

Jake winced. Myrtle's carriage! How could he leave without finishing it? Should he wait until it was done? And what about the wedding? He could hardly enlist and then in two months' time ask for leave to attend his sister's wedding. No telling where he might be by that time; and, heaven forbid, what if he got wounded? What kind of a wedding day would Myrtle have under those circumstances?

They crossed the Square and came upon George Scott, fiddling with a tangled mess of wire in front of his store. "Damned Rebels!"

Pa called, "Do you need some help?"

"Nah, too late for that. I went to all the trouble to take the telegraph wire down when I heard the Rebs were coming, now it looks like they must've cut the line somewheres else. Probably 'tween here and York, that's where the bastards headed." Mr. Scott spit and adjusted his chaw of tobacco. "No telling when we'll receive messages again."

"I guess we won't be hearing from Myrtle any time soon," Pa grumbled.

Jake tried to estimate how far his sisters may have gone by the time the Confederates left Hanover. If they had gotten back on the road right after meeting up with Faith, then they might have made it to York ahead of the cavalry, but if not . . . "Do you think if they heard the army was close, they would have gone to Uncle Robert's in Dover?"

"With twelve kids of his own, I don't know where your Uncle Robert would put them all, but I'm sure he'd do whatever he could. All we can do for them now is pray."

The rest of the way home, Jake prayed: for his sisters and their families, for his future with Eliza, and for the impending discussion with Pa about enlistment in the Confederate Army.

-13-

Jake walked Skipper into the pasture and unclipped the lead. The chestnut stallion nudged his master under the arm.

"Sorry boy, no sugar cube today," Jake said, patting Skipper's neck.

The horse shook out his mane and trotted to the far corner of the field, head held high above his graceful neck. Skipper had become Jake's favorite of the several Morgans they had owned over the years. Now that they were down to two horses, Jake loved him all the more.

Upon their return from Manassas in '61, Pa sold a pair of horses to the U.S. Army, who had put out a special call for teams to pull caissons in artillery units. The Morgan breed, renowned for its compact stature, powerful hindquarters, and great endurance, was a favorite among cavalrymen and teamsters alike. Pa wanted to help with the cause, and he figured his horses had a slightly better chance of survival pulling caissons than they did charging into battle as cavalry mounts.

Unfortunately, their second pair of Morgans fared less well. In October of '62, Jake and Pa delivered a new wagon to a farm just outside Westminster, Maryland. As usual, they had planned to ride the wagon's team back home, but a squad of Union cavalry caught up with them not long after they left Westminster. The Union men politely suggested Pa might like to trade his Morgans for their two hardest used mounts; after all, it was his patriotic duty.

Rather than subject the exhausted cavalry horses to further abuse, Jake and Pa walked them to Union Mills. Andrew Shriver, owner of the mill, gladly loaned his friends two horses, arranging to trade back when he came to Hanover in a couple of days. But one of the ex-cavalry horses died that night. Pa sold the other one a week later.

". . . Jake?"

"What? Oh, sorry, Pa. I was just thinking about . . ."

"Losing Venus and Jupiter to the Union cavalry?"

Jake smiled ruefully. "How did you know?"

"So was I. They're all special creatures of God, aren't they?"

"Yeah." Jake's voice choked with emotion.

"They'd do anything for you, and you'd do anything for them," Pa said wistfully.

"Yeah . . ."

Pa slapped Jake on the back. "Good. Then get the shovel and muck out the storeroom. I'll get started on the rear bench for the carriage."

At the sound of the slap, Skipper and Streak lifted their heads, looked at Jake, and swished their tails. Jake groaned. Was that a blink, or had Skipper just winked at him?

-14-

Dear Diary:

    What a day! Two men fought over me in town today! One was Jake (of course!) and the other was a <u>very</u> handsome Captain—you won't scarcely believe this—in the cavalry of THE ARMY OF NORTHERN VIRGINIA! Yes I could scarce believe mine own eyes. Oh how I hoped those brave men had come to take me home, but alas, it is not yet my time.

    Now for the best part. Before he left, the Captain <u>kissed my hand</u>! I commenced to swoon, but as I was about to collapse who should catch me but Jake Becker? Well, you should have seen how angry Jake got at that Captain! His face got so very red. He yelled at the Captain to let me be. I saw the look on the Captain's face, like he wanted to take on the whole Yankee army for the right to wrap his strong arms around me. Such a rogue! But

The bedroom door burst open.

Eliza slammed the diary shut and slid it under a pillow.

Kat flounced into the room and plopped down next to Eliza on the bed. "Watcha doing?"

"Nothing. Go away!"

"I thought so," Kat sniffed. "You're writing in your diary, aren't you."

"What's it to you?"

Kat undid her bun and combed her fingers through her long tawny hair. "I don't care. I'll just read it later when you're done." She slid off the bed and headed for the door.

Eliza snickered. "You don't even know where I keep it."

Kat turned, putting a finger to her chin. "Hmm, let me see. If I were you, where would I hide my diary? Think, think, think." Her eyes lit up. "Behind the baseboard in the left corner of the closet?"

"You are such a brat!" Eliza tossed a pillow at her sister's head.

Kat caught the pillow and cocked her arm to counterattack but instead, stopped and struck a pose. "I know. But at least I'm a lovable brat!"

"It's so unfair! How come everyone in our family loves you more than they love me?" Eliza flung herself across the bed and buried her face in her arms.

After a long moment, Kat said softly, "That's not exactly true. I love you more than I love me."

Eliza rolled onto her side and stared up at her sister. "What? That doesn't make any sense."

Kat flopped onto the bed, looking more worn and drawn than Eliza had ever seen her. "It means I love you, Eliza. A lot. Even more since we came north." She picked at a loose thread on the patchwork quilt. "That's why I wanted you to promise to include me in your secret talks. I'm tired of being enemies all the time."

"Well, you sure choose an odd way of showing it." Eliza took a deep breath and slowly released it through pursed lips.

So now what? Could they possibly be friends again, like when they were children? Eliza felt a pang of loneliness. She looked at her sister and pondered for a long moment, then sat up, pulled her diary from beneath the pillow, and handed the book to Kat. "Here. Read whatever you want."

Eliza was about to add, *You've already read the rest of it, you may as well read the new part,* when one of Kat's words finally sunk in. *Enemies?* "Do you really feel like we've been . . . enemies?" Eliza's stomach knotted at the sound of the word. "Have you hated me that much?"

"Oh, you've made me plenty mad. Lots of times! But I never really hated you." Kat plucked the loose thread from the quilt and balled it up between her thumb and finger. "I just hated the things you did to me."

"What? You're the one who's always starting things."

Frowning, Kat flicked the balled thread onto the floor. "I'm sorry. I guess . . . it's just . . . I didn't know any other way to get you to pay attention to me. We used to play together a lot when we were little, but over the past few years you've treated me like, like . . ."

"I know. We used to have such fun together." *But that was back home in Manassas, a lifetime ago,* Eliza thought bitterly. Had the little girl in her died when her father sent her away two years ago?

Tears slid down Kat's cheeks. "Can we be like we used to be? Will you forgive me?"

Could it be that easy to turn back the clock? Eliza doubted it, but she found herself yearning to rejoice in the sisterly love she had once known. "Indeed yes. Will you forgive me, too?" She opened her arms to Kat and they hugged each other, tight.

"I'll forgive you on one condition," Kat said quietly. She stood, looking anxious. "Will you please call me by my real name? I'm not a little girl any more."

A flood of affection filled Eliza's heart, washing away the emptiness, purging the loneliness she had felt since she had left Manassas.

"Of course, *Kathleen.*"

-15-

Jake placed the two panels together and held them up in the lingering ray of late day sun. He closed one eye and studied the pieces' edges, looking for the slightest imperfection. Seeing none, he stood the panels on the workbench, closed both eyes, and ran his index finger around the perimeter of the wood.

"Ah, there's one." His finger continued on its path. "And two." The finger resumed its search. "And . . ." The finger stopped, went back and forth over one spot a few times, and then completed its circuit of the panels. "Nope. Just two."

Jake opened his eyes, picked up a piece of sandpaper, and rubbed the imperfect panel's two offending spots. After blowing away the dust, he closed his eyes and rechecked his work. "These side panels are done, Pa."

"Are you sure they're *exactly* alike?" Pa said with mock seriousness. "After all, they'll be separated by seven feet of bench, we can't have anyone notice they aren't perfectly symmetrical."

Jake put on a pretend glare, carefully removed his apron, and shook it out in Pa's direction. The fine particles of oak shot about two feet, then floated aimlessly in the fading sunlight. "And there's lots more where that came from, too!" Jake plucked a small piece of oak from his shirtsleeve and flicked it at his father.

Pa snorted. "Little dog with a big bark."

"Hey, you and Ma always said, 'Leave no good work unfinished.' If you didn't want me to be so thorough in my work, you should have told me sooner. Think of all the time I'd have saved."

They shared a hearty laugh. The Becker family may have abandoned a few of their German ancestors' traditions, but attention to detail remained as integral a part of their existence as breathing.

Jake smoothed out the valuable piece of sandpaper and placed it back in its nook above his bench. "How did you ever get along back in the old days before they invented sandpaper, Pa?"

"I didn't have to. It was when they invented sandpaper that I decided to build carriages, now that I would have this new-fangled convenience to help me out."

Jake nodded as though he had just learned one of the secrets of God's creation. "Ah, I see."

"Speaking of sandpaper," Pa pointed toward the unfinished bench seat stretched across the sawhorses in front of him, "this is ready for some."

"Are you asking for the sandpaper, or for my help?"

"Well, seeing as how you have your sanding arm all loosened up . . ."

Jake took out two pieces of sandpaper, grabbed his stool, and went to work with his father. Though the bench would eventually be covered with padding and leather, the men wouldn't think of slighting any detail. The bench would someday need reupholstering, and they wanted whoever did the job to see only their finest work.

While they sanded, Jake gathered his thoughts in preparation for broaching the subject of enlistment. Pa whistled a heartfelt rendition of Stephen Foster's "I See Her Still in My Dreams." As the last note faded, Jake decided the time was right.

"Pa, I've been thinking on what we talked about on the way home this afternoon. I figure it's time I make a plan for my future, and I very much want Miss Eliza Bigler to be a part of that plan. Now I know Mrs. Bigler doesn't think I'm good enough for her daughter—"

"Then she don't know you," Pa said angrily. The sanding stopped. "You've grown up to be a fine young man. You've done your Mama proud."

Jake winced. "You know what I mean."

"I surely do not!" Pa set the sandpaper on the bench and balled his fists on his knees. "Outside of the journey when we brought Mrs. Bigler and her daughters up here, what has she had to do with us, and you in particular? She knows you're sweet on Eliza. Oh, she was the picture of graciousness while we traveled, but once here, she's had no use for us! We're good enough to make her carriages and haul her away from danger, but a young man as fine as you isn't good enough to court her daughter?"

Jake swallowed hard. On the one hand, he basked in his father's praise, but on the other, getting his father's dander up did not bode well for the rest of the discussion.

Pa leaned closer, his eyes dark. "Hear me well, Jacob. Any woman who would try to make a hardworking, God-fearing man think he isn't good enough . . . well, *she* is the one who isn't good enough!"

No use bringing up enlistment now. Jake remembered his father's adage, "Don't make decisions when you're angry. Anger clouds the mind." *Maybe after dinner.*

Pa punctuated his words with his finger. "And you can tell them I said so when you go calling tomorrow. And don't be a bit surprised if Henry and Ida Wertz shout the amen! They know what I'm talking about."

"Yes sir."

Pa picked up the sandpaper and went back to work, muttering, "I won't cotton with anyone saying your Mama raised a young man not good enough."

Lost in thought, Jake sanded. For the first time in his young life he felt as if he understood the full measure of his father's love for his mother. Tears filled Jake's eyes. He coughed to clear the lump in his throat, then sang the words to Foster's song.

> *While the flow'rs bloom in gladness and spring birds rejoice*
> *There's a void in our household of one gentle voice.*
> *The form of a loved one hath passed from the light,*
> *But the sound of her footfall returns with the night;*

Pa joined Jake in the chorus, both men struggling through the tears streaming down their faces.

For I see her still in my dreams,
I see her still in my dreams,
Though her smiles have departed
from the meadows and the streams.
I see her still in my dreams.

The final note faded beneath the scritch-scratch of sandpaper on oak.

Jake reflected on his mother and father's love. Did Eliza love him like that? He realized he had a lot more thinking to do.

-16-

After an easy-to-make dinner of pork chops over sauerkraut with boiled potatoes, Jake and Pa shared the clean-up duties. There were never leftovers in the Becker house, of course, but tonight it took every spare inch in Jake's belly to make sure the rule remained unbroken. Neither man seemed to have much of an appetite.

Whenever Myrtle put up food, she filled each jar with enough to feed the three of them. Yet another adjustment he had to make if she was to be gone for any length of time.

Jake dried the last serving fork and slid it into the drawer. "Pa, this morning I heard Colonel White when he spoke in the Square. He said that he and his men were gentlemen, and that they fought for a cause they believed to be right." Jake hung the towel on the hook and turned to look into his father's eyes. "Do you believe they have a righteous cause?" From his father's expression, Jake knew he had found the right opening.

Pa reached into his pocket and pulled out his pipe. "Well now, that would depend on what they say that cause is, wouldn't it?"

Jake smiled with anticipation. Since the war had begun, discussions on politics or philosophy had often followed the evening meal. The pipe acted as moderator. As long as Pa puffed, the other person had the floor. When the pipe came out of Pa's mouth, it was his turn to speak.

"I'll light this up and then join you on the porch, Jake."

The gray clouds had returned, making for an early twilight. The air felt a bit warmer than during the day, but it was still unseasonably cool, probably not even seventy degrees. Best of all, the humidity was low. Jake sat in his rocker, leaned back, and allowed his eyes to wander among the maple trees lining the street. Sparrows and squirrels flitted and hopped, chirped and chattered, staking claims on their beds for the coming night.

The sweet aroma of cherry pipe tobacco announced Pa's approach. He settled into his rocker with a groan. "Your grandfather used to say that a man knew he was getting old when he made sounds sitting down and sounds getting up." He took a puff on the pipe.

Did that mean Pa wanted Jake to start? The pipe came out: evidently not. As usual, Pa opened the discussion with a series of rhetorical questions.

"How righteous is the cause that allows one man to force another to work in his fields in exchange for a meager living? How righteous is it to sell another man's children? Is it a righteous cause that denies a whole race of people the chance for an education? Refuses to allow them to even learn to read?"

Pa took a quick puff on his pipe, held it for a moment, and then exhaled slowly, which usually meant he was about to deliver his most important point. "How righteous is it for a man to refuse his 'servant' a copy of the Bible, God's word? Surely, God will not bless such a cause." Having said his piece, Pa settled back and started to rock.

Jake didn't want to get bogged down with a rehash of previous discussions. "You know I certainly agree with you on the need to eliminate slavery, but do you really think that is the cause the colonel meant? This war didn't really start in order to free the slaves, did it? If the Federal government hadn't treated the Southern states the way it had, would they have left the Union? Remember when we were at the Biglers'? Time and again we heard soldiers and regular folks say that this was their second War of Independence."

Pa's eyes narrowed as he nodded.

"But independence from what, Pa? I hadn't given it much thought until today. Seeing the army in town brought back memories of the last time we saw Confederate soldiers, fighting for their lives against tens of thousands of Union troops in Manassas." Jake shook his head sadly. "Those were American soldiers, Pa—I just can't get over this—American soldiers sent by our President to kill other Americans in their own home state! What kind of a government does that? And packs up a picnic lunch, puts their family into a carriage, and goes to watch?" His fists tightened on the arms of the rocker and he took a deep breath to quell the seething anger.

Pa puffed faster on the pipe, but said nothing.

"I don't know, Pa, what was Mr. Lincoln's plan? Did he think the invasion of Virginia and the ruination of innocent farmers' lands would bring the Union back together? How is that any different from a slave owner who thrashes not only his runaway slave, but that slave's family as well?"

Pa nodded and rocked. The sparrows and squirrels had settled their disputes; only the rhythm of the rockers and the chant of the crickets remained, heralding the impending night.

Jake searched for a way to consolidate his thoughts. "I think it all goes back to the Declaration of Independence. Funny how I can still remember it all. What has it been, six years since Miss Henze made me memorize it for recitation?

"Anyway, it's clear the Federal government lost the consent of the governed in those states that seceded, right? Each state's legislature voted and approved the secession, just like the Declaration calls for." Jake slipped into the rhythm he had used to memorize the famous text. "'That whenever any form of government—becomes destructive to these ends—it is the right of the people—to alter or to abolish it—and to institute new government—laying its foundation on such principles—and organizing its powers in such form—as to them shall seem most likely—to effect their safety and happiness.'"

Jake leaned forward in the rocker with his hands on his knees. "Well, isn't that exactly what the Confederate States of America did? And like the Declaration says, 'It is their right, it is their *duty*—to throw off such government—and to provide new guards for their future security.'"

The pipe came out. "So, you are saying the colonel's cause—indeed, his right and his 'duty'—is the establishment and protection of this new, independent Confederate States of America?"

Jake considered this idea before answering. He sensed there might be more to it than that. "Well, yes, but I'm not so sure it was in anyone's mind to do that until the Northern states exerted their will through the Federal government in ways that drove the Southern states to do what they did."

Jake wrinkled his brow and grinned wryly. "Did that come out right? Let me try again. I think the Southern states realized that if the Federal government had its way, it would only be a matter of time until things became intolerable. Why, their whole society would fall apart! They saw they couldn't solve things through the Congress or the courts, and if that was true, then wasn't secession their best course of action?"

Pa sighed heavily and stood. He went to the edge of the porch and turned his eyes toward the charcoal sky. "You know, Jacob, sometimes seeing God's plan is like looking for the moon behind those clouds. You may have a general idea where it is, but it can take a while before things clear up enough to see it plainly."

He turned and leaned against the railing. "Both sides in this war invoke the name of God in support of their cause. We know they can't both be right. You have stated the Confederate cause well enough to *almost* make a believer of me." He took a puff on the pipe and returned to his rocker.

Once again, Jake appreciated the way his father respected his opinions. And when they were in disagreement, his Pa often posed questions to lead him to the error in his reasoning, instead of correcting him.

"I think the big problem, Jake, is that the war may not have been about slavery when this all started, but it certainly is now. How can any government obey the Constitution and yet deny Negroes the 'right to life, liberty, and the pursuit of happiness'?"

Agitation filled Pa's voice. "Old Ben Franklin had it right. 'We must hang together, else we shall most assuredly hang separately.' If the slave states are allowed to have their own country, how long before someone wants a third? And a fourth? Before you know it, we'll have more countries and more wars than Europe." His tone grew angry. "Your great-grandfather didn't lose a leg in the Revolution for that! We *must* have a *United* States of America, and the Negroes must go free."

Jake drummed his fingers on the arm of the rocker. Lightning bugs flickered in the yard. He swatted a mosquito in mid-bite on his arm. No use putting it off any longer. Time to get to the main point. *Here we go. Help me, Lord.*

He turned his chair to face his father and spoke with a calm, measured tone. "I think that when Mr. Lincoln issued his proclamation freeing the slaves, he ruined any chance for reconciliation. Mere words do not have the power to transform an entire society's way of life." Jake's voice rose as his agitation grew. "How can the Confederate states rejoin the Union knowing that the day they do, Negroes everywhere will have the right to go wherever they want?" He threw up his hands. "Think of the chaos. What will become of hundreds of thousands of former slaves who will probably have only the clothes on their backs?"

After taking a moment to slow his racing heart, Jake continued firmly, "As desirable as the end of slavery may be, it simply cannot be achieved in a single day. I believe the Confederacy deserves its freedom from the tyranny of the Federal government. The issue of slavery must be dealt with, but over time, and with the helping hand of the government, not at the end of the government's whip."

Jake swallowed and took a deep breath. The moment had come. "Pa, I believe it is my *duty* to join with the Confederacy in their fight for this freedom—"

The pipe in Pa's fist hit the arm of the rocker with a loud crack. "Is this all because of that Bigler girl? Is it?"

Jake gulped. "No, sir, I can honestly say it is not. At first, part of the reason I wanted to go was to gain Eliza's favor, but you've helped me to see things more clearly in that regard. The more I have thought about this, the more convinced I am that this is the path I must take."

Without a word, Pa rose and went into the house.

Jake's whole body trembled. *What is he thinking? What have I done?*

Pa kicked the screen door open and strode onto the porch. He held Jake's Springfield in his hands. "Private Becker! Stand at attention!"

Jake's jaw dropped as he rose to his feet.

"Private Becker. Take your weapon, proceed down Frederick Street to the Forney farm, and shoot as many of those Yankee bastards as you can."

Jake's knees buckled. "Pa, you know I'd never do that."

His father seemed to grow three feet taller as he stepped in front of him. "That is an order, soldier! Do you know what we do to men who disobey orders?"

"That's not fair! You know it won't be like that."

Pa's tone softened. And was all the more terrible because of it. "Oh? And just who do you think you'll be shooting at, son?"

So this is it. He is right. But not about the cause itself. Jake stiffened his resolve and met his father's stare. "You know I have seen what happens in war. You and me, we carried so many mangled bodies from the fields of Manassas. And how many men did we bury? Men whose crime was not owning slaves, but defending their families and their homes from invaders. Pa, I must follow my convictions. Like you taught me."

Pa gave one slow nod, propped the rifle against the wall, and sat back down in the rocker. He stared straight ahead into the night. His voice cracked as he spoke. "And what of Myrtle's carriage?"

"I know, Pa." Jake sank into his rocker.

"Will you wait to go until after it's finished? And what about her wedding?"

Jake shook his head. "I don't know. My heart tells me to stay, but I better think more about that."

"And pray."

"You can count on that, Pa."

They rocked without speaking for a while. Jake felt drained. And something else. A void in the pit of his stomach? No. Something was there. Like a tiny worm, gnawing at his insides. And it was growing. Jake watched his father rock. Suddenly, Pa looked so much older than his forty-five years.

Pa sighed. "Well, this has certainly been a day to remember."

The words rang in Jake's ears as if they had crossed a great chasm. For the first time in his life, he felt distance between himself and his father. It was not a pleasant feeling. Soon the distance would become real.

In that moment, Jake wanted to crawl onto his father's lap and cry. *Papa, make this awful war go away! I don't want to ever leave you. And please, can you bring my Mama back to me? Please, Papa? You can fix anything.* He closed his eyes and bit his lip. *Get a hold of yourself! Is that any way for a* man *to think?* When Jake opened his eyes, he left the last vestige of childhood behind.

Pa stood and held his arms wide.

Jake sensed he would cherish that embrace every day for the rest of his life, along with his father's prayer: "Dear God and Father of us all, *please* guide and protect us. *Thy* will be done."

Sunday, June 28, 1863

-1-

Such a glorious day for a walk! Jake wore his white linen shirt, gray woolen church pants, and spit-shined church shoes. Eliza looked more resplendent than ever in her pink dress. Her hair hung in tight ringlets, exposing the sensuous curve of her neck. The creamy white skin above her bosom seemed to glow in the late afternoon sun. Her lustrous brown eyes made his heart tingle. And she had done something to her lips to make them look especially red and full, inviting his kiss?

They strolled past the Henry house arm-in-arm and made their way to the top of Bald Hill. Eliza said she always enjoyed the view from up there, and what a view! Rolling hills and rich Virginia farmlands from horizon to horizon.

In the midst of a particularly robust field of corn stood a jagged gibbet, from which hung a gangly scarecrow adorned with a tattered black greatcoat and bent stovepipe hat. The straw man wriggled free from the stake, leapt to the ground, and danced a floppy jig. Then he put his fingers to his mouth and loosed an ear-piercing whistle. Lifting his head to the heavens, the scarecrow screamed, "Harvest time!"

The crops did indeed look ripe for the harvest: bloated horse carcasses, severed body parts, broken weapons, and mangled men splayed like discarded rag dolls as far as the eye could see.

Eliza's hand flew to her cheek. "Oh dear, I think there may be fisticuffs!"

A dark cloud scuttled in from the east. Blue crows. Thousands and thousands of them. The scavengers dove onto the crop of men and horses, pecking and tearing in their frenzy to feed. Eliza gasped and buried her face against Jake's chest.

"Dear God," Jake whispered. "Do something!"

A gray storm cloud swept in from the south, driving the crows back from whence they had come. Jake peered skyward, hoping to see the sun break through the darkness, but the clouds only thickened.

On the ground nearby, a blue-clad man rolled over and sat up. It was the Smiling Man! He arched his back and stretched his arms high over his head. His left arm fell off. He tried to stand, but when he had rolled over, his right foot hadn't budged. Now his leg twisted backward, the toe of his boot stuck in the mud of the blood-soaked ground. "Oh dear, I think there may be a delay in my return home."

The Smiling Man turned to Jake, bloodshot eyes pleading, "Can you tell my wife I will be late? And tell my children I am so very sorry. Perhaps you can carry on the fight in my stead?" He yawned and lay back down, pillowing his head on the disembodied arm.

Jake lurched awake, drenched with sweat. He rolled off his side and tried to sit up, but found his left arm useless, a dead weight. Then the pins-and-needles sensation set in. He had fallen asleep on his arm. He struggled to a sitting position and a bead of sweat trickled down his spine.

In the darkened bedroom it was impossible to tell the time, but Jake guessed morning couldn't be far off. With his emotions in turmoil it had taken hours to fall asleep. A dog barked in the distance. A breeze rustled through the tree outside the window. The birds weren't warbling yet, so he figured there was at least another half-hour before dawn.

Jake flopped back onto the down-filled pillow and flexed the fingers on his left hand to chase away the last of the stinging sensation. Images of the Smiling Man flashed through his mind. He closed his eyes and tried to recreate the image of Eliza in the dream, but now her face looked like the crone on the oxcart. He started to yawn, but that reminded him of the Smiling Man again.

Jake threw off the light quilt, got out of bed, and groped his way downstairs. Dull light from the front windows revealed his father, asleep on the divan in the parlor. Jake tiptoed past the doorway.

"So," Pa's voice broke the silence like a thunderclap. "Are you making the coffee today?"

Jake banged his funny bone against the doorframe as he whirled to face the sound. "Youch! You scared the bejeebers out of me, Pa!" He rubbed his tingling right arm. *Is God trying to tell me something? Both arms in one night.*

Pa chuckled. "Remember when you and Myrtle used to hide so you could jump out and scare each other?"

Jake imitated a little boy's voice. "She started it!"

"I don't know about that, but I seem to recall you were way ahead in the accounting before you both outgrew it. So mark that one up on Myrtle's tally."

The muffled chirrup of an awakening sparrow floated through the open window. A few more sparrows responded, then a chorus.

Pa sat up on the divan. "Breakfast or horses?"

"Seeing as how you're still dressed, you do the horses, I'll make breakfast."

"What about Old Jack?" Pa's voice grew somber. "Do you want me to do it?"

They had planned to eat the rooster, Old Jack, for Sunday dinner. Jake had named the feisty Rhode Island Red in honor of General Thomas Jackson, hero of the first Battle of Manassas. Jackson's courage in the face of fierce Union fire rallied the Confederates to victory and earned him the nickname Stonewall Jackson, but to his men, Jackson was always Old Jack.

"Oh, yeah. I've been thinking about that, Pa. Can't we hide Old Jack in the root cellar if an army comes by? It don't hardly seem fair to eat him, you know what I mean?" Jackson had been accidentally shot by his own troops several weeks ago. While recovering from the loss of his arm, he contracted pneumonia and died.

Two dark shadows sped past the windows, accompanied by the sound of hoof beats. A dog howled just down the street. More dogs answered on the edge of town.

Jake and Pa gaped at each other, then ran through the house and out the back door. Jake squinted through the gloom. The barn stood wide open, its door drifting back and forth in the breeze.

They sprinted to the barn.

Skipper and Streak were gone.

-2-

Jake sat on the edge of his bed, staring at the white linen shirt in his hands. Could things get any more complicated? When should he leave to enlist? What should he do about the wedding and finishing Myrtle's carriage? Had his sisters and their children reached safety in time? Did Eliza really love him, and if so, how could he win her parents' approval? Even if he did, would Pa approve? Now on top of all that, their last two horses, stolen. At least Old Jack had managed a reprieve, though Jake wanted to wring the rooster's neck for failing to sound the alarm when the thieves had come.

Pa figured Skipper and Streak had been taken by raiders from one army or the other. Over the years, Jake had been careful to avoid getting attached to their livestock, but now he realized how deeply he cared for Skipper. How could part of his heart feel so empty, yet hurt so much?

Someone knocked on the front door. "Hallo!" John Forney's voice called from the porch.

Pa called from the kitchen, "Come on in, John. No need to knock."

Jake quickly finished dressing and clomped down the stairs. John and Pa, both already dressed for church, stood in the middle of the parlor.

"The Forneys have invited us to Sunday dinner," Pa said.

John fidgeted with the hat in his hands, working his fingers around the wide brim. "You know Ma. She can't abide the thought of you two fending for yourselfs whilst Myrtle's away. And since Sam went with her, Ma figured mebbe the two of you can manage to eat what Sam woulda et."

Pa clapped him on the shoulder. "That's thoughtful of your Ma. We're delighted to come."

"Oh, and Pa said to tell you that when he rode out around our fields this morning, he found fresh horse tracks along the north thirty, heading toward the McSherryville Road. At least two sets, not more than four."

John's father, Karle, had heard horses gallop past their house just before dawn. He went to investigate, but by the time he got outside all he saw was David and Jake, looking down the empty street.

Pa shook his head at the news. "They'd have reached Gettysburg by now, and you know how the roads branch off in every direction from there."

He went over to the melodeon and lifted the family Bible from the music rack above the keyboard. "Jake, do you have your New Testament?"

Jake patted his pants pocket. "Yes, sir."

"Then we're on our way."

The banjo clock on the wall chimed the quarter hour.

"We'd better hurry," John said.

Many of the worshippers at the Methodist Church stood outside until the last minute, exchanging stories of yesterday's excitement. Jake and Pa took their usual pew, third row, right side. The opening hymn didn't sound the same without Myrtle's alto to balance Jake's tenor and Pa's bass. Even during the hymns, Jake had difficulty paying attention as his mind turned from one dilemma to another.

At first, he wondered if the theft of the horses was God's way of telling him not to enlist. Then he remembered the money he had saved. Though he hoped to use it someday to start out his marriage with Eliza, there was enough to buy a very good horse. Several days ago, at Governor Curtin's order, all the banks in the county had sent the bulk of their deposits to Philadelphia for safekeeping, but surely Pa's banker would work something out for him.

Maybe this was God's way of testing his resolve, his willingness to make sacrifices and bear hardships. Or should he forget about cavalry service and join the infantry? Or forget about the whole idea? Harkening back to Pa's words the previous night, Jake peered at the ceiling, as if "searching for the moon behind the clouds."

Rev. Guyer stepped to the lectern and cleared his throat. "Today's first text, found in the gospel of Luke, has particular meaning in light of yesterday's grim events."

Interest piqued, Jake sat up straighter and focused on the pastor.

"Turn with me in your Bibles to the ninth chapter of Luke, beginning with the fifty-seventh verse."

Jake pulled out his New Testament and thumbed through the well-worn pages. He scanned ahead while the passage was read aloud. His eyes lingered on the closing verses.

> *"Lord, I will follow thee; but let me first go bid them farewell, which are at home at my house."*
> *And Jesus said unto him, "No man, having put his hand to the plough, and looking back, is fit for the kingdom of God."*

Was that the same thing as waiting for Myrtle's wedding before he enlisted? Jake swallowed hard. He believed his duty was clear: to fight for the cause of the Second War of Independence. Were these dilemmas examples of putting his hand to the plough and then looking back?

Rev. Guyer expounded on the verses, reminding the congregation to remain steadfast in their support of the Union cause. Meanwhile, Jake grew more certain he must leave the family business behind in order to fulfill his duty. But he still struggled with leaving the carriage unfinished and missing Myrtle's wedding.

"Turn over to the fourteenth chapter of Luke, the twenty-fifth verse," the pastor intoned.

Again, Jake read ahead.

> And he turned, and said unto them, "If any man come to me, and hate not his father, and mother, and wife, and children, and brethren, and sisters, yea, and his own life also, he cannot be my disciple."

Jake gulped. He knew Jesus' words were in the context of commitment to faith, but didn't they also apply to the works one was called to do?

> "For which of you, intending to build a tower, sitteth not down first, and counteth the cost, whether he have sufficient to finish it?"

Pa had quoted verse twenty-eight often enough! "Count the cost." Jake was counting. The problem was, he didn't like the way the costs were mounting.

> "Lest haply, after he hath laid the foundation, and is not able to finish it, all that behold it begin to mock him, Saying, This man began to build, and was not able to finish."

Pa's axiom rang in his ears, "Don't start what you can't finish!"

Jake only half-listened to the pastor's sermon on commitment. One by one, he mentally listed the factors holding him back from enlistment and, at the end, he felt more determined than ever. His sense of duty demanded he do his part to finish the job the founding fathers had begun: to ensure all people the freedoms the Constitution envisioned, especially freedom from an intrusive, tyrannical government.

Jake bowed his head and prayed. *I will leave all and follow the path You have shown me.*

Rev. Guyer announced the closing hymn, "Soldiers of Christ Arise."

Jake stood with the congregation and turned to the popular Wesleyan hymn. Now that he knew what he must do, he felt as though a tremendous burden had been lifted from his shoulders. But what about the queasiness in the pit of his stomach? Was this how a condemned man felt awaiting the gallows, knowing the hour of his death drew nigh?

3

Sunday dinner finished, Karle Forney pushed back from the table and invited Jake and Pa to the front porch for cigars. Jake's stomach reeled at the mere thought of it. He hadn't been able to resist extra helpings of Mary Forney's scrumptious ham, *schnitz,* and dumplings. He imagined he might have better success rolling than walking to the hymn-sing at the Wertzes. Of course, those two slices of blueberry pie he'd had didn't help any.

"What time is it, Pa?"

Pa pulled out his pocket watch and held it where his eyes could properly focus. "Twenty-five, no, twenty-six until four."

"I guess I better get going." Jake turned to Mrs. Forney. "Thank you very much for the kind invitation and the delicious dinner." He stood and rubbed his stomach. "I may never be hungry again."

John Forney swallowed his last bite. "Thanks, Ma. May I be excused to go to the Albrights?"

"Of course, dear, and tell Deborah we look forward to having her family here next Sunday."

John's sister, Susan, cleared the table while the young men headed off to visit their beloveds.

As he walked, Jake reflected on the decision he'd made during the church service. It would be hard to leave Hanover, but he knew he was ready. He would wait to tell Pa until after he got back from seeing Eliza.

Jake stopped by the house, hoping Skipper and Streak had somehow managed to escape and find their way back home, but all he found was Old Jack, pecking away at some grit in front of the A-framed chicken coop that Myrtle had jokingly dubbed the "Poulet Chalet."

Well, I can't very well sign up for the cavalry without a horse. If the Confederate Army had horses to give away, there'd be no infantry. So, Lord, let that be the final sign. If you want me to go, I'll need a horse. No horse, no enlistment.

As he passed the unfinished church foundation, the crone's words rang in his mind. *Best hope dat ain't your own graves you're diggin'.*

From the trench, a ghostly image of the Smiling Man flashed a fleshless grin and beckoned with a bony finger. "Will you join the fight?"

Jake blinked and shook his head to chase away the specter. He turned toward the Square and saw the usual Sunday afternoon traffic: couples and families out for a stroll, an occasional buggy—

A buggy suddenly veered and headed in his direction. The driver cracked the whip above the horse's back. The steed broke into a fast trot, head bobbing as if trying to understand the unaccustomed urgency.

In the Square, a few of the women separated from their companions and scurried out of sight. Most of the men huddled together, some pointing down Carlisle Street.

As the buggy flew past, the driver shouted, "Rebels!"

"Not again," Jake muttered. Lengthening his stride, he half walked and half ran to see what was going on.

By the time he got to the Square, three mounted men in dingy gray uniforms had arrived. Jake moved to the back of the small crowd and looked out Carlisle Street. He expected to see another column of Confederate cavalry on the way, but the street stood empty.

One of the soldiers, a squat man in his thirties with tufts of red hair poking from beneath his forage cap, cleared his throat and growled, "Where can a fellow get something to wet his whistle around here?"

Mr. Lookenbaugh scoffed, "If your whistle were any wetter, you'd like to drown in it."

Nervous chuckles rippled through the small crowd.

Jake scrutinized the soldier's face, noting the bleary bloodshot eyes. Drunk as a skunk, no doubt. The man put his hand on his belly. Jake's eyes followed the path of the hand, and— *No! It can't be!* Jake craned his neck for a closer look. The soldier sat atop Streak! The man behind him rode a bay, and the other—was on Skipper!

Mr. Gobrecht waved for calm, both palms down. "Now let's be hospitable. I'll be glad to tell you men where you can get a drink." He turned and pointed behind him. "You go past the Market Shed there, go out Baltimore Street, oh . . . about forty miles or so, then turn right, and keep going 'til you hit Virginia."

The soldiers scowled.

Jake wanted to scream. *No, don't leave! How can I get Skipper and Streak back?*

Mr. Lookenbaugh added, "Or maybe they would like to see the little tavern we have *under* the Market Shed."

The townsfolk laughed. The excavation beneath the market building served as the town jail.

Should I just shout that those men stole our horses?

A pistol suddenly appeared in the redheaded soldier's hand. His shirt hung open at the belt, exposing his grime-encrusted paunch. The soldier on the bay brandished a shotgun. The jeers stopped. The click of the pistol's hammer sounded all the more ominous in the silence.

Jake felt a surge of despair. *How do I get those scoundrels off our horses? I can't very well invite them back to our house for a drink. They may be too drunk to realize they've looped their way back to the same town, but surely they would recognize our place.* Then it came to him. "I know where you can get something to drink."

The townsfolk turned to glare at Jake. Ignoring the looks of shock and disgust, he gestured over his shoulder toward the apothecary. "Captain Myers of the 35th Virginia Cavalry got some whiskey from Mr. Scott yesterday." Jake tried to sound jovial. "That Mr. Scott, he's always ready to help a man in need."

The soldier gently lowered the hammer of the pistol.

But then a shrill voice rang out, "He'd not help the likes of you!" Jake gulped. It was Mrs. Scott.

"And that's an apothecary, not a brewery," she scolded. "My husband doesn't even drink, so you scallywags can just take your mischief elsewheres!"

The soldier leveled his gun at Mrs. Scott. "Well then, how 'bout you show us to the nearest tavern, and we'll do just that."

Since he was no longer the center of attention, Jake scanned the crowd for help. His eyes stopped on Mr. Stonesifer, whose vest bulged above the right hip. A pistol? Jake inched in his direction.

Mrs. Scott huffed. "Well! This is the Lord's Day. Every tavern is closed. Don't you Rebels observe the Sabbath?"

Mr. Gobrecht scoffed, "They're slavers, they don't know nothin' 'bout the Lord."

The soldier turned the pistol on Gobrecht. "Well maybe I should send you to the Maker, so's you can introduce me. You can tell Him Corporal Raymond Biggins sent you." He pulled back the hammer.

Jake stood behind Mr. Stonesifer and whispered, "Do you have a gun? Those men stole our horses."

Stonesifer nodded slightly and brushed against his right side.

"Good. I'm going to look for a couple more men to help. Be ready—"

A gravelly baritone voice rang out from the doorway to the Central Hotel. "What seems to be the problem, gentlemen?" It was Mr. Dellone.

Someone muttered, "Danged Copperhead."

Dellone proceeded down the steps. The crowd parted, allowing him to reach the soldiers.

"I'm Joseph Dellone, publishing editor of the *Hanover Citizen*. Would you gentlemen care to join me in the hotel for a bit of refreshment? Perhaps you would allow me an interview over dinner?"

The soldiers exchanged wary looks.

Mr. Gobrecht exclaimed, "Joseph Dellone, may you rot in hell!"

Apparently satisfied that Dellone meant no harm, Corporal Biggins lowered the hammer on his pistol and returned the weapon to his belt. The men dismounted and led the horses to the hotel hitching post.

Jake saw an opportunity. "I'll take your horses around back to the hotel stables. I'll feed them and make sure no one bothers them."

Dellone gave the soldiers an assuring nod. "That sounds like a good idea. Thank you, Jake." He gestured toward the doorway. "Gentlemen?"

Jake could barely hide his glee. *Thank you, Lord! All I have to do is stable the bay, then take Skipper and Streak out to the Forneys' and get—*

"Jefferson!" Biggins shouted.

The man on Skipper drawled, "Yessir?"

"You go with the lad here and guard the horses. After we eat, I'll send O'Brian out so's you can get something to eat, too."

Market Shed and Central Hotel (1850's)
Frederick Street exits the Square behind the Shed.

Now what? Jake tried to calm his nerves. At least there would be only one soldier to contend with. He took Skipper's and Streak's reins from the soldiers. Both horses nuzzled him and Skipper nickered softly.

Biggins' eyes narrowed.

Stonesifer interjected, "Horses can always tell when they're around a good handler."

Skipper sniffed Jake's pockets.

The corporal again drew his pistol.

"I've know Jake's family for years," Dellone said in a soothing tone. "He's been around horses all his life."

Jake willed Mr. Dellone to stop speaking, but as usual the man rambled on.

"In fact, his father always has at least one pair of Morgans, just like you fellows, right Jake?"

Biggins aimed the pistol at Jake.

With all the speed and dexterity of a magician, Stonesifer drew his pistol and thrust it against the corporal's neck. "Any of you Rebels move, and he dies where he stands."

Biggins gagged from the pistol's pressure. "All right. Enough."

Gobrecht stepped forward and took the gun from the corporal's hand.

"What is the meaning of this?" Dellone sputtered.

Jake could restrain himself no longer. "Those men stole our horses this morning! That's Skipper, this is Streak, and that's our tack."

"That ain't true," O'Brian shouted. "We took 'em off two darkies. They was runaways, for sure."

Dellone looked like he wanted to believe them, but then suspicion clouded his face. "If that is true, then where are the slaves now?"

The crowd murmured.

O'Brian bit his lower lip and glanced nervously at the throng. "Um, where are the slaves now? Uh, we left 'em by the stream next to the cornfield they was comin' out of."

Jake's heart sagged. The Forneys' north thirty acres were planted in corn, and the horse tracks had gone through that field. A stream bordered the northern edge. Could it be true after all? Had escaped slaves stolen Skipper and Streak?

Dellone didn't look convinced. "We'll have to see about that. Ruben and Benjamin, bring that man and we'll go check out his story." He turned to the rest of the crowd. "Maybe you other men can take these two to our 'little tavern' until we sort this all out."

No one muttered "Copperhead" now. More than one man cast a grudging look of approval at Dellone.

Jake asked no one in particular, "What about Skipper and Streak?"

Dellone considered for a moment. "Why don't you go ahead and take them on home."

Half expecting someone to raise an objection, Jake kept a tight hold on Streak's reins and mounted Skipper. The crowd parted. Jake and the Morgans cantered for home. *I guess I have my sign, Lord.*

The clock on St. Matthew's struck four. Jake groaned. What would Eliza and her mother think when he was late?

-4-

David used Karle Forney's cigar to light his own, then both men settled into their rockers on the Forneys' small front porch.

"Cool today," Karle said, cigar smoke billowing around his head.

"Thick clouds," David added. He rocked slowly, mulling over Jake's demeanor during church. Why such deep attention to the Bible passages?

Two hens squabbled over some scrap in the yard. When the rooster swooped in to investigate, they ran under the porch. David's eyes followed the big bird as he strutted away with the morsel. Turning to Karle, he announced, "Jake will enlist soon."

"That so."

David took a puff and held it for a long moment, then let it go in a thin stream. "Confederate Army."

Karle's face didn't change. "Ya don't say."

"Hope you don't mind Samuel's bride bringing a Rebel into the family."

The rockers stopped. Karle looked David in the eye. "Too late. Our grandfathers wore that title with pride."

"True enough." The rocking resumed.

Karle's eyes narrowed, his bushy white brows protruding like snow-covered caterpillars. "Jake favor slavery?"

"Nope."

"Ah. States' rights."

"Yep."

Karle knocked his knuckles on the arm of his rocker. "You know, if that 'temporary income tax' ever becomes permanent, I'll join up myself!"

David snorted. "Three percent of all I make. We didn't stand for taxes like that from King George! Americans won't long put up with that from our own government, that's for certain."

"Indeed!" The men vented their agitation with several rapid puffs on their cigars. Karle reached over and swatted David's arm. "You raised a fine young man in that Jacob. Not to worry."

David smiled. "True enough. And with a mind of his own."

"Thank God," Karle said, a twinkle in his eye.

The distant thud of horses' hooves echoed up the street. David stood for a better look. A single rider atop a chestnut horse approached at full gallop; a similar horse ran close behind.

Karle stepped off the porch and went out to the road. "That looks sorta like . . ."

"It is!" David hastened to meet his son.

Jake reined Skipper to a halt and Streak pulled up next to them. Both horses bobbed their heads and swished their tails, excited to be back in familiar hands.

"Pa, look what I found!" Jake dismounted, tied the horses to the big iron loop on the hitching post, then breathlessly related the events in town.

"Well, thank the Lord," David said, rubbing Streak's neck. "It's so good to have you boys back." He looked sadly at Skipper. *But how much longer will you be here?*

"Pa, I have to get over to the Wertzes. I figured I'd ride Skipper and leave Streak here with you. We're going to have to keep a close eye on them, I guess."

David sucked a thread of ham from between his teeth and nodded. "Sounds right. Best you get on your way, I heard the clock in the withdrawing room chime the hour a few minutes ago."

"Yes, sir." Jake untied Skipper, eased into the saddle in one fluid motion and cantered off.

Karle spoke around his cigar. "That young man will do you proud."

"He'll do us all proud," David said, swallowing the lump in his throat.

-5-

The soothing strains of "O God Our Help in Ages Past" greeted Jake as he rode up to the Wertzes' porch and tied Skipper to the hitching rail. Two warbling sopranos dominated the other voices in the final lines: "Be Thou our guard while troubles last, and our eternal home."

Jake took off his hat, smoothed his hair, then knocked on the front door. After the sound of rushing footsteps, Kat opened the door. Eliza stood behind her in the hallway.

Kat performed a very proper curtsey, and said, "Good afternoon, Jacob, won't you come in?"

Barely noticing Kat, he entered, his eyes fixed on Eliza.

Kat reached out her hand. "May I take your hat, sir?"

He slowly handed over the hat. Eliza did not look pleased to see him. A clock chimed the half-hour. "I'm sorry I'm late, Eliza."

Mrs. Bigler appeared from the parlor. "Ohhh, hello, Jacob." Her voice sounded as though she had just discovered a clod of dung on her shoe.

Jake flashed his warmest smile. "Good afternoon, Mrs. Bigler. Thank you for allowing me to join your hymn-sing. I'm sor—"

"It is not *my* hymn-sing, young man, it is the Lord's." Mrs. Bigler spun on her heel and returned to the parlor, billowing contempt in her wake.

Mr. Wertz entered the hallway. "Howdy, Jake. Glad to have you with us. Come on in."

"Thank you, sir." Jake tried to make eye contact with Eliza, but she turned away and went back into the parlor.

Kat stepped in front of him, her green eyes twinkling mischievously, as usual. "How come you're late, Jake?"

"There was some trouble in town."

"Oh really? Tell us!" Kat took him by the hand and led him into the parlor.

Eliza sat at the spinet, her back to him. Mr. and Mrs. Wertz shared the divan. Mrs. Bigler sat enthroned on the large wing chair, and Lydia shared the loveseat with Jonas Serff, her beau. Next to the spinet stood two cane-backed chairs from the dining room set.

Kat took a seat in one of the empty chairs and patted the other for Jake to sit. She looked up at him, her eyes bright. "Trouble? More soldiers?"

Eliza turned to face Jake when he spoke. Her eyes grew wide as his story unfolded. "So was it slaves that done it, or those soldiers?"

"I believe it was the soldiers, because when I came back through town the three of them were tied up in the back of a wagon."

Kat's eyes gleamed. "Golly!"

"That's no way for a young lady to speak, Kathleen," Eliza corrected.

Jake cocked his head and gave the younger sister an appraising look.

He broke out his best Irish brogue, his inflection dropping at the end of each question. "So, 'tis Kathleen now? Is there a more glorrrious name for such a beeauutiful young lass?"

Kathleen blushed and looked away. A smile spread across her face.

A dissonant chord rang out from the spinet. "Oh dear!" Eliza exclaimed. Had her elbow slipped and fallen on the keys?

Mrs. Bigler ostentatiously cleared her throat. "Perhaps we should take that as a sign for us to remember why we are here?"

Mrs. Wertz added, "Kathleen, dear, why don't you get Jacob from the cupboard a hymn book?"

Lydia cleared her throat, and said, "But Mother, we only have these five." Eliza had one book at the spinet, Mrs. Bigler held one, and both of the couples shared a copy. Kathleen's was the last.

"I suppose Jacob can share mine," Kathleen offered.

Eliza looked askance at her sister.

"That's very kind of you, Kathleen," Mrs. Wertz said. "Jacob, we've each selected a hymn to sing, so it is yet your turn. Have you a favorite?"

"Yes, ma'am. 'And Can It Be?'"

Flipping through the index, Kathleen found the number first. "It's number 301."

While the others found the page, Mr. Wertz asked, "Tenor or bass?"

"Tenor."

"Perfect," Mr. Wertz grunted. "Now Jonas can stop straining for those high notes."

Jonas grinned and turned to Lydia. "So that means you can stop pinching me to sing higher." Lydia smiled and squeezed his hand.

Eliza played the chorus for the introduction, then they all began to sing. As Jake had suspected, the "pouter pigeon vibratos" came from Mrs. Wertz and Mrs. Bigler. Lydia and Eliza sang solid altos, and the men produced a nice rich bass. But to his surprise, it was Kathleen's voice that sent chills up his spine.

At the end of the first stanza, Kathleen sang the three ascending arpeggios with such perfection of pitch and beauty of tone, Jake could hardly believe his ears. When the soprano and tenor lines moved in parallel harmony on the chorus, their voices rang with fervor, finally joining as one on the final note.

"Ladies alone on the second stanza," Mr. Wertz directed.

Jake had a hard time concentrating on the words. He kept his eyes on the page, but his ears reveled in the sound of Kathleen's mellifluous voice.

"All right, men, we have verse three," Mr. Wertz said.

Now that Jake sang the melody, his voice stumbled a bit on the arpeggios. Kathleen shot him a crooked smile and gave him a gentle nudge with her elbow.

"Parts!" Mr. Wertz announced.

The group sang the rousing final verse with all the gusto the text demanded. With Kathleen's voice ringing in Jake's ear, the chorus was even more exhilarating the final time around. As the amen faded away, Kathleen slid her hand under the hymnal and gave Jake's wrist a quick squeeze. He turned his head to look at her, but she averted her eyes.

Mrs. Wertz fanned her face with her hand. "That was simply glorious!" The others murmured in agreement. "Jake, you have a fine voice. What a difference it makes having you here."

Eliza turned to face the group. "How could we possibly do better than that?" Her inflection implied she wanted to stop.

"So glorious, how could we end now?" Kathleen quickly added.

Jake saw the sisters exchange a look, but it was one he couldn't read.

Evidently, Mr. Wertz agreed with Kathleen. "All right, then, let's each select another. Kathleen, what would you like us to sing next?"

She chose "When I Survey the Wondrous Cross," which happened to be another of Jake's favorites. So when it came time for him to select the final hymn, he searched his memory for the perfect song.

"How about 'Blest Be the Tie that Binds?'" Jake liked its heart-warming message, but he mainly chose it for the way its soprano and tenor lines intertwined throughout the song. The tenor line sometimes supported the soprano, at other times it soared above, leading the way. As they sang the last stanza unaccompanied, the text pinged Jake's heart:

> *When we asunder part, it gives us inward pain.*
> *But we shall still be joined in heart, and hope to meet again.*

Eliza stood and opened the spinet's bench, rearranged a stack of sheet music to make room for the hymnal, then turned and faced the gathering with an expectant look on her face.

Mrs. Wertz cleared her throat. "Would you help me in the kitchen, Irene? And Kathleen?"

The men stood as the ladies left the room. Mr. Wertz gestured toward the divan, and said, "Jacob, why don't you and Eliza sit here, I'll take the chair."

Jake waited for Eliza to settle on the couch, then sat a respectable distance away from her. The clock ticked. No one spoke.

Just before the silence became awkward, Jonas said, "Jake, are there any rumors in town of troop movements?"

"None that I heard of. Sam Forney is due back tonight. He took my sisters to Lancaster yesterday, and presuming they weren't waylaid, he should have some news."

Mr. Wertz sniffed. "I hope he didn't run into the Rebel cavalry that left here."

This small talk was not at all what Jake had in mind. Then again, he hadn't really given much thought to how the afternoon visit would pass.

How could he possibly be alone with Eliza to tell her his plans? Time was running short, and he couldn't discuss something this serious in front of everyone, not without telling Pa about his decision first.

Kathleen returned from the kitchen and set a silver tray on the coffee table; everyone oohed and aahed at the fruit pastries. Mrs. Wertz circled the room handing out linen napkins. Mrs. Bigler entered, surveyed the seating situation, and cast an imperious eye upon the couple on the divan.

"Jake and I will take our sweets on the porch, Mama," Eliza said, perhaps a bit too eagerly.

Her mother's look only darkened.

"And Kathleen, too, of course," Eliza added reluctantly.

Mrs. Wertz handed her sister-in-law a napkin. "Well, that sounds like a splendid idea, don't you agree, Irene?"

Mrs. Bigler didn't look like she agreed in the least, but she acquiesced and stepped aside. The trio each plucked a pastry from the tray and left for the porch.

Once outside the front door, Eliza leaned over and whispered in Jake's ear. "Did you talk with your father?"

Her breath sent a shiver down his spine. He turned to face her and got lost in her expectant, brown eyes.

"Well, what did he say?" Eliza implored, tugging on his arm.

Coming up beside the couple, Kathleen licked some icing from her finger and thumb. "What did who say?"

Jake hesitated. He had decided to leave tomorrow, but hadn't told Pa yet. Should he say good-bye to Eliza now, or wait and stop by on his way out of town? He walked to the far end of the porch, the young women trailing behind him. Remembering the Bible verse about not looking back, Jake made up his mind.

He set his napkin and pastry on the porch rail and turned to face his beloved. "Eliza, I spoke with my father last night. I have made my decision. I am leaving tomorrow to join the Army of Northern Virginia."

Eliza squealed with excitement. "Wait here, I'll be right back." She hurried into the house. Jake and Kathleen exchanged quizzical looks.

From the parlor Mrs. Bigler called, "Eliza! Did you leave your sister and Jacob alone on the porch?"

The scornful reply floated down the stairs. "Mother! It's just Kathleen . . ."

Kathleen sagged as if physically wounded.

Hating to see her like that, Jake put his hand on her shoulder. She started, then relaxed and glanced up at him.

"Kathleen, you sing like an angel."

She blushed and looked away.

He gave her shoulder a gentle squeeze. "Really."

She looked at him. Her eyes seemed to penetrate his very soul.

As Jake removed his hand from her shoulder, his fingertips brushed her bare arm and a small shiver went through him. "God has blessed you with a wonderful gift, Kathleen. A miraculous treasure. I hope someday you—"

Eliza bustled through the door, clutching a photograph in one hand, a scissors and length of ribbon in the other. She strode over to Jake and held out the picture. "Would you carry this picture of me? I'm sorry it isn't my best, but it's the only one I can take without angering Mama."

Jake's eyes pored over the photograph. Eliza and Kathleen stood side by side. They wore matching square-necked, flowered frocks. Eliza's bonnet framed her pretty face in a very lady-like manner; Kathleen's perched at a jaunty angle, and in spite of the custom to maintain a serious visage, a mischievous smile played on the corners of her mouth.

"Eliza, you know I hate that picture," Kathleen protested. She turned to Jake. "That was taken three years ago. I was just a girl and had a hard time standing still."

"Don't worry, I could never forget your face," he soothed.

"Kathleen, would you cut a lock of my hair for Jake?" Eliza handed over the scissors, lifted the hair from her shoulders, and turned her back. "Make sure to cut along my neck, so it doesn't show."

Instead, Kathleen quickly gathered a short length of her own hair in one hand and held the scissors to it. She turned to Jake and mouthed the words, *Would you—*

His heart warming at the thought, Jake stopped her with a quick nod and again squeezed her shoulder. Were those tears in her eyes?

"Can't you find a good spot?" Eliza prompted.

Kathleen snipped her own lock before cutting one of her sister's. "Let me have the ribbon, Eliza, and I'll cut a piece of it for you."

Eliza handed over the ribbon, then turned to Jake. "I am so proud of you. But you must promise me not to do anything foolish. I already know how brave you are, no need to go getting yourself shot."

While Eliza chattered on, out of the corner of his eye Jake saw Kathleen cut two lengths of the pink satin ribbon. She tied each lock separately. Finished, she looked up at him, her eyes filled with sadness and—what else? Love? He looked directly at her. The loosened tress on the left side of her face clung to her tear-dampened cheek. The spot where she had cut a lock was plain to see. She wiped her cheek with the back of a hand, then used her fingertips to comb her hair back toward her bun.

". . . proper good-bye," Eliza said.

Jake blinked. "I'm sorry, Eliza. What was that?"

"I asked if you wanted to go somewhere so I can give you a proper good-bye," Eliza repeated insistently.

Kathleen muttered, "Mama wouldn't like that."

Sounds from inside the house told them the get-together was coming to an end.

Eliza humphed. "Then I shall have to say good-bye right here." She took Jake's face in her hands and nearly devoured his lips. Her tongue poked its way into his mouth. She pressed her body against him, and her bosom literally warmed his heart.

Jake hugged her and imagined the two of them in their wedding bed, finally free to express their love in the fullest measure. Eliza moaned softly as his hands gently stroked her back.

"Eliza Marie Bigler!"

The couple sprang apart. Mrs. Bigler stomped to their side. "What is going on here!"

Kathleen interjected, "Mama, Jacob just told us he is leaving tomorrow to join the army. The *Confederate Army*, Mama, isn't that exciting? We decided it only fitting to send our hero off with a kiss—on behalf of all the grateful women of the South." And with that, Kathleen elbowed Eliza aside, placed her hands on Jake's cheeks, rose onto her tiptoes, and shyly touched her lips to his.

Her lips tasted like the blueberry tart she had eaten. But that was not what Jake would always remember. Her kiss was gentle at first, then a bit more urgent. It lacked the passion of Eliza's kiss, but carried with it a sense of love and tenderness beyond anything he had ever imagined. Her lips left his, then she laid the side of her head against his chest and whispered, "God be with you, Jacob."

He wondered if she could hear his pounding heart. Aware of Eliza and Mrs. Bigler's presence, he reluctantly ended the embrace, put his hands on Kathleen's shoulders, and looked into her ethereal green eyes. "Thank you, Kathleen, and may God be with you, too."

Hands on hips, Eliza glared at her sister. Mrs. Bigler stared from one daughter to the other, apparently at a rare loss for words.

Jake decided there might never be a better time to speak his mind. "Mrs. Bigler, I shall leave on the morrow to volunteer my services with the Army of Northern Virginia. God willing, upon my return I will ask your permission to court your daughter."

Eliza's eyes lit up and she clasped her hands together.

An odd expression appeared on Kathleen's face.

Brow furrowed, Mrs. Bigler looked Jake up and down. "Tell me, why are you going?"

Jake looked Mrs. Bigler straight in the eye. "For two years now, the memory of what Unionists did to the men defending their own free state has never been far from my mind. Any government that would order such a thing cannot be allowed to stand. Now that I am a man, I believe it is my duty to help the Confederate states win their Second War of Independence."

"I see." Mrs. Bigler's face actually softened. "You are making a highly honorable commitment to fight for our cause. For that you have our thanks and admiration." She stared off into the distance for a long moment, then focused her eyes upon Jake. "As for my daughter, I shall have to discuss the matter with Mr. Bigler."

Jake's breath returned. At least she didn't say no, that was good progress. But there was more.

"However, if God grants you a safe return, Jacob, I may be favorably disposed to consider the possibility."

If . . . may . . . possibility . . . hardly a yes, but far better than he had expected. "Thank you, Mrs. Bigler."

He turned to speak to Eliza, but Kathleen's slight movement caught his attention. What could he read in such an expression?

Her head tilted slightly—questioning? The corners of her mouth quivered. Her eyes . . . again, that penetrating look. Her hand rested on her heart, fingers curled around the lock of hair she had cut for him.

Jake's heart suddenly burned with feelings for her. New feelings. Different from any other he had ever experienced. He wanted to hold her in his arms and protect her from all the evils of the world. He wanted to do something, anything, to make her smile, to make her *happy.*

He looked at Eliza. Her eyes met his and glowed with the promise of fantasies fulfilled. His body stirred, but he chased the carnal thoughts from his mind.

"And you are leaving tomorrow?" Mrs. Bigler asked.

Jake gulped. Was she in such a hurry to be rid of him?

"He's leaving tomorrow, Mama," Eliza said. "And I have a lock of my hair that he promised to carry over his heart." She snapped her fingers at Kathleen, who quickly produced the lock. Eliza kissed it and slid the treasure into Jake's shirt pocket.

Her mother said, "That's very sweet of you, dear. I'm sure he will cherish it. Now why don't we go inside and tell the others about Jake's decision?" She led the way and Eliza followed.

"I'll be right in, Mama," Kathleen said. "I'll clean up out here first." As Eliza and Mrs. Bigler went into the house, Kathleen tugged on Jake's shirtsleeve for him to stay.

He turned to face her.

"Know that my thoughts and my prayers go with you, Jacob." She held up her lock of hair, kissed it, and slipped it into his pocket. Her eyes never left his as she put a hand on his heart, stood on the tips of her toes, and gave him another tender kiss on the lips. Then she quickly gathered up the napkins and hurried into the house.

His thoughts racing crazily, Jake sagged against the porch post to catch his breath before going inside. Never had his mind been so befuddled. And his emotions? He didn't even know where to begin. He knew he loved Eliza. But what about Kathleen? What in heaven's name was going on in his heart over her?

Good thing I'm going off to war. I need some time to figure this out!

-6-

While Kathleen pulled out the trundle bed, Lydia went around the candlelit bedroom and drew the curtains. Eliza had already stripped down to her chemise and short bloomers.

Lydia snapped the last pair of curtains shut, turned to her cousin, and said with mock accusation, "Did you hope Jake was out there, trying to catch a glimpse of you in your unmentionables before he leaves?"

Eliza flinched. How did Lydia know? Finally realizing it was a joke, she retorted, "More likely that Jonas is out there, wishing to see you."

Blushing, Lydia went to the closet and stepped out of her dress. "Actually, I have some news for you." She disappeared into the closet.

"What news?" Kathleen asked, lolling on the trundle bed.

Lydia's muffled voice came from the closet. "News about Jonas." She peeked around the corner. "And me."

Kathleen ran to the closet and dragged her cousin into the room. "Tell us!"

"Well . . . tomorrow night . . . Jonas is going to ask Pa for my hand!"

The three young women squealed and hugged. The questions came in a flood. "Do you think Uncle Henry will say yes?" "How soon 'til the wedding?" "Can I be a bridesmaid?" "You aren't with child are you?"

Lydia looked horrified. "Kathleen! Perish such a thought!"

"I'm sorry, I didn't mean anything by it. It's just, you know, I happened to be in one of the stalls a few weeks ago when you and Jonas went up into the hayloft."

It was Eliza's turn to pretend to scold. She narrowed her eyes and waggled her finger at Lydia. "Were you allowing Mr. Serff to take liberties, young lady?"

"And what if I was," Lydia replied with a petulant grin. She pulled off a stocking and threw it on the floor. "There's winning your man," she removed the other stocking and flung it over her shoulder, "and then there's keeping your man." She wiggled her bloomer-covered bottom at the window.

The three girls broke into fits of laughter. Kathleen took her turn changing while Eliza continued, "Well, you've got nothing on me. Jake asked Mama for my hand today."

Kathleen's disheveled, tawny head peeked from the closet. "Asked for permission to court you, you mean."

"Same thing."

"Is it really?" Kathleen wedding-stepped into the room. Her inside-out dress hung off the back of her head like an elaborate veil. She held her rolled-up stockings like a bouquet.

"Very nice, sis," Eliza snickered. She turned her face to the mirror and stroked her hair. "By the way, don't think I didn't notice the way you acted toward Jake this afternoon. I'm glad you care for him so. He can be the big brother you never had."

One of the crumpled stockings hit Eliza on the rump.

Lydia sat on the bed and chuckled. "So, did you give him a good-bye present, Eliza?"

"My picture and a lock of my hair, which I tied in that pretty pink ribbon we had left over from my new dress."

"You know what I mean," Lydia said with a sly look.

Eliza crossed to the dresser and picked up her brush. "Kathleen, would you be a dear and—" As she turned, she bumped into her sister, now dressed in a cotton nightgown. Eliza handed Kathleen the brush and they joined Lydia on the bed.

"Well? Did you or didn't you?" Lydia persisted.

Kathleen began the ritual hundred brush strokes while Eliza slowly tilted her head from side to side. Eliza always looked forward to this bit of daily pampering. She smiled at the thought of teaching Jake how to brush her hair when they were married.

Lydia put her face directly in front of Eliza's. "I guess not, then."

"Actually, I gave him a kiss he'll never forget."

Lydia giggled.

The brush caught in Eliza's hair. "Ouch! Careful!"

"One hundred!" Kathleen announced, handing the brush over Eliza's shoulder.

"Already? Hmm. Anyways, I wished we were somewhere private, but then Mama came out on the porch, right in the middle of the kiss!"

Lydia stood and pulled back the quilt and top sheet. "So that's why she yelled at you. We all heard her clear in the house. What did she say?" Lydia crawled under the covers while Kathleen sat on the trundle bed.

Eliza put the brush away and then got into the other side of the double bed. "Wait a minute." She moved to the middle of the bed and patted the vacant spot next to her. "I promised Kathleen she could be part of our secret talks from now on."

Lydia smiled at her younger cousin. "Good, I'm glad. Oh, could you make the candles out before you get in?" Kathleen wet her fingers and dashed around the room to pinch out all four flames.

Once the three young women got settled under the sheet, Lydia prompted, "Your mother said . . ."

"She said, 'What is going on here!' I was too shocked to speak on account of Jake's kiss addling my mind. Lucky for me Kathleen was there." Eliza grasped her sister's hand and gave it a squeeze. "I'm so glad we're friends now, Kathleen. Tell Lydia what you said."

"No, you can tell it." Kathleen's voice cracked as she spoke.

"Well, don't you know, Kathleen answered right up with, 'Jake told us he's joining the Confederate Army. We decided it only fitting to send our hero off with a kiss—*on behalf of all the grateful women of the South.*'" Eliza and Lydia chortled. "And then she gave him the sweetest little kiss, didn't you, Kathleen?"

Kathleen rolled over on her side and faced the door.

Eliza sat up. "Oh . . . that was your first kiss wasn't it? Lydia, isn't that exciting? Today my little sister got her first kiss! Of course, it don't count for much, Jake being my beau and all, but still, I'm glad it was Jake that done it, aren't you? If that isn't the sweetest thing. I shall have to add that to my diary for today."

Someone knocked on the door. Without waiting for an answer, Irene Bigler entered the bedroom, lantern in hand. She set the light on the dresser, pushed the end of the trundle bed aside, and took a seat on the double bed next to Kathleen, who promptly curled into a ball.

Eliza couldn't remember the last time her mother had come to see them at bedtime. "What is it, Mama?" And was that the smell of whiskey?

Her mother's voice sounded strained. "Everything is changing. Nothing will ever be the same."

Kathleen pulled the pillow over her head. Eliza reached over her sister and laid a hand on their mother's arm. "What's the matter, Mama?"

"What won't ever be the same?" Lydia asked, sitting up.

Staring at the lantern's flame, Mama shook her head slowly. After a long moment, she laid a hand on top of Eliza's. "I got a letter from your father yesterday."

The pillow stirred. Kathleen's muffled voice cried, "Is Papa all right?"

"Yes, he's fine," Mama said, her voice slurring. "It's just, well, sometimes things happen. Things change."

Eliza couldn't imagine what horrible thing could have happened to make her mother act like this. "Just tell us, Mama."

Her mother took a shaky breath and slowly let it out. The reek of alcohol permeated the air. "You girls saw what happened to our fields after the battle two years ago. Then there was the second battle in Manassas last year. What crops survived were mostly taken by one army or the other." Her voice grew angry. "And no one has paid for any of it!"

"Don't worry, Mama." Eliza was about to add *Papa has lots of money*, but she suddenly realized she hadn't the slightest idea about such things. "This year will be different."

"I doubt it. The war has been hard on everyone. The McLeans even left their farm and moved to Appomattox. Your father decided it would be prudent to sell some of the slaves." She moved her hand to Kathleen's shoulder. "One of them was Abigail."

The pillow flew off the bed as Kathleen erupted from beneath the covers. "No, not Abby!" she cried.

"Now don't carry on so. You girls have no more need of a nanny. Abigail has a good disposition, is a hard worker, and is still of breeding age. She brought twice as much money as—well, never mind about that."

"What about Joey and Savannah and Danny and Bekka?" Kathleen asked tremulously.

Mama's voice resumed its usual austere tone. "Joseph was sold to a buyer from Atlanta. The letter didn't mention the other children." She stood and smoothed her skirt.

"Oh no, poor Joey!" Kathleen dissolved into tears.

"I am sorry I disturbed your sleep," Mama said coldly. She tottered to the dresser, picked up the lantern, and left without closing the door.

-7-

David rocked and rocked, ignoring the pipe in his hand. His son was going off to war. Images of Manassas filled his mind: the dead, the dying, all bearing the face of his one and only son.

Jake's earnest voice chased the phantasms away, ". . . to William Shriver's first. Herb also wants to join up."

David took a puff on the pipe and discovered it had gone out. No matter, this was no longer a discussion. He rested the pipe on his thigh. "The Shrivers? Yes, they're good folk. Funny, how a staunch Union man like Andrew owns slaves, yet right across the road, his brother William don't own a one. Good folks don't always have to make sense, I guess."

Jake nodded. "Herb's brother Kei left the infantry and is now with a medical unit in Richmond. I'm not sure where Lum is. Maybe Herb and I can find out and get into the same company as him. I figure even if Herb's parents won't let him go, his Pa might give me a letter of introduction."

"Sounds like a good plan, but if yesterday is any sign, you might not have to go far to find Lum." David puffed on the unlit pipe.

Jake bit a piece off his thumbnail and spat it out. "Before I go to sleep tonight I'll write a letter to my sisters." He fiddled with the ragged thumbnail for a moment, then stopped rocking.

"Pa, I hope you know how hard it is for me to ask you this, but, will you finish Myrtle's carriage without me? Last night I couldn't imagine leaving that job undone and missing her wedding, but during the sermon this morning, those Bible verses; it's like God was talking to me, Pa, telling me that there *are* causes even more important than family, and I believe this is one of them."

Though his heart felt like crumbling, David managed a smile. "Of course I'll finish it. I understand." But did he, really? Jake's reasoning seemed sound, and he truly believed he was following God's will. What more could a father ask?

Jake leaned forward in his rocker. "Oh, did your pipe go out? Here, let me go light that for you."

Numb, David handed the pipe to his son, who then disappeared into the house. Leaning back in the rocker, David remembered how Jake had looked that morning in church, bent over his New Testament, almost literally wrestling with its words. The last time he had looked like that was when he struggled for days to memorize the Declaration of

Independence. How many times had Jake wanted to give up? But his determination had won out. David would never forget the look of pride on his son's face after the perfect recitation.

Would Jake feel so strongly about his duty to this "Second War of Independence" if he had never learned so much about the first one? Funny how a seed could lie dormant for years, then suddenly bloom, bearing its unexpected fruit for all to see. How might life be different had that seed never been planted? What if David had allowed his son to leave that particular memorization assignment unfinished? But Jake was his mother's son, too. Rose's sense of fairness and justice ran strong in him.

David closed his eyes and images of Rose and Jake paraded through his mind: Rose cradling her newborn son to her breast . . . changing his diaper . . . feeding him his first oatmeal . . . holding her arms out to catch him at the end of his first steps . . . hiding her fear when he rode his first horse . . . her wan smile when Jake came to kiss her good-bye on her deathbed . . . the light and love in her eyes when she breathed her last . . . Jake dropping a rose on her casket as they lowered it into the—

"Here you go, Pa."

David blinked back a tear. Jake stood in front of him, holding out the pipe. The father looked into his son's eyes. "Tonight, it is yours to smoke."

Jake's mouth dropped open. His face broke into a broad smile. "Thank you, Pa. That means a lot to me." Jake settled into his seat, took a puff on the pipe, and resumed rocking.

The pipe came out. "Would it be all right with you if I take Skipper?"

David stifled a smile. Not at the question, but at the thought of how much Jake probably looked like he had twenty-odd years ago. "Oh, yes, Skipper." He sighed. "All in all, that's probably a good idea. Having your own horse is probably your only chance of getting into the cavalry, and it will make a big difference starting out on a horse you know so well. Of course, you realize what will probably wind up happening to him."

"Yeah, I thought about that. I'd hate to have to make that sacrifice, too, but either I'm willing to put my all on the line or I'm not."

"Glad to see you're counting the cost."

Jake saluted with the pipe. "You raised me, how could I not?"

"Oh, and maybe you should buy a pistol tomorrow. I'll dig up one of the jars of money we buried in the flower garden. Buy a lot of bullets and do some practicing as you get the chance."

Jake took a quick puff on the pipe. "Guess I'm going to have to learn to use a sabre, too."

Trying to sound old and wise, David said, "I believe the idea is to put the pointy end into the other fellow."

Both men chuckled more than the old joke was worth, then David added, "You might want to buy a new pair of shoes while you're in town. You can take your old ones along in case you're assigned to the infantry. If nothing else, you can always trade or sell them. And when are you going to go say good-bye to Eliza?"

A troubled look filled Jake's face. "I did that this afternoon."

"I see. Probably better that way."

They rocked in silence for a while. A sense of disquiet descended upon Jake.

"What is it, Jake, Eliza?" David thought he knew the problem. That girl just seemed to exude feminine wiles.

Jake nodded. "But not just her. Something about Kathleen. I can't describe it. You know I love Eliza, but today—Kathleen—I don't know—I think she might have feelings for me. And today I discovered I feel a lot for her, but it's different than my feelings for Eliza." He shook his head and buzzed his lips as if freezing. "I don't know what to make of it."

David nodded knowingly. "I guess I should have warned you about the effect we Becker men have on women."

Their eyes met and the men burst into laughter.

A voice called from the street. "Hey, do you want to keep the noise down over there? How's a neighbor to sleep with all that caterwauling?" It was Karle Forney. His wife and son walked at his side.

"Come on in," David said, rising to his feet. "We'll turn this into a going away party for Jake."

The Forneys stepped up onto the porch, Mrs. Forney in the lead. She handed a woolen bundle to Jake.

"We can't stay, we just came to give this to you, Jake. I knew the Lord wouldn't count this as working on the Sabbath, so I sewed it up for you this afternoon. It's a bedroll. I made it from the blanket Myrtle gave to Samuel, but I know they'd both want you to take it with you."

Jake looked mystified. "How did you know I was going?"

Karle grunted, then said, "Your Pa told me this afternoon."

"What? How?"

David shrugged his shoulders. "I figured it out after dinner."

John stepped forward and shook Jake's hand. "We're proud of you taking a stand. Just don't go shootin' at any Hanover boys now, hear?"

When Jake winced, David wondered if it was from remembering the demonstration with the rifle on the porch last night.

"Just the ones who shoot at me," Jake said resolutely.

The young men stood, eye to eye. A look of understanding seemed to pass between them.

Mrs. Forney said, "You need anything, you just let us know. And that goes for you, too, David."

On their way back down Frederick Street, John turned to wave. He stopped and stared into the sky over the Becker house. "Pa, what do you make of that?"

Karle peered up into the night. David and Jake dashed from the porch to look. The sky along the northeastern horizon glowed orange!

Mrs. Forney's voice quavered. "Is that York? Is York burning?

Monday, June 29, 1863

Jake held the pistol at arm's length, concentrating to keep the barrel of the gun on the same line as his arm. He imagined pointing with his index finger, then tried to align the sight at the end of the barrel with the notch on the nose of the hammer, all while atop a moving horse. "Mr. Gitt was right, Skipper. This is next to impossible." Jake carefully lowered the hammer and holstered the revolver.

Stopping next to a young plum tree, Jake dismounted and tied the reins securely around the trunk. "Steady now Skip, this time it's for real." Jake stroked the horse's cheek with his left hand, while his right hand eased the gun out of the holster. He stepped back a few paces, aimed the pistol at the woods across the road, and cocked the hammer. "Here we go, Skipper, easy now."

He squeezed the trigger and the hammer fell. The noise and the jolt were more than he expected, especially since his primary concern was Skipper's reaction to the close gunfire. The horse lurched and tried to shake his head free, but Jake quickly holstered the gun and rushed to calm him. "Skipper. Skipper. Easy, boy. Easy, Skipper."

After a few more sidesteps and tail swishes, Skipper calmed enough for Jake to remount. Though the puff of smoke had already evaporated behind them, the stink of sulphur still clung to Jake's nose. He pulled out the pistol and laid it across his thigh, tilting the weapon to highlight the engraving on the cylinder: two ships in combat, an odd image for a 44-caliber Colt Army revolver. Mr. Gitt had explained how the 36-caliber Colt Navy revolver came first, but Jake didn't understand why Mr. Colt wouldn't bother to engrave an appropriate army scene on this model.

Jake looked for another target. Mr. Gitt told him not to bother shooting at anything over a hundred feet away, since it was hard enough to hit something from half that distance. Jake picked a tall birch about forty feet from him and cocked the hammer. "Good boy, Skipper. Ready for another go? Steady—"

Again, the shot missed. Wanting to run, Skipper jerked and strained at the reins. Jake reassured him, and the stallion recovered his composure sooner this time.

"And steady, Skip." Seven feet closer to the target and another miss! Skipper neighed in complaint but didn't try to run.

"Good boy, Skipper!" Jake thumbed the hammer back and fired. A piece of bark flew end over end from the side of the tree. A few feet closer and another shot. The bullet pierced the trunk with a loud thunk.

"Golly!" Jake flushed with exhilaration. He recalled Eliza's chiding voice, *That's no way for a lady to speak,* and grinned at the memory of Kathleen's rueful smile.

Skipper shook his head and pulled at the reins. Jake patted the horse's neck and leaned over to speak in his ear. "That's a good boy, Skipper. I think we're getting the hang of this. Fifth shot wounded, sixth shot would've put a man down. Not too bad for our first round." He tried not to think about how that average would fare with hundreds of guns firing in the heat of battle.

Jake holstered the revolver and gave the horse its head. The road to Union Mills was a familiar one because they made the trip a couple of times every month. Skipper broke into a trot, then a canter. "Can't wait to get away from that smell, huh, boy?"

About a mile down the road, the horse slowed to a walk. Jake reached back to check on the saddlebags. Everything seemed to be in order. The bag on the right held three leather cases, one for the paper cartridges of black powder, one for bullets, and one for percussion caps—fifty-four of each item. Two empty cylinders for the .44 Colt and a small jar of grease lay on the bottom of the bag.

Mr. Gitt had warned him how long it took to reload the gun, and he strongly advised having two additional cylinders loaded and ready to exchange when under fire. "That oughta hold you over. If eighteen shots don't see you through, then you best be skedaddling out of whatever trouble you got yourself into."

The revolver set Jake back $27. The extra cylinders, cases, and ammo cost him another $36. He had never gone through that kind of money before; two months' wages for a lot of folks. "War is an expensive proposition," he had observed. Mr. Gitt guffawed as though Jake had made a joke.

Skipper headed for an algae-covered pool near the side of the road. Jake reined him in. "You don't want that nasty stuff, boy. We'll be at Pipe Creek soon enough."

After riding in peace and quiet for a while, Jake practiced drawing the revolver. Sometimes the sight on the end of the barrel caught the lip of the holster. He'd have to remember to slide the gun up and back when pulling it in a hurry. "What do you think, Skipper, should I practice changing cylinders now?"

The horse lifted his tail and littered the road.

Jake chuckled. "If you could only speak as well as you seem to understand! Sorry, boy, but I need the practice."

He reached back and pulled a spare cylinder from the saddlebag. The oil-coated cylinder slipped from his hand, bounced twice on the road, and then rolled down into the weed-choked gully.

"Drat!" Annoyed, Jake dismounted, tied the reins around the trunk of a poplar sapling, and sidestepped to the bottom of the gully. As he rummaged among the weeds, he heard the sound of running feet on the road. Skipper whinnied loudly. Jake scrambled out of the gully and discovered a Union soldier fumbling to untie the reins while Skipper struggled to pull himself free from the tree.

"Hey! Get away from my horse!" Jake bellowed.

The man spun to face Jake. "I mean to have this horse." He drew a Bowie knife from the sheath on his belt. "Stand aside or I'll have to cut you."

Jake drew the revolver. Mr. Gitt's advice rang in his mind. *Unless you've had a lot of practice, make sure you hold your arm out straight. If your arm's bent you'll be lucky to hit a horse let alone a man, even at close quarters.*

The soldier froze.

Jake cocked the hammer. Then he remembered. *Oh no! This cylinder is empty!* He gulped. *But this man doesn't know that.* Hoping to sound menacing, he lowered his voice. "Drop the knife and kick it away."

The man let the knife fall to the ground. "Don't shoot, I'm doing what you said." He used the instep of his boot to kick the knife toward the gully. As he did, the front of the boot flopped away from the sole, exposing filth-encrusted toes. He held his hands out at his sides, palms up, his rheumy eyes downcast. "I just want to get back home."

"Move over there." Jake gestured with his head and the man inched away from Skipper. Jake slowly made his way to Skipper's side, careful to keep the gun trained on the would-be thief. "So you 'just want to get back home.' What are you, a deserter?"

The soldier spoke slowly at first. "A deserter? No . . . I was taken prisoner." His voice rose as he spoke. "A prisoner, you see. And I was paroled. You know, in exchange for my promise not to fight any more. If you let me go into my pocket, I'll show you my parole paper."

Jake took a step closer and eyed the man's pockets. No bulges that might indicate another weapon. "All right, but only use your thumb and one finger."

The weight of the revolver began to take its toll on Jake's arm. The eight-inch barrel started to quiver. He took a step back and steadied the gun with both hands. Should he just mount up and gallop away?

The soldier pulled a folded piece of paper from his pants pocket. "Here you go, see?"

"Bring it to me."

The soldier walked slowly, the paper in his right hand.

Jake reached for the paper with his left hand. In a blur of motion, the soldier suddenly grabbed Jake's hand, yanked him forward, knocked the Colt from his grip, and sent him reeling with a ferocious uppercut. Jake bounced off Skipper and slumped to the ground. The edge of a broken tooth jagged at his tongue. Then the pain set in. He blinked, trying to make sense of what had happened.

"Crawl away from the horse," the soldier ordered, waving Jake's gun.

Jake looked up at the blue-steel barrel of the 44-caliber Colt. It looked so much bigger from this angle! The rush of fear cleared his mind. *The gun is empty.* He slid his right hand under his pants leg, pulled his knife from its sheath, and boldly stood.

The soldier skirted to his right. "Drop the knife and move away from the horse."

"The gun is empty. Drop—"

"Do you think I haven't heard that one before? Move away from the horse and I'll let you live."

Jake went into a crouch and planned his attack. "As you said, I don't want to have to cut you. Give me back my gun and you can go your way."

The man circled to his right, the gun waist high, aimed at Jake's chest. "Last chance."

Was the soldier moving to avoid having Skipper in the line of fire? Jake saw an opening and made his move. He feinted left, darted right, planted his foot, and swung the knife in an arc for the man's gut. As Jake felt the concussion and heat of the gun blast, the knife glanced off the soldier's lowest rib and plunged into his belly. Behind them, Skipper made an ungodly sound. Screaming in agony, the man dropped the gun, clutched at his stomach, and slid off the knife. Jake spun in time to see Skipper collapse.

Eyes bulging, mouth frothing, blood spurting in red streamers, the horse somehow managed to regain his footing. Jake dropped the knife and rushed to cover the wound with his hand. "Skipper! No!" Hot blood squirted between his fingers as he tried in vain to staunch the flow. Skipper went down on his haunches. He struggled to get back up, but his forelegs started to spasm. He made a gasping sound and crumpled to the ground at Jake's feet.

Jake retrieved his knife and cut the reins, as if that freedom might somehow allow Skipper to stand. Dropping to his knees, Jake gently patted Skipper's cheek. "Easy, Skipper, easy boy . . ."

But Skipper was gone.

How did this happen? Didn't I fire all six rounds? This is all my fault; I should have counted my shots! "Pride goeth before destruction."

A low groan came from behind him. "Pocket . . . envelope . . . family."

Jake turned on his knees and saw the widening pool of blood next to the deserter. He picked up his knife and stared at it; his mind raced, his heart pounded. He had used the weapon in self-defense, now would he use it in anger? *"Thou shalt not kill,"* rang in his mind. *But there has to be an exception for war,* he argued. Bitterness and rage filled his heart. *That man killed Skipper and tried to kill me!*

He stood and walked slowly to the prostrate soldier. The heat of his anger turned to cold fury and his heart grew hard. Cut the bastard's throat? Or maybe stomp on his windpipe and crush him like a bug.

The soldier opened his glazed eyes. "Bury? Write . . . family?"

With all his effort Jake fought against his baser urges; he must obey his Christian duty. "Are you a God-fearing man?"

The soldier groaned a weak "yes."

A gust of wind blew a piece of paper against Jake's foot. It looked like the soldier's letter of parole. Jake picked it up and discovered it was actually a tally of gambling debts the man owed his comrades! Fury flooded over him, along with a surge of hatred far beyond anything he had ever felt before. Jake used the paper to wipe Skipper's blood from his hands, wadded it into a tight ball, and tossed it over his shoulder. His tone frosted as he said through clenched teeth, "Then you better pray for God's mercy, for you shan't have any of mine." He recovered his revolver and slammed it into the holster.

To the accompaniment of the soldier's gurgling death throes, Jake knelt down and kissed his beloved horse goodbye. Steeling himself, he went to work freeing the saddlebags, bedroll, and rifle holster. He removed the saddle, blanket, and tack and hid them in the gully. After looping the bedroll around his neck, he draped the saddlebags over one shoulder and slung the rifle over the other.

Jake paused to look at the corpse. There had been a lot of dead men at Manassas, but none of them by his hand. Now he had killed a Yankee.

Thou shalt not kill, a pious voice scolded in his mind.

"But I am at war now," Jake said aloud. He gritted his teeth, turned his back on the body, and set off on the last mile to Union Mills.

I was so sure the gun was empty! Mr. Gitt warned me to count to six, but oh no, not me, I can keep track of something so simple as that. How could I have been so careless?

The voice of Reason chided, *And how long do careless men live in war? Someone must always pay the price for carelessness.*

Jake muttered bitterly, "War is an expensive proposition."

He stopped in the middle of the road, dropped his burdens, and sat down. Reaching into the saddlebags, he pulled out the ammo cases, cylinders, and jar of grease. He took the Colt, thumbed the hammer to the half-cocked position, and removed the spent cylinder. "Sure, you're empty now."

Jake bit the end off a paper cartridge and carefully poured the black powder into one of the cylinder's chambers. He put a bullet on top of the powder and swaged it down with the loading lever. "One!" He repeated the process. "Two!" Again. "Three!" And again. "Four!"

After filling the two remaining chambers, Jake opened the jar and smeared some grease over the open end of each chamber. He wiped the excess grease on the rim of the jar and then cleaned his finger in the crook of his knee. He grabbed the cap case and pulled out a small brass percussion cap. Following Mr. Gitt's advice, he applied just enough pressure with his thumb and forefinger to bend the cap slightly out of round. "Less chance of falling aside and causing a misfire that way," Mr.

Gitt had said.

Jake pushed the cap into place on the back of the first chamber. "One!"

He finished with the first cylinder and proceeded to load the other two. A good fifteen minutes passed before the job was finished.

Jake reassembled the Colt and holstered the loaded weapon. He put the cases away, gathered up his equipment, and gazed into the gray sky. Six turkey buzzards circled above. Thick clouds obscured the sun.

"Lord, why did you let Skipper be stolen and then found, only to die like this? Am I to be an infantryman after all? Or do You want me to go back home?"

He started to turn, to look back up the road to Hanover, but froze. He would not put his hand to the plough and then look back. He had known before setting out that his horse was not likely to survive the war. Yet, if Skipper's death was the cost of the lesson that might ultimately save his life, then so be it. He hiked the burden farther up his shoulders and resumed the march south. God's will be done.

-2-

At the sound of an approaching horse, David dropped the adze and rushed to the workshop window. Had Jake forgotten something? It was Samuel Forney!

By the time David flung open the door, Sam had already tied his black mare to the hitching post and was in the process of combing his fingers through his wavy, blond hair.

"Sam! What news?"

"They're all safe at your brother's." He put his hat back on, the brim at a jaunty angle.

David sighed with relief, but he had to be certain. "Benjamin's or Robert's?"

"Oh, sorry. They're across the river and at Benjamin's now."

"Thank God."

"We had quite a time of it. Everyone we passed on the road had a different story about whose army was marching where. We saw a squad of thieving gray-coats on the other side of Spring Forge, but no Union men until we got to the York Pike. Even those men looked to be foragers.

"By the time we got to York it was mid-afternoon. The city was full of rumors of Rebel armies about to invade from the west. Folks in town said we should stay the night. There were plenty of rooms available at Metzel's Hotel, as so many people had already fled east across the river."

David gestured to the kitchen. "Come inside. I've got a few of Myrtle's blueberry muffins left, and I can reheat the coffee."

"Well . . ." Sam said reluctantly.

"I understand, you need to get on home. Tell me the rest of the story quick, so you can let your Ma and Pa know you're safe."

With a rueful smile, Sam continued, "On Sunday morning I led us all in our own little worship time in a corner of the hotel's drawing room, then I went out to see if it was safe to continue our journey.

"As the morning church bells rang, a man rode up Market Street yelling that the Rebels were on the way. A few minutes later came the scruffiest looking band of men you're ever like to see. They spread out along the street and put out the word they were just guards to 'assure our safety.' I went back in the hotel, got your daughters up to their room, and then went back outside.

"The Rebel flags waved and the band blared. It would've been a grand sight, if not for the men who marched in the lead. I expected well-dressed officers, but instead they were just dust-covered infantrymen, toting shovels and pickaxes like they were rifles. A lady screamed, 'Oh my Heavenly Father protect us, they are coming to dig our graves.'

"One of the Rebs laughed at her and told us their job was to widen the road and clear obstacles—like dead Yankees and horses."

The mare nudged Sam's back. "It's all right, girl, I know we're close to home. We'll go soon, I gotta finish the story first."

Not wishing to delay his future son-in-law's return home any longer, David said, "I'll walk with you while you finish the telling."

"Good idea, thanks." Sam untied his horse.

David grabbed his hat from the peg in the hallway, then caught up with Sam in the street. "What happened next?"

"I saw one of their commanders, General Gordon, when he stopped at a house on the corner. He rode his horse up onto the pavement and spoke to several women on the porch."

Sam lowered his voice and took on a Southern drawl. "'Ladies, I have a word to say. I suppose you think me a pretty rough-looking man, but when I am shaved and dressed, my wife considers me a very good-looking fellow. I want to say to you we have not come among you to pursue the same warfare your men did in our country. You need not have any fear of us whilst we are in your midst. You are just as safe as though we were a thousand miles away.'"

Resuming his normal tone, Sam continued, "He told of how his men had just read in the *Philadelphia Inquirer* about the Federal Army destroying the towns of Buford, South Carolina and Darien, Georgia, and that some of his soldiers were from Darien, but that they were motivated by the duty of self-defense, not retaliation—that they were here only to fight the armies who were invading their soil and destroying their houses. And he promised to deal most severely with any of his men who disturbed private property or insulted a woman.

"As he rode away, a young girl, maybe twelve years old, ran up and gave him a bouquet of flowers. She must have written him a nice note, because he pulled a piece of paper out of the bouquet and, after reading it, looked around to thank her, but she had disappeared."

David muttered, "Not a big surprise, since we know there are a lot of Copperheads in York."

As they neared the Forney house, Sam quickened his pace. "Another officer announced that all of their men knew that any insult or injury to a female was punishable with death. Then he pointed to the guards along the street, nodded, and went along his way. And you know, I believed him.

"Since the army appeared to be stopping in town for a spell, I decided we might be better off trying to cross the river whilst we could. If they continued east, no telling how long the bridge would stand."

David patted Sam on the back. "Sound thinking." Once again he thanked the Lord for providing his youngest daughter with such a fine future husband, and he felt doubly blessed that Sam lived nearby.

Sam stopped in front of the house. With his father and brother at work in the fields and his mother and sister most likely busy in the kitchen, this was a good place to finish the story without interruption. "We had no problems leaving town. The Johnnies were very polite, nearly all of them doffed their caps to the ladies as we drove past. I could tell Myrtle's heart went out to them, so many looked half-starved. She kept glancing back at the chickens. I reminded her that we didn't know but that those birds might help keep her nieces and nephews alive.

"We traveled freely until we got to Wrightsville. A lot of the streets were barricaded. The militia had built a line of earthworks around the entrance to the bridge, and there was a crowd of folks waiting to cross the river. The crowd got so big the Union militia ordered the toll-takers to let people pass for free. We made it over the bridge about an hour before they had to blow up a portion of it to stop the Rebels. Sadly, the whole bridge caught fire and burned."

David sighed. "What a shame. Such a beautiful bridge." Crossing the mile-long covered bridge had been a treasured highlight on every family trip to Benjamin's. "What time was that?"

"Shortly after dark. It burned for hours as section after section fell into the river and floated away. Some sparks caught on a few houses on the Wrightsville side. In no time, there was a real conflagration."

David smiled wistfully, remembering when Jake had struggled with "conflagration" in spelling class. How he missed him already!

Sam looked at him as if wondering why he smiled at such news.

"Oh, pardon me, I was just thinking of something else," David said. "So, it was the bridge and Wrightsville that burned, not York?"

He nodded. "I got ferried across the Susquehanna well south of the burnt out bridge early this morning. I skirted south of the city and came back through Seven Valleys and Jefferson. Rebels already went through there and tore up the railroads and bridges and telegraphs."

David slid a speck of sawdust out of the corner of his eye. "You missed some excitement here shortly after you left Saturday morning. A battalion of Confederate cavalry stopped in town to buy supplies, can you believe it?"

"What happened?" Sam asked eagerly.

"A couple of men got shot at, and there were a few complaints about thievery and worthless Confederate money, but other than that . . ."

A flash of anger coursed through David. *And that Rebel colonel enticed my son to go off to war, but other than that! Well, that's not really true. No call for blaming somebody else. Jake made his decision based on a lot of good reasoning. I just don't like his ultimate conclusion.*

". . . in town?" Sam cocked his head, waiting for a reply.

David blinked. "I'm sorry, Sam, I was thinking about Jake. What did you say?"

"I was just asking after him. Is he in town?"

It hurt to say it. "He's, uh, gone off to enlist." The words rang with such finality, as if he had gone, never to return.

Sam's eyes brightened. "Really? Is he going to join the Marion Rifles or the 28th Pennsylvania with the other Hanover boys?"

"It's not like that." David briefly explained the reasons behind Jake's decision to fight for the Confederacy.

"Yep, that sounds like Jake. Likes to look at a problem from both sides and, more often than not, he winds up going with the minority. When did he leave?"

"About two hours ago. He's heading for Union Mills. Thinks Herb Shriver's ready to join up, too. He figures they might be able to get into the same company as one of the other Shriver boys."

Sam put his hand on his horse's back. "Do you want I should go catch him up and tell him his sisters are safe?"

David glanced at the sweaty mare. "No, your horse has already had a good run today. You best tend to her and then get inside. Your Ma was expecting you last night. I'll give a letter to the Winebrenners next door. Since their son David is married to a Shriver girl and Wirt Shriver is courting Mary Winebrenner, I'm sure one of them could give the Shrivers a letter to pass on to Jake."

David thought of going himself to tell Jake, but decided against it. How would it look for a young man to go off to war, only to have his Pa come running after him with news from home?

Sam tugged a good-bye on the brim of his cap and led his mare to the barn.

Figuring it was as good a time as any for lunch, David headed home, closed up the shop, and went into the kitchen. Ready and waiting at the head of the table was a napkin-covered plate Jake had prepared. It was the same food Jake would eat for lunch; thus they could have one more meal together, in spirit if not in fact.

David paused in the middle of pulling out his chair. *Why eat alone?*

He went to the parlor and took Rose's picture off the mantel. "May I have the honor of your presence at lunch?" Her face seemed to brighten.

Back in the kitchen, David pushed his plate from the head of the table to one of the places along the side. He stood the framed picture in front of the seat next to him. They hadn't sat next to each other at a meal since Grace was an infant. He put his hand atop the frame, bowed his head, and prayed. Uncovering the plate, he found a slab of smoked ham, a hunk of goat's cheese, two thick slices of oat bread, and some mushy blueberries.

"Well, Rose, here we are, alone at last. And on my first day alone in the workshop in over five years. Jake left this morning to fight in the war." He reached for the crock of butter and spread some on the bread. "Grace and Faith and Myrtle and the grandchildren are all over to Benjamin's." He cut a slice of ham and a corner of cheese, stabbed them together with the fork, and started to eat.

David and Rose shared a pleasant lunch, reminiscing about the children and the life they had all shared together. When he was done eating, David wiped his mouth with the napkin and picked up the picture. He looked lovingly into his wife's eyes.

"We did it, Rosie, we did it. We finished what we set out to do. Five wonderful children, each a blessing from God. They're in His hands now."

Bittersweet tears rolled down his cheeks. He returned Rose to her place over the family hearth and then went back to work on Myrtle's carriage.

-3-

As Jake reached the edge of the Shriver farm, a young woman called, "Look, Emily! Did you ever see such a funny-looking horse?"

Jake craned his neck to see around the saddlebags on his shoulder. At the top of a knoll stood fifteen-year-old Mary Shriver, berry bucket in hand. Her sister, Emily, aged thirteen and youngest of the thirteen Shriver progeny, poked her head over a cluster of huckleberry bushes.

"That's no horse, Mary, but you're right about the funny-looking part," Emily rounded the bushes and wiped her hands on her frock, then bounded down the knoll, cocked her head sideways, and gave Jake a droll look. "Are you man or horse?" She gasped. "Oh my, are you a centaur?" She spun on her heel and waved to her sister. "Mary, come see! I do believe I found a centaur!"

After killing a horse thief, losing his beloved Skipper, and trudging with heavy gear the last mile to get there, Jake was in no mood for banter. He sloughed off the saddlebags and laid the holstered rifle across them. Sliding the sweat-soaked bedroll over his head, he growled, "Here, Emmy, make yourself useful." He held out the bedroll.

Emily scowled. "Well! Excuse me for breathing *your* air!" Mary arrived, her short pigtails bobbing as she nodded in agreement.

Jake dropped the bedroll and plopped down on it. "I'm sorry, Em. Skipper died on the way here."

"Awww . . ." the girls responded in harmony.

"Is that dried blood?" Mary dabbed Jake's forehead with her finger.

He wiped his head with the back of his hand. "I guess so."

A motherly tone permeated Emily's voice. "What happened, Jake?"

"I ran into a Yankee deserter up the road a piece. He shot Skipper." Struggling to steady his voice, he muttered, "Then I killed him." Struck with a surge of guilt, he dropped his head into his hands.

The girls gasped at the news. Emily took charge. "Come on, Mary, let's help Jake get his things to the house."

Jake held up a hand. "Thanks, but wait a moment." He unbuckled the left saddlebag, pulled out the canteen, and gingerly opened his mouth to drink. The stab of pain in his battered jaw felt torturous. His eyes narrowed as he placed the canteen firmly on his lips and drank deeply, purging his guilt with the agony,

Mary examined his chin. "That's a nasty bruise. Are you all right?"

"I am now." He screwed the cap back in place and climbed to his feet. The girls gathered up his gear, then they all headed toward the house.

As they passed the cornfield, Mary yelled to her brothers. "Mark! Herb!" She waved them in from their field work.

Although Mark was four years older than Herb, the younger brother's exuberance often made him the leader of the four youngest siblings. When Herb got close enough to the road to recognize Jake, he tugged his hat tight and ran. Clumps of fertile Maryland soil flew up behind him. Once on the road, he stomped the mud from his boots.

"Jake, what brings you out in the middle of the day? And on foot, no less. Where's Sk—"

Mary frantically waved for her brother to stop.

Jake took a deep breath and puffed it out. "That's all right, Mary." Mark jogged up as Jake continued, "How about we go to the house and I'll tell everyone the whole story."

Herb took the rifle from Mary while Mark relieved Emily of the saddlebags. Jake shouldered the bedroll and they all headed for the large white house.

The front door opened and William Shriver came out on the porch, looking every bit the Biblical patriarch with his long white beard and thinning silver hair. "Jacob! Good to see you, son." He glanced up the road. "Is your father coming?"

"No, sir, not on this trip."

Emily dashed up the steps and gave her father a bear hug. "Guess what, Papa? Jake kilt a Yankee on his way here!"

Mr. Shriver looked thoughtfully over his glasses at Jake. "That so?"

"Yessir."

"With that there pistol on your hip, or your rifle?"

"Actually, it was with my knife."

The girls gasped.

Herb's eyes shone. "Hand to hand combat, huh? Tell us all about it!"

Mr. Shriver sighed. "Best come on inside. This sounds like a tale the neighbors mightn't want to be hearing." He nodded to the house across the road, the Shriver family homestead, where his brother Andrew lived. Andrew's son, Wirt, had joined the Union Army two weeks ago.

Herb led the way to the parlor. As Jake passed through the foyer, Mrs. Mary Shriver appeared in the kitchen doorway at the other end of the hall.

"Hello, Jacob. Won't you stay for dinner?"

He removed his hat and dropped it atop his gear behind the front door. "Gladly, Mama Shriver." He met her halfway down the hall and kissed her cheek.

Sally peeked over her mother's shoulder. "Where's my hug?" Unmarried and in her early thirties, Sally shared the household management with her mother, who, having borne thirteen healthy children in less than twenty-three years, had more than earned the help.

Jake held his arms wide. Sally wiped her floury hands on her apron and went to his embrace.

The tangy aroma of pork and barbeque sauce drifted from the kitchen and Jake's stomach rumbled. "You must have known I was coming, you made my favorite dinner, 'Barbeque à la Maison Dupuys.'"

Mrs. Shriver laid her hand on his elbow. "I'll just have to make it more often, then." She had learned the recipe several years ago from a traveler from New Orleans. Her eyes fixed on his pistol and she wagged her finger. "Of course, you'll have to leave your firearm at the door."

He winced. "Yes, ma'am."

Herb called from the parlor, "Come on Jake, we're all waiting. Mama and Sally, you might want to hear this, too."

"You go ahead, Mama, I'll mind the kitchen." Sally held out a hand to receive her mother's apron, then returned to the dinner preparations.

Mrs. Shriver sat next to her husband in their matching gray wing chairs. Mary and Emily perched on the green divan, and Mark and Herb shared the deacon's bench. Mr. Shriver pointed to the cane-backed rocker. "Since you're the storyteller, you may as well make yourself comfortable."

Jake didn't know where to begin—the reason for the visit or the encounter on the way? He chose the former, but decided to save the part about his hope for enlisting with Herb until after he told about his misfortune. Besides, there was a good chance Herb would suggest the idea himself by that point.

Jake cleared his throat. "Well, sir, I find myself in sympathy with the Confederate States' struggle for independence. Therefore, it is my duty to go and join their fight."

Herb blurted, "Good for you!"

"Though my father strongly supports the ideal of re-establishing the Union, he respects my decision and has given me his blessing."

Mr. Shriver nodded thoughtfully. His wife pulled a handkerchief from her sleeve and dabbed her eyes.

"On my way here, I was accosted by a Yankee deserter, who tried to steal Skipper whilst my back was turned. I pulled my pistol on him, but then I realized it was out of bullets, as I had been practicing with it."

Determined not to whitewash the story, Jake proceeded, his eyes downcast. "I foolishly allowed the man to get close enough to knock me down and grab the gun. I pulled out my knife and told him the gun was empty and, if he gave it back, I'd let him go. But he didn't believe me, he wanted Skipper. He was aiming to shoot me when I stabbed at him with my knife. The gun went off." Jake swallowed his pride and continued. "I didn't count my practice shots. As it turned out, there was one bullet left, and it hit Skipper in the chest."

The clock on the wall struck the quarter hour. Doleful looks awaited the last chime of the Westminster tune.

"Skip fought hard, but the bullet must've struck an artery. He didn't suffer long. The Yankee wasn't so blessed, but he had expired by the time I gathered up my things."

Jake's voice grew hard. "Skipper paid for my carelessness. Now I have to make sure I've learned my lesson."

Mr. Shriver cleared his throat and stood. "Well, we're so glad you're all right. I'd better send a couple of men to tend to the bodies and retrieve your tack." He left the room.

Emily went over, knelt at Jake's feet, and patted his hand. "I'm so glad you're safe."

"And I take back what I said about you looking like a horse," Mary said from the divan.

"But not the funny-looking part?" Emily said, wrinkling her nose.

Herb impatiently interrupted, "So what are your plans, Jake?"

"Well, I'd hoped to enlist with a Virginia cavalry unit, but after buying a gun and supplies this morning, I don't have enough money left for a horse." He sighed. "So it seems I will be joining the infantry."

Herb shifted in his seat. "Mama? You know I've been wanting to join up, too. May I go with Jake? This is—"

"Thomas Herbert, you are too young to go to war," Mrs. Shriver said sternly. "Besides, two boys in the army are enough from one family."

Mr. Shriver spoke solemnly from the doorway. "If the war is still going on when you turn eighteen, you may volunteer with our blessing."

Mrs. Shriver looked as though she might have other thoughts on the matter, but she kept them to herself.

Jake's spirit sagged. *Great. No horse, no friend to join up with, no plans. Now what, Lord?*

-4-

Uncle Henry pushed back from the dinner table and announced, "First thing in the morning, I want to take the horses up into the Pigeon Hills. Alan Zimmerman has a cabin up there where we can hide our livestock till the Rebels, um, armies leave the area."

Eliza saw her mother stiffen. Had she taken offense? Evidently not.

"Would you like some help?" Mrs. Bigler asked, her face bright. Her voice took on a girlish lilt. "I simply adore riding in the hills, I miss it so very much."

"Why, it will be nice to have you along, Irene. And if Ida and all three girls come along, that will account for all six of the horses."

"But Papa," Lydia said, "don't you remember? Jonas is coming for dinner tomorrow night. I need to be here all day to get everything ready."

Kathleen added, "I have girls' choir rehearsal in the morning at eight, and I promised Reverend Alleman I would help make bandages."

Uncle Henry held up his hands in surrender, "That's fine girls, we can manage with four." He looked over his spectacles at Eliza. "And I suppose you, too, have a previous engagement?"

Eliza froze. She loved to ride, but with the arrival of her "monthly visitor," she didn't relish the thought of a jaunt on horseback, not to mention the long hike back down the hill. How could she explain that to her uncle?

"No sir, I do not." Should she offer to stay and help with the dinner preparations? No, that wouldn't work. Everyone knew she was next to useless in the kitchen. Besides, Lydia was going to make hog maw, and the thought of stuffing onions, diced potatoes, and spiced sausage into the stomach of a pig made Eliza want to retch. But what about . . .

"Uncle Henry, if you don't mind, I'm not feeling very well. Maybe I can ride as far as Uncle George's, then I'll tend my cousins so Aunt Linda Jane can ride with you?"

Mama exclaimed, "That sounds like a fine idea!" She turned to her brother. "Just think, Henry, it will be like before we all had children. We should pack a lunch and have a picnic."

"Splendid!" Aunt Ida agreed, her blue eyes sparkling.

"Hmph. Like before we had children," Uncle Henry said gruffly. "I think I can remember that far back. Well, now that that's settled, let's get to the evening chores."

Lydia and Kathleen left to tend the horses while Eliza gathered up the dishes. Mama and Aunt Ida went to ret up the kitchen.

Uncle Henry hurried to the window, leaned down, and hollered after the girls, "And don't forget to throw the horses over the fence some hay!" He tucked in his shirt, went to the sideboard to select a cigar from the humidor, and headed for the front porch.

Eliza called toward the kitchen, "Mama? Would you like some help fetching the dish water?"

Mama's face appeared around the corner of the door, smiling for the second time that night. "Yes, that would be nice." They each took a bucket from the back porch and went to the water pump. Eliza worked the handle while her mother held a bucket under the spigot.

Eliza screwed up her courage. "Mama, I want to talk to you about last night."

"Whatever do you mean?" she asked innocently.

"When you came into our room to—" Eliza paused. She was about to say "kiss us goodnight," but realized it had been years since that had last happened. She let go of the pump handle and decided to get right to the point. "—to tell us about the letter you got from Papa."

"Oh, that." Her mother set the full bucket on the ground, then held the empty one up to the spigot. "I'm sorry I brought that up. You don't need to concern yourself, darlin'."

Eliza lifted her foot meaning to stomp it, but gently lowered it to the ground instead, deciding never to do such a childish thing again. She grabbed the pump handle and thrust down with all her might, sending a gush of water sloshing into the bucket. "Mother, I want to know if father is having troubles with the farm. Are we running out of money?"

Her mother trembled slightly as she set the bucket down. "Why do you want to know?"

"Shouldn't I know about things that affect my prospects?"

Mama scratched her head and pondered for a moment. "Things will probably be different after the war." She caught a stray tress and tucked it behind her ear. "And they may be difficult for some considerable time."

"I thought so," Eliza sighed. "Papa wouldn't have sold Abby unless—"

"Yes, his precious Abby," Mama spat.

Eliza's jaw dropped. She knew her father must have liked Abigail because she had seen him treat her kindly on many occasions. Like the time in the hallway when he helped Abby remove something from her eye. He often gave her hugs in out of the way places. And then there was that afternoon when Eliza burst into her father's bedroom and found him tending Abby, who must have taken ill and was resting in his bed . . .

Eliza sank to the ground. Her stomach heaved. "Oh, Mama." She covered her mouth and choked back the bile. Why hadn't she realized it before? How could her father? And with—? In their house? And Mama must have known!

Mama crouched and spoke softly in her ear. "Are you all right, darlin'?"

Eliza held up a shaky hand, nodded once, and then looked away. She didn't even want to look at her mother, not yet; but she had to be certain.

"Did my father—with Abigail. You know what I mean. Did he?"

There was a long moment of silence, broken by a terse, "Yes."

A single, toneless word, and Eliza felt her world change. She wasn't sure she would like being a grownup after all. Children could be cruel to one another, but this was despicable, villainous. Eliza turned and looked her mother in the eye. "Couldn't you stop it?"

Her mother's eyes hardened. "What for? Men have their needs. After I finally gave him the son he wanted, he let me be. Abigail kept him from sowing his wild oats all around the county, so you see, it was all for the best." She swallowed hard. "We all have our needs."

Eliza stood and brushed herself off. *Well, Jake would never treat me like that!* And that was when she knew she wanted to marry him. She held out her hand and helped her mother up.

"Remember my mother's advice to me," Mama continued morosely. "Separate bedrooms have made many a marriage tolerable."

If my husband ever treats me that way, the only separate bedroom he'll ever see is a pine box, six feet underground, Eliza vowed.

Mother and daughter stood in the farmyard, face to face, no longer merely parent and child. For the first time in her life, Eliza felt someone else's heartache. Her throat tightened as she fought off the sensation of drowning in emptiness. She took her mother into her arms. "I love you, Mama."

"I love you, too, Little Eyes." The women exchanged bemused glances, then burst into laughter.

"You haven't called me that in ages!" When Eliza was a child, her mother had taught her the song "Li'l Liza Jane," but Eliza thought the words were "Little Eyes of Jane." Thus, Papa had dubbed her Little Eyes.

Papa. How did she feel toward him now that she knew the unimaginable? She wanted to slap his face and tell him what a scoundrel he was, though he had never shown her anything but love. Oh, he doted on her little brother, but that had never bothered her. She figured that was to be expected since Richard was his only son. Her frown deepened.

"What is it, Eliza?"

Or were some of those worry lines there all the time now? Eliza searched her mother's eyes. *I guess if Mama can forgive him, I can learn to as well.* She decided she needed to change the subject.

"Mama, what do you really think of Jake Becker?"

Her mother's face softened. "I believe that young man will make some lucky lady a wonderful husband someday." She reached for Eliza's hand. "And I would be proud to call him my son."

"Really?" Eliza's spirit soared. "Thank you, Mama." She gave her mother's hand a squeeze, then they each took a bucket of water and headed into the house.

Perhaps Jake will solve all our problems, Eliza mused. *We might not be able to have as big a wedding as I dreamed of, but after we're married, Jake can help Papa restore the farm and rebuild our fortunes. We'll build a big house and host lots of parties and go to lots of parties and . . .*

-5-

Jake sat up, fluffed the lumpy pillow, folded it in half, and lay back down. Across the small bedroom, Herb's snores didn't miss a beat.

What would it take to fall asleep tonight? Jake couldn't get his mind to stop churning. Surrendering to fitfulness, he sat up, opened the nightstand drawer, and groped for the box of matches. He scratched a match along the bottom of the stand, lifted the glass chimney from the candle, lit the wick, and shook the match out. A soft yellow glow flickered on the flowered wallpaper.

Jake picked up his New Testament. Too bad he didn't have the whole Bible with him. Reading any chapter in Leviticus usually put him to sleep in no time. He glanced around the room, but the dim light failed to reveal a Bible anywhere. Just as well. The Shrivers were devout Catholics, and he didn't know what to make of the Catholic Bible with all those extra books stuck in between the Testaments.

His eyes came to rest on the pink-ribboned locks of hair lying on the nightstand. He set the New Testament on his lap and picked up Eliza's lock. The candlelight revealed a few auburn highlights. A whiff of perfume reached his nose. She must have put some on her neck, but he hadn't noticed it when he was with her—yesterday? It seemed longer ago than that.

Jake opened the New Testament to Ephesians 3:14-21, one of his favorite passages about God's love. He kissed the lock of hair and placed it between the pages. The grandfather clock chimed in the parlor below. He counted eleven strokes.

Kathleen's lock of hair seemed to beckon to him from the nightstand. Jake held the lock up to the light. Every strand had its own subtle hue, from a shy blonde to a brassy gold, sometimes within the same strand. He grinned. *Now that's Kathleen all over!* He lifted the lock to his nose and sniffed. No perfume. No surprise.

Jake pondered a moment. Which verse should he bookmark with Kathleen's lock? He turned back a page to Ephesians 2:8-10. His eyes lingered on the last line: "For we are his workmanship, created in Christ Jesus unto good works, which God hath before ordained that we should walk in them."

The sound of approaching horses floated through the open window. Lots of horses!

Jake marked the verse with Kathleen's lock, snapped the book shut, and dropped it on the nightstand next to Eliza and Kathleen's photograph. He rushed to the window and poked his head out. It was too dark to distinguish what was going on, but there had to be dozens of horses.

He went over to Herb and shook his shoulder. "Herb!"

Herb sat up, nearly bumping heads with Jake. "Wha—?"

"Come look," Jake whispered. "I think there's some cavalry outside."

By the time the young men reached the window, a knocking sound came from the homestead across the road. Men's voices. Horses nickered, snorted, and pawed the dirt. The knocking turned into pounding.

The homestead door creaked opened. A slave with a lantern stepped out onto the porch. The light revealed four soldiers, standing in an arc. Gray uniforms? Must be, Jake decided. Blue uniforms would probably look black in the dim light.

A soldier in an officer's hat spoke for the group. His soft Virginia accent removed any doubt as to which army he represented. "Summon your master." He gestured toward the mounted officer at the gate. "Tell him he has the honor of a visit from General Fitzhugh Lee and his men, and we are very hungry."

"Yessir!"

But before he could comply, Andrew Shriver and his son, Austin, arrived on the scene. Andrew stepped forward, his nightshirt partly tucked into his trousers. "What can I do for you *gentlemen?*" His scorn was evident for all to hear.

Jake nudged Herb. "You better go get your Pa, before your uncle gets himself in trouble." Herb dashed from the room.

The officer snapped, "Would you prefer to see Union troops?" He pointed over his shoulder. It sounded as if the road was full of horses, clear down to Westminster. "Well, sir, I can tell you that you are in the midst of thousands of Rebels."

Andrew harrumphed. "Well, sir, I can just tell you that I am a Union man!"

"Well, I like to see a man speak out, and as that is the case, that you are a Union man, I want to know where your horses are."

"I am sorry to inform you, sir, that our horses are not receiving visitors this evening."

The officer loomed over Andrew. "Then we shall have you as *our* guest unless the horses are speedily produced, although I would much rather entertain the horses." The soldier gestured to one of his aides. "Take some men and search the stables."

Turning to Andrew, the soldier continued, "Now, about that food for our men?"

Andrew called into the house, "Paul! Tell Ruth and her girls to make some flapjacks for our *guests.*"

The officer reached into his pocket and then held out his fist. "We shall pay you for your ungrateful hospitality."

"What would I do with your worthless Confederate paper?" In the light of the lantern, his sneer looked malevolent. "Perhaps I *shall* take some—as a curiosity."

"Damn it, if that is all you want with it you will not get it!"

Anna and Eliza, Andrew's daughters, burst from the house and ran crying to his side.

Still atop his horse at the gate, General Lee called something to the officer, but Jake couldn't make out the words. The soldiers left the porch.

The Confederates in front of the homestead dismounted. It sounded as if the other cavalrymen were moving into the fields on either side of the road. Andrew hung the lantern on a hook and led his sobbing daughters back into the house.

Hurried footsteps sounded behind Jake, first in the hallway, then down the stairs. A moment later William Shriver, Mark, and Herb bounded into the road.

William went up to General Lee. "May I help you, sir?" The eagerness in his voice was unmistakable.

Lee chuckled, then said, "I daresay, you do not sound like a Union man." A few of his men laughed.

"No, sir, I am not. I am William Shriver, and two of my sons serve in the Army of Northern Virginia."

"I am General Fitzhugh Lee. It is a pleasure to make your acquaintance, I assure you."

William clasped the general's outstretched hand. "Won't you please come in? My family and I are at your service."

"Thank you, sir." Lee handed the reins to a lieutenant. "Please see to my horse. Her name is Nellie Gray."

Jake had seen enough. He hurriedly dressed, then patted his pockets, sensing he had forgotten something. The New Testament and photo! He picked them up from the nightstand, and when he placed the picture inside the book his eyes fell on the verse ". . . good works, which God hath before ordained." Could it be? Had the Lord brought him to this place at this time to meet up with the Confederate Cavalry? Jake pocketed the New Testament and took the stairs two at a time.

Hat in hand, General Lee stood in the middle of the parlor. Dust clung to his uniform, turning the gold brocade on his jacket a mustard yellow. His full, dark beard extended halfway down his chest and a thick moustache obscured his mouth. But it was the general's eyes Jake found most striking: alert, kind—and with a hint of sadness?

Mr. Shriver gestured toward the wing chairs. "Won't you please sit down, General Lee? I'll have my daughter prepare a room for you."

"Thank you, but I should get back to my men. I prefer to sleep outside, as they do. It is better for morale, you see. I did want to ask, have you heard of the whereabouts of any Union troops?"

"Just in Westminster, but as you have come from that direction, I presume that information is of little use to you now."

Herb pointed to Jake. "My friend Jake killed a Yankee deserter a few miles north of here this afternoon."

Lee turned and looked Jake up and down. "Is that so? Tell me."

"Well, um . . ." *Speak up, fool, this is no time to act the child!* Jake stiffened his back and spoke firmly. "I was on my way to volunteer to fight for the Confederacy when a Yankee soldier accosted me. He tried to steal my horse. He took advantage of my inexperience and got my revolver away from me. I still had my knife and I managed to slay him, but not before he shot and killed my horse."

"Very impressive," Lee said, his eyebrows arching.

Jake was about to ask if he might volunteer for one of the general's cavalry units when Mr. Shriver interjected, "Jake and his father are two of the finest wagon makers for miles around."

"Oh really?" General Lee replied, eyeing Jake. "So, how are you at handling a team?"

"He's a great teamster," Herb boasted. "And he's almost as good a rider as me, too."

Lee nodded. "Excellent! We can always use a good man who knows how to handle a team. Especially now. We've captured over a hundred Union supply wagons. The drivers are Union men, so it will be good to have one more of our own in the line."

"Thank you, sir, I shall do my best." But Jake's spirit sagged. How would he impress the Biglers if all he did for the Confederate cause was drive a supply wagon?

"Come see me first thing in the morning, and I shall have a member of my staff take care of your assignment."

"Yes, sir. It will be an honor to be under your command." Jake found comfort in the words. It was official! He was to be part of the Army of Northern Virginia. Not in a role he'd ever imagined, but it was a start, and he vowed to do his very best.

Gen. Fitzhugh Lee (1862)

Part Two: Days of Destiny

Tuesday, June 30, 1863

Jake, wake up!"

Jake sat up and rubbed his eyes. The dim glow of dawn infiltrated the room, and Herb's face slowly came into focus. Why did he look so eager?

"Come on out to the barn when you're dressed," Herb said. "Let's show General Lee some riding! I'll see you out there."

By the time Jake got outside, Herb was already in the saddle. "Hey, Jake, you should see how well Traveler jumps now." Herb had named his horse after Robert E. Lee's famous mount. Had he shouted the horse's name in order to catch the attention of Robert's nephew, Fitzhugh Lee? Herb flicked the reins and Traveler cantered into the paddock, where several obstacles had been laid out.

Jake wrinkled his nose at the smell of smoke in the air. As far as the eye could see, rows of dingy white tents and clusters of horses filled the orchards and fields of Union Mills. Fortifying themselves for the day ahead, soldiers in uniforms of butternut and gray gathered around various campfires.

A contingent of Confederate horsemen crested the south hill. Jake's eyes fixed on the long, black plume fluttering gaily from the hat of a particularly well-dressed officer. When the riders drew abreast of the paddock where Herb put Traveler through his paces, the dapper officer signaled with his hand and his men spread out along the fence to watch.

Jake hurried over to join them. Herb was right; Traveler was in rare form. The dappled gray easily cleared a stack of firewood about three feet high. Herb spurred Traveler into a gallop and headed directly at Jake. Just as Jake thought he would have to jump out of the way, Herb tugged the reins and Traveler made a nearly impossible cut, veering away less than a yard from the fence. The horse gathered speed and leapt into the air, this time for distance, clearing a cluster of logs a dozen feet wide.

"Bravo, I say, bravo!" The officer in the black-plumed hat stood in the stirrups, his gloved hands emitting a small cloud of dust as he applauded. "Young man, come here. I wish to meet you."

Flushed with obvious excitement, Herb walked Traveler over to the split-rail fence. "Hello, sir, my name is Thomas Herbert Shriver but people call me Herbert or my friends call me Herb but you can call me anything you like, of course, and this here is Traveler." Finally out of breath, Herb reached down and patted his horse's neck.

"That was a superb piece of riding you displayed there, son. You are a fine horseman."

"Thank you, sir!"

"We can always use men who ride as well as you. Why aren't you already in the cavalry?" The officer cocked his head. "Don't tell me you are a Federalist."

"No sir! My parents say I must wait 'til next year to join up, sir."

The officer glanced down the fence line at his entourage. "Well, we shall see what they have to say if Jeb Stuart does the asking." The men laughed knowingly.

Jake gawked. Jeb Stuart!

The famous general turned his piercing eyes upon Jake. "And who might this young man be?"

Herb spoke for his tongue-tied friend. "That there's Jake Becker. He's a fine rider, too, General Stuart."

Jake's heart pounded. Might he become a cavalryman after all?

"He wanted to join the cavalry," Herb continued, "but last night General Lee asked him to drive a wagon for him."

"I see," Stuart said thoughtfully. "I'm sure General Lee will put you to good use, son."

Jake fought to keep the disappointment from showing on his face.

Turning back to Herb, Stuart said, "How about you take me to meet your father."

"Yes, sir!" Herb dismounted, climbed over the fence, and led Stuart and his men to the house. The general dismounted and handed the reins to a Negro in his company.

Servant or slave? Jake wondered.

Mr. Shriver came out onto the porch and Herb made the introductions. "General Stuart, this is my father, William Shriver. Father, this is General James Ewell Brown Stuart."

"General Stuart, your fame precedes you. Welcome!" The men shook hands heartily.

Stuart pointed to his nearest companion. "And this is my adjutant, Major Henry McClellan."

The tromping of boots echoed from the front hallway. Fitzhugh Lee exited the house, beaming. "Good morning, General, you're just in time for breakfast."

Mr. Shriver held the door for Stuart and his officers. Herb and Jake brought up the rear. Mrs. Shriver appeared from the kitchen and ushered the men into the dining room, where several more officers soon joined them. Jake took his breakfast in the kitchen with the Shriver daughters. The flapjacks and fat biscuits filled his stomach, but the hashed browns were a lot spicier than Myrtle made them. Fortunately, the fresh milk soothed the mild upset.

As the Shriver girls brought the empty dishes from the dining room, Jake heard Stuart ask, "Was that a piano I spied in the parlor?"

"Yes, sir! A fine Steinway it is," Mr. Shriver said. "Do you play?"

"Yes, sir, I do. May we have a round of singing?"

"Splendid idea!" Mrs. Shriver answered.

The men relocated to the parlor; Jake and the girls joined them. Stuart went around the room with a quick introduction of each of his staff officers, then in a booming baritone voice, he led the impromptu glee club in "Dixie," "My Old Kentucky Home," and "Annie Laurie."

Stuart stood, went to the window, and called out, "Sam, we could surely use your banjo."

A few moments later Stuart introduced his servant, Sam Sweeney, who carried a well-worn banjo. Sam plucked a few arpeggios to give everyone the key. "Ready for your favorite song, General?"

The soldiers clapped and stomped in rhythm as they belted out Jeb Stuart's theme song:

If you want to have a good time, jine the cavalry!
Jine the cavalry! Jine the cavalry!
If you want to catch the Devil, if you want to have fun,
If you want to smell Hell, Jine the cavalry!

Sam vamped the opening chord and announced, "Here's a new verse for you, General." Familiar with the pattern, the rest of the soldiers joined in after the first line.

Now we're goin' into Pennsylvania,
Into Pennsylvania, into Pennsylvania!
Now we're goin' into Pennsylvania,
Bully boys, hey! Bully boys, ho!

Lee circled his hand in the air for Sam to continue playing, and said, "I have a verse, too."

The big fat Dutch gals will hand 'round the breadium,
Hand around the breadium, hand 'round the breadium!
The big fat Dutch gals will hand 'round the breadium,
Bully boys, hey! Bully boys, ho!

As the song ended, Mrs. Heard, a Shriver friend who "just happened to be passing by," joined the festivities and took a turn at the piano while General Stuart acted the *bon vivant*.

When the grandfather clock struck the hour of eight, Stuart sighed and said, "This has been the most pleasant start to a day I can long remember." He crossed to Mrs. Shriver and bowed deeply. "And your gracious hospitality, ma'am, shall always be a treasured memory."

Mrs. Shriver looked radiant. "You are most welcome, General Stuart. My only regret is that our entertainment was so inadequate for the occasion, but you make us feel as though it is elegant. I hope you may return someday in happier times."

"I shall most assuredly plan to visit you again, ma'am, should I ever get within twenty-five miles of here." Stuart's eyes twinkled.

Mrs. Shriver stood and offered her hand, upon which Stuart bestowed an eloquent kiss. She flashed a smile around the room. "Now if you will please excuse me, gentlemen, after being awake all night, I must take my leave." She curtseyed and left the parlor. Her delicate footsteps echoed from the hallway as she made her way upstairs.

Stuart asked Mr. Shriver's permission to use the dining room table for his maps, and the officers adjourned to plan the day's route. On their way out of the parlor, Stuart pulled Herb and Jake aside. "I'd like you two lads to join us. I have some questions about the roads north of here."

McClellan handed Stuart a rolled-up map, which he spread out on the table. Stuart found Westminster with his finger, then traced the road north to Union Mills. He leaned over the table for a closer look. "Young man, I want to know about the dirt or country roads up yonder leading to Hanover." He turned and looked over his shoulder at Herb. "Are they wide enough for artillery?"

"Sir, I have never seen artillery, but heavily loaded wagons pulled by four mules can travel on them."

The general nodded. "That's fine." He stood up and put his hand on Herb's shoulder. "Now listen. I want you to come with me. You aren't afraid, I'm sure."

Eyes wide with excitement, Herb shook his head.

"Are you?"

"No, sir!"

"That's more like it. Now, take me up to your mother's room and I will ask her permission. Is that all right with you?"

"Yes, sir, General Stuart." Herb nudged Jake, and the two young men followed Stuart up the stairs.

On the top landing, Stuart stepped aside and Herb led the way to his parents' room. Starting to feel like a third wheel, Jake decided to wait at the top of the stairs. Herb knocked on the door and his father opened it.

"What is it, Herb? Your mother is resting."

"Pa, General Stuart would like to speak with her."

The door creaked fully open and Mr. Shriver stepped into the hall, an anxious look on his face. "Is everything all right, General?"

"Oh, yessir. However, there is one last request I would like to make. I apologize for the imposition."

Mrs. Shriver called enthusiastically from the bedroom, "Not at all, General Stuart. Please, do come in."

Stuart's voice took on a soothing quality. "Mrs. Shriver, I know you have two sons already serving our cause, for which we are indeed grateful. As our army moves into enemy territory, it is essential we have knowledgeable men to guide us on our way. I would be most obliged if your son Herbert might serve us in that capacity. With your kind permission, of course."

There was a brief silence. Mrs. Shriver's quavering voice replied, "If you need him, yes. But isn't he too young?"

"My dear lady, no. And I promise both of you that I will keep him by my side at all times. And furthermore, when things are more settled, at the earliest possible time, I will personally send him to the Virginia Military Institute and, when he is graduated, I will put him on my staff."

"Oh, General Stuart, you are most kind. Thank you, sir."

Jake shuffled to Herb's room and sank dejectedly onto the bed. While he wanted to be happy for his friend and the great opportunity afforded him, he could not help feeling jealous. From outside, the banjo plucked the chorus of Stuart's theme song and dozens of men joined in singing, "If you want to have a good time, jine the cavalry!"

Jake sighed and slumped backward across the bed. *Lord, why can't I jine the cavalry?*

-2-

David took a break from digging, pulled a wrinkled handkerchief from his pocket, and wiped the sweat from his brow. He propped his shovel against the side of the trench and leaned back to stretch his aching muscles. The clock on St. Matthew's chimed the hour of eight. Immediately afterward came the melodious strains of the girls' chorus, singing "My Country 'Tis of Thee."

Harvey Stremmel leaned on his shovel. "That Josiah Daniels sure is a stickler for punctuality."

Peter Frank smirked. "Actually, the clock must be a few seconds early, otherwise the chime and the first note would have happened at the same instant."

As the girls sang *Land where my fathers died,* one glorious soprano voice rang out above the others.

David exclaimed, "Shew! Now that young lady can sing!"

"Who is that?" Peter shaded his eyes and looked intently toward the church, as if trying to see through the brick wall.

From the west, out Frederick Street, came a soft rumble, building in intensity. David climbed from the trench and ran into the middle of the road; Peter and Harvey followed close behind.

Another cavalry column. Blue or gray? Shaded by the trees, the distant flag flashed glimpses of red, white, and blue, but David couldn't make out whether it was the Stars and Stripes or the Stars and Bars.

Mrs. Meckley, a half-filled basket of huckleberries careening from her arm, hurried past the men on her way toward the Square. "The hills are full of Rebels! You better see to your households."

David exchanged worried looks with Peter and Harvey. Across the road, Mrs. Stahl shooed her two toddlers inside the house.

The soldiers drew nearer to David's house, and he was finally able to determine under which flag they marched. "Federal troops!"

His words seemed to echo as the news passed up Frederick Street to the center of town. By the time the front of the column reached the building site, dozens of cheering and clapping citizens lined the road.

Josiah Daniels ushered the girls' chorus into two rows along the side of the street. They quickly launched into a rousing rendition of "Columbia, the Gem of the Ocean."

Perfectly situated above the thoroughfare hung a large thirty-four star American flag that had been strung up in celebration of Hanover's Centennial Anniversary. The appearance of the Union Army had evolved into a spontaneous parade.

Leaving his fellow workers behind, David followed the regiment up the street. The front rank halted near the Market Shed in the Square. Several soldiers dismounted, including one particularly striking young officer. Flowing blonde locks spilled from beneath his wide-brimmed hat and down the back of his black velveteen uniform coat. The epaulette on each shoulder bore a single gold star. Gleaming gold lacework decorated the coat sleeves. A silver star glistened from each end of the wide collar on his blue sailor shirt, and he sported a bright red bandana like a tie around his neck. David wondered what kind of man would go off to war as if dressed for a masquerade.

One of the other officers addressed the gawking crowd. "Is there anyone here who has a map of the area?"

David stepped forward. "I know Jacob Wirt has a large map of the county on his wall. He lives just a few doors down."

An officer with deep-set eyes, a beakish nose, and unkempt mutton chops turned to David. "Splendid! Why don't you take us there? You may make the introductions. I am General Judson Kilpatrick, this is General Elon Farnsworth, and that young man," he gestured to the officer with the fancy uniform, "is our newest general, George Custer."

Gen. Judson Kilpatrick   **Gen. George Armstrong Custer**

David led the way, followed by Custer, Kilpatrick, and a few other officers. Although Jacob Wirt had left Hanover to accompany the bulk of his bank's deposits to safety across the Susquehanna, Calvin Wirt cheerfully ushered the soldiers into the house. David stood in the back of the parlor while Calvin showed Kilpatrick the map. Custer went to the front window, crossed his arms, and leaned against the window jamb.

The front door opened and Rev. Zieber entered. "Is there anything I can do to be of service?"

"I pity my men," Kilpatrick said, "for they have had no breakfast, and they're very hungry. We have been marching hard ever since we crossed the Potomac and have been short of rations for three days. I don't have all my commissary wagons with me."

"Our people are thoroughly loyal and we are glad to have you come," Rev. Zieber said. "We have been expecting the approach of the enemy for the past two days. All you have to do is give the word, and we will see that your soldiers are fed."

"Thank you very much, sir," Kilpatrick said. "You are most kind."

The reverend went out onto the step and addressed the crowd. "These soldiers are our friends and protectors. They are tired and hungry. The best thing we can do is to feed them."

In no time, the streets filled with citizens bearing bread, pie, coffee, milk, beer, pretzels, berries, meat, cheese, cigars, pipes, shoes, and many other items the townsfolk thought the men might need. The cavalrymen ate in the saddle, but when someone pulled out a fiddle, several men dismounted and danced with the many willing young ladies.

David decided to go home and raid his root cellar for jars of provisions to share. On the way, he passed the girls' chorus, distributing glasses of milk and slices of pie to the men in blue. Kathleen Bigler sang as she worked, earning many admiring glances from the soldiers.

"That young lady has a heavenly voice," David murmured.

"She sure looks like an angel," a young cavalryman added wistfully.

David waited for one of the soldiers to finish chewing a bite of biscuit, then asked, "How many of you are there?"

The young man wiped the crumbs from his moustache. "Several thousand. We left Littlestown first thing this morning."

Mrs. Marks called from her upstairs window, "The Lord bless you!"

The soldiers cheered. A pudgy, middle-aged man stood in the stirrups and shook his fist. "Seen any Rebs we can kill for ya, ma'am?"

David's heart sank as he thought of Jake. Should he have tried harder to dissuade his son from going? Would more effort have made a difference? He reminded himself that Jake was an adult, responsible before God and man for his own decisions. Thank heaven Jake had already gone on his way south; hopefully, far from where the armies were gathering. Sooner or later the enemies would meet, and when they did, David didn't want his son to be anywhere in the vicinity.

-3-

Jake stood on the Shrivers' front porch and watched while Herb walked his horse to the head of the long column of cavalry, where General Stuart sat astride a different bay mare than the one he had ridden the day before. The black plume in Stuart's hat flittered in the breeze, mimicking the flutter in Jake's heart. His best friend was about to embark on the adventure of a lifetime without him.

General Lee's voice rang from the hallway. "Thank you again, ma'am." He came out onto the porch and pulled up his gauntlets. "Well, Private Becker, looks like a fine day for riding. Tell me, is June always this pleasantly cool around here?"

"No, sir, we're usually a good twenty degrees warmer." Jake wondered if he should have saluted, but from what he had seen thus far, the officers didn't seem to stand much on formalities in casual situations.

"I'll be taking my men on a separate route from General Stuart's. General Hampton will take charge of the wagon train. Do you remember which one he is?"

"The one with the curly hair and bushy beard?"

"Right. A member of his staff will be looking for you when the wagons pass by here. It will take some time, as they're still down by Westminster. One of his men will assign you a wagon to drive." Lee put a hand to the brim of his hat, nodded curtly, and left to mount up.

At General Stuart's gesture, Colonel John Chambliss' brigade led the column down the incline toward the Shriver homestead, past the brick gristmill, and over Pipe Creek's stone bridge. Stuart and his staff followed next in line. Jake stood with Herb's family at the picket fence and waved until Herb passed from sight.

A half-hour elapsed and still the cavalry paraded by. Feeling fidgety, Jake re-organized the gear in his saddlebags and practiced changing the revolver's cylinders. Finally, the horse-drawn caissons and cannons rolled into view. Jake grinned. *At least I got to see artillery before Herb did.*

A column of Conestoga wagons appeared at the top of the hill. Jake draped his bedroll and saddlebags over his left arm, grabbed his rifle with his right hand, and clomped down the porch steps.

General Wade Hampton and a member of his staff rode up to the porch. Hampton nodded to Jake, then pointed with his thumb toward the young officer at his right. "Lieutenant Hampton here will show you which wagon is yours." The general continued on with the column while the lieutenant reined his horse out of line. Was this the general's son?

"All you need to do is follow the wagon ahead of you. If you have any problems, let one of the outriders know. They'll be riding patrol on either side of the column. Any questions?"

"No, sir." Jake gulped. That wasn't completely true. "Well, sir, if you don't mind my asking. Are you—"

"Yes, yes, I'm the general's son, Lieutenant Wade Hampton. Wade Hampton, the fourth, if you must know."

The young lieutenant held up his hand and waved the next wagon off the road. He pointed at the elderly driver. "Thank you for your service, sir. You are free to go. You may take your things and leave."

The old man dropped the reins, reached under the bench for his gear, and climbed off the wagon. "Thank you. Sir." He spat a long stream of tobacco juice, bowed stiffly, and then headed off toward Westminster.

Bemused, Jake recognized the name of the wagon's maker, John Studebaker from Hunterstown, who had underbid Pa for a big army contract two years ago. Jake slid his gear under the bench, set his rifle in the foot well, then walked to the front of the mule team. He scratched the animals' necks while they got his scent.

"You might wish you were a little quicker once you see how much dust there is the farther back in line you are," Hampton said.

"Yes, sir." Jake climbed into the wagon, flicked the reins, and joined the column. The pair responded well, so Jake settled in for the ride. As they passed the tannery, he checked the time on Andrew Shriver's homemade, wall-mounted sundial. It was shortly after nine o'clock, if the rod was adjusted properly. Knowing Andrew, it was.

As the wheels clattered across the stone bridge, Jake glanced down at Pipe Creek and thought, *General Stuart may not be Julius Caesar and this wagon is certainly no chariot, but there lies my Rubicon. I'm a member of the Confederate Army now.*

The Rebel Raid into Pennsylvania

Fortunately, they were headed for Littlestown, a dozen miles west of Hanover. Jake only knew a few people there, so the odds of being recognized were negligible. What would the Biglers think if the army went through Hanover and instead of seeing Jake as a dashing member of the cavalry, they saw him driving a supply wagon?

Supplies? He turned in his seat and studied the contents of the wagon: burlap bags, stacked waist-high, labeled, "50# OATS—Robinson and Palmer Mills—Baltimore." Fifty-pound bags of oats! Knowing that oats were a far superior feed to grass, Jake realized his cargo would save the cavalry many hours in grazing time. *Huh. I always wished I'd find an important task to accomplish someday. I just figured it would be more significant than serving as feed master to a bunch of horses, even if they are in Jeb Stuart's cavalry. Well, at least the greatest danger I'll face is the teeth of a ravenous horse—better that than the bayonet of a raving enemy, I guess. Well, Lord, a cavalry isn't much good without its horses, and the horses gotta eat, so I guess I'm pretty valuable after all.* He flicked the reins and encouraged the team up the hill from Union Mills.

A cavalryman appeared from the north, his horse at a gallop. He reined up smartly in front of General Hampton and his staff. The brief encounter ended, and the general and most of his staff rejoined the procession, leaving Lieutenant Hampton and the rider behind.

As Jake's wagon drew abreast of the two men, Lieutenant Hampton pointed to Jake. "Pull your wagon out of line."

Jake nervously obeyed. What had he done wrong? Was he about to lose his job?

"Wait here for the corporal," the lieutenant commanded. Hampton nodded to the rider, then reined his horse about and trotted to regain his place in the column.

The corporal hurried toward the rear of the wagon train. He returned several minutes later with a black mare in tow. "Get your things and come with me. Be quick about it."

Jake hurriedly transferred his gear to the horse. A middle-aged Negro left a passing wagon to take control of Jake's vehicle.

The corporal stared at Jake, openly curious. "Come with me. General Stuart wants you."

Jake's jaw dropped. *General Stuart wants* me?

Without waiting for a reply, the corporal turned his horse and spurred her into a gallop. Jake's new mount sprang into action as if delighted at the opportunity to show off her strength and speed, adding to Jake's exhilaration in no small measure.

Had Herb said something to General Stuart on Jake's behalf? In any case, what possible reason could there be for such haste?

The corporal led Jake to a brick farmhouse in front of which General Stuart and his staff waited. Herb waved discreetly.

"Jake, hurry here, my boy," Stuart said. His saddle creaked as he leaned and pointed to the cut in the hill for the road up ahead. "My scouts tell me there is a large force of Federal troops in Littlestown. Young Herbert has shown me this back road into Hanover. Tell me, do you know how we can get through the gap in the Pigeon Hills north of the town?"

"Yessir, General Stuart. I know a couple of different routes you could take. The shortest is directly through town." Jake trembled, both with excitement and fear. While it was exhilarating to think of Eliza seeing him in the company of Jeb Stuart, what if a few Hanoverians acted foolishly and someone got hurt?

"Very good. Now tell me, young man, is it your desire to become a soldier in this army?"

Jake's fears vanished. "Yessir, it truly is!"

"Major McClellan," Stuart called over his shoulder, "please administer the oath."

McClellan joined them. "Raise your right hand and repeat after me."

His mind in a blur, Jake repeated each phrase with all the conviction he could muster. "I, Jacob Becker, do solemnly swear . . . that I will bear true faith and allegiance . . . to the Confederate States of America . . . and that I will serve them honestly and faithfully . . . against all their enemies or opposers whomsoever . . . and that I will observe and obey . . . the orders of the President of the Confederate States . . . and the orders of the officers appointed over me . . . according to the Rules and Articles of War."

Golly! I've really done it. It's official!

General Stuart nodded grimly to the patiently waiting corporal. "Take Private Becker back on patrol with you and have him show you the way to the Pigeon Hills. He can bring your report back to me. I may have more questions for him by then."

Major McClellan cleared his throat. "What about a uniform for the lad? If they run into trouble, he'd be considered a spy in civilian clothes."

"No time," Stuart said. He turned to Jake. "You're from Hanover, so if the Billies take you, just act happy they've rescued you. We'll get you dudded up proper later."

"Yessir." Jake shifted uneasily in the saddle. Didn't they hang spies?

McClellan gave Jake an appraising stare. "Don't forget your oath."

"No, sir." Jake met the major's eyes without flinching. "I know whose side I am on." *Everything is happening so quickly! Is this a dream?*

"Let's go," the corporal said impatiently.

They set out at a canter and soon caught up with a small squad of Confederate cavalrymen atop Conewago Hill. Across the way, Jake picked out the Mill at Josiah Gitt's farm.

The corporal reined up next to one of the officers. "Major Gillette, sir, this here's Private Becker. He's from these parts. General Stuart sent him along to help scout out our new route."

"Excellent, Corporal. Take him up ahead to the advance patrol."

Jake let his eyes drift up the road toward home. He did a double take, startled at the sight of a band of blue uniformed cavalrymen over by Gitt's Mill, a few hundred yards away. "Um, sir? Aren't those—"

A shot rang out, followed by another and another. The corporal toppled from his saddle and thudded on the road like a sack of oats.

The Confederates pulled out their carbines and returned fire. Jake managed to bring his rifle to bear just as the Yankees turned and fled northward. Should he fire anyway? He decided against pulling the trigger; he would not shoot at a man whose back was turned. His new comrades felt no such compunction. They fired off a volley of bullets and epithets at their fleeing foes.

"Ha! That oughta send them right into the arms of our patrol," Major Gillette said. He turned and studied Jake while two of his men dismounted to tend to the corporal's body.

For the second time in the past fifteen minutes, Jake found himself under a major's scrutiny. Did this one also question his loyalty? Jake quickly explained, "I just enlisted, sir. Major McClellan swore me in, and General Stuart sent me on without a uniform."

"I see," Gillette said, clearly impressed. "Well, Private, perhaps I best send you right back to him—"

Jake's heart sank. His hopes for an important mission, dashed.

"—with a message," Gillette continued. "Tell him we've heard reports that General Early is in York, and we just ran across some Yankee scouts. No telling how many more are about. I'll send word as soon as I hear from our patrol."

"Yes, sir!" Jake saluted and turned his horse to go.

One of the dismounted men added, "It's high time we made the Yankee farmers suffer, just like our folks did back in Virginia."

Jake cringed. Must York County suffer such devastation, too?

-4-

For two hours a stream of Union cavalry passed through Hanover, each unit pausing in turn to rest and eat. David stood in front of his house and handed out jars of peaches and other canned goods. He knew he was giving away more food than he should, but with Jake and Myrtle gone, he figured he could always make do.

A rosy-cheeked cavalryman called from just down the street. "Mr. Becker, hello!"

"John? John Hoffacker? How are you?" David hurried over to where the slender young man sat astride his roan stallion, waiting for the column to resume the march. "Do your parents know your troop is here?"

"No, sir, I'm sure they don't. Would you tell them you saw me and that I am well?" He pointed to the insignia on his sleeve. "Only two months, and I already made corporal!"

"Congratulations, Corporal Hoffacker! I'm sure they'll be very proud of you. I don't expect to see them before church on Sunday, but I'll get word to them, even if I have to ride out to West Mannheim myself." The column of troopers crept forward. "You take care now, hear?"

David decided he should return to his work on the church foundation and headed up Frederick Street. The smell of baking bread hung over the town like a heavenly perfume.

Just up the street from the building site, the girls continued to dole out food and drink, though now they only had bowls left to hold the beverages. David caught sight of Kathleen as she served a towheaded youngster in a blue uniform. A shiny bugle dangled at his side. The boy accepted a small pie, took a big bite, and washed it down with a drink from the bowl. Judging from the expression on his face, the lad was more than a little enamored with his attractive benefactress.

Something boomed off in the distance, louder and deeper than a rifle shot. A cannon salute from the troops? A rippling crackle echoed from the west end of town. A string of firecrackers? Not likely, it sounded more forceful than that.

An officer on a black horse trotted up the street and shouted, "Citizens will please go to their homes and into their cellars. In a few minutes there will be fighting on your streets."

Stunned, David gaped in disbelief. Moments later, several wagons and dozens of Union cavalrymen galloped up Frederick Street toward the Square. A host of gray-clad troopers, firing pistols and brandishing sabres, followed hard on their heels! Some of the dismounted Union men dashed for their horses, others hid where they could. The girls' chorus ran for the church. The bugle boy disappeared behind the flow of cavalrymen.

David ducked behind a tree at the edge of the church lot and squinted down the street toward his house. Confederates swarmed around several abandoned wagons. The vehicles slowly turned around and headed off with a Rebel escort.

The sound of gunfire rang up and down the street. Sabre clanged on sabre. Men shouted and cursed. Most horrifying was the thunk of sabre against flesh and bone. David doubted he would ever forget that sound— or the gut-wrenching shrieks of pain that followed.

Several yards to the right, a Union man slumped and fell from his saddle. The next horse and rider tried to leap over the body, but the horse went limp in mid-jump and crumpled to the ground with a sickening thud. Somehow, the rider landed clear of the dying horse, rolled, and scrambled to his feet. Just then, a Rebel cavalryman rode up, slashed with his sabre, and sent the defenseless man to meet his Maker.

With bile rising in his throat, David turned away from the gory scene. He looked toward the Square and could scarcely believe his eyes. Why did townsfolk stand on the edges of the street, watching the battle unfold as if it were a pageant?

Down the block, Mrs. Wolf held out a piece of pie to a passing Union cavalryman. Horrified, David was about to shout for her to get to safety, when a pursuing Confederate fired his pistol and the man in blue tumbled to the street. As the puff of smoke faded, the dead man's horse reared, then fled toward the Square. Mrs. Wolf looked bewildered—and eerily oblivious to any danger.

Gunshots erupted from the fields behind him. David spied several Confederate riflemen in the half-grown corn. They quickly crouched out of sight, apparently to reload.

Just beyond the church lot, a band of Confederate cavalrymen bore down on four Union troopers fleeing on foot. The leading Rebel's horse suddenly spouted a bloody plume from its chest and went down in a heap. The officer dove from the saddle, hit the ground rolling, and jumped to his feet. He started for the horse tethered nearby. David groaned. Harvey Stremmel wasn't going to like hearing that a Rebel had stolen his horse.

Surrounded and outnumbered, the Union men threw up their hands. Two of the Confederates led the prisoners away. The rest of the Rebels spurred their mounts and headed in David's direction. He slunk down, pressing his back against the trunk of the tree.

The horses rose from the ground, one after the other, and leapt over the far end of the foundation. Despite the rush of fear, David marveled at the animals' grace and beauty. The earth trembled as the cavalrymen galloped down the center of the lot, cleared the near end of the foundation, and burst onto the street. Whooping and hollering at the top of their lungs, the troopers raced for the center of town.

David rolled onto his stomach and peered around the tree. The road was littered with the corpses of soldiers and horses. Wounded men moaned and writhed in the dirt. The few Federal troops still on their feet had guns trained upon them. A cannon boomed in the distance while sporadic gunshots continued, near and far. The devilish stench of sulphur hung in the air. A bugle sounded from the direction of the Square. Shouts. Gunfire. Galloping horses.

The Confederate cavalry retreated out Frederick Street as a swarm of Union forces countercharged through the Square! From sidewalks, windows, and doorways the dauntless townsfolk applauded and cheered at the rapid turn of events.

A cannon shell whistled through the air, finding its mark in a Union cavalryman. The soldier's right leg turned into a pulpy mass, the horse's innards splattered the road, and the pair collapsed in a hideous heap.

Expecting more shells to follow, David ran for home and the safety of his cellar. In the few moments it took to get there, the wave of battle swept around the bend in the road and out toward Karle Forney's home. Across the street in front of the Trone house, a Union man jubilantly waved a Confederate battle flag. Several sheepish looking men in blue crept out of the basement of Henry Long's silversmith shop.

The gunfire continued unabated at the edge of town. Help had arrived just in time and, judging from the thousands of men in blue who had paraded through Hanover all morning, there were plenty more Federal soldiers on the way.

On the road in front of David's house lay a dead roan, pinning its erstwhile rider. David rushed to aid the sergeant who knelt by the trapped man's side.

"I warned him not to ride ahead of us," the sergeant told David sadly. "But he said, 'Oh God, I am too close to my home to die.' That was just before he took a pistol ball in the forehead."

David stared in horror at John Hoffacker's lifeless body.

-5-

Though not particularly pleased to hear of the encounter with the Yankee scouts, General Stuart looked delighted at Jake's news of General Early's whereabouts. "Excellent! York it is, then. What is the fastest route, Private Becker?"

"Through Hanover, sir."

A vision of riding through Center Square at Jeb Stuart's side flashed through Jake's mind. Who would have imagined it was possible to feel both jubilant and horrified at the same time? True, Colonel White's men had come and gone with little damage done, but what were those couple of hundred troopers compared to Stuart's several thousand? And three days ago there hadn't been any sign of Federal troops threatening to cause a ruckus.

Jake decided to amend his answer. "Actually, sir, I know a short cut to the York Road that will avoid having to go through the town."

"Perfect. We need to proceed with all haste," Stuart said. "Major, send someone to hurry that blasted wagon train along."

Just as McClellan finished assigning one of the lieutenants to the task, a noise like a thunderclap roared up ahead. A faint crackling sound followed.

"Captain Cooke, go see what that firing is all about," Stuart commanded.

"Colonel Chambliss' men probably came upon those Yankee scouts and are enjoying a little 'squirrel hunting,'" Lieutenant Hagan quipped.

"With a cannon?" Lieutenant Robertson asked, sardonically.

Combat near Hanover? Jake's mind reeled. He frantically scanned his surroundings, hoping to see the Smiling Man or the talking scarecrow—anything that would prove this was just a bad dream.

Stuart set off at a canter, and his staff followed close behind. Jake's apprehension grew as they neared the site of the corporal's death. He half-expected to crest Conewago Hill and see another Manassas unfolding before his eyes. Fortunately, there were no signs of conflict, but the distant battle sounds were growing louder.

Cooke intercepted them just before they reached the ridge overlooking Hanover. "General Stuart, Chambliss' men have encountered some Yankees and are driving them through Hanover."

"Good! Tell him to push on and occupy the town, but not to pursue them too far."

Jake's heart pounded. Occupy Hanover? What had he gotten himself into? Good thing he was with Stuart's staff and wouldn't take part in any of the fighting.

The jovial Jeb disappeared as General Jeb Stuart issued a flurry of orders. Major McClellan carefully penned the commander's words, then handed the directives to Lieutenants Garnett and Dabney, who galloped away to deliver them.

Stuart turned in the saddle. "Tell me, Jake, how far does this ridge extend?"

Jake bit his lip as he hurriedly gathered his senses. "A bit more to the west and a couple of miles east, sir. Cemetery Hill is at the eastern end of the ridge." Jake felt a pang of grief. His mother and sister lay buried in that cemetery.

"Major Beckham! It sounds as if Colonel Payne has already employed a battery. Prepare to deploy your guns east along this ridge."

"Yes sir!" The major galloped off.

Stuart issued a few more orders, then called for his other mount, Virginia. His colored servant, Bob, promptly brought the horse.

"Bob, give Highfly some oats but not much water, in case I need her later," Stuart said. He traded mounts, started toward town, and called back over his shoulder, "Herbert! Jake! Stay with me."

The young men exchanged worried looks, then rushed to catch up with Stuart and his staff. Jake's holstered rifle bounced and bumped against his knee. Pa's words filled his mind. *Private Becker. Take your weapon and proceed down Frederick Street to the Forney farm and shoot as many of those Yankee bastards as you can. That is an order, soldier! Do you know what we do to men who disobey orders?*

The image of John Forney's guileless face added, *Just don't go shootin' at any Hanover boys now, hear?*

Jake's heart sank. When would he awaken from this nightmare?

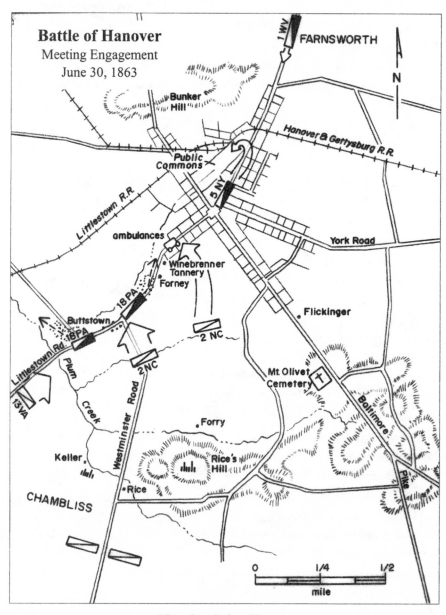

Battle of Hanover
Meeting Engagement
June 30, 1863

Map by John Heiser

-6-

At the first sign of Union troops, Eliza scooped Sarah into her arms and hustled her other two cousins toward their house on the Abbottstown Road. Six-year-old Christopher insisted on running back to retrieve his toy boats from the watering trough. And of course he had to fetch the little turtle he'd found that morning.

His sister, Emily, eight years old and self-proclaimed queen for the day, stood with hands on hips, scolding from the porch. "Mama said you're to mind Eliza. Mama said you're to mind Eliza. Mama said . . ."

Seventeen-month-old Sarah picked that moment to fill her diaper to overflowing. The smelly mess ran down Eliza's arm and onto her frock.

"Sarah! I told you not to eat so many berries," Eliza moaned. "Eww disgusting!" She felt on the verge of tears.

The toddler parroted, "Eww gussy! Eww gussy! Eww . . ."

Emily droned, "Mama said you're to mind Eliza. Mama said . . ."

And the Union cavalry drew ever nearer.

Eliza lost her last ounce of patience. "Ca-riss-toe-fer!"

The three youngsters immediately fell silent.

"To your room," Eliza said coldly.

Unable to manage the boats and his new pet with only two hands, Christopher tapped his index finger on the top of the turtle's shell. The critter quickly retreated into its abode. The grimy lad put the shell between his teeth, scooped up the toys, and waddled into the house.

Sarah pulled at her diaper. "Eww, 'Liza."

Groaning, Eliza wondered when her mother, aunt, and uncle would return from hiding the horses. How could anyone handle three young children all alone? "Emily, let's see how much mothering you want to do now. Go and get a wet rag and meet me in your parents' room."

The curly-haired girl folded her arms and started to make a face, but then wilted under Eliza's glare. Ten minutes later, the toddler was somewhat cleaner and in her crib; Christopher romped in his room; and Emily, given the choice between setting out the lunch and keeping the baby company, sagely chose the former.

Between her headache and body aches, Eliza just wanted to strip down and soak in the big oaken tub. And if Kathleen would pour some nice hot water over her back . . . Kathleen! Eliza ran to the hallway window and glanced down at the passing soldiers. They must have come through Hanover. Was Kathleen all right? Remembering her sister was at a chorus rehearsal, Eliza took a deep breath and tried to relax. Surely the Yankees wouldn't bother anyone in a church. Then again, what were the chances Kathleen would stay inside St. Matthew's?

The first in a row of artillery pieces rattled past. Eliza's eyes were drawn to a particularly rotund teamster, who pawed through a basket on the seat next to him and pulled out a small loaf of pumpernickel. She took a closer look at the other cavalrymen. They all seemed to be busy with everything *but* soldiering: eating, laughing, drinking, smoking, bragging about the girls they had encountered in town. "It's like a picnic on horseback," Eliza grumbled. She looked to the heavens and begged for a downpour, or at least a plague of ants to ruin their outing.

Dismayed at yet another gray sky, Eliza dreamt of a sunny day after the war. She decided she would go on a picnic with Jake up on Bald Mountain, and she'd wear her pink dress. All the young men at her cotillion had told her how beautiful she looked in it.

Ruining the reverie, a small group of cavalrymen raced back toward Hanover at a gallop. Eliza followed them with her eyes while her thoughts turned to her present situation. Now that her mother approved of Jake, why couldn't he just come on home so they could be together?

Excited shouts rippled along the line and accordion-like, the column of soldiers came to a halt. A jar slipped from one trooper's grasp and crashed to the ground, spilling juicy peaches across the road. The column of men turned their horses and headed for Hanover at a canter.

In the midst of the turmoil, the teamster on one of the caissons jackknifed his rig near the house. Eliza stared, intrigued with the man's maneuverings to correct his course. One of the big wheels slid off the edge of the road and down into a small gully. The driver cracked his whip and the six horses pulled as one. When the wheel popped free of the ditch, the caisson bounced onto the road, and the sudden jar detonated the contents of the caisson. The explosion rattled the windows of the house. As sparks flared above the fireball, Eliza felt a wave of heat on her face. The driver flew through the air and tumbled to the ground like a rag doll. The wheel pair of horses lay mangled in the road; blood flowed down the flanks of the panicky middle pair; and the lead pair whinnied and reared, struggling to break free of the harness. Eliza's hands flew to her mouth. She willed her eyes to close, but they refused to obey.

Going into Action, W. H. Shelton (1887)

Shouts of horror filled the air. Several soldiers swiftly dismounted and ran to the fallen man's side. One of them shouted, "Not Jimmy!"

"Yes, Jimmy Moran," an officer replied sadly.

Four men lifted Jimmy's broken body and carried him toward the house. Another ran ahead to open the door.

Eliza heard the men enter—without so much as a knock. She turned to go downstairs and bumped into Christopher and Emily, huddled behind her.

"What happened, Eliza?" Emily asked, sounding very much the little girl now.

Christopher went to the railing and shouted indignantly down the stairs. "Who's in our house?"

Eliza ushered her cousins into their parents' bedroom. "You stay put now, hear? One of the soldiers got hurt and they brought him into the house. I'm going to go down and take care of things. You stay here!" Too frightened to disobey, the children nodded and clung to one another.

A dust-covered soldier awaited Eliza at the bottom of the stairs. "We're sorry to intrude, ma'am. Are your parents at hand?"

"What do you want?" she asked coldly, bristling at the implication she was incapable of dealing with the situation. All the while, part of her secretly rejoiced in the Yankees' misfortunes.

The cavalryman's eyes arched. "We have a seriously wounded man here and—"

Eliza brushed past the trooper and entered the parlor. Her temper flared at the sight of the blood-soaked man lying on the divan. "You are ruining our furniture," she snapped.

Two of the soldiers glowered at her. The other two kept working on the injured man.

Anger surged through her and emerged as invective. "What's the matter, did you run into the Confederate Army? Is that who you're running away from?"

The man with the two shiny bars on his collar spoke in an icy tone. "We do not run from anyone or anything, *miss*. We are returning to Hanover to counterattack the Rebel dogs who hit the rear of our column."

Eliza froze; suddenly fear for her loved ones displaced her anger. If there were a battle, Kathleen would surely be in danger. And what of Mr. Becker? And Lydia was home alone!

A middle-aged soldier looked up from the wounded man's side, and said grimly, "There's nothing more I can do for him." Eyes pleading, he turned to Eliza. "Miss, if you would be so kind, would you see to this man during his most urgent time of need?"

The unexpected compassion in his eyes melted Eliza's defenses. Praying her beloved Jake would never face a similar fate, she nodded solemnly.

The officer nudged the older man. "How do we know she won't help him to his grave?"

The expression on his face said it would probably be a mercy.

One of the other men took out a pencil and scrap of paper, leaned on the coffee table, and began scribbling. "This here's his name and such. If anything happens, well, if he don't . . ." He folded the paper and handed it to Eliza.

The officer knelt by the prostrate man and mumbled a prayer, then shuffled from the room, eyes downcast. The rest of the contingent followed suit.

Eliza opened the scrap of paper and read:

> *Pvt. James Moran*
> *Battery M, 2nd US Artillery*
> *attached Custer's 1st Michigan*

Numb, she eased into her aunt's chair. Michigan was so very far away. Lord forbid Jake should ever meet such an end.

Now what was she to do, wait and watch the man die? Her mind flooded with painful memories of the dead and dying Virginians in her father's fields two years past. Long repressed feelings erupted within her. She cursed the men in blue who always brought such unspeakable devastation and horror. She even cursed the God who allowed such things in the name of "freedom." What good was one man's freedom when it enslaved another in a lifetime of agony and despair, his loved one dead or maimed beyond recognition?

The dam finally gave way. Sobbing loudly, Eliza buried her face in her hands. *Why, God? Why can't you find a better way to end this horror?*

The man on the couch groaned and stirred. "P-p-priest."

Eliza looked up, shocked at the sound of the dying man's voice. Somehow, her outrage emerged from the maelstrom in her mind. "You want a *priest?*"

The soldier blinked a few times, then passed out.

Great, and he's a papist besides!

And yet another shock: was that the smell of smoke? From in front of the house a man shouted, "Fire! Get water!"

Dear God, when will it end? Eliza had never felt more overwhelmed than in that moment.

Emily's frightened voice called from the top of the stairs, "Eliza?"

Wiping the tears from her cheeks, Eliza turned her back on the Yankee and dashed up the stairs to tend to her charges.

-7-

Passing the rear elements of Chambliss' brigade, Stuart and his men crested the ridge overlooking Hanover. Jake anxiously scanned the area below. Dozens of Confederate troopers swarmed a line of Conestoga wagons between Karle Forney's farm and the Winebrenner tannery on the edge of town. Any men in blue stood with their hands in the air. Jake picked out the Becker carriage workshop and the back of the house. Between the buildings and trees he glimpsed flashes of muzzle fire and swirls of blue and gray uniforms. Farther along the right, toward the Square, his eyes fell upon the church building site where—*Pa is digging the foundation today! Oh Lord, how can this be?*

The chatter of gunfire punctuated distant shouts and screams. Jake moaned at the sight of Confederates firing on the town from the fields behind the church building lot.

Major McClellan pressed a pair of binoculars to his eyes, then proclaimed, "We've got them on the run, General! The Yankees are fleeing through the center of town, and our boys are chasing them. Hard to see with the houses and trees . . . but . . . it looks like some hand-to-hand is still going on . . . and we've got a few dozen prisoners here and there." He handed the glasses to Stuart.

Jake prayed this was nothing more than a skirmish and that his fellow townsmen were all holed up somewhere safe.

"Hold on . . . no!" Stuart said, standing in the stirrups. "It looks like a counterattack. In force! Tell Captain McGregor to open up with his three-inch guns. Send word to Captain Breathed to have his battery move up on our right and unlimber." Orderlies hurried off with the commands.

"Colonel Payne," Stuart called, guiding his horse to the officer's side. "Would you lead the charge into town and drive the Yankees out?"

"Of course, General!" Payne replied.

"Take the outside street," Stuart said, pointing out the alley that ran parallel with Frederick Street. "Penetrate deep into the body of the town and cut off the force."

Jake gasped. Payne's troops would ride right behind his house! And what was happening on the street in front of it?

Payne's 150 troopers galloped down the hill and raced along the alley, unimpeded. When they cut left to enter the town, some of the men rode directly through the church building lot.

"Here we go, men. Follow me!" Stuart shouted.

Stuart led the advance down Westminster Road. McClellan and Blackford rode on either side of the general, with Hagan, Kennan, and Robertson riding just behind them. Jake and Herb brought up the rear.

The sounds of battle reverberated above the thrumming of the horses' hooves. Jake gulped for air like a swimmer struggling to stay afloat. When his horse started to overtake the leaders, he reluctantly reined her in. The mare had Skipper's power plus speed to spare! As Jake focused on becoming one with his mount, his fear and anxiety dissipated.

Stuart slowed the pace to a trot as a dozen Conestoga wagons and a cluster of Union prisoners slowly made their way up the hill. One of the Confederate officers accompanying the procession had a blood-soaked kerchief tied around his neck. Despite the man's sunken eyes and blanched face, Jake recognized Major Gillette. Stuart shouted a few words of encouragement to Gillette, then led his small band off to the right, through a broad meadow of timothy grass. They soon emerged on the Frederick Road. Karle Forney's farm stood a short distance away.

Jake patted his horse's neck, more to steady his nerves than hers. As they cantered toward town, he prayed the Forneys would stay out of sight. Where was Pa? The Lord forbid any harm befall him.

The sounds of gunfire drew nearer. Confederate cannons blasted away on the ridge, their reports echoed like rolling thunder. Up ahead, a squad of Union cavalry suddenly appeared at the bend in the road. Jake's heart froze. The enemy outnumbered them at least three to one!

Stuart drew his sabre and laughed heartily. "Come on, Blackford, let's ride for it. Stay with me boys!"

The general urged Virginia to the right and she cleared the low hedge with ease. Blackford, atop Magic, jumped next; followed by Jake, Herb, and the rest of the general's staff. From the road came sounds of the Union cavalrymen in pursuit, but the Confederates found a more urgent situation confronting them in the meadow.

"Halt!" Thirty feet to their left, a couple dozen Union cavalrymen spurred their horses and charged.

One of Stuart's lieutenants fired his pistol. A Yankee fell across the horse of the Union officer next to him. The officer shoved the body to the ground and drew his pistol. To Jake's left, Blackford's sabre clashed and rang as he exchanged strokes with an equally skilled foe.

Fighting off the rush of panic, Jake reached for his Colt, but he fumbled pulling it free of the holster, and the revolver slipped from his grasp. He watched in helpless horror while the weapon flipped end over end to the ground. Should he dismount and retrieve it? No time!

"Follow me, boys!" Stuart put his heels to Virginia and the mare shot forward through the tall grass. Jake and his comrades dashed for the ridge, crouching in their saddles to make themselves smaller targets.

Jake knew that a stream bisected the meadow. In some places the gully was a good fifteen feet wide and a dozen feet deep. He shouted with all his might, "General Stuart, bear right! Jump!"

But his words couldn't compete with the gunshots, pounding hooves, and swishing grass. Stuart and Blackford must have seen the stream in time because Virginia and Magic leapt majestically over the obstacle. Virginia cleared the gully with a few feet to spare, though one of Magic's rear hooves left a divot on the edge of the far bank.

Herb's well-trained mount had no trouble with the jump. Kennan, however, was not so fortunate. His horse tried to stop but slid into the creek. Though Kennan managed to dive free, he rolled down the bank and into the water. Robertson's horse offered what looked to be a half-hearted effort as she belly-flopped into the stream, sending up a spout of water. Even in a crouch, Hagan looked massive. His overloaded horse didn't stand a chance, and they toppled ingloriously into the gully.

Bullets whistled past Jake, seeking more valuable targets than the lad in civilian garb. He took little comfort in remembering how difficult it was to shoot and hit anything from a moving horse. Praying his earlier estimation of his horse's strength was accurate, he gave the mare her head. She judged the take-off point perfectly. For one heart-stopping moment he wondered if they would ever land. The world took on an eerie silence but for the rush of wind in his ears. When the horse's front hooves hit the opposite bank, Jake doubled over from the impact, the breath momentarily knocked from his lungs. He made a mental note to lean back the next time they made such a jump. The mare burst into a gallop and soon caught up with the others.

"Good boy, Sk—" Jake flinched. "Good girl!" He would have to decide on a name for her later.

Jake turned and looked over his shoulder. Kennan and Robertson managed to find their way out of the gully, dripping and muddy. None of the Union riders had attempted the jump. Meanwhile, Confederate skirmishers, positioned halfway down the hill, opened fire. A cannon shell whistled from the top of the ridge and exploded near the pursuers. The Yankees turned their mounts and fled toward town.

Stuart pulled up near John Forry's farm, just below the ridge. Heart pounding, Jake reined-in next to Herb. Kennan and Robertson joined them soon after. But where was Hagan?

A bedraggled bear emerged from the stream: Lieutenant Hagan, caked with mud. He flicked his goopy hands and brown slime splattered the grass next to his dripping boots. The beleaguered horse struggled up onto firm ground. Hagan groped for the reins, mounted, and hurried to join his jeering comrades.

Now that Jake was safe, he had time to berate himself over the loss of his revolver. Dare he ask the quartermaster for another pistol?

Herb stared at Jake's empty holster. "What happened to your gun?"

"I dropped it during our escape," Jake said dejectedly. "Do you think I should try to go back for it?"

"Well, that horse of yours sure is fast enough for the job. She runs like a scared cat!" Herb's face turned thoughtful. "Hey, maybe you should name her Scaredy Cat."

Jake considered the name as General Stuart began to hum a chorus of Stephen Foster's "Her Bright Smile Haunts Me Still." Jake grinned. He had the perfect name for his spunky mount. "I'll just shorten that to Cat."

-8-

David blinked away the tears that blurred his vision and Jake's image vanished, revealing John Hoffacker's vacant stare. Heaving a trembling sigh, David closed John's eyes. The sergeant helped him free John's leg from under the dead horse, then they carried the young man's body to the porch and gently laid him in front of the empty rockers.

A soft rustling in the street drew David's attention. A Union soldier squatted next to John's horse and his hand rummaged inside John's haversack. David burned with rage. "Hey! What do you think you're doing? Get away from there, thief!" He charged from the porch, fists ready for action. The looter blanched, ran down the alley on the opposite side of the street, and disappeared from view behind the Trone house. The sergeant followed in hot pursuit.

David gathered John's things and retrieved the crumpled kepi cap from the road. He covered John's face with the hat and put the rest of the gear inside the front door. Now what should he do with John? No telling when it would be safe enough to take him home. David's heart ached at the thought of breaking the tragic news to the Hoffackers.

Up the street, soft moans became screams of agony. David's eyes flew to the source of the cries: a wounded Confederate had just regained consciousness. Sylvia and Heinrich Metzger hurried from the front of their home to aid the stricken man.

Deciding he could be of more use to the living than the dead, David stepped into the road in search of wounded men in need. Dozens of bodies and dead horses littered the ground. Fortunately, it appeared that all of the injured soldiers already had someone tending them. Most of the injuries looked like sabre wounds, which probably caused less damage than a bullet. Perhaps someone could use his help nearer the Square.

With sporadic gunfire rattling in the distance, David headed for the center of town. As he passed the alley to St. Matthew's, a young woman dashed from the passageway. David caught her in his arms. "Whoa, little lady! It's not safe to be out here." He set her back on her feet.

"I want to help the wounded men," Kathleen Bigler replied, her face filled with anxiety. "Please, let me come with you."

David gestured with his arm toward the distant sounds of battle; but just then, the gunfire dissipated like the final bursts in a pot of popping corn. Still, he didn't think it wise to take such responsibility for someone else's daughter. "I don't think your mother would want you to—"

Kathleen clutched his arm. "Mr. Becker, I want to do it for—" She bit her lip. "It's the right thing to do." She looked up at him with eager eyes. "I'm not a child. I've seen war before, remember?"

The urgency in her voice weakened his resolve. David recalled how unflinching Kathleen had been when she helped the wounded men in Manassas. "Tell me, do you girls still have the bandages you made?"

She shook her head and a few strands of tawny hair escaped from her loose bun. "We already gave them to the troops as they passed by earlier. But I have these." She tugged open a drawstring bag and pulled out several strips of white cloth. "I have another petticoat and chemise at home," she explained sheepishly.

How could he deny a woman willing to make such sacrifices? "All right, but stay close to me. I don't want anything to happen to you."

David took Kathleen's arm and they dashed across the street. Keeping close to the buildings on their right, they hurried up the block to the Square.

From Center Square viewing east onto Broadway (c. 1870) Schmidt's Apothecary is on the left. At the rear of the photo, Abbottstown Rd. branches to the left, York St. to the right.

An injured Confederate lay writhing in the churned earth near Schmidt's apothecary. Blood streamed down his forehead. David and Kathleen rushed over, arriving at the same instant as Rev. Zieber. The pastor lifted the poor man's head.

"Where am I?" the Rebel asked through gritted teeth.

Rev. Zieber's face softened. "You are a wounded man and in need of assistance. I come to help you."

The dazed man tried to sit up but fell back, overcome with pain. "Have the Yankees got me?"

"No matter where you are, you are in the hands of friends." The pastor gestured with his head toward David and Kathleen.

That seemed to bolster the soldier. "God bless you. I was forced into this war and compelled to enter the army." He struggled to swallow, choking and coughing with the effort. "Are you a surgeon? If you are, do what you can for me." He went limp.

"I am a preacher," Rev. Zieber said. Kathleen handed him a strip of cloth, and he worked to staunch the flow of blood.

"Pray for me." The man's strength flagged. "My wound is serious. I am suffering . . . extreme pain."

The pastor offered up a prayer for healing, for relief from pain, and for the man's eternal soul.

"I'm Sgt. Isaac Peale," the soldier gasped. "Second. North. Carol—" His words ended in an agonized squeal.

Dr. William Bange arrived, examined the man's wounds, and gave a small shake of his head. "Do what you can to make him comfortable," he said sadly. He pulled a wet sponge from his bucket, handed it to the pastor, and then moved on. Rev. Zieber washed the dying man's face.

David turned at the sound of approaching horses. Confederates! What happened to all the Union men? He stood and shielded Kathleen behind him.

A band of nine Rebels rode up. An officer dismounted. "Halt! What are you doing to that man?"

Rev. Zieber didn't look away from his ministrations. "We are trying to aid a wounded man, and we will take care of him."

A hundred yards away at the intersection of Broadway and York Street, a dismounted Union trooper yelled, "There's some Johnnies!"

The Confederate officer climbed into his saddle and called over his shoulder, "Thank you, sir." He led his men in a mad dash south across the Square and out Baltimore Street.

Kathleen handed the pastor a clean strip of cloth to bandage Isaac's head. The chest wound was another matter.

"Maybe we should try to get him inside," David suggested.

Rev. Zieber nodded. "Where?"

Two men carrying a Union soldier in a makeshift litter entered the Square from Broadway. David called, "Where are you taking him?"

"Marion Hall," one of the men replied.

A horseman approached from the east. A lone Union officer, his horse drenched with lather, galloped into the Square. Torn remnants of wheat and corn stalks hung from the horse's tack.

The Union soldiers in the vicinity joined in a loud hurrah. An officer appeared in the doorway to the Central Hotel. "General Kilpatrick, over here, sir!" The general rode over, dismounted, and handed the reins to a Negro stable hand.

David saw three letters branded on the horse's sweat-soaked flank: CSA. Confederate States of America. The captured horse looked so spent, David half-expected it to drop dead at any moment.

Kilpatrick called to the soldiers, "Boys, look at me. I am General Kilpatrick. I want you to know me, and where I go I want you to follow.

Stuart is making a call on us, and we are going to whip him." He nodded grimly, then disappeared inside the hotel.

More Federal troopers streamed into the Square from Broadway. A waiting officer conferred with the lead elements, and a column of cavalrymen headed out Baltimore Street.

"I do believe there will be more fighting soon," Rev. Zieber said, looking pointedly from David to Kathleen, then back again.

David took the hint. "Kathleen, let's head toward my house. A lot of the battle took place near there. Surely we can find someone who needs our help." *And I can protect you in the root cellar if the battle resumes.*

Before Kathleen could respond, General Custer and several of his men rode into the Square. Custer dismounted and tied his bay to a young maple tree. He spoke briefly with the colored man who had followed him, then went inside the hotel, leaving his horse in the servant's care.

Kathleen turned to David, determination in her eyes. "Let's go."

About halfway down Frederick Street, they came upon an odd-looking procession. A small group of Union men escorted a chagrined Confederate officer, his uniform and skin stained brown. One of the captors explained to the astonished onlookers, "Danged fool fell into a tanning vat when I shot his horse from under him."

A flurry of activity erupted back in the Square. At the head of the street, Union men and townsfolk erected a barricade of wagons, boxes, and barrels. Iron bars and ladders protruded at threatening angles.

Taking Kathleen's arm, David hurried for home. On the way, they had to skirt around several horse carcasses and pools of blood. David stole a glance at Kathleen to see how she was coping with the carnage. Her determined expression never wavered.

Being with Kathleen made David miss his daughters, though he was glad they were far away and wouldn't witness such things. Like John Hoffacker's— David stopped and gave Kathleen's arm a gentle squeeze.

"Kathleen, dear, I must prepare you for something. On my porch, when we get there, well . . ." Looking into her eyes, he momentarily lost his train of thought. Only in Rose's eyes had he seen such—how to describe it? Depth? Richness of spirit? No wonder Jake felt so *ferhoodled!* What was it about these Bigler girls?

Kathleen's eyes clouded over, then fear flashed across her face. "Is it Jake?" She grabbed both of David's hands and her voice grew frantic. "Has something happened to Jacob?"

"No, dear, not Jake," David reassured her, "but a young soldier I know. He's been killed. I'll have to get word to his family."

Her initial look of relief quickly changed to one of sorrow. "That's awful. How sad." She bit her lip. "We must do what we can for him. You know, before his parents see him."

Touched by her compassion, David gave her hands another squeeze before letting go. "That is very kind of you, but I can't ask you to—"

"You didn't have to ask," she gently interrupted.

His eyebrows arched and he nodded. "All right, thank you Kathleen." *Maybe Jake is interested in the wrong Bigler girl. There is something very special about Ka—*

A pair of cannons blasted from the hills southwest of town. Two shells screamed overhead. David threw an arm around Kathleen's shoulder and steered her for cover behind an ancient maple tree. A loud blast erupted from the rear of the Winebrenner house, quickly followed by a series of crashes and crunches. When the noises finally stopped, David peeked around the tree.

The Winebrenners' front door opened and Henry tossed an unexploded shell into the small front yard. He winked at David. "Good thing Martha and my wife just left the balcony." He went back inside as if nothing out of the ordinary had occurred.

David gripped Kathleen's hand. "Let's make a run for it, before they fire again. We'll head for the root cellar." She stood, gathered her skirt with her free hand, and ran with the agility of a boy.

As they reached the porch, the cannons again boomed from the ridge. Nearby, gunshots echoed in reply. Reluctantly leaving John behind, David threw open the front door and led Kathleen down the hall to the kitchen. He snatched the lantern off the hook, grabbed a box of matches from the counter, and flung open the door to the cellar. He stepped aside and gestured for his young charge to start down the stairs. "I'll be right down as soon as I get this lantern lit."

Safely ensconced in the root cellar, David pulled the small flour barrel away from the wall and offered Kathleen a seat. He hung the lantern from a hook on one of the beams, then sat atop the potato bin.

An explosion shook the house. David and Kathleen's shadows did a macabre dance in the quivering light of the lantern. The jars on the shelves rattled, and a sprinkling of dust fell from the beams. David's eyes searched Kathleen's. How would she respond to this new danger?

Kathleen grinned impishly. "Do you like to sing?"

He cocked his head, bemused. What was it about stressful situations that seemed to invite incongruous responses? First the townsfolk watching the battle as if it were a pageant, then Henry's quip about the shelling of his house, now this. But then again, what better way to pass the time? "Yes, I do. Do you have a song in mind?"

In the flickering glow of the lantern, her eyes took on a faraway look. "How about, 'And Can It Be?'"

-9-

Transfixed, Eliza watched from the front door while flames enveloped one end of the corncrib. Two Union men dipped buckets into the watering trough, ran across the road, and tossed water onto the fire, but the flames only seemed to intensify. A few more men joined the effort.

Christopher's little feet pattered down the stairs as he ran to join his cousin in the doorway. "I smell smoke, Eliza." He pointed a grubby finger. "Fire! Eliza, the corn shed's burning!"

Emily's frightened voice called from the top of the stairwell, "The corn shed?"

The wounded soldier on the divan moaned loudly, then shouted, "Help me, please . . . help me! Oh, Lordy."

Eliza turned just in time to see the soldier spew an acrid combination of blood and bile.

Christopher scolded, "Hey, don't *kutz* in our house!"

"Hush, Christopher!" Eliza said. Ignoring the disgusting Yankee's plight, she grabbed Christopher's hand and led him back up the stairs, where Emily threw her arms around Eliza's waist. Freeing herself from the hug, Eliza took Emily's hand, but Christopher shook free and ran to look out the hallway window. Figuring the boy was safe enough for the moment, Eliza led Emily to the bedroom to get Sarah from the crib. With the whimpering toddler perched on one hip and Emily's arms again clutching her waist, Eliza made her way back out into the hallway. "Christopher, let's go! Down the back stairs and outside. Now!"

He ignored her command and stared out the window. Exasperated, Eliza fumed, "Of all God's creatures, little boys have the least sense!"

She headed for the rear staircase and called over her shoulder, "Come with me *right now*, Christopher Isaac, or I won't let you help put out the fire!"

Christopher beat them down the stairs.

Once they got outside, the imp dashed for the front of the house. Resisting the temptation to let the little terror get himself into trouble, Eliza yelled, "You're gonna need a bucket. Go to the barn and get one."

Christopher's legs churned across the yard. Eliza caught up with him on his way back from the barn. She lost her grip on the squirmy youngster's arm, but managed to hold onto his shirtsleeve. "Not so fast. You need to—"

"But 'Liza, you said—"

"What's burning?" Uncle George shouted from the lane next to the hay field. Eliza's mother and aunt trailed close behind him.

Cupping a hand to her mouth, Eliza called, "Corncrib."

Her uncle ran the rest of the way, grabbed the bucket from Christopher, and raced for the front of the house.

Eliza shouted after him, "Not to worry. There are some Yankees throwing water on it."

Emily wailed, "Is our house gonna burn down, too?"

"I wanna help! You promised," Christopher shouted over his sister.

"Lord forbid I ever have a boy," Eliza muttered.

Sarah made a face and held her belly. "Ouchy."

Christopher stuck out his tongue and tried to squirm free. "I wish Kat was here instead of you!"

"You ungrateful little—so do I!" Her feelings wounded, Eliza let go of the sleeve. Christopher lost his balance and sprawled in the dirt.

Emily spotted her mother at the edge of the field. "Mama, Christopher stuck his tongue out at Eliza."

Another foul odor wafted from Sarah's diaper. "Eww gussy," she whimpered.

"Not again!" Eliza stood Sarah on the ground and unpinned the diaper, letting it plop around the toddler's feet. "Come on, you, let's get—"

Stepping free of the malodorous mess, Sarah chanted, "Neck-ed baby, neck-ed baby," and scurried toward her mother.

Beaming with angelic smiles, Emily and Christopher ran to their mother's arms. Irene Bigler stooped to intercept Sarah and held her out at arms' length. "Let's go get you a clean diaper, darlin'."

Just in case Mama expected help with the baby, Eliza decided to go out front and have a look at the fire. On the way, she fretted over her cousins. They could behave perfectly well when their parents were around, so how come they acted like horrid little beasts for her? Would her own children act like that some day? What if she turned out to be an awful mother? *I'll just have to find a nanny as good at raising children as Abby. Being old and ugly will be an absolute requirement, though.*

Rounding the corner of the house, Eliza found the corncrib engulfed in flames. The roof caved in. Flames leapt into the sky, then retreated behind a shower of sparks and dying embers.

Uncle George dipped a bucket in the trough, went to the corner of the house opposite the fire, and splashed the water as high up the building as he could.

Meanwhile, the Union cavalry streamed back toward Hanover. The men who had tried to save the shed stacked their buckets at the side of the trough, untied their mounts from the hitching post, and joined the frantic countermarch.

Aunt Ida's muted scream rang from the house. "Good Lord! Who? What?" Uncle George dropped his bucket and dashed inside.

Rather than go in and explain the Yankee's presence on the divan, Eliza decided to take advantage of her hard-earned break. Fascinated, she crossed the road for a closer look at the burning shed. The flames reminded her of the bonfire at the harvest festival three years ago. Jasper Wilson had wanted her to sneak off into the shadows with him, but she was too taken with the dancing flames: a giant kaleidoscope of reds and oranges and yellows. They had been her favorite colors ever since.

She took a step closer to the conflagration, closed her eyes, and basked in the warmth. Her thoughts turned to Jake. The feel of his lips on hers, his hands caressing her back, the way she stirred, deep in her core, as their bodies pressed together.

One of the passing cavalrymen called, "Hey, beautiful, ride with me!"

"To the devil with you!" Eliza screamed, shaking her fist at the despicable brute. Another trooper reached out and batted at her hair as he rode past. Eliza shrieked, "The devil take you all!"

-10-

After their narrow escape, General Stuart and his men hurried to the top of the ridge. Colonel Chambliss' staff was overjoyed to see the commander, especially after having heard he had been captured. In the midst of their congratulations, several bullets whizzed overhead and ripped through a nearby cherry tree. Two Confederates jumped from the tree and hugged the ground.

"What's the matter, boys?" Stuart called. "Those cherries sour?"

Laughing uproariously, everyone moved into the woods for cover, where Stuart set about establishing his command post and issuing orders for the disposition of his troops.

"Private Becker!" Major McClellan called.

"Here, sir," Jake said, his voice sounding strangely high.

"Come tell us about Hanover," McClellan ordered.

Jake handed Cat's reins to Herb and hustled to join the cluster of men surrounding Stuart and McClellan. Jake snapped to attention and saluted. "What would you like to know, sir?"

"At ease, Private," Stuart said, stifling a smile.

McClellan narrowed his eyes. "First off, tell us how many Federal troops were in town when you left."

Jake flushed in dismay. Did they think he had led them into an ambush? "Oh no, sir, there were no Union soldiers in Hanover when I left. In fact, Colonel Elijah White's 35th Virginia cavalry were the last soldiers in town, just three days ago."

With an approving nod, Stuart turned to McClellan. "Satisfied, Major?"

Looking only slightly mollified, McClellan continued, "Militia?"

"No militia, sir, though some passed through a few days ago and headed east. Many men from Hanover have enlisted in the Union Army, but I believe I am the only one to have joined up with the Confederacy."

"How many citizens? Houses mainly wood or brick? Are there any fortifications?" McClellan pressed.

Despite feeling traitorous, Jake answered as duty demanded. "About 1,600 folks live in Hanover, sir. There are a lot of wooden houses and just as many brick buildings, but there are no fortifications at all."

Lieutenant Dabney returned and McClellan nodded for him to deliver his message. "The first artillery battery is ready, General Stuart."

"Very good," Stuart said. "Tell Captain Breathed to fire a few rounds. Let's try to see what they've got out there." McClellan wrote down the orders and handed the paper to Dabney. As the young rider galloped away, Stuart added, "I do not want a major engagement here."

Jake had read about the Union Army's shelling and burning of Fredericksburg, Virginia, the previous December. It had marked the first time Americans fired on a civilian center. Fortunately, most of the residents had already been evacuated before the scandalous attack.

A cannon blasted on their left. Cat nickered and tossed her head. Jake rubbed her neck and leaned over to speak in her ear, but a second cannon drowned out his soothing voice. A Union shell exploded in the woods about a hundred yards behind them. Through the ensuing two-hour artillery exchange, Jake prayed for the safety of his father and fellow Hanoverians.

By the time the firing ceased, Chambliss' troops held a line across the fields on either side of Westminster road. If Stuart decided to assault the town, his forces would have to pass through Karle Forney's farmlands. Jake shifted uneasily in the saddle. *Where is John? Has Sam returned from getting Grace, Faith, and Myrtle to safety? At least Eliza and Kathleen should be out of harm's way at the other end of town.*

A freckle-faced orderly rode up, his strawberry blonde hair poking from beneath his cap like straw from a haymow. He delivered a snappy salute, then reported, "General Stuart, sir, General Lee sends this message, and I am to tell you it is with his compliments, sir." He pulled a folded piece of paper from his blouse and placed it in Major McClellan's waiting hand.

McClellan opened the message and read aloud, "Greetings and salutations, General Stuart. The 2,200 men of the 1st through 5th Virginia Cavalry are in the woods on your left flank. They await your invitation to attend the dance. At your pleasure, your obedient etc. etc., Fitz Lee."

Stuart threw back his head and laughed long and loud, while Virginia swished her tail and shook out her mane. Taking a deep breath to set aside the levity, the general wiped the sweat from his brow and turned serious. "Now tell me what that paper really says."

McClellan feigned innocence. "Just what I said, sir. Lee occupies the woods over yonder." He turned to Blackford. "Your glasses?" Blackford handed his binoculars to McClellan, who passed them on to Stuart.

With a commanding view from Forney's Hill, Stuart scanned Lee's position through the strong glasses. "Perfect." Humming a tune that Jake didn't recognize, the general surveyed the rest of the Confederate lines.

Another orderly rode up, this time from the south. McClellan read the report and summarized it for Stuart.

"General Hampton and the wagon train have arrived. The wagons have formed a square."

"Good," Stuart said, clearly relieved. "Tell him to prepare to torch the wagons, just in case. We cannot let the enemy have their supplies back."

McClellan wrote out the reply and handed it to the orderly, who promptly raced back the way he had come. Herb pulled fresh bread and salted beef from his saddlebag and offered some to Jake, who traded two half-squashed blueberry muffins from his stash. The two young men slouched in their saddles and munched their makeshift meal.

Stuart held the binoculars out for Jake. "Where does that road go, east of that hill occupied by the Union artillery?"

Jake wiped his mouth, then cleaned his hands on his pants. Never having used binoculars, he slowly moved the glasses toward his eyes. The jiggling close-up view made him dizzy.

Blackford chuckled. "Take a deep breath and hold steady. Those are the most powerful binoculars I have ever found."

The advice enabled Jake to get a close-up view of St. Matthew's steeple. What a marvel! Everything looked so much closer, though a bit blurry. He squinted for a better look.

"You can improve the focus with that ring in the middle," Blackford suggested. He walked his horse over to Jake's and showed him how to make the adjustments.

"Golly!" Jake tried to locate his house, but everything flashed past so quickly that by the time he stopped moving, he found himself viewing the back of the Winebrenner tannery on the west end of town.

"The road?" General Stuart prompted.

Distracted by a flurry of action near the tannery, yet knowing there were two roads that fit the general's description, Jake asked, "Do you mean the road that runs northeast, or the one that jogs to the east?"

"I believe that would be northeast."

Jake answered without changing his view. "That road leads to Abbottstown, sir." Through the glasses, he spied several hundred Union cavalrymen crowding the road between the tannery and the Forney farmlands. The men dismounted, took their carbines, and started to form up. One particular rider caught Jake's attention. "Um, sir? Who is that officer with the fancy uniform and long blonde hair?"

Stuart took the field glasses and had a look. "How far out the road to Abbottstown do you mean?

"Oh, sorry, sir. I saw him by the tannery, directly below us."

The general shifted the binoculars. "What the devil? McClellan, who is that dandy? He looks like a lost circus rider!"

McClellan peered through the glasses. "That may be George Custer. He was a captain, last I knew. Looks like he has a single star on his epaulette, so I guess it is Brigadier General Custer now. Did you see how many men he has with him?" He handed the binoculars to Stuart.

"Yes, I did. Have the signal officer prepare to call for a flank attack from Lee. Order Beckham to target his artillery on the area by that stream we jumped. Any attackers will have to pause there, and I don't want them using the creek gully for cover."

McClellan handed the written orders to Hagan, who assigned them to Dabney and Hullihen. The junior officers nudged their mounts into action and galloped off.

Stuart took another survey of the battle lines. "There aren't enough Yankees down there to take this hill. That is either a defensive force or a diversion." He turned in the saddle and gestured Jake to come to his side.

"Jake, you know these hills better than any of us. What lies east of the town?"

"The road to York, sir, and there are a lot of open farmlands all around there." Jake's heart pounded. Henry Wertz's farm was only a couple of miles north of the York Pike.

Stuart turned to McClellan. "I think we need to extend our line to the east. We can't have any Yankees circling around behind us. I doubt they are foolish enough to try an assault on our high ground, so if there is to be an attack in force, it will likely be in those fields to our east."

A rush of fear coursed through Jake's body. Had Eliza and Kathleen traveled all those miles from Manassas only to find themselves once again surrounded by a maelstrom of death?

Gen. J.E.B. Stuart   **Gen. Wade Hampton**

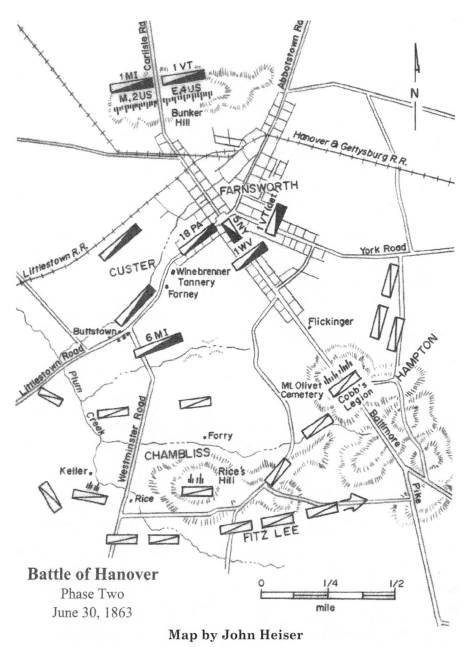

Battle of Hanover

Phase Two

June 30, 1863

0   1/4   1/2

mile

Map by John Heiser

The Becker and Winebrenner houses are northeast of the Winebrenner Tannery, at the left edge of the marker for 18 PA. The Henry Wertz farm is near the N in the directional marker. George Wertz's farm is off the map, a few miles out the Abbottstown Road.

-11-

For nearly two hours, David and Kathleen chatted and sang in the musty root cellar. He found her combination of youthful exuberance and budding maturity fascinating. In the rare instance when she paused to search for the right words, her expressive face spoke volumes. He fondly recalled the days when his own daughters had passed through that precious stage: one moment a girl, the next instant a young woman. How he missed his family! And then there was that marvelous singing voice. More than once, David stumbled on the lyrics while basking in the warmth and beauty of Kathleen's dulcet tones.

"It was so nice of you girls to sing for the soldiers today. Thank the Lord none of you got hurt when the bullets started flying."

Kathleen frowned. "Except for poor Lizzie Sweitzer. When everyone started running hither and yon, someone knocked her down and she took a nasty tumble. Then a horse rode right over her! God spared her life, but her left ankle was bleeding something fierce. A kind Yankee stopped to help. He wasn't sure if it was a bullet or if a hoof had cut her. Mr. Daniels made us all go back into the church before I saw where they took her."

"We must pray more folks don't get hurt, especially with all these cannon shells flying about," David said somberly.

When the bombardment slowed and finally stopped, David waited another thirty minutes before reluctantly suggesting he leave the cellar to check out the situation. "Don't worry, Missy. I'll be right back."

On his way up the steps, David realized he had just called Kathleen by the same pet name he had used for his daughters when they were young. Now that they had grown and gone, it felt good to have someone else to care for in their place, if only for an afternoon.

Looking out the kitchen window, David spotted three Union riflemen, crouched behind stacks of firewood in the Winebrenners' woodshed. Only the occasional distant gunshot broke the silence.

David hurried to the front door and looked outside. Several Union cavalrymen patrolled the road. To his horror, he saw two crows and a cloud of flies working on John's head. David threw the door open. "Shoo!" The crows cawed and flapped away, but the flies were not as cooperative. He fetched a clean sheet from the cedar chest and covered the body.

Henry called over from next door, "Hey David! You oughta come see what that shell done to Sarah's chest."

David's jaw dropped. He felt sickened by the grotesque image.

"No, not *that* chest. It blew a hole through her drawers," Henry elaborated.

Both men's brows furrowed.

Henry slapped his forehead. "You know what I mean. *Chest of drawers.*"

In spite of the gravity of the situation, David chuckled. "Sure, I'll be right over, but first I should go get Kathleen Bigler out of my root cellar."

Henry looked confused. He cupped a hand to one ear. "What kinda wiggler you got down there?"

"Never mind. I'll be right back."

Kathleen stood at the bottom of the cellar stairs. The light from the lantern flickered across her worried face as she spoke in a rush. "What's going on? Are they done fighting? Can I come up now?"

"The soldiers are still here, but I think it'll be safe for us to go next door for a little—"

Kathleen gathered her skirt, held the lantern high, and clambered up the steps. David turned the lantern off and set it on the table, then led the way out the front door.

Kathleen paused on the porch and glanced at the shrouded body. Her eyes grew misty. "Poor man."

A squad of Union officers trotted their horses out Frederick Street from the direction of the Square. The troopers rounded the bend, and David stepped out into the road to watch the riders join a column of dismounted soldiers in front of the Forneys' house. He didn't like the look of things. Was the action about to resume?

Martha Winebrenner called from the porch next door. "Kathleen, what are you doing at Jake's? Is Eliza there, too?"

"No, she's babysitting our cousins out at Uncle George's and Aunt Linda Jane's," Kathleen replied.

David turned to usher Kathleen back to the cellar, but she was already on the Winebrenners' steps. A fierce, undulating wail echoed from the hills above the Forney farm. Moments later, gunfire erupted on the outskirts of town.

The young women followed Henry into the Winebrenner house, with David close behind. By the time they all got into the hallway, the unearthly sound ceased and the gunfire died away.

"Danged skirmishers," Henry muttered.

Martha looked frightened. "What was that hideous noise?"

"That was a Rebel yell," Kathleen explained proudly.

David grimaced, remembering the afternoon in Manassas when the Union Army had disintegrated in the face of that sound. They dropped their weapons and ran from the charging banshees, as far and as fast as they could go. Fortunately for the Union cause, the Confederates were too exhausted to do much more than rejoice in their hard-won victory.

Sarah Winebrenner called from upstairs, "Kathleen, is that you? Come up and see what happened to my room."

Kathleen and Martha hurried up the stairs. David and Henry started for the parlor, but fifteen-year-old Henry, Jr. blocked the doorway. His longing eyes followed Kathleen up the steps.

"Pa, may I go to my room for a while?"

Henry winked knowingly at David, then turned to his son. "I'd rather have you go to your sisters' room. Keep 'em safe. If the cannons start up again, then you bring those girls right down to the cellar, hear?"

"Yessir." The love-struck lad took the stairs two at a time.

Someone tromped up the porch steps and Henry opened the door. "Back already, Nathan?"

Nathan McCreary entered, a grim look on his face. Henry turned to David and explained, "Nathan left for Westminster early today. He took along your letter for Jake, planning to drop it off at the Shrivers."

Henry cocked his head at Nathan. "How did you get through the Rebel lines?"

"I got back by skirting around their right end," Nathan said, fidgeting with the hat in his hands. "Came up Becker's Mill Road just ahead of a bunch of those rascals." He looked solemnly at David. "And I think I know where Jake is."

"Have you seen him?" David asked anxiously.

"No, but early this morning, about a mile this side of Union Mills, I came upon a long column of Rebel cavalry. They stopped me and I told them I was going to Westminster; so they let me pass, as long as I promised to stay there."

Mind racing, David considered the possibilities. *What if Jake and the Confederate Army were in Union Mills at the same time?*

"When I got to Union Mills, William told me that Jake and Herb had gone with Stuart's army, heading for Littlestown," Nathan continued.

Anxiety gnawed at David. "If they were marching to Littlestown when you passed them, there's no way they'd have taken part in the attack here." He relaxed a bit with that thought.

Nathan winced. "I'm afraid it ain't necessarily so. The last of the Rebs left Union Mills before ten. I waited for the road to clear so I could ride back to Hanover with the news. On the way, I found out they had changed directions. They came here instead."

"You mean Jake's with that army up in the hills?" Could it be? Had Jake taken part in the attack on his own hometown?

"Not exactly. William told me Jake's horse got shot on the way there."

"Oh no, poor Skipper," David groaned.

"When one of the Reb generals found out Jake was a good teamster, he asked him to drive a supply wagon."

David felt as if a huge weight had been lifted from his back. At least his son was somewhere in the rear of the action. He closed his eyes and rubbed his throbbing forehead.

Henry prompted, "You said his horse got shot?"

Nodding, Nathan added, "One of the Shriver girls couldn't wait for her father to tell it, so she gave me the story. Said a Union deserter tried to steal Jake's horse, and during the fight the horse caught a bullet. Jake killed the soldier with his knife."

David exclaimed, "Jake ki—"

"Thank God Jake is alive!" Kathleen's voice rang from the middle of the stairs. Tears welling up in her eyes, she grasped the railing and sank onto a step.

Feeling the same relief tenfold, David hurried to Kathleen's side and put his arm around her shoulder. "Yes, Missy, thank God." He laid his hand over hers and offered up a fervent prayer—for the dead and dying, for everyone's safety, and for an end to the devastation, once and for all. From the top of the stairs and the hallway below, everyone joined the "amen."

-12-

A very small man in an oversized gray uniform rode up from the south and handed a dispatch bag to Major McClellan. The major laid the bag across his saddle, removed a sheet of paper, quickly skimmed it, and spoke without looking up. "This report is from Hampton. His men are ready for deployment, and the wagons are arranged as you ordered."

He reached back into the bag "And what have we here?" He pulled out a newspaper and unfolded it. "This morning's edition! How in the world . . ." McClellan's lips moved as he read, then he exclaimed, "General, it says here that General Early's army has left York!" He read on. "But it does not say which direction he took."

"I see," Stuart said. He pondered for a long moment. "Draft the order for General Hampton to move his men into position on our right flank. He is to extend from the cemetery, across the Baltimore Pike, and as far to the east as he can hold in strength. I do not wish to re-engage the enemy today. He is to protect the flank and screen the movements of the wagons as we withdraw. We *must* find General Early!"

McClellan finished writing and handed the directive to the diminutive orderly. The cavalryman galloped off, his baggy uniform flapping like a flag in the breeze.

For the third time, Chambliss' dismounted brigade loosed their Rebel yell and charged down the hill. A line of Union carbiners sprung from hiding in the tall grass and opened fire—a lot of fire.

From the vantage point on Forney's Hill, Jake had a clear view of the action. Either those men were taking their good old time aiming, or . . .

Blackford spoke from behind his binoculars. "General Stuart, those Yanks." He adjusted the focus. "Sir, they have repeater carbines!"

Jake had never heard of such a thing. Did they work like revolvers?

Stuart reached for the binoculars. "Are you certain?"

"Yes, sir." Blackford handed over the field glasses. "I just saw four puffs of smoke from the same gun before the man ducked back into the grass."

"And their line has moved much closer to the creek," Stuart

observed. He gave the binoculars back to Blackford and called to the signal officer, "Tell General Lee to attack that flank now!"

The officer unfurled a red flag with a white square in the middle. He walked to the northwest corner of the hill and waved the banner back and forth over his head. Below and to the left, a man at the edge of the woods answered in kind. The signal officer then held the flag straight up over his head, snapped it to the ground twice on his left side, held it overhead, and repeated the sequence. The flagman in the woods reiterated the signal. The signal officer snapped his flag to the ground directly in front three times, his counterpart did likewise.

Moments later, Lee's cavalry burst from cover behind the trees. The riders were nearly atop the enemy before the first man in blue realized his peril. He dropped his gun and threw up his hands. The fellow next to him turned to shoot, but Confederate gunfire mowed him down.

The Union line quickly withdrew. Some of the men fired as they retreated, others ran for their lives. Jake counted at least a dozen Yankee prisoners before Lee's men returned to the woods.

Herb reached over and nudged Jake. "Ha! Billy Yank won't try that maneuver again, I bet."

Stuart laughed. "Yes, a fine bit of 'dancing,' wouldn't you say McClellan? Be sure to add the name of Fitz Lee to my dance card."

"As you say, sir." McClellan chuckled, then cleared his throat. "Are you ready to hear the rest of the dispatches?"

The general nodded.

"Quartermaster Fitzhugh says we have 626 captured horses at hand, but that we are running low on ammunition. He asks if there is any word as to when he can expect a new supply." McClellan looked up, as if expecting an immediate reply. Stuart seemed lost in thought.

Jake studied Stuart's pensive face. Those piercing eyes didn't seem to miss a thing. What stratagem was the great commander mulling?

Stuart slapped his thigh. "I find myself with a sudden hankering for blueberries. Jake, do you have any more of those blueberry muffins you shared with Herbert a while ago?"

"Oh, uh, yes sir, I do." He reached into his saddlebag and handed his commander a flattened muffin while McClellan read another message.

"Major Ryals reports the prisoner count is at 337."

Blackford lowered his binoculars. "You can make that 338."

Wiping some muffin crumbs from his beard, Stuart dismounted and pulled a map from inside his shirt. "Jake, come show me the best way to get the wagons from here to York without going any nearer to Hanover."

Glad to get down and stretch his legs, Jake hurried to the general's side. His finger traced the various roads and turns on the map. "I think the best route is to swing over that way. Take Fuhrman Mill Road, pass Dubs Church, head for Jefferson, go through Seven Valleys, then on to York." Anticipating the question, he added, "The wagons can handle those roads, sir."

"I see. Thank you." Stuart tucked the map away and mounted up. "McClellan, order General Lee to withdraw behind cover of the woods. He is to escort the train of wagons with all haste to York via Jefferson. He will have Private Becker for his guide. Tell him . . ."

Jake only half-heard the rest of the order for Lee to travel through the night. Was this a dream? He would be riding at the head of an army, side by side with General Lee. Well, it was General Robert E. Lee's nephew, but Fitzhugh Lee was no slouch! What would the Biglers think of their prospective son-in-law now?

-13-

While Eliza watched from the parlor window, Uncle George pulled a burning plank from the ruined corncrib and dragged it over to the pyre surrounding the dead horses. Eliza looked away. "Poor innocent things. What did they do to deserve that?" The smell of roasting meat permeated the air.

The wounded soldier groaned from the divan. Mama rose from the wing chair and went to check on him. "Can I get you anything, sir?"

Slipping back into unconsciousness, the man made no reply.

"Eliza, keep an eye on Mr. Moran." Mama went to the hall and called to Aunt Linda Jane in the kitchen. "Do you need any help with dinner?"

Eliza scowled at the soldier and wished he would just get it over with and die. She couldn't wait to get away from his dreadful stench. Even so, given the choice of tending the children or caring for the wounded man, she chose the latter, though she vowed not to "care" one whit. She was convinced that given the chance, the Yankee would've gladly used his cannon to blow Jake to smithereens.

Mama returned and joined Eliza at the window. "Aunt Linda Jane is making your favorite ham and green beans to thank you for tending your cousins. She's picking the snap beans while the ham hock is cooking. Do you want to slice the potatoes?"

Eliza gave her mother a you've-got-to-be-kidding look. "You know me and knives."

"Well, at least do the snap beans when they're ready," Mama said. "And be sure to leave the tendrils on. My Aunt Elaine is coming to join us, and you know how much she likes them like that."

"Yes, Ma—" Eliza stared out the window and felt a strange sense of satisfaction as the last wall of the corncrib keeled over, hit the ground, and sent up a shower of flames and sparks. Uncle George used a large set of tongs to free a piece of the burning wall to add to the horses' pyre.

Uncle George was in his late thirties and strong as an ox. Eliza thought he rather looked like one, too. She turned to her mother. "So, you said Uncle George shimmied up a tree to find out where the cannon sounds were coming from? I'd like to have seen him do that!"

"Oh, my little brother was always such a *crottler*. He could go farther up a tree than anyone. And your Uncle Henry was the best runner."

Astonished, Eliza couldn't remember Mama ever talking about her siblings when they were young. "Tell me more!"

"The only man I ever saw who could run faster than Henry was your father . . ." Mama's voice trailed off, and her eyes took on a dreamy look that Eliza couldn't recall having seen before.

"When did you see Papa *run*?"

A smile played at the corners of Mama's mouth. "Here in Hanover, at a church social. I was seventeen and he was twenty-two." Her voice sounded younger, almost girlish. "Wavy brown hair, bright blue eyes, and those parentheses around his mouth from so much smiling. He was up from Virginia, making business deals with several of the local cigar makers. Anyway, he beat Henry in the footrace by a lot. I knew right then and there that any man who could beat my big brother like that had to be somebody quite special."

Fascinated at the glimpse into her parents' past, Eliza tried to keep her usually reticent mother talking. "Is that how you met?"

Mama winked. "Well . . . I 'accidentally' bumped into his father, causing him to spill his tea all over my sleeve. I stained my dress, but I wound up catching your Papa's attention."

"Wait a minute," Eliza said, mystified. "I thought Grandpa Bigler died when Papa was twelve."

"You're thinking of Grandpa Bygylor. B-y-g-y-l-o-r. That's the original Welsh spelling. Grandpapa B-i-g-l-e-r was really your father's Uncle Howard. After your father was orphaned, his Uncle Howard brought him over from Ireland and adopted him."

"Papa was an orphan? And he grew up in Ireland?" Eliza's mind reeled at the revelations. "Why haven't I ever heard about that?"

With a heavy sigh, Mama led Eliza to a seat on the deacon's bench. "He only told me about it once." She met Eliza's troubled eyes. "I guess it's about time you knew." She took a deep breath and launched into the story.

"Your father grew up in Ireland near the little town of Carrickshook. During the time known as the Tithe Wars, he went into town on an errand. A mob of Catholic farmers, angry over being forced to pay a tithe to the protestant Church of England, started a riot. Your Grandpa Bygylor was a policeman, and it was his duty to restore the peace. The mob only carried farming tools, but they used them to kill your Grandpa and seventeen other men." Her voice grew softer. "And your Papa witnessed it all."

"Oh, how dreadful!" Eliza's stomach roiled at the image of enraged farmers wielding their tools on human flesh.

"Unfortunately, it gets worse. When your father ran home to tell his mother the horrible news, he found the house had burned down. His mother, brothers, and sisters were inside. No one saw how it happened, and no one could explain how the family was unable to escape from a one-story, four-room house. Some people whispered it was Catholics that done it. Your father believes that is the truth of it. You know how he goes on about the papists."

How could God allow such evil? Eliza seethed. "And all because of money! Those farmers didn't want to tithe to the church."

"It's not just money, dear. Catholics and Protestants have warred against each other for centuries before that." Her eyes and voice grew hard. "Some men would rather kill you than allow you to think differently, especially when it comes to religion. They claim to worship the same God, but—"

The soldier lurched and cried out in pain. Eliza pursed her lips. Was he getting a foretaste of the eternal flames? She'd heard somewhere along the way that Catholics wanted to see a priest before they died and that they thought it important to be buried in a Catholic cemetery. This Yankee had asked for a priest. Should she tell someone? Images of the burning cottage flashed in her mind.

No. Let his corpse rot in a cemetery full of Protestants. Maybe an eternity among "heretics" might soften his views.

-14-

As the column crossed Beckers Mill Road, named for his grandfather's mill, Jake turned in the saddle and surveyed the long line of cavalrymen and wagons. The white-canopied Conestogas bobbed and wove like a flock of sheep trailing its bellwether.

"Impressive, isn't it? And more than a little comforting," General Fitzhugh Lee remarked.

"Yes, sir." Jake faced forward. He would have said the army looked daunting rather than comforting, but as he thought more about it, he understood the general's point. If you were traveling through enemy territory—odd, calling his own county enemy territory—what better comfort than to have an army behind you?

A lieutenant rode up, saluted General Lee, and reported, "Sir, one of the details has returned with some fresh horses and an odd story. A man named Jacob Leppo told them he'd given the 'Knights of the Golden Circle' a dollar to learn a secret sign to show us that would prevent us from taking any of his animals. Do you know anything about this?"

"Not a thing," Lee said, obviously perplexed. "What did you do?"

"We told him he should save his hand-waving for General Stuart and took his three horses," the lieutenant replied with a grin.

"Very good, lieutenant, carry on," Lee said. He flicked the reins and resumed the march.

When they rounded a small bend in the road, Jake stood in the stirrups and pointed. "That's the Mannheim schoolhouse on the Baltimore Pike, and over there's the Brockley farm."

Lee cocked his head. "Yankees have a whole farm just for broccoli?"

It took Jake a moment to realize the misunderstanding. "Oh, no sir. That's the farmer's name. Brock-ley. Anthony Brockley."

"It has been so long since I saw prosperous farmlands, I couldn't help wondering," Lee said.

They took the Baltimore Pike south the short distance to Fuhrman Mill Road and turned east, toward Jefferson. One of Lee's staff officers rode ahead and knocked on a farmhouse door. A burly man with a thick black moustache and beard came out onto the stoop. A boy, maybe twelve years old, stood behind him in the doorway.

As the head of the column drew near, Jake heard the lieutenant ask, "Y'all seen any Yankees in the area?"

The farmer tilted his head. "*Es tut mir leid. Ich verstehe Sie nicht. Ich spreche ein bisschen Englisch.*"

The lieutenant looked at his commander and shrugged. Lee turned to Jake. "Do you know this man?"

"Sorry, sir, I don't. He spoke in German about not understanding, but that's all I could make out."

The farmer smiled obsequiously and made a grand gesture toward the column of men and wagons. "*Der Teufel nimmt Sie alles.*"

Jake scowled. He knew that bit of German. *The devil take you all.* He'd been told it was the most insulting profanity a German could utter. Should he let General Lee know?

The officer tried again, shouting, "Yan-kees. An-y Yan-kees." He swung his arm in a sweeping arc.

The farmer shook his head no.

The youngster stepped from the doorway. "Oh, yes, sir. I saw some Yankees. They went into the woods over there." He pointed to a copse of trees atop a small rise on the other side of the road.

Lee issued the command for some of his men to go investigate. About sixty Confederate cavalrymen, each with his pistol or sabre drawn, charged up the hill. Jake dismounted and studied the woods from behind the lead wagon. Several puffs of smoke arose from the tall brush in front of the tree line, followed by the crackle of gunshots. The riders closed the distance in a matter of seconds, but not before one man slumped in his saddle, wounded. Two others toppled to the ground when their horses fell victim to the unseen enemy. Some of the troopers rode directly into the woods, others dismounted at the edge and scoured the area on foot.

The skirmishers returned empty-handed. A lanky captain rode up to General Lee with a report. "Must've been a squad of scouts. They probably fired one round and took off. Do you want me to send some men after them?"

"We have our orders. We must keep moving." Lee shifted his eyes to the two men who were now without a horse. "Have those fellows wait here for new mounts. We've got several hundred captured horses following behind us. Get the wounded man to the surgeon." Turning to his adjutant, Lee continued, "Take that farmer prisoner. We don't need him giving information to the enemy."

The major moved to obey, then hesitated. "What about the boy, sir?"

"He can stay. Thank him for his help, and tell him that his father will be set free when we reach our destination." Lee looked over his shoulder and waved for the column to move out.

Scowling, Jake remounted. Somehow that didn't seem fair, especially since some Yankees had already seen the column and gotten away.

As if reading Jake's mind, Lee said, "Information is often more valuable than bullets, Private. Those Yanks that got away might never make it back to their lines. Even if they do, they only saw part of our force. That farmer would see it all pass right in front of his doorstep."

"Yes, sir, I understand." But did he? It was easy to imagine how he'd feel if soldiers carried Pa away. Jake wanted to ride back and promise the lad that his father would be all right, that General Lee was a kind man and would see no harm came to him. Then he remembered the fire in the general's eyes when he saw his wounded man return. What would Lee do to anyone who betrayed his entire army?

-15-

After dinner with the Winebrenners, David went out front to see if he could learn any news. There was activity over on his porch. A Union lieutenant knelt by John Hoffacker's body.

David called, "I know that man. He's a local boy, lives south of town." Instantly recognizing the absurdity of his statement, he hurried over to explain. "I'd take him home, but I presume the Confederates aren't likely to let me pass."

Exuding an air of self-importance, the soldier stood and said, "Indeed, but there's a burial detail just down the road. Let them take care of it." He waved dismissively. "You can go along and let the family know his whereabouts later."

The casual tone grated on David's nerves. He hadn't realized how much tension had built up within him, and now this weaseling soldier had offered himself as a target. Resisting the temptation, David took a deep breath and turned his back on the man.

There came the sound of a page flipping, then the lieutenant inquired, "Name?"

"David Becker," he replied over his shoulder.

A pencil scratched on the paper. In a bored tone, the man continued, "And do you know what company this David Becker was with?"

David spun and let his anger free. "*I'm* David Becker, you inconsiderate dingleberry!" He pointed to John's body. "This is Corporal John Hoffacker, and until his life was cut short several hours ago, he was one of the finest young men you'd ever hope to meet. So fine, in fact, he gave up his life so a self-centered fool like you might live free in the United States of *all* of America." He put his face within an inch of the quailing officer and lowered his voice to a menacing tone. "So you better search that tiny brain of yours and find the proper respect for this man— or I shall pry open your head and pour some in!"

"Yes, sir," the lieutenant said feebly. He cautiously bent down to retrieve the pencil and notebook he had dropped during the tirade.

The burial detail arrived. David took one look inside the wagon, then glared at the driver. Bodies lay stacked atop one another like firewood.

The young officer hurried over to the wagon. "Corporal, make sure these men receive a proper burial. Then come straight back here and take this brave soldier to his rest." He gestured over his shoulder to John's body on the porch.

"Hee-yah!" The corporal flipped the reins, and the wagon took off up the street.

Not trusting himself to even look at the lieutenant, David muttered, "Glad to see you learn quick."

David decided the workshop would be a good place to cool off. Besides, Streak would want tending by now.

After mucking out the storeroom and refilling the water and feed bins, David went outside and dared to glance around the corner of the building. It was difficult to notice anyone moving up on the ridge, since both armies did their best to stay out of sight. No one wanted to become sport for sharpshooters. With less than an hour until dark, several smoky plumes floated skyward. The Rebels seemed satisfied to eat and watch.

David thought of doing some more work on the carriage but decided against it. His heart wouldn't be in it, and he didn't want Myrtle's wedding present to be born of such an attitude.

As he entered the kitchen, the mantel clock struck half past the hour. If not for the ticking of the timepiece, the house would have been silent. David went into the parlor and rewound the clock.

A wave of loneliness washed over him. He crossed the room to the melodeon, opened the lid, and took a seat on the bench. Pressing the keys for a C-major cord, he pumped the pedals, and the reeds wheezed to life as the air drew across them. Not much of a keyboard player, David tried to pick out the melody for "I Still See Her in My Dreams," but he didn't have the ear for it. He stopped pumping the pedals and the bellows emptied with a gasp.

David spun slowly on the bench and glanced around the room. His eyes rested on Jake's tenor horn, standing on its bell in the corner to his left. He went over, picked up the instrument, and worked the valves. The second and third valves stuck down. He figured it was all for the best. If the valves had worked, he'd have tried to play a tune, though it had been how many years since he had last played? No telling what awful sound would come out of the bell. His neighbors would likely think he was hiding a sick cow. Maybe after things settled down he would take up the horn again. After all, someone had to replace Jake in the town band while he was away.

Peals of girlish laughter cascaded from the Winebrenners' house. David realized that with the armies still in position, Kathleen would need to spend the night in town.

His face lit up at the thought of even temporary company. He went up to Myrtle's room and opened the window to let in some fresh air. He ran his hands over the quilt on her bed, even though it didn't need smoothing. The tension on the ropes was fine, but he snugged them anyway. After fluffing the pillow, David went outside to Rose's garden and tried to guess what flowers Kathleen might like.

Tiger lilies, the perfect flowers for a young woman like Kathleen. He pulled out his knife, cut a handful of the most colorful blooms, and took them to the kitchen. Rummaging through the pantry, he discovered a red glass vase just the right size. He added some water from the bucket on the counter and carried the flowers upstairs.

David set the vase in front of the mirror on Myrtle's dresser. He did his best to arrange the orange blooms evenly and, after a few minor adjustments, was finally satisfied. The clock struck the quarter-hour. It would soon turn dark.

David hurried over to the Winebrenners. As he entered the front door, Kathleen came bounding down the stairs. She froze a few steps from the bottom of the staircase and flashed a dazzling smile. "Oh, good. I was just on my way to see you."

The sight of her animated face made David miss his daughters even more. He began, "I was wondering—" and in the same instant Kathleen said, "Martha and Sarah—" They paused, then did the same thing all over again.

Kathleen giggled. "Go ahead. What did you want to say?"

David smiled. "No, you first."

She came the rest of the way down the stairs and looked up into his eyes, her pert face aglow. "Martha and Sarah invited me to stay with them tonight. Since you've been watching out for me today, I thought I should ask your permission."

His heart ached. Why did it seem as though he was about to send away one of his own daughters? He did his best to ignore the feeling and mustered up a smile. "That sounds like a lot of fun. The good Lord knows, you deserve it after the day you've had."

Kathleen's eyes lit with joy. "Thank you, P—" She put her hand to her cheek and blushed. "May I call you Papa Becker?"

David felt too choked up to do anything but nod.

"Thank you—Papa Becker." She threw her arms around him and gave him a big hug.

Without a second thought, David said, "God bless you, precious lamb." It was the goodnight blessing he had always said over his own children.

Kathleen stood on tiptoe and kissed his cheek. "Thank you for everything." She gave his arm a quick squeeze, gathered her skirt, and hurried back up the steps. "Papa Becker says I can stay!" Two delighted squeals answered from the hallway above.

David waited for the joyful sounds to fade, then headed for home. He stood on the front porch and stared at the empty rockers. Closing his eyes, he offered up a fervent prayer for his daughters, their families, and for the blessing of Kathleen's company during such a trying day. *And, dear Lord, please watch over my one and only son, Jacob. Keep him safe in the palm of Your almighty hand. Amen and amen.*

Once in the parlor, David eased into the armchair with a groan. Rose seemed to smile at him from the tintype photo on the mantel.

"I miss you so much, Rosie." How he yearned to hold her in his arms one more time! He reached for Rose's knitting basket, still in its accustomed place next to the chair, and tenderly withdrew the unfinished scarf. Imagining it was Rose's cheek, he held the treasure against his face and savored the soft warmth for a few long moments. Heartened, he returned the scarf to its home.

Grunting as he stood, David went up to Myrtle's room, shut the window, picked up the vase of flowers, and took them back down to the parlor. He placed the vase next to Rose's picture. "Never as beautiful as you, Rose." He blew his wife a kiss and settled down on the divan to spend the night.

He had a hard time getting to sleep. Like walking all day with a pebble in his shoe, his irritation with the war had grown and festered, but what could *he* do about it?

-16-

Enemy territory. Jake's fellow soldiers used the phrase so casually. A Confederate might well face hostility from many folks in York County, but to Jake, these were his people and this land still represented home.

The column rode past the Klinefelter farm. Their son Amos had enlisted in the 26th Pennsylvania Emergency Regiment. Did that make the Klinefelters Jake's enemies? And there was the road to the Hoffacker farm. Surely that must be enemy territory. Jake remembered the Sunday at church a couple of months back, when the congregation had prayed for John Hoffacker before he left to join the 18th Pennsylvania Regulars. John was about six years older than Jake, so they had never been much more than acquaintances. They certainly held no animosity toward one another; in fact, they were brothers in the Lord. If they should meet on the field of battle, who would pull the trigger first? If and when such a time came, which calling would win out: patriotic duty or Christian love? Or would fear trump all, forcing one of the young men to turn tail and run?

From what Jake had witnessed at Manassas, he knew that until a man faced the chaos of that first moment under fire, there was no way to predict which way he would react. Jake took comfort in knowing he had passed the first test when he didn't hesitate to attack the deserter trying to steal Skipper. He just hoped he'd never have to fight someone he knew.

As the column crossed the stone bridge over Codorus Creek, a small herd of deer broke from cover and dashed through a wheat field on the right. A flurry of shots rang out. Two does and a fawn fell into the wheat; the other whitetails zigzagged their way back into the woods. Several riders cantered into the field to retrieve the fresh meat.

Someone yelled, "Woo-hoo, fresh venison tonight!"

Another man drawled, "How ya gonna cook it on horseback?" Everyone knew the order to keep the wagons moving at all cost.

The first man snapped, "If I have to eat any more salted meat, I'll shrivel like a slug. I'll find a way to cook that deer, or I'll eat it raw."

Progress slowed while the mules strained to pull the wagons up the hill heading out of the hamlet of Sinsheim. It took another half-hour to cover the remaining mile into Jefferson. Riding through the empty town square gave Jake the creeps. From near and far, a chorus of dogs howled and barked. A craggy, toothless old man gaped from a second story window over Kroft's store. Was that really Albert Kroft?

At the sound of breaking glass, Jake turned in the saddle. A fellow Confederate reached through a broken pane and unlocked the door of William Christ's hardware store. Several troopers dismounted and traipsed inside. Other men forced their way into Jacob Rebert's store.

Kroft's store was next, but the apparition from the window met the raiders at the front door with a Kentucky long rifle in his hand. Albert spit his chaw of tobacco at the feet of the nearest Confederate soldier. "This here store ain't open 'til eight A.M."

When a rock smashed the display window, Albert flinched and turned to look. Two soldiers wrenched the rifle from his hands. The hammer fell and the gun fired, emitting a feeble *pooff*. The soldiers carried the kicking old man by the elbows and set him down on the edge of the porch.

"Y'all's clock must be a little slow," one of the Confederates snarled. "Mine says it's exactly eight A.M."

The column moved inexorably onward and the confrontation passed from view. Jake glanced at General Lee to gauge his reaction, but Lee seemed unconcerned. Meanwhile, the cacophony of breaking glass and overturned shelves echoed through the village.

Anger surged through Jake. He felt bad enough about the thievery; did his comrades have to wantonly destroy things as well?

As if reading Jake's mind, Lee said, "There are two ways to win a war, Private Becker. You can destroy the enemy's *ability* to fight, or you can destroy his *will* to fight."

Jake started to argue that such actions as these were only likely to rile Pennsylvania Dutchmen to just fight all the harder, but he decided it best to keep his thoughts to himself. He was surprised that the general bothered to speak to him in the first place. Certainly, Lee wouldn't be interested in a lowly private's opinions.

"Speak your mind, son," Lee said gently.

Jake took a moment to organize his thoughts; he didn't want to ruin the moment. Even in the darkness he sensed a kindness in General Lee's demeanor that reminded him of Pa. "Well, sir, since we already have a whole wagon train full of supplies, is it really necessary to, um, help ourselves to what's in those little stores, and to bust them up, besides?"

The general sighed. "I once heard it said that there are two things a man can't be: too rich and too good-looking. My Uncle Robert would add that there are two things an army can't be: too well-disciplined and too well-supplied."

It made sense, but Jake still didn't like the feel of it. "Yes, sir, I understand." And how disciplined were those looters in Jefferson?

Lee added, "That goes double in enemy territory."

There was that phrase again, "enemy territory." What about after the war? Would York County always be enemy territory to Jake? How would his fellow Hanoverians treat him when this was all over?

He imagined being back home after the war and suddenly felt nauseous. Suppose a Hanover boy died in an engagement with Jake's unit and the information got back to the folks in town. It wouldn't matter if the bullet hadn't come from Jake's gun, many would hold him to account for it. How could he carry on the family business, regardless of which side won the war?

Maybe it wasn't too late. He could sneak away in the dark. No one would—

His father's adage rang in his ears. *Don't start what you can't finish.* And then his Heavenly Father's words about "not looking back."

Jake renewed his resolve; duty demanded that he follow his conscience. The Confederate States of America must be allowed to stand, especially after the actions taken by the Federal government. York County had voted overwhelmingly against Lincoln in the '61 election; surely many Hanoverians would not fault Jake for standing up for his convictions. And if he did become an outcast, he could always start his own business in Virginia. Eliza would like that.

-17-

Eliza wanted to scream. Would the moaning never stop? It was bad enough she had to share Emily's small bed and lumpy mattress with her snoring mother, how much longer must she put up with the infernal groans of that dying Yankee in the parlor below? The one time in her life she wished Beelzebub would do his worst, and Old Mr. Scratch was off on some other mischief. She rolled onto her stomach and crushed the pillow over her head.

The motion woke her mother. Mama stirred in mid-snore and turned on her side to face Eliza. "Are you awake, darlin'?"

She yanked the pillow from her head and turned to face her mother. "How does Kathleen sleep on that trundle bed every night? Our dogs have better beds than this."

"I remember how delighted I was when my Papa made me this bed," Mama snapped. "There are folks who'd consider this a blessing."

Eliza gulped. She'd forgotten her mother grew up in this house. Was this the original mattress, too? Her mind flashed back to the time several years ago, when she had caught a glimpse inside the little shed Abby and her children called home. Danny and Bekka were only a few years old then, and Abby was taking them in for a nap. She'd spread an old horse blanket over a mound of straw in one corner of the dirt floor, laid her children on top of it, and told them to stay put until she got back. The rest of the afternoon, Abby tended to Eliza and her siblings, with no break until her charges went to dinner. Later that night, Eliza asked her mother who Abby's children had for a nanny and tutor.

"Don't be silly, girl. Slaves don't need nannies or tutors."

"But who teaches them their ABC's and numbers?"

"Slaves don't need book learning. They don't have the brains."

"Slaves don't have brains?"

"God made them for working, not thinking. It's part of their curse." Mama had gone on to explain that back in Bible days, God cursed a man named Ham for doing something bad. God put a mark on Ham, and told him that from then on, his people would have to serve normal folk. And that mark was dark skin.

At the time, Eliza had barely understood. Now the explanation smelled a little fishy, but maybe she remembered it wrong. Then again, it seemed to be common knowledge in both Hanover and Manassas that Negroes weren't the equal of whites. Besides, what about the Negroes who had lighter skin? Were they less cursed? No, judging from the way she'd heard folks talk, light-skinned ones must be more cursed.

Poor Danny and Bekka. Sold away from their mama, and they had lighter skin, besides.

The pieces suddenly came together in Eliza's mind. She knew white cream turned black coffee to light brown. Dear Lord, was it possible?

When her father and Abby . . .

Mama was snoring again. Eliza wanted to shake her awake and demand the whole truth, but how much did she really want to know?

So much had happened in the two days since she'd learned about her father and Abigail. Jake had gone off to war, the fighting had come to Hanover, and Yankees patrolled the road, talking about an attack at daybreak. Eliza didn't even know where Kathleen had spent the night.

She groaned and shifted to find a more comfortable position. She'd gone from her plush canopied bed in Manassas to the double bed she shared with Lydia. Now this. Was the barn to be her next bed?

From down in the parlor an agonized scream knifed through the floorboards, echoed in the stairwell, and set Eliza's heart to pounding. The hideous noise died away beneath Aunt Linda Jane's soothing tones. "Can I get you something, Mr. Moran?"

Then came the most pitiful whimpering Eliza had ever heard. She pictured the Devil, cat-like, toying with the man before he took him.

Somehow, the chilling image didn't give her as much pleasure as she'd thought it might. True, she hated the Yankees, but it occurred to her that not all Northerners were bad. Take Jake, for example, and most of the people she'd met around Hanover. Even those who supported the Union cause, like her aunts and uncles and Mr. Becker, were all decent, tolerable folks. They had never treated her poorly just because she was a Virginian. They had never treated her poorly at all.

Then there was Lydia, gladly sharing her room with her Southern cousins. Eliza tried to imagine how she'd have felt if the situation were reversed. Would she welcome such an intrusion in her own domain? Though she liked Lydia a lot, she had to admit it would be difficult to share her room with her. She cringed at the thought of Emily and Sarah so much as setting foot inside her bedroom back in Manassas.

Eliza wondered what condition her room was in now. Had anyone done anything to take care of it during the two years she had been gone? How many slaves did her father still own? She pictured the house and farm, lying in ruins. What awaited her in Virginia after the war?

Maybe the people who hated slavery were right. Plenty of folks in the Hanover area seemed to do fine without slaves. On the whole, darkies just weren't worth all the trouble.

Perhaps she and Jake should live in Hanover after they got married. He could keep working with his father and someday the carriage business would be his. While Mr. Becker didn't treat her as warmly as most of the men she met, he was never unkind. And it would be nice to get to know Jake's sisters, as long as they didn't expect her to tend their children.

The clock struck ten. Eliza groaned. Less than seven hours until dawn and the voice in her mind just wouldn't shut up.

-18-

The grandmother clock in John Ziegler's stone farmhouse began to strike the hour of ten. Jake lifted his weary head from his hands, then sat up straight on the bench as General Stuart entered the parlor.

Stuart nodded to his brigade commanders, seated on a well-worn, overstuffed couch. "Lee, Hampton, Chambliss. Good, let's make this brief." He strode to the new-fangled bentwood rocker and eased into the upholstered seat. A look of utter delight passed over his face. "Ah . . ."

McClellan spoke from the doorway. "Perhaps we don't need to be so brief, General."

"Thank you, Major, but we must keep moving. This wagon train has become a source of embarrassment, yet I do not wish to leave it behind." Stuart sighed and waved for his adjutant to have a seat in the wing chair next to him. "We must be near General Early's troops by now." He turned to Jake. "How much farther to York?"

Jake did some quick mental calculations. "About eleven miles, sir. Six to the Pike, then another five or so after that."

"Good." Stuart made a scribbling motion to McClellan. "When we get to the pike, write the order to release the civilian prisoners we took along the way. There will be no need for secrecy after that. That goes for you, too, Jake. We appreciate all the help you have given us, but now . . ."

As Stuart continued, Jake's mind raced. Was he to be packed off home already? Had he acted upon a mistaken sense of duty? This could be his "out," if he wanted it.

McClellan cleared his throat and laid a hand on Stuart's arm. "Sir, perhaps it has slipped your mind. This is *Private* Becker. He enlisted this morning."

Stuart took a deep breath and puffed it out a corner of his mouth. "Right you are." He turned to Jake. "I do apologize, Private Becker."

When relief washed over him, Jake knew in his heart that he was on the right path. "Yes, sir. Thank you, sir."

Stuart continued, "Major, make sure Private Becker gets a proper uniform. And issue him a sabre while you're at it." McClellan scribbled on a piece of paper and handed it to Jake.

"Now then, Private, show me where we are," Stuart said.

McClellan spread a map across the coffee table in front of the couch. Stuart scooted the rocker over to get a better look.

Jake knelt by the table and took a moment to get oriented. He traced his finger along the map. "That is Hanover. We came through Jefferson, and now we're right about here. See Hanover Junction there?"

Stuart looked up. "Has that railroad junction been dealt with?"

"Yes, sir," McClellan said. "Our scouts reported that Colonel White's men went through there a couple of days ago."

Irritation rang in Stuart's voice. "And where are they now?"

The brigade officers exchanged embarrassed glances. McClellan said, "We have no recent reports on the exact whereabouts of any other troops, sir, ours or theirs—excepting Kilpatrick's, of course."

"Hampton, are your men all caught up at the rear of the column?"

"Yes, sir. Colonel Chambliss' men are directly in front of us."

Stuart tapped his fingers on the arms of the rocker. "And how recent is the information on General Early, Major?"

McClellan didn't need to check his dispatches. "Nothing since this afternoon, sir."

The general glanced at each of his officers in turn. "Well, gentlemen. Where do we go from here?"

Before anyone could answer, some horses trotted up outside. Muffled voices and heavy footsteps sounded on the porch. Hat in hand, Captain Blackford burst into the parlor. "General Stuart, sir. Scouts."

"Good. Show them in."

The two scouts couldn't have looked more different. The older man was dark-complected, very short, and thick-bodied; his beetled brow gave him an ominous look. The skeletal lad stood a few inches taller than Jake, and he was very blonde, very pale, and very wall-eyed. Judging by his snaggletooth grin, he was quick to laugh at even the mildest humor.

The man with the trollish features snapped to attention and saluted smartly. "We have located 3,000 Union cavalry commanded by General Gregg. They are encamped east of here. We learned from two different people that his army is heading west, toward Hanover."

Stuart looked grim. "Did you get word on the location of our troops?"

The affable scarecrow replied, but his Southern drawl was so thick that Jake had a hard time understanding him. From the gist of it, an important bridge over the Susquehanna had been burned, thwarting General Early's advance, so he had gone west toward Shippensburg; but rumors in York still had the Confederates preparing to launch an attack on the state capitol in Harrisburg. Jake couldn't help wondering how effective the young man could be as a spy, what with those bumpkin looks and that telltale accent. Nevertheless, he had delivered the goods.

"Anything else to report?" Stuart asked. Having nothing to add, the scouts were quickly dismissed.

Stuart rose and paced the room. His knee-high boots thudded on the parlor's wide pine planks. "Which way should we go when we reach the York Pike? West to catch up to General Early, or northeast toward Harrisburg?"

The officers needed little discussion. They unanimously decided to follow General Early toward Shippensburg.

As the meeting adjourned, Stuart took Jake aside. "Now don't forget to get that uniform right away. We don't want you to get hanged as a spy in enemy territory."

A shiver raced up Jake's spine.

Execution, by hanging, of two Rebel spies, Williams and Peters,
in the Army of the Cumberland, June 9, 1863
Harper's Weekly, July 4, 1863

Wednesday, July 1, 1863

-1-

The nonstop march, moonless night, and rough backcountry roads took their toll on the already exhausted Confederate soldiers. In a never-ending battle to keep the wagon train from becoming too spread out, junior officers rode up and down the column waking drivers who had fallen asleep at the reins. Trusting their weary horses to stay in line and keep pace, most of the cavalrymen slept in the saddle. More than one man joined the casualty list after toppling from his mount.

Jake's ears buzzed. His eyes felt dry and swollen. He was too fuzz-brained to guess the hour. Surely dawn must soon break, he was surprised they hadn't reached the York Pike already. Were they covering even one mile every hour? His agitation grew as the army wormed its way toward daylight and better roads. The homespun gray uniform shirt the quartermaster had given him scratched the back of his neck, and the slouch hat was just a little too tight. The sabre and scabbard's unaccustomed weight irritated his left hip. And then there were the clouds of mosquitoes. No telling how many of the pernicious insects he had splattered on his butternut colored pants. At least the season for black flies was over.

General Stuart tried to keep spirits high by leading those around him in song, but the worn-out men lacked the energy to sing the boisterous tunes with conviction, and the ballads only served to beckon Morpheus. Trying to stave off sleep, Jake hummed along with improvised harmonies. The soothing vibrations in his head only increased his drowsiness.

Jake finally managed to find a balanced position against Cat's neck with his arms draped on either side. Sleep came quickly. He had no idea how long he was out. He awoke to find strands of Cat's mane between his lips, and he was so groggy he couldn't even remember which Bigler girl he dreamt he was kissing.

Herb reached over and nudged him. "Is your stomach all right?"

"Huh? Yeah. I think so. Why?"

"You were moaning something awful."

Jake remembered more of the dream and felt his face flush. Finally, the dark night proved useful for something. Herb would tease him for days if he figured out why he had moaned. "I'm fine. How are you keeping awake?"

Herb leaned over and lowered his voice. "I gotta pee so bad, I'm afraid if I fall asleep I'll wet myself."

Stuart finished a chorus of "Maryland, My Maryland," turned in the saddle, and called, "Major FitzHugh, we need you."

One of the general's aides rode back along the column to fetch the quartermaster, Norman FitzHugh. A few minutes later, FitzHugh rode up, his voice heavy with sleep. "Yes, sir, is there a problem?"

"Yes, one that I think you are best equipped to solve. As you may have noticed, some of the men seem to have difficulty staying awake. Perhaps if you would be so kind as to regale them with a story or two?"

The sound of fatigue disappeared from FitzHugh's voice. "Did you have one in mind, sir?"

"What do you think, young Herbert? Would you rather hear about Indians or spies?"

Both sounded intriguing to Jake. Herb blurted, "Spies, sir."

"Good choice," Stuart said. "But we'll have an Indian tale or two after, if you don't mind, Major?"

"Not at all, sir. Well, my adventure began last August when I was captured at Verdiersville by the 1st Michigan. General Stuart barely escaped, or things would have been worse. As it was, they caught me in possession of some papers detailing General Lee's current offensive. They threw me in the Old Capitol Prison in Washington City, and guess who occupied the cell next to mine?"

Jake and Herb had no idea, of course. After waiting for the suspense to build, FitzHugh announced, "Belle Boyd."

The name sounded vaguely familiar to Jake. Herb whooped, "Yeow, Belle Boyd the spy! Is she as handsome as they say?"

"Oh, let me tell you, boys. Nineteen years old, long brown hair in a braid down to her bountiful buttocks. And buxom? Like to poke your eyes out! She's a danger, for sure."

As though wise in the ways of the world, the boys chuckled.

"And she has the finest ankles you'll ever lay eyes on. Feisty as all get out, too. On the Fourth of July in '61, she shot a Yankee who tried to fly a U.S. flag from her house.

"Anyways, I'd probably still be rotting away in that jail if not for her. She got herself paroled—again—and," his voice lowered to a suggestive tone, "I was assigned to escort her back to Virginia."

The men responded with the obligatory *aahs*.

"We had quite the excursion: a carriage ride to the *Juniata*, which took us down the Potomac, and then another carriage ride to Richmond, where the newspapermen swarmed to her like bees on sweet clover."

Captain Blackford called, "And did *you* do any 'swarming' on the way, Major?"

"A gentleman never tells."

Jake grinned. If the major's inflection was any indication, he had done enough swarming for an entire hive of bees.

Stuart prompted, "Tell the story of how she used to send her nigra Sophie with messages hidden inside a pocket watch."

Before FitzHugh could continue, a squad of riders approached from the rear. Stuart gestured for the column to proceed while he and his staff moved into the field on the right.

Five Confederate cavalrymen escorted six blindfolded riders in civilian clothes. One of the cavalrymen acted as spokesman. "Sir, we've captured some spies, though they deny it, of course. Shall we try to see what we can get out of them, or just go ahead and shoot them?"

The first signs of dawn brightened the eastern horizon as Stuart said, "Let's have a look." He motioned and the blindfolds were removed.

In the dim light, Jake thought he recognized one of the captives. He eased Cat to the left, behind Herb. While Stuart asked a few questions, Jake peeked around Herb's shoulder. There was no longer any doubt. One of the "spies" was Charles Diehl.

Charles, a spy? Jake couldn't fathom it. The Beckers had made several wagons for Charles' father, Peter, who owned a tannery in New Oxford. The Diehls also ran a freight line down to Baltimore. Charles was no spy. Then again, how many Hanoverians would be surprised when they heard Jake had joined the Army of Northern Virginia?

One of the strangers with Charles pleaded for their lives. "I swear to you, sir, we're just on our way to take our horses to safety across the Susquehanna."

Major McClellan glared at the prisoners. "And how did you propose to get them across when the bridge burned two days ago?"

Jake wondered if he should say something on Charles' behalf, but would it be wise to reveal his allegiance? Only a few people in Hanover knew he had joined the Confederate cause, and they were family friends. When he bought the revolver, Mr. Gitt presumed Jake was joining the Union Army. Though it twinged his conscience, Jake did nothing to dissuade the merchant of that notion. Might it be easier to return home after the war if no one else discovered for which cause he had fought?

One of the captors brandished his pistol by the barrel. "Shall I use my 'persuader' to loosen their tongues?"

Charles looked shocked at the suggestion.

In a flash, Jake knew what he must do. He realized he could never live the lie it would take to cover up his true involvement in the war, and how could he stand by and watch an innocent man suffer?

"Excuse me, General Stuart," Jake called out. "I know one of these men. That's Charles Diehl. Our fathers have done business together for years."

Charles stared. "Jake?" he said, incredulously.

Stuart scrutinized Jake's face. "So. You vouch for these men?"

Stifling a gulp, Jake paused to consider. Charles, yes, but what about the five strangers? Trusting his instincts that Charles had not taken up with ne'er-do-wells, Jake nodded. "Yes, sir, I do."

"Very well," Stuart said. He turned to Lieutenant Dabney. "Until our column has passed, see that these men are put to good use. Have them haul water for the horses, help with the wounded, or whatever other jobs need tending. Now let's get on with our work, gentlemen."

Dabney motioned for the captors to escort the prisoners toward the rear of the line. Charles nodded his thanks to Jake, and a look of understanding passed between the two young men. Perhaps there was one more person who wouldn't object if Jake returned home after the war.

-2-

David awoke with a start. The hair on the back of his neck prickled. Was someone watching him? Feigning sleep, he peeked through half-closed lids; seeing no one, he sat up and scanned the parlor. Gray light poured through the front windows. He strained to listen. What *was* that sound in the kitchen? Maybe a soldier raiding the pantry?

He eased off the sofa and tiptoed to the door. Peeking around the corner and down the hall, David spied a faint shadow on the floor as someone passed in front of the kitchen window. Deciding to address the situation from the safety of the hallway, David barked, "What are you doing in my house!"

"Oh dear!" a woman screamed. A plate crashed to the floor.

Recognizing the voice, David rushed down the hall. "Kathleen? Is that you?" He entered the kitchen and found Kathleen, one hand covering her mouth, the other balled in a fist over her heart.

Their eyes met and Kathleen relaxed. "You frightened me!"

"I'm sorry, I thought a soldier might be helping himself to my pantry. I had no idea it was you."

She pulled a stray hair from her eyes. "Oh . . ." She pointed to the mess on the floor. "I'm sorry, I dropped one of your plates."

"Not to worry, I have plenty more." Then he noticed the food on the table. "What is that?"

A shy smile crossed Kathleen's face. "I made breakfast for you at the Winebrenners, then brought it over here to surprise you."

"For me?" Warmth filled David's heart. "Thank you, that is very kind of you. You didn't have to do that."

Kathleen flashed a feisty look. "I know. That's partly why I did it." She pulled out the chair at the head of the table and patted the seat. "If you would please sit right here, Papa Becker, I'll serve it right up."

As David sat, she lifted the cover off an iron skillet and used a wooden spatula to transfer a hefty omelette onto a plate. Fragments of cheese, onions, and ham protruded from the eggy concoction. She ladled a generous helping of home fries from one of the Winebrenners' bowls. "I'm afraid there's only water to drink. I'm good at making coffee, but your crock only had a few beans left in it."

"I know, but water is fine. This is all quite a treat, thank you."

She wrinkled her nose. "You might want to wait until you taste it."

"If it tastes half as good as it smells . . ."

Kathleen served herself and then took a seat.

The omelette tasted even better than it smelled. David rolled his eyes and patted his stomach. "This is delicious!"

"Thanks." She beamed. "Omelettes are my favorite food to make."

Between bites, they reminisced about the trip from Manassas to Hanover. Kathleen told of how she missed her home in Virginia, but she had come to love Hanover just as much. She missed her father and brother, but she had made a lot of new friends in Pennsylvania, especially Jake and her new "Papa."

Then, her face clouded over. David couldn't stand the thought of his "daughter" bearing the burden of melancholy. "What is it, Sunshine?"

She frowned and stared at her plate. David wondered whether to press the issue or let it pass.

Kathleen lifted her head. "I was just thinking about something my Mama told us the other night."

"Go on," David said sympathetically.

"She said that things back home aren't going very well. Papa had to sell some of the slaves. Worst of all, he sold our nanny Abigail and her children. And," her voice choked, "he didn't sell them together." She covered her face with her hands.

Remembering the sorrowful parting between the Bigler girls and the Negro woman two years ago, David moved to the chair next to Kathleen and put his arm around her shoulders. "That must have been very painful to hear."

She leaned against him and let the tears flow. After a few moments, she recovered her composure and dabbed her eyes with a napkin. "Sorry. I don't want to ruin your—"

David shushed her and put on a tone of mock seriousness. "I won't let you call me Papa Becker unless you let me act like a Papa when you need one."

Her face lit up and her eyes sparkled behind the tears. "Thank you, Papa." She leaned over and gave him a big hug.

Deciding the situation called for a treat, David stood and went to the pantry, returning with the last two blueberry muffins. "Do you like blueberries?"

"My fav-o-rite!"

David smiled to cover the sinking feeling in his stomach. She over-enunciated "favorite" exactly like Jake did. She even savored every bite in much the same manner.

Finished, Kathleen used a pinky to wipe a crumb from her chin, then licked the morsel from her fingertip. "Aren't blueberries Jake's favorite, too?" Her green eyes seemed to fade to gray. "I miss him so much. You know, Eliza said that when she marries Jake, he'll be like the big brother

I never had. I hadn't thought about that before, but I've thought about it a lot since then, and maybe she's right." She swallowed hard, though she hadn't put any food in her mouth. Her voice sounded tight. "It might be nice to have a big brother like Jake."

"I think he'd be mighty blessed to have a little sister like you." David chuckled. "Probably do him a world of good!"

Kathleen bit her lip, then smiled wanly. "I hope so."

She abruptly pushed back from the table, went to the counter, and dumped a bucket of water into the washbasin. Her voice took on a hopeful tone. "Do you think that now the Confederate Army has come north the war will end soon?"

David stood and started clearing the table. "I don't know. If it did, that would mean the Union would be dissolved, and I fear that would only lead to more wars in the future."

"Oh, that's bad. I never thought about that. My Mama says men are always looking for excuses to fight." She washed the dishes and David dried them.

"Unfortunately, there may be a lot of truth to that. My father and grandfather both fought in wars. I was hoping my son would never have to do likewise."

Kathleen handed him a fork to dry. "Well, I'm proud of the way Jake is standing up for what he believes in, but I wish it didn't mean he had to go off to war." She cocked her head. "Do you think the same way as Jake does about the Confederacy?"

It was David's turn to bite his lip. "No. As I said before, I think we need to keep all the states united." He decided to avoid the issue of slavery, though from the way Kathleen suffered over the news of Abigail and her children, she might be open to the abolitionist position.

"Last one," Kathleen said, handing over another fork. While David dried it and put it away, she leaned up over the counter to look out the window.

"Surprise, looks like another cloudy day." Smoothing her dress, she turned to face him. "Would you like some help today? Or maybe I could go help out with the wounded men, like I did after the battle back home."

While David welcomed the chance to spend more time with this intriguing young lady, he feared he might become too fond of her. How often would he see Kathleen when things returned to normal? While his new "daughter" seemed like a balm sent from God, he needed to deal with the demon of loneliness sooner than later. But looking into her eager eyes weakened his resolve. What was it about daughters that made it so hard to say "no" to them? "First, let me go outside and see what's going on with the armies."

The Confederates had slipped away during the night, but Union soldiers still patrolled the streets. One of the men in blue instructed David that citizens could pass freely in town, but travel outside was prohibited for the time being.

Karle Forney's voice boomed down the street. "Hey, David! You ought to come see what happened over to our place. And if you have the time, we could use another pair of hands dealing with some dead horses."

So there was David's answer. Kathleen wouldn't want to keep him company on a task like that. "Sure, Karle, I'll be over as soon as I can." He started up the porch steps.

Kathleen stood in the front doorway with a look of sadness in her eyes. "I heard. Since I'm going to be in town for a while longer, maybe I should go over to the church and see if anyone can use my help. Is that all right?"

"That sounds like a fine idea."

Her eyes gleamed. "Meet you back here for lunch at noon?"

"Indeed!" What a nice treat to look forward to, David thought, especially after the onerous task of hauling dead horses.

She was already down the porch steps when David called, "Kathleen, wait a moment, please. I'll be right back."

Looking puzzled, Kathleen followed David into the house. She waited in the hallway while he hurried up the stairs to his bedroom.

Once in the room, he paused. Though initially surprised at the impulse that had brought him there, the more he thought about the idea, the more he felt it was the right thing to do. He went to the closet, reached up, and lifted a jewelry box from the top shelf. The piece was right where he remembered: the middle compartment in the middle drawer.

On his way back downstairs, the image of Hope's delighted face filled his mind. Her voice rang as clearly as if she was right beside him. "Oh Papa, just what I always wanted! It's so beautiful, thank you, thank you, thank you!"

He knew his other daughters liked the lockets he had given them, but if he had known how much Hope would treasure such a thing, he would have given her the locket much sooner. As it turned out, she only had a few months to enjoy it before she died. He had wanted to bury it with her, but Rose convinced him to hold on to it, assuring him there would come a day when he would find just the right young lady to give it to—someone who would cherish it as much as Hope had, and that would be a much more fitting tribute to their precious daughter. David figured he would someday give it to one of his granddaughters or maybe Jake's wife as a wedding present. Was it too late to change his mind? Maybe he should wait.

But when he saw Kathleen's smiling face at the bottom of the stairs, all doubts vanished. He took her hand and led her into the parlor.

"Kathleen, I would like you to have this." He opened his hand to show her. "It was—"

Her eyes brimmed with tears—tears of utter joy, if her smile was any indication. "Oh, Papa Becker, a locket! It's just what I've always wanted! How did you know? May I?" She reached tentatively toward his hand.

Too choked up to speak, David circled with his finger for her to turn. Kathleen turned her back to him, lifting the bun of hair away from her neck. He undid the clasp, draped the heart-shaped golden locket around her neck, and refastened the clasp.

Kathleen lifted the locket and examined its gleaming cover. Her voice took on a reverent tone. "It is so beautiful. Thank you so much." She turned and looked into his eyes, searching. "But why me?"

Why indeed? How could he explain what he didn't fully understand himself? The words came unbidden. "Because you are such a blessing."

Her eyebrows arched. "Me?"

David nodded. "This used to belong to Jake's sister, Hope. She died when she was nine. My wife told me that someday I would find a young lady who would like having this as much as Hope. Well, today I did."

His eyes misted. He struggled to keep his voice steady. "You've probably heard your parents say this a thousand times but, someday when you have children, you'll understand. You'll know what a precious blessing from God they are. Kathleen, you not only bless me by calling me Papa, you honor me. And I thank God for sending you at such a time as this. What with Jake and Myrtle—"

Kathleen threw her arms around him and squeezed like she'd never let go. "I understand plenty. Thank you, Papa Becker. I love you."

A flood of peace and joy washed the emptiness from David's heart. "I love you, too, precious lamb."

-3-

Still accompanying the wagon train, Jake and Herb finally arrived in Dover shortly before eight in the morning. General Stuart and his staff, who had ridden ahead of the column and arrived hours earlier, waited in front of Jacob Fries' Upper Hotel.

A rider approached at top speed from the outskirts of town. "Hopefully, news at last!" Stuart exclaimed.

A rotund lieutenant, sweat pouring down his cheeks, reined up and quickly dismounted in front of the commander. He saluted smartly, then gave his report. "General Early headed west toward Shippensburg yesterday afternoon, but you shoulda seen what we'uns took off them folks in York." He reached into his shirt pocket and pulled out a piece of paper. "We managed to get a copy of the requisition General Early gave them, and I heard they was so anxious to avoid any trouble, they nearly wet themselves getting most of this stuff together by the deadline."

General Stuart took the paper, ran his eyes down the page, and chuckled. His eyes lingered at the bottom of the page. "He got *all* of this, including the $100,000.00?"

"Pretty near," the lieutenant said.

Stuart held the paper up and read for all to hear. "165,000 pounds of flour. 3,500 pounds of sugar. 300 gallons of molasses."

A voice called out, "What's he gonna do, cook a birthday cake for the whole army?"

Stuart continued, raising his voice to be heard over the laughter. "28,000 pounds of bread. 1,200 pounds of salt. 32,000 pounds of beef or 21,000 pounds of pork. And 2,000 shoes, 1,000 pairs of socks, and 1,000 felt hats."

Jake was impressed. York was a city of fewer than ten thousand people, so this was quite a haul. He wondered if all of Richmond could have met such a demand after two years of war in Virginia.

Stuart finished perusing the requisition and looked up. "No oats?"

The messenger looked doubtful. "Not that I heard of."

"Well, there you have it, gentlemen," Stuart said triumphantly. "We are indeed fortunate to have retained these wagons. Now General Early can feed us and we shall feed his horses. Thank you for your report, Lieutenant. Now let us return to the task at hand."

He called to his Provost Marshal. "Lieutenant Ryals, place guards in front of any establishment where spirits may be procured. The men must all remain alert."

Ryals set off to put the order into motion.

"Lieutenant Kennan," Stuart continued, "I want a room for the surgeons to tend our wounded, and see about ordering breakfast for us."

As the young lieutenant headed into the hotel, Jake tried to imagine Mr. Fries' face when presented with a request to feed several thousand famished men. He knew the general must mean to include only the staff officers, but his sleep-deprived mind preferred to conjure up images of the hotel's guests gawking as the entire army crowded into the dining room.

Stuart fired off a series of orders. "Major Johnson, disperse rations and let the men know we will rest here for a few hours. Remind them of General Lee's order against plundering. And see that the hay we acquired from the Zieglers is spread along the gutters, so when the rest of the wagons arrive the mules can eat.

"Captain Cooke, send scouts in all directions, concentrating on the area between here and Carlisle."

The provost returned and waited expectantly until Stuart nodded permission to speak. "Sir, what shall I do with the prisoners?"

"Feed them. I'll have General Hampton oversee their parole following breakfast, but do not tell them yet."

Lieutenant Kennan emerged from the hotel. "The hotel dining room is ready, sir. The parlor is being emptied for the surgeons."

"Thank you, Lieutenant. You may tell the medical staff." He took a deep breath and sighed. "Gentlemen, shall we dine?"

Jake dismounted, expecting to follow Stuart into the dining room to eat, but the surge of pain in his cramped thighs brought him back to reality. Privates did not dine with generals. In his fatigue, he had nearly forgotten his station.

Stuart put his arm around Herb's shoulders and engaged him in conversation as they went in to the hotel. Jake was far too tired and sore to be jealous.

He wobbled over to the corner of the hotel and tied Cat's reins to the post. As he turned to sit, he noticed a familiar face in the hotel window. He rubbed his bleary eyes. Yep. He knew that scruffy young man with *stroobly* hair and in desperate need of a shave and a wash. It was his own reflection. He tugged the brim of his hat down, took a seat on the edge of the low porch, and eased his aching back against the hitching post.

Three wagons rolled to a stop in front of the hotel. Some of the wounded managed to climb out under their own power, but many more needed assistance. Two able-bodied soldiers barked directions, and several cavalrymen carried the most severely wounded men into the hotel. Those less critically injured formed a line on the porch.

Wary townsfolk appeared in windows and doorways all along the street. Small clusters of Confederate soldiers wandered aimlessly, some of them gnawing on a hunk of salted meat or hardtack. Several small fires had already been started in the road. The clank of coffee pots and cups sounded like the old pie tins Mama used to hang in the garden to scare the birds away. In stark contrast, the soft clinking of silverware and fine dishes floated through the hotel windows.

Jake's stomach rumbled. He decided to eat the last of the food he'd brought from home; there'd be plenty of time to learn to digest the infamous hardtack later. He stood and reached into the saddlebag. Cat turned and gave him a pleading look.

"Don't worry, girl, I'm going to feed you before I eat my grub." He pulled out the feedbag and went to get some oats. While Cat munched hungrily, Jake retrieved the last of Myrtle's bread from the saddlebag.

He nearly dropped the bread at the sound of the gut-wrenching scream that erupted from inside the hotel. The scream devolved into a long wail of agony. Jake caught a whiff of burning flesh, and he shook his head sadly. He had learned what that smell meant when he assisted with the wounded men back in Manassas. How could they perform amputations in the room right next to where General Stuart and his staff ate breakfast? Had the surgeon used the hotel's cook-fire to heat the cauterizing tool?

His appetite ruined for the moment, Jake stowed the bread in the saddlebag, then stripped everything from Cat's back and gave her a thorough brushing. Finally, using the saddle as a backrest, he stretched out on the porch and covered his face with his hat.

Even though he had never stayed awake this long before, sleep eluded him. His head throbbed. His thighs felt as if they'd been trapped in a vise for hours. Drifting on the edge of consciousness, he willed his mind to silence, but with no success.

From about twenty yards away, a harsh voice railed, "Repent, you evil man-stealers! Slavery is an abomination before the Lord!"

Jake groaned and reached for Cat's blanket, hoping to block out the diatribe. Did this fool think to win converts in the Confederate Army? Jake knew the arguments well enough, he even held many of them in common with the self-appointed evangelist, but here? Now?

". . . stealing their pay, fornicating with their women, selling them like animals. Repent while the Lord is yet merciful!"

Did he know that voice? Jake sat up and straightened his hat. A glance at the speaker confirmed his suspicion. The would-be preacher was his cousin, Richard, a devotee of William Garrison's particularly vitriolic brand of abolitionism.

Jake scanned the area in search of other kin. Since the army was here, he didn't expect to see any women, but was Uncle Robert in town, too? Jake wouldn't put it past any of his Dover relatives to make a scene if they spied him in a Rebel uniform. He turned his back on the scene.

Richard's voice drew nearer. "Repent, I say! You may bravely face the fire of the Union Army, but dare you face the eternal fire of Hell?"

Jake felt a hand on his shoulder. His cousin's voice rang in his ear. "Will you be the first to repent?"

-4-

The Forneys had their hands full clearing horse carcasses from their lands. Though some of the dead horses in town were taken out to the stone quarry for burial, Karle decided it would be a lot easier to just burn the nine bodies on his property. David suggested they go to the barn and make a travois to haul the horses into three separate pyres. While Sam and John harnessed the draft horses, Karle and David built the travois.

"So, you must have had a good view of the fighting out your windows," David thought aloud.

"We saw the troops sooner than that," Sam replied. "John and I were plowing in the north thirty when our troops first passed by. We, uh," he glanced at his father, "well, we took a bit of a break, you see, and sat on the fence so we could talk with some of the men as they went past."

Karle clicked his tongue. "And what did your idle ears hear?"

Both sons reddened at the mild rebuke. John picked up the story. "We were talking to a lieutenant when a soldier in gray came up. Turns out, he was a captured scout. They let him stop and talk with us a little piece. He said he was from North Carolina and wished he was back home plowing corn like us."

"Pa," Sam asked earnestly, "do you think that now that the Rebels are here, this will all soon end?"

"Can't say," Karle said grimly. He shrugged. "Time will tell."

"Anyways," John said, "we went back to the plow, and a couple of hours later we heard shouts and gunshots. The next thing we knew, the fields were full of cavalry. We unhitched the horses and took off toward McSherryville so the soldiers wouldn't take them. We went to the Geiselmans until things died down in the afternoon."

Bedraggled and exhausted, Mary Forney entered the barn. "That Rebel is about to breathe his last."

The men left their work and followed her into the sitting room. Karle's daughter, Susan, looked up from the stool next to the dying man's pallet. She looked drained and on the verge of tears.

The baby-faced soldier lifted his bloodied arm and groaned as he reached for the pocket of his grimy gray shirt. He pulled out a New Testament and held it up to Susan. "Take this book and send it to my home." Hands shaking, he opened the cover and pointed to the flyleaf. "That address will reach my sister." He tensed, waiting for a wave of pain to pass. "She gave me this book when I left home two years ago," His slow drawl grew thicker. "And she asked me to keep it and bring it back again when this cruel war shall have ended." His hand fell against Susan's leg, then he broke into a racking cough. Foamy blood spewed from the corners of his mouth. "It has ended now for me."

Tears rolled down Susan's face. "God be with you, Samuel Reddick."

The Confederate soldier wheezed his final breath and went limp. Karle knelt down, closed the man's vacant brown eyes, and folded the hands in a peaceful posture. Susan sobbed quietly.

After leading a brief prayer for the man's family and loved ones, Karle stood and motioned to his sons. "Let's dig him a grave out by the locust trees."

"We'll wash him up," Mary said, giving her daughter a nod.

Squawking crows settled on the slate roof of the barn while the men prepared the burial site. David marveled at how scavengers always knew when Death paid a visit. Unfortunately, the only things Karle could spare for a burial shroud were three burlap feed bags, compounding the soldier's inglorious demise.

When they lowered Samuel Reddick into the ground, a voice in David's head warned, *That could be Jake someday, and you might never know where they plant him.*

David thought Life had annealed his emotions over the years. He had thought wrong. As the men returned to the task of dealing with the dead horses, worry for Jake's safety gnawed at David's heart.

Work again halted when John pointed to a metal object glistening in the nearby grass. "Lookie here!" He picked up a shiny revolver.

David gasped. "Why that looks like—" It was a .44 Colt. "May I see it?" John carefully handed the weapon over.

While checking out Jake's new gun on Monday morning, David

couldn't help noticing its palindromic serial number: 53135. With trepidation, he flipped the weapon upside down and examined the brass trigger guard. "Dear Lord," he murmured, reading the engraving: 53135.

Karle put his hand on David's shoulder. "What is it?"

Shaking, David scoured the blood-soaked, trampled grass in search of any signs that might indicate what had happened. "This gun. It's Jake's. I remember the serial number."

Had Jake been captured, wounded, or worse?

-5-

The hand tightened on Jake's shoulder. His cousin's voice rose in intensity. "Be a leader! Be the first to repent of your wickedness! Others will follow your example."

Jake leaned his head on Cat's neck and lowered his voice. "Leave me be, I'm no slaver."

Richard removed his hand but didn't walk away. "Thank the Lord for that, but if you fight for their cause you are still under condemnation. Kneel with me and pray for forgiveness before it is too late."

"Leave me be, I say!" Jake didn't dare turn around. He knew that when Richard set his mind on such matters, there was no reasoning with him; he was like a terrier on a rat.

"Do you dare resist the Lord's call? Jesus says, 'Behold, I stand at the door and knock. If any man hear my voice and open the door, I will come in to him and—'"

"—will sup with him, and he with me," Jake said gruffly, completing the well-known verse. "See? I know. I'm a believer, too."

"Then why do you keep company with these sinners?" Richard put his hand on Jake's arm, as if expecting him to turn around.

"Excuse me, I have to use the privy." Jake ducked under Cat's neck, strode toward the hotel entrance, and hoped his cousin would seek a fertile soul elsewhere. But as he walked across the porch, he heard the sound of someone's boots right behind him.

General Stuart emerged from the hotel. "There you are, Private Becker."

Herb came out and stood at the general's side. "Why didn't you eat with us, Jake?"

Jake cringed; would Richard connect the names? Before Jake could turn to explain, Stuart added, "Becker, I want you to serve as one of my couriers."

"Yes, sir." Jake blanched. Surely his cousin would connect the names now.

But Richard had already resumed preaching from the other end of the porch. "Repent, man-stealers . . ."

Stuart looked askance at Richard, then turned, went back into the hotel lobby, and called, "Lieutenant Ryals, I believe there is someone out here who might benefit from your attention."

Coffee cup in hand, Stuart's Provost Marshal strolled out onto the porch. Jake peeked over Herb's shoulder and spotted several men in gray huddled near his cousin—and they had mischief in their eyes. Ryals drained the cup, handed it to a passing Negro porter, and then went to join the impending confrontation.

Jake held his breath. What if Richard got into a fight? Though his cousin was big enough to hold his own against most men, no one would last long at the hands of this angry bunch.

Ryals strolled over and tapped Richard on the shoulder. Ryals was only in his mid-twenties, but his soft Virginia drawl took on a fatherly tone. "Y'all have a very persuasive way about you, young man."

When Richard turned to face the lieutenant, Jake ducked behind Herb. Ryals continued, "How would you like to meet the man who probably owns more slaves than anyone else in the country?"

"Who?" Richard's eagerness gave way to suspicion. "Why do you ask?"

"Right inside this very hotel you can meet General Wade Hampton, who owns thousands of slaves. But you should know that his grandpappy fought in our First War of Independence, and then again in the War of 1812. He fought for your right to stand here and spout whatever is on your mind."

Richard's face clouded and his eyes narrowed. Jake knew that look. His cousin was about to vent his wrath.

Ryals gestured to the growing mob of soldiers in the street and raised his voice. "How many of y'all have ever kidnapped a man? Hold your hand high for us to see." There were guffaws and a few obscene wisecracks, but no one raised a hand. "And how many of you men own at least one slave back home?"

Jake craned his neck to see the response. Of the fifty or sixty soldiers in the crowd, only eight hands went up.

The lieutenant spoke with exaggerated surprise. "Well, well, well. Do you see that, boy? It appears we are not an army of man-stealers after all. This brings to mind a saying you might do well to heed. Have you heard of Oliver Wendell Homes?"

With a condescending glance toward the men in gray, Richard shook his head. "No, sir."

"Well, Holmes wrote, 'The right to swing my fist ends where the other man's nose begins.' Do you see all these noses standing here in front of you?"

Richard sneered and remained silent.

"I dare say your fist has gotten about as close to those noses as any sane man would dare to go. Now, it is my job as Provost Marshal in this here army to make sure these men behave like gentlemen. Surely you would agree, there comes a time when in order to retain his honor, a gentleman must employ the manly arts in his defense."

Richard's eyes widened, but the fire in them remained.

The lieutenant brushed at some dust on Richard's sleeve. "I do hope you resolve to guard your tongue whilst we are guests in your town. It would be a shame if I have to look the other way while these gentlemen defend their honor."

"Yes. *Sir*." Richard looked like a branded bull, itching to be freed.

"Another thing Holmes said that you might do well to learn." Ryals put his face within inches of Richard's. "'The greatest act of faith is when a man understands he is not God.'"

Jake saw his cousin's fists clench, then slowly relax. Was that a thoughtful expression on his face?

Ryals stepped back and addressed the throng. "We'll only be here a couple more hours. I suggest y'all try to get some sleep whilst you can."

Some of the soldiers grumbled as if disappointed the show was over, but the men dispersed as ordered. Richard walked away, head held high. Jake noticed the disquiet in his cousin's eyes. Had someone finally managed to put Richard in his place?

Now that trouble was averted, exhaustion swept over Jake. Every muscle threatened mutiny. He nudged Herb. "Let's find a place to nap."

They went around the corner of the building and took the last two empty spots along the shady side of the hotel. Jake pulled the New Testament from his pocket and let it fall open to the photo of Eliza and Kathleen. His sleepy eyes pored over their faces, though memory had to fill in the details of Kathleen's out-of-focus features. Their smiles sent a wellspring of warmth and hope through his being. He turned thoughtfully to each of the pages that held the locks of hair, first Eliza's, then Kathleen's. The exhaustion that came with his first day of enlistment had displaced the conflict he felt over the two sisters, and for this, he felt a strangely disquieting wave of gratitude. He remembered with mild amusement that he had been glad to go off to war so he'd have time to figure things out. How foolish! He had had no idea how *hard* it could be to simply stay awake and keep moving.

Jake closed the book tenderly and returned it to its place in the pocket nearest his heart. But this time as he slipped into unconsciousness, he remembered which Bigler girl he had kissed in his dream the night before. And he wanted to kiss her again.

-6-

About an hour after the last of the Union Army headed north past Uncle George's farm, James Moran finally gave up the ghost. Relieved the cursed Yankee was finally dead, Eliza went upstairs. The last thing she wanted to do was help clean up after him. From her cousins' bedroom doorway, she overheard her aunt and uncle discuss burying the soldier at their church, Abbottstown's Lutheran. A small voice in Eliza's head urged her to go downstairs and reveal the man was Catholic, but she ignored the prompting. She moved to the hallway window and watched her mother help her aunt and uncle carry the dead man out to the wagon, then Uncle George set off for Abbottstown.

After a quick lunch, Eliza said good-bye to Aunt Linda Jane—and a silent "good riddance" to her little cousins—and set off with her mother for home. The ninety-minute walk turned out to be the best time they had spent together since leaving Virginia. Mama shared stories from her youth, and Eliza chattered about dreams of her future with Jake.

When they rounded the corner of Uncle Henry's house, they found Lydia with her hand on the pump handle. "Eliza, I'm so glad you're back!" She filled the water bucket with one more stroke. "We can use your help. We have a wounded Yankee inside."

Eliza responded with a look of abject disbelief. Somehow, she managed to stifle the scream welling up inside. Why must God torment her so? She trudged into the kitchen after her mother and cousin.

Leaning heavily on Uncle Henry's arm, a man in a blue uniform limped from the dining room. Lydia set the water bucket down and rushed to pull out a chair from the kitchen table. The soldier hobbled toward it and Uncle Henry helped him sit. Lydia turned over an empty bucket to put under the man's bandaged leg for support.

"Thank you, dear Lydia, you're very kind," the red-haired Yankee said. He flashed a buck-toothed smile around the room. "Everyone has been so kind."

Lydia blushed deeply. "I was the only one here yesterday when he crawled up onto the porch. Gave me quite a fright, he did."

The soldier's face filled with disappointment. "I'm sorry, Lydia. I'd have wanted to make your acquaintance under better circumstances."

Eliza groaned. Which was worse, a dying Yankee, or one all agog over her cousin? At least he didn't look to be in much physical pain. How long would she have to put up with this one?

As if reading her mind, Uncle Henry explained, "They're coming this afternoon to take Corporal Darcy to one of the hospitals in town."

Mama glanced out the window. "Is that them now?"

Eliza hurried to her mother's side. A buggy approached from the direction of town. Since there was no trailing cloud of dust, she presumed the driver was in no hurry.

Mama exclaimed, "Is that Kathleen?" She ran outside and waved at the buggy. "Kathleen, thank God you're safe!"

Eliza recognized the driver. Why was Mr. Becker bringing Kathleen home? She'd make it her business to find out. Aunt Ida and Uncle Henry joined the gathering on the porch as the buggy came to a halt.

Smiling brightly, Kathleen waited for Mr. Becker to lift her down, then she reached inside her frock, pulled out a shiny gold object, and rushed over to her mother. "Look what Papa Becker gave me!"

Eliza fumed inwardly, *Papa Becker? Where does Kathleen get the nerve to call him that? And why in the world would he give her a locket?*

Mama glared. "What did you say? Papa who?"

Her tone sent a shiver down Eliza's spine.

Oblivious to her mother's anger, Kathleen bubbled on. "Mr. Becker watched out for me during the battle. He was so kind, I asked him if I could call him Papa Becker, and he said he didn't mind. So after I made breakfast for him this morning—"

"You slept in his house?" Mama turned on Mr. Becker. "Who else was there? What of her reputation, sir?"

A stunned silence engulfed the scene. David looked too flabbergasted to speak.

Kathleen's eyes turned stormy. "I stayed with the Winebrenners last night—*Mother.* Why must you see evil in everything? When Mr. Becker looked out for me, it reminded me of how Papa took care of me during the battle back home, so that's why I asked if I could call him Papa Becker. If that offends you, just remember that *you're* the one who took me away from my Papa in the first place! We didn't *have* to leave home."

The shocking challenge left Mama speechless.

Suspicion wormed its way into Eliza's thoughts. Was her little sister trying to win over her beau's father? And steal her beau? Why else would Mr. Becker give her such an expensive-looking locket?

Mama's face reddened. "Please forgive me, Mr. Becker. I— Oh, dear Lord." Her eyes darted from Kathleen to Mr. Becker. "I am so very sorry."

"Apology accepted," he said brusquely. Then his face softened. "I have three daughters of my own. If I thought someone had compromised their reputations, I would have said far worse than you, madam."

Aunt Ida offered in a conciliatory tone, "We've all been through a lot these last two days."

Uncle Henry moved to his sister's side, shrugged his shoulders, and gave a look as if to say, *Women! What can you do?* "Why don't we all go inside? Ida can make us a pot of coffee."

"Thank you, but I must be going." Mr. Becker's voice grew somber. "I must give the Hoffackers news no parent should ever have to hear."

Kathleen brushed past her mother and threw her arms around Mr. Becker. "Thank you again for everything, Papa Becker. God bless you."

Eliza heard him whisper something in reply, but couldn't make out his words. A surge of jealousy coursed through her, but this time it was because she realized how much she missed her own Papa's affection. She had foolishly thought she had outgrown such a need. Now she ached for the safety of his loving embrace.

After giving Mr. Becker a kiss on the cheek, Kathleen turned and cast a wary glance at her mother. The locket sparkled in the sunlight.

Mama apparently found just the right words to ease the tension. "What a lovely locket, Kathleen. That was very nice of your Papa Becker to give it to you. Would you like to show it to us?"

Kathleen's face lit up, and she held out the locket for her mother to examine. Eliza moved to look over Mama's shoulder.

Mama reached out and cradled the locket in the palm of her hand. "May I open it?"

"Certainly. I haven't even looked—"

Inside was a tiny picture. It was Jake! Scowling, Eliza snapped, "What are you doing with a picture of my beau?"

Mr. Becker looked surprised. "There's a picture in there?" He took a step closer as Kathleen held it where they both could see. "Huh. That's Jake when he was nine years old." He looked up from the photo, his face filled with sadness. "This locket belonged to my daughter, Hope. She died when Jake was ten. I always wondered what happened to that picture."

Kathleen carefully slipped her fingernail into the locket, pried the photo loose, and handed it to Mr. Becker.

"Thank you, Kathleen." He studied the picture for a moment before speaking. "Do you have a locket, Eliza?"

"Yes, sir, I do."

He turned to her mother. "Perhaps you all might call on me sometime soon, and with your permission, Mrs. Bigler, Eliza could select a picture of Jake for her locket. I only have a few recent ones to choose from, but I believe he would be happy for her to have one."

Eliza couldn't wait for the day when she, too, could call this kind man Papa.

-7-

David flicked the reins and Streak set off at a trot. He waited until they were out of earshot before striking up a conversation with his horse. "Can you believe that woman? How did Kathleen ever grow into such a nice young lady with a mother like that?"

An even bigger question, what if Jake married Eliza? David knew all too well how tiresome a meddling mother-in-law could be. Though he had never wished ill upon Rose's mother, he was not a bit sad when Colleen O'Neill and her husband went west during the gold rush, never to return.

Streak slowed when they neared the intersection. David gave a tug on the reins and the horse turned onto Black Rock Road. Signs of the

Confederate Army's occupation scarred the land. Trampled fields and empty pastures lined the dung-covered road. Though no fighting had taken place on this side of town, ruined crops and stolen livestock would no doubt cause hard times for many of the farmers.

The buggy bounced over the ruts left by cannons and caissons. Jake's Colt revolver spilled from the box under the seat and bumped against David's foot. He reached down to pick up the gun, and all the fears came rushing back. Before meeting Kathleen for lunch, David had scoured the makeshift hospitals in town. No sign of Jake. What if he had died and someone had buried him yesterday? David might never know what had happened to his son. All he could do was pray and wait.

David had decided not to tell Kathleen about the revolver; he could worry enough for the both of them. He remembered one of Kathleen's comments in the root cellar during the bombardment, and a smile played across his face. When he had asked if she was worried, she flashed a crooked grin, and said, "Not really, but maybe I should be. Back home, our Pastor Cook says that worrying *must* work, because most of the things we worry about never happen!"

The buggy neared the intersection of the road from Fuhrman's Mill and David noted the telltale signs of a large army headed east toward Jefferson. So much for the hope the Confederates would retreat south. He continued out Black Rock Road. The surface was much smoother now, and the half-grown grain fields looked untouched. Unfortunately, the lush pastures were devoid of livestock.

The horrors of the devastation at Manassas flooded David's mind. And now similar scenes, right here in Hanover.

His anger flared. An accusatory voice in his head prompted, *So, are you just going to complain, or are you going to do something about it?*

-8-

Somewhere in the small town of Dover, a clock chimed the hour of eleven. Jake sat up and adjusted his hat. Though the week-long cloud cover remained, the diffused light seemed blinding after such a sound nap.

A pock-faced sergeant clapped his hands and walked down the line of dozing men. "Let's go, *ladies,* everybody on your feet."

Someone groaned, "Come on, Sarge, we need our beauty nap."

"There ain't enough naptime in the world to pretty up the likes of you, Jeffries." The sergeant kicked the complainer's foot. "Last man up gets to water my horse."

On the word "last," the man next to Jake scrambled to his feet. Jake and Herb hastened to do the same; even so, they were among the last men to stand.

The sergeant clapped the loser on the back. "You're it, Jeffries."

"Aw Sarge, that ain't fair."

"You're right, boy, you deserve more than that. Next time we stop, you can brush Margie as well as water her."

One of the men called out, "Hey, Margie's my girl. You keep your hands offa her," which set off a round of catcalls from the others.

Herb nudged Jake. "We better get back to General Stuart."

As Jake saddled Cat a young lieutenant strode up. "Are you Private Becker?"

"Yes, sir." Jake recognized Lieutenant Dabney from Stuart's staff. He looked even younger than Jake, though his broad forehead, rosy cheeks, and small mouth probably had a lot to do with that.

"General Stuart wants us to ride together so I can teach you what you need to know about being a courier."

"Thank you, sir." Jake wondered if Dabney's somber tone meant he viewed the assignment as a burden or if the young man just had a dour disposition. "I appreciate that, Lieutenant Dabney."

Dabney grinned. "Hey, not bad! How did you know my name?"

"I have a good memory for faces. Remember yesterday at the Shrivers when General Stuart introduced everyone in the parlor?"

"Hey, maybe you can teach me how you do that."

Jake put his knee to Cat's flank and pulled the girth strap tight. "Yes, sir." When he turned around, Dabney stood with his hand out.

"You can call me Chis, short for Chiswell."

They shook hands while Jake stifled the urge to smirk at the unusual name. "And I'm Jake."

"How old are you, Jake?"

"Eighteen. Until next month, anyway."

"Great! I'm glad I won't be the youngest any more. I turn nineteen on the 25th." Chis glanced over Jake's shoulder. "We better hurry."

The general's staff gathered on the street at the far end of the hotel. Jake and Chis mounted up and walked their horses over to join the group. Since Herb was deep in conversation with Captain Blackford, Jake decided to learn more about his new friend.

"So, where are you from, Chis?"

Pride filled Dabney's voice. "Campbell County, Virginia. My family has lived there for over two hundred years, ever since our Huguenot ancestors came over from France."

Stuart gave the signal and the army resumed its westward march toward Carlisle. Herb rode with Blackford, while Jake and Chis rode with the other couriers and aides-de-camp. The column of cavalry, four men per rank, came next. The wagon train would eventually bring up the rear.

They passed through the sleepy town of Wellsville and completed the several miles to Dillsburg with ease, especially compared with the previous night's arduous trek. Along the way, Jake told Chis all about Hanover and how it felt to see the war literally reach his own backyard. Chis explained that in the fall of '61 he had gone from being a freshman at the University of Virginia to being a courier for General Stuart. Jake was delighted to learn Chis had earned his promotion to lieutenant in only a few months' time, in spite of the fact that he had been furloughed home with typhoid fever when the promotion came through.

When Jake related his encounter with the Yankee deserter, Chis nodded excitedly. "A few weeks ago during the battle at Brandy Station, Major Von Brocke and I were riding down upon a pair of Union cavalrymen, firing our pistols all the while. We came upon a hill fronted by a ditch full of water, and my man's horse didn't make it the whole way across. The Yank crawled up the other bank and started fiddling with his carbine. Mind you, I had counted and knew my gun was empty—"

Jake winced, remembering the consequences when he had miscounted.

"—but I figured the Yankee don't know that. So I leveled my pistol and ordered him to drop his gun or I'd blow his head off. I made him wade on over so I could take him prisoner. Now the bullets were flying pretty thick, and the Yank said, 'Don't keep me here or I will be shot by my own men.' So I sent him running toward our rear like a scared deer, where I saw the provost guard collect him."

They passed into the shadow of a thick bank of clouds and the steady rhythm of the horses' hooves finally caught up with Jake. He shook his head to clear his bleary eyes. Now that the road grew steep, he dismounted and walked for a while to give Cat a break. Chis joined him. It was late in the afternoon by the time the weary men cleared the craggy precipice of South Mountain and descended into the Cumberland Valley.

Chis pulled out a picture of a lovely young lady with dark hair. "This is the woman I hope to marry someday, Lucy Fontaine. Her Pa's on General Stuart's medical staff."

Jake took out his picture of the Bigler girls. Chis seemed suitably impressed with both Eliza and Kathleen, though Jake figured his new friend was just being polite with his comments about Kathleen. After all, the fuzzy photo didn't begin to show the incredible beauty of her eyes, or the softness of her lips, or the playful way she smiled. His face flushed, remembering Kathleen's kiss good-bye. Then Eliza's image filled his mind—the passion in her kiss, the feel of her voluptuous body pressed against his.

"Do you want some of my water?" Chis held out his canteen. "You're sweating like a demon at the judgment. You sick? It ain't all that hot."

Jake blushed and pulled out his own canteen. "I'm fine, thanks."

A pair of Confederate cavalrymen galloped up the road from Carlisle. Jake couldn't hear their report, but he did hear General Stuart's order.

"Major McClellan, write a letter to General Smith ordering the surrender of Carlisle. Our requisition for food and supplies will follow." A few minutes later, the scouts took off back the way they had come, this time with a letter and a white flag.

Stuart issued more orders. McClellan copied the information down, then handed two pieces of paper to Lieutenant Hagan, the Chief of Couriers. Hagan bellowed, "Dabney! Becker!" Jake followed Chis to the front of the column. "Dabney, take these orders to General Hampton. Becker, these go to General Lee." Chis turned his roan and set off at a gallop. Jake and Cat followed hard on his heels.

Jake found Fitzhugh Lee at the head of the second brigade. Lee gave Jake a small nod of recognition and read the orders. "Thank you, Private. You may tell General Stuart we are on our way."

Jake rode to the small knoll where Stuart's staff had taken up position and delivered the message to McClellan. A few minutes later, Lee and his cavalry brigade trotted into view. Stuart waved his plumed hat and led a chorus of cheers to reinvigorate the exhausted troops. Six horse-drawn artillery pieces brought up the rear of the procession.

Lee's men quickly took position along the southeastern approach to Carlisle. The gun crews hurriedly prepared for action.

The scouts soon returned from town. Stuart did not look pleased at their report. "Major McClellan, a word with you."

After an animated discussion with Stuart, McClellan waved to Jake. "Becker. Deliver this new order to General Lee."

Lee read the order, his face impassive. He handed the paper to his adjutant and signaled the captain of the artillery battery.

Even though Jake knew it was coming, he still cringed at the din of the opening salvo. When the Yankee artillery responded in kind, the Confederate gunners whooped with joy and adjusted their fire to center on the new target. After three rounds, the big guns went silent. Pungent smoke drifted over the battery like ground fog on an autumn morning.

Jake followed the progress of the two scouts in the distance as they returned to Carlisle. Their white banner flapped in the breeze like a sheet on a laundry line. Lee's adjutant broke the reverie.

"Orderly! Take this to General Stuart."

By the time Jake delivered the message, Chis had returned from his mission. Jake motioned to Herb and Chis, and the trio dismounted to chat until the scouts arrived with the Union commander's response.

Upon hearing the reply, Stuart raged, "That man thinks his little band of militia can stand in our way? Then bomb the impudent fool! We must have those supplies. We *will* have those supplies."

Soon Jake was on his way back to Lee's command post with orders to burn the nearby lumberyard, the gas works, and the militia barracks. Three squads of cavalry trotted off, torches in hand, while all six cannons opened fire.

Darkness closed over Carlisle. Jake's eyes followed the glowing path of each shell as it screamed its way through the black sky. He prayed the Union leader would relent and surrender, before General Stuart turned several thousand hungry men loose on the town.

-9-

After the trauma of breaking the bad news of John's death to his family, David felt the need to spend some time close to Rose; so on the way back from the Hoffackers, he decided to stop at the cemetery. He tied Streak to a rail near the entrance, picked a bouquet of wild flowers from along the edge of the road, and headed for the family plot.

David laid half the flowers on Hope's grave, the other half on Rose's, then sat cross-legged facing the two headstones. No matter how many times he saw Hope's stone, his heart always ached to hold her in his arms one more time.

In loving memory of
Hope Daisy Becker
March 11, 1846—June 5, 1855
aged 9 years 2 mo. 25 d.
Now she plays in God's garden
And brings a smile to His face.
She has laid down earth's burdens
And lives in His marvelous Grace.

David's faith taught him that Hope was in a better place, and though he firmly believed that to be true, his heart often struggled to understand why God had called his precious little girl home while she was still so young. Two images warred in David's mind: Hope's mischievous smile while playing with her siblings—and the look of death in her sunken eyes moments before she passed. No amount of time would erase the feelings of helplessness and despair he had felt watching his little girl die.

When Rose died two weeks later, David felt like crawling into the grave with her, but he never dared show it. His children needed him, almost as much as he needed them. Though the path would be immeasurably harder, David vowed to finish the job he and Rose had started. Now that the children were adults, what was left for him to do?

For perhaps the thousandth time, David's eyes traced the words on Rose's headstone.

In loving memory of
Charity Rose Becker
Feb. 17, 1817—June 19, 1855
aged 38 years 4 mo. 2 d.
Her life was her family
Her home filled with love.
She is at rest now
In God's mansion above.

David stood and let his eyes wander among the neighboring family plots. Signs of the Confederate Army's occupation were everywhere. Heavy ruts showed where their artillery had unlimbered just west of the cemetery proper. Piles of horse dung littered the normally pristine pathways and refuse dotted the hillside. Frustration and anger coursed through David. Wasn't it enough to terrorize the living, must they also disturb the dead?

"Well, what do you think Rose? Americans shooting and killing other Americans. Is this what our fathers and grandfathers fought for? And now our son." His voice grew grim. "Is Jake with you, or is he still among the living? I don't even know." He nearly choked on the words.

David paced back and forth in front of the family plot. His place next to Rose was ready and waiting; there was room for five more. Would Jake be next? Or was he doomed to become one of those nameless and forsaken young men who wound up in an unmarked grave far from home? And what of David's future grandsons? How many of them would some day have to go off to war?

Helplessness and despair threatened to overwhelm him. He balled his fists in anger, refusing to give in. He was not helpless. Perhaps there was something he could do to help bring this madness to an end, to finish the work the founding fathers had started. With darkness fast approaching, David bowed his head and prayed. This time, for guidance.

-10-

Guided by the light of the buildings General Lee had ordered burnt, the bombing of Carlisle continued. A few townsfolk sought refuge among the attackers. While Jake nibbled on his last chunk of hardtack, a wrinkled woman with wispy white hair shared her story.

The Rebels Shelling the NY Militia in the Main Street of Carlisle

"Our place was ransacked by soldiers, but not you fellows. They were our own boys, and a lot of them were raised right around here. In fact, a hired man who used to live with us showed them through the premises! They broke open the desk, expecting to find money, I guess. Lucky that my husband hid it all away yesterday. They took all our food, killed all the chickens, and even took all our books. I asked them when they planned to do all that reading, and one of them laughed and said they were taking them for privy paper."

She leaned on her cane, turned her head, and spat a stream of tobacco juice on the ground. "Now if you fellows had done it, everybody would raise a fuss and say what barbarians you all are. But it was *our* men, yet their officers done nothing against it! One of our neighbors said some New Yorkers shot a steer and several hogs and just left them to rot. So I say, the sooner you boys can end this thing, the better I'll like it."

The bombardment finally ceased and Jake's ears throbbed in the sudden silence. It was almost midnight. Hoping to get some shut-eye while he could, Jake lay down between the mossy roots of an ancient maple tree, closed his eyes, and fell into a dreamless sleep.

-11-

David checked on Streak in the storage room, took inventory of the depleted food supplies in the root cellar, and then went to work on Myrtle's carriage. Shortly before midnight he finished the last of the benches. When the upholsterers finished covering them, he could mount the seats on the painted carriage frame and start the final trim work.

He shook his head sadly. Now that so much had changed, they should probably reschedule the wedding. He closed up the shop and trudged to the house.

The mantel clock struck midnight as David entered the parlor. He strode to the desk, settled in the sturdy oak chair, and rolled open the desktop. After pulling paper, ink, and pen from their nooks, he took a moment to pray for his family and the course he was about to take. Strengthened, he uncapped the ink, dipped the pen, and began to write.

My dearest daughters . . .

Thursday, July 2, 1863

The sudden cannon blast rattled the maple tree and shook Jake awake. A second cannon fired, then another, and another. Jake groaned, stretched, and sat up.

Herb's wry grin flickered in the cannon fire. "It's just past midnight. Time to rise and shine!"

With every muscle screaming for mercy, Jake climbed to his feet. "There, I'm up. But you'll have to shine for the both of us." He rolled his head to chase the cricks from his neck and caught a faint whiff of coffee mingled with the cannons' sulphurous stench. Who was making coffee under these conditions?

Fifteen feet away, several men gathered around a low fire. Major McClellan held a guitar by the neck, while next to him a colored man tuned a left-handed violin. The scene reminded him of the story of Nero fiddling while Rome burned. His eyes continued to scan for coffee. Sure enough, there it was! A large tin coffee pot sat on a rock at the edge of the flames.

Jake elbowed Herb. "Come on, grab your cup and—"

Herb held up two empty cups. "Ready when you are."

"Charge!" Despite his aching muscles, Jake won the sprint to the coffee pot, but only because he caught Herb unaware. He picked up the pot and filled the cups in Herb's outstretched hands.

Though a little bitter for Jake's taste, the heavenly brew did wonders for his spirit. He finally felt human enough for conversation.

The man to his right, Quartermaster Norman FitzHugh, entertained Chis with another story. "True enough, young man. I spent twenty years out west, a lot of that time as adopted son to a Sioux Indian chief. And Frank Robertson over there is a di-rect de-scen-dant from none other than Pocahontas herself."

"Golly," Chis said, starry-eyed.

Finished tuning, the fiddle player launched into a chorus of "Turkey in the Straw." McClellan picked up the guitar and joined in. Though the blasting cannons often obliterated the music, the barrage did nothing to dampen the men's spirits. While dozens of soldiers danced and hooted, others stomped their feet and clapped their hands. The musicians picked up the tempo with each new chorus. Even the most exhausted man had a smile on his face.

About a half-hour into the revelry, a rider trotted in out of the darkness. General Stuart rushed to greet him. "Major Venable! Have you found General Lee?"

Venable reached into his jacket, pulled out a letter, and handed it to Stuart. "Yes, sir, (cannon blast) you to join him in Gettys— (cannon blast) possible, and for your troops to follow with all (cannon blast)."

Jake read the obvious relief on the general's face. Stuart shouted for McClellan to stop the bombardment. Then, deep in discussion, the two men moved out of earshot. As the nearest crew limbered their cannon, Jake overheard one man mutter, "Well, that turned out to be a waste of 134 shells."

Another man responded, "Not a total waste. At least we found out those new fuses burn too long. I'd hate to think how we'd have fared if we were in a real battle and didn't know that."

A surly sergeant put an end to the carping. "Hurry up and get those pieces limbered, or you can find somewhere else to make your eleven dollars a month."

Jake started. He hadn't even thought about getting paid for his service, not that thirty-five cents a day was a huge windfall. He quickly did some more arithmetic in his head. After what he'd paid for his equipment, he'd break even in six months.

"Private Becker!" McClellan stood near the dying fire with his hands still cupped around his mouth.

"Here, sir!" Jake stepped from the shadows.

"Come with me." The major led the way to General Stuart, who sat astride his mare, Virginia. They both looked eager to be on their way.

"Private Becker, do you know the roads from here to Gettysburg?"

Was he going to get to ride through the night with General Jeb Stuart? Jake's heart raced. "Yes, sir, I do. Much of the way is just like going to Hanover."

"Good. I want you to go with Major McClellan here, who will carry my orders to General Hampton. He's at the rear of the column with that infernal wagon train, probably around Dillsburg. You will accompany General Hampton and his men and guide them to Gettysburg." Stuart leaned closer and winked. "If you get them there by noon, I'll put you in for a commission."

And with that, Stuart waved a hand and his staff followed him toward the road to Gettysburg. Herb shouted as he passed, "See you in Gettysburg, Jake!"

Jake nodded dumbly. General Stuart's last word rang in his ears. Commission? Jake ran for Cat, but tripped twice along the way. The second fall ended in a forward roll. In the process, he bumped his chin on his knee and sent a bolt of pain through his bruised jaw. Had it really been less than three days since that encounter with the Yankee deserter?

Thick clouds diffused the glow of the full moon, but there was still enough light for Jake and McClellan to make good time in finding Hampton. It took them only two hours to traverse the eleven miles to Dillsburg.

Rousted at three in the morning, the teamsters brayed even louder than their mules. Could the wagons cover the twenty-three miles to Gettysburg in less than nine hours? At least the Harrisburg-Gettysburg Road had a macadam surface. The hard-packed gravel would surely ease the strain on the exhausted animals and drivers. Jake figured the chances were good the column could meet General Stuart's challenge— unless someone or something got in the way.

-2-

Unable to sleep, David rose and turned off the chimes on the mantel clock. While he was up, he decided to amend the letter to his daughters. He rewrote the epistle, this time leaving out the part about finding Jake's gun and the probability of his presence during the battle on the Forney farm. No use causing the girls greater anxiety.

He blotted the pen and returned it to its stand. After blowing the last lines dry, he picked up the paper and held it out to where his eyes could focus.

> *My dearest daughters, Faith, Grace, and Myrtle,*
>
> *It is with a heavy heart that I pick up my pen to write to you. Things have changed mightily since you left. A couple hundred Confederate cavalrymen spent some time here on 27th June. However, it was on 30th June that Hanover lost her innocence. Several thousand Federal troops passed through town that morning, only to be attacked by Confederate cavalry and artillery.*
>
> *Do not fear. Our home is safe and I am well.*
>
> *You must pray for John Hoffacker's family. Poor John met a most terrible end in front of our house early in the battle.*
>
> *A shell struck the Winebrenners' house. God be praised, no one was hurt. Sarah and Martha left the balcony moments before the missile arrived.*
>
> *The Confederates took positions on the ridge south of town, leaving quite a mess around the cemetery near your beloved mother and sister. Both armies left the next day. Many dead soldiers and horses needed tending, along with several dozen wounded men from both armies.*
>
> *Now I must give you news you will no doubt find most distressing. Our beloved Jacob has found it to be his duty to volunteer his service for the cause of the Confederacy. It is his strong belief they are fighting a true war of independence, brought on by our Federal government. You know our dear Jake, and I know he will be the subject of your constant prayers.*

*Now it grieves me to cause you yet another worry. As you
know, your grandfather and great-grandfather both fought to
gain our country's freedom. With each passing day, the
presence of Confederate troops on Union soil increases the
chance that Northern hearts will fail and our people will call
on President Lincoln to end the war. If the South stands as a
separate country, I fear the day will come when your sons and
their sons and their sons will have to fight in a never ending
series of wars. I must do all in my power to see that that day
never comes. Only God and country may cast a higher calling
than family. I believe both now require my service. Thus, I
leave today to offer my aid in the effort to restore the Union.*

*I hope to be granted a 90-day enlistment. God willing, I
hope that will be sufficient time to accomplish the expulsion of
the Confederate armies from Pennsylvania. I promise to
return home to you at the earliest opportunity.*

*I thank you for the prayers I know you will send
Heavenward on behalf of Jake and me.*

With much love and many prayers,
Papa

David set the letter on the desk and bowed his head again in prayer.

Was that music he heard? It sounded like a great host of men singing "We Will Meet You in the Promised Land." David rolled the desktop down, grabbed his hat, and ran out into the street.

Cavalrymen filled the torch-lit Square. Was another battle about to begin? David hurried to find out.

In spite of the late night hour, townsfolk once again served up food and drink, this time from York Street into the center of town and out Carlisle Street. From what David could gather, a few thousand Union cavalrymen were on their way to join the battle that had broken out in Gettysburg yesterday.

Never one to ignore Providence, David ran home and gathered together his rifle and ammo. He threw his extra pair of socks into a rucksack and raided the root cellar for enough dried food to fill out the pack.

Hands trembling with a mixture of excitement and anxiety, David took the letter from the desk, put it in an envelope, and carried it next door. Fortunately, Henry had already been awakened by the commotion in the Square.

Henry took one look at the letter in David's hand and frowned. "Does this mean what I think it means?"

"You know me too well, old friend. Will you—" The lump in David's throat kept him from finishing.

"Certainly. I'll get this to Sam Forney first thing in the morning. You can count on him to take this to your family as soon as possible."

By the time David and Streak cantered into the Square, the head of the Union column was again on the move. David rode up to the first officer he saw and explained his purpose.

The soldier looked David over and nodded slowly. "Well, whaddaya know. Come with me. I think the general ought to meet you."

As dawn broke about an hour later, they caught up with General David Gregg at the head of the column in McSherryville. The corners of Gregg's baggy eyes crinkled as he smiled at his new volunteer. "We can always use another brave soldier." He motioned to a nearby captain. "Since this is a local man, take him to Colonel McIntosh. He can fight with the 3rd Pennsylvania boys."

In short order, David met the colonel and received a hearty handshake; then he was taken to his new commander, Captain William Miller of Company H. "Glad to have you in my squadron, Becker. Cinch your belt tight. I think we may be in for quite a ride. There's Rebels ahead."

David took a deep breath and joined the file of cavalry on the road west to Gettysburg. He hoped Jake was well on his way east with General Stuart's troops. And for the first time in David's life, he prayed his son would keep his distance.

-3-

Eliza crowded into the buggy with Kathleen and Mama. Mama snapped the whip over the horse's head, and the buggy set off for town.

Each clip-clop of the horse's hooves and every turn of the iron-rimmed wheels brought Eliza closer to her beau's home. Her heart thumped in anticipation of calling on Mr. Becker and picking out a picture of Jake for her locket. Mama had apparently felt so guilty about insulting Mr. Becker yesterday, she quickly consented when Eliza suggested the idea of the visit.

But Mr. Becker was not at home. Nor was he in the carriage shop. Kathleen raised an eyebrow quizzically. "Maybe he's at the Concert Hall helping with the wounded. Remember Isaac Peale? You know, the man I told you we tended during the battle."

Eliza rolled her eyes. Leave it to Kathleen to get to help a brave hero from Carolina while she got stuck with a loathsome Yankee.

Kathleen motioned toward the center of town. "Mama, would you and Eliza like to come with me to the Concert Hall? I know the wounded men would be glad of the company."

Just the thought of a room full of injured men turned Eliza's stomach, but before she could object, Mama agreed. They crowded back into the buggy and set off on the short jaunt to the Square.

Dr. Hinkle was just finishing a cigar as Mama tied the reins to the hitching post in front of the Concert Hall. His eyes lit up. "Kathleen, so good of you to come again. And you brought more helpers, bless you." He cast an admiring look Eliza's way.

Eliza wasn't sure she liked how the doctor eyed her figure. She had always enjoyed such harmless flirtations in the past, but now that she was "spoken for," she should probably learn to discourage such attention.

"How is Sergeant Trowbridge today?" Kathleen asked, starting up the steps to the makeshift hospital.

The doctor flicked the cigar stub away. "He is coming along splendidly! The area around the amputation is already showing laudable pus. Would you like to learn how to help him keep his muscles from withering while he . . ." The doctor and Kathleen disappeared inside the building.

From a second story window, a barely human voice whimpered, "Oh, Lord, let me die."

Her skin crawling, Eliza climbed back into the buggy. "When should I come back to pick you up?"

Mama was not amused. "Eliza, think of those poor Virginians in there, so far from home, suffering for our freedom. Surely you can—"

"Mother, I just don't have the stomach for it! You know that."

"Well, you better grow one, then," Mama said coldly. "And there's no better time than this."

Eliza stomped her foot on the floor of the buggy. "Mama . . ."

"And stop that infernal whining, your Papa isn't here to spoil you. After two years away from home, I'd have thought you'd have learned that by now."

Eliza opened her mouth to protest, but her mother had more to say.

"If you want me to give permission for Jake Becker to call on you someday, then you better do some growing up. Though that boy is besotted with you now, I can assure you he isn't likely to cater to your whims once you marry. No man—"

A flurry of shouts erupted in the Square behind them.

"Halt!"

"Get back here, Cowell!"

"Stop or I'll shoot!"

Eliza gasped with horror as three Union soldiers leveled their rifles at a disheveled man in blue, who sprinted from the direction of the Market Shed. A single shot rang out, sounding like several as the report echoed around the Square. The fleeing man screamed and collapsed like a deer brought down in mid-leap. He writhed in the dirt and clutched his right thigh. Blood flowed through his grimy fingers.

A whiff of sulphur burned Eliza's nose. She turned and stared in disbelief at the shooter. A fading cloud of white smoke floated above the steely-eyed rifleman.

"Dear Lord!" Mama shrieked. "Haven't y'all had enough of killing? Must you hunt down your own?"

A Yankee with a silver bar on his collar glared at Mama. "You would do well to mind your own business, madam. He's a deserter."

Mama glared at the officer, then started for the whimpering soldier in the dirt. "May the Lord—"

"I said, mind your own business, madam!" The Yankee reached for Mama's arm to restrain her. She raised her hand to fend him off. Eliza bolted from the buggy and pounded her fists on the impudent man's back.

"What's going on here, Lieutenant?" A doctor in a bloodied apron stood in the doorway of the Concert Hall. Eliza stopped her pummeling and the officer stepped away from Mama.

"Just taking care of a deserter, Dr. Gardner." The officer pointed to the prostrate man.

"Well, get him in here," the doctor said. "I'll—"

"Too late for that," the shooter announced, kneeling at the deserter's side. He closed the dead man's eyes and gestured for a buddy to come help remove the body.

Dr. Gardner shook his head, muttered something under his breath, and went back inside.

The officer looked askance at Eliza and Mama. "You *ladies* don't sound like you're from around here."

"We are from Virginia," Eliza said haughtily. "And you men would do well to mind your manners, before Bobby Lee and Jeb Stuart's men catch up with you."

The soldier chuckled. "It'll be a cold day in, well, a cold day before that happens, missy. There's a hundred thousand men hunting those rascals down right now. Johnny Reb will be hightailing it back to Virginia any day now, you wait and see."

Kathleen's voice called from an upper floor window of the hospital. "Mama, news of Mr. Becker!"

Eliza shielded her eyes and looked up at her sister. "Is he here?"

"No." Kathleen looked on the verge of tears. "Mrs. Winebrenner told me that last night he went and joined the Union Army!"

The Union Army? The thought of her beau's father as an enemy of the Confederacy sent Eliza reeling. *How could he?* Her imagination ran amok, picturing Jake and his father on the same battlefield in armed combat—*and* on opposite sides. "No! It can't be!" She wanted to scream. It had to be a nightmare. *My future father-in-law is a Yankee soldier?*

-4-

General Gregg's column of 2,600 cavalrymen came to a halt in the shade of Geiselman's Woods, several miles east of Gettysburg. Word came down the line that the general and his staff had gone on ahead while Colonel McIntosh, who had suddenly taken ill, received treatment from Surgeon Tate in the Geiselman farmhouse.

Captain Miller turned his horse about and shouted, "Dismount! We'll have a short rest."

Bleary-eyed troopers sprawled in the shade at the edge of the road. David followed the example of the other cavalrymen and tied Streak's reins around his wrist before lying down in the weeds to nap.

Finding himself too restless to doze, David fished the watch from his pocket. It was ten after eight in the morning. The only time he had gone longer without sleep was the night Rose died. He tucked the painful memory away, right alongside his fears for Jake. Instead of fretting, he turned to memories of playing hide-and-go-seek with his granddaughters. The joyful images soothed him into a state of half-sleep.

About an hour later, a young lieutenant worked his way down the line. "Mount up, you slackers! This ain't a picnic."

David slowly stood, rolled his neck to chase away the cricks, then swung up into the saddle. His sleep-starved brain felt like it was stuffed with cotton. Both ears throbbed in rhythm with each heartbeat.

The column rode quietly through the hamlet of Bonaughtown. Leery villagers peeked through shuttered windows. The soldiers' dust-covered uniforms now looked more like Confederate gray than Union blue. About a mile past Bonaughtown, the column slowed at the marshy brook known as White Run. The men of Pennsylvania 3rd Cavalry, Company H, took turns watering their horses and refilling canteens.

Since Jake had taken their only canteen, David had planned to get by with a bottle, but in the rush to leave he had forgotten to get one out of the root cellar. So he rode Streak upstream, past the flotsam from the recent rains, in search of unsullied water to guzzle.

The cool water soothed David's dusty throat. He cupped his hands and splashed his face. Wetting the back of his neck, he stood and sighed with delight as the water dribbled down his chest and back. Thirst slaked and mind refreshed, David walked Streak back onto the road.

Once the Company reassembled, Captain Miller announced, "We're deploying straight ahead." He led his men over a moderate rise to the intersection with a rutted country lane, Low Dutch Road.

Colonel McIntosh met them at the crossroads and waved the troops off to the right. "You men go into this clover field. We are to wait here in reserve."

A smattering of gunshots could be heard from over the next rise. "Skirmishers," someone muttered.

In spite of the ever-present gray clouds, the air felt thick and hot. Streak nickered softly as if relieved to walk in the lush, green clover. David found a good spot to dismount and tied the reins around his wrist. He couldn't wait to take a long nap.

Unfortunately, Captain Miller had other plans. "Becker, this is Sergeant Fosnaugh, our quartermaster. He'll see you have everything you need." The introduction complete, the captain left to see to other matters.

Fosnaugh gave David a firm handshake. "Glad to have you with us, Becker. The supply wagon ought to catch up with us in a little while. In the meantime, let's figure out what you'll be needing." He leaned toward Streak's saddle and examined David's rifle. "With that long of a barrel, that must be an old smoothbore, 1842 model."

David nodded, impressed. "Yes it is, but I had the barrel rifled a few years back."

"I can fix you up with a Sharps carbine if you like. You're sure to want a breechloader on horseback. Besides, unless you brought a lot of ammo with you, you'll have to get used to one sooner or later any way."

Too tired to care, David agreed.

"How about a sabre and pistol?"

David flinched at that last word. Somehow, he felt guilty using Jake's revolver. "Um, I have a loaded .44 Colt. No extra cylinders or ammo, though. And I've never held a sabre."

"I'll get you one. The Johnnies seem to prefer pistols in close, so you probably don't need much experience with a blade. All you really need to know is that the pointy end goes into the other feller." Fosnaugh laughed as if no one else had ever thought of the joke. "No need to kill 'em, just slash and parry, slash and parry. Besides, a wounded man puts more of a strain on their resources than a dead one."

David stifled a yawn with the back of his hand. "I see."

"Just let me point out our blacksmith, Steve Hepfor," Fosnaugh indicated a short, ruddy-faced man, playing cards several yards away. "Oh, and here comes our saddler, Bill Over." The men exchanged nods.

Fosnaugh chuckled as David yawned loudly. "You're right, Becker. We'd better get us some shut-eye whilst we can."

Since the other men left their horses saddled, David did likewise. He curled up in Streak's shadow and cradled his head on his arm. Moments later, horse and rider slept soundly.

-5-

After passing through Hunterstown and enjoying the hospitality of the many townsfolk who handed out food and drink, General Hampton halted his men on the Harrisburg Pike a few miles northeast of Gettysburg. Those fortunate enough to be near the head of the line were granted permission to dismount and seek respite from the noontime heat.

Jake walked Cat underneath a towering elm tree, dismounted, tied the reins around his wrist, and stretched out in the cool shade. Cat munched on the wild grass while he tried to doze. At the sound of approaching horses, Jake lifted his head and trained his groggy eyes on two gray-clad riders, who joined General Hampton a few yards away.

A pimply-faced orderly held out a piece of paper. "Orders from General Stuart, sir."

Hampton read the message and sighed. "No rest for the weary, gentlemen. We are to proceed to the York Pike and deploy along General Ewell's left flank. It seems we are heading into a major engagement. At least we are finally to be rid of that blasted wagon train. They are to proceed directly ahead."

The orders were repeated down the line. The bugler blew "To Horse," and the troopers groaned in unison.

"You're a good girl, Cat," Jake said, as he remounted. He leaned over to pat the mare's neck and spotted a gray squirrel scampering across the road. The furry creature paused, twitched its bushy tail, then scrambled up an oak tree. Jake smiled, remembering the last time he had seen such a sight. A few weeks earlier, Kathleen had kept him company on the Wertzes' porch while he waited for Eliza to come out. They saw a squirrel bound across the yard, scurry up an old maple, and bounce from branch to branch as if enjoying the time of his life. Kathleen's wistful, "I want to be a squirrel," perfectly summed up her playful, adventurous spirit.

Other memories of Kathleen filled his mind. The word games they used to play . . . the way her eyes lit with glee whenever she pulled a prank on him . . . the look on her face after she had kissed him . . . and he'd never forget the way his entire body tingled as she rested her head against his chest.

Overwhelmed with yearning to see Kathleen again, Jake considered turning east once the column reached the York Pike. He knew a shortcut across Low Dutch Road that would get him to the Hanover Road in no time, and from there . . . he would be a deserter. Jake dismissed the cowardly idea from his mind.

More riders approached from the south. Jake recognized them as one of the bands of scouts General Hampton had sent out earlier.

A dark-haired man with a long drooping moustache spoke from beneath his dusty slouch hat. "Sir, a heavy force of Union cavalry is advancing from the southeast toward Hunterstown. If left unchecked, they will be able to get to our rear."

Hampton rose up in the stirrups and called, "Private Becker!"

Jake flicked Cat's reins and moved out of line. "Here, sir!"

"What is the fastest route to Hunterstown from here?"

"Back up the road, sir, there's a turn-off near where we last stopped. The town is a few miles east of there."

Hampton nodded curtly. "So be it. Captain Barker, order the countermarch. We are off to Hunterstown. Private Becker, ride with me."

Jake joined Hampton and his staff as they cantered past the weary troops. The riders made it to the outskirts of Hunterstown in half an hour. Jake nudged Cat's flanks and they pulled even with General Hampton and his mount.

"Sir, that road to the right is another route to Gettysburg."

"Very good. Thank you, Private." Hampton raised his hand and the group halted. "Lieutenant Kelly, wait here and direct the column to follow in this direction. As for the rest, let us see how large a force the Yanks are sending our way."

The route south to Gettysburg crossed a low hill and wound past two farms in the dale on the other side. The impromptu scouting party crested the next hill and trotted along the quiet lane for another quick mile. Jake called to Hampton, "The York Pike is only a few miles away."

Hampton raised a hand and his men reined to a halt around him. "Let's take a short rest. We must be nearing Ewell's pickets by now."

Jake slid from the saddle. Limping from the cramps in his thighs, he led Cat to a shady patch of grass. His eyes were closed before he reached the ground.

Moments later, a gun fired in the distance and a Minie ball whistled overhead. Jake rolled onto his stomach. Were there more shots to come? He watched in awe as General Hampton galloped toward a thicket a few hundred yards away, where a blue-uniformed soldier, seated atop the trunk of a fallen tree, hurriedly reloaded his carbine.

Hampton stopped at a distance of a hundred yards, turned his horse to the side, raised his pistol at arm's length, and took aim. The Yankee lifted the carbine to his shoulder. The weapons fired at the same instant. Splinters flew from the trunk by the Yankee's feet. The carbine shot missed its mark. Hampton thumbed back the hammer of his revolver for another shot. The Union man raised one hand, waved it back and forth over his head, and then pointed to his carbine. Hampton nodded and lowered his weapon.

Jake's jaw dropped. The Yankee soldier sat on the trunk and went to work cleaning his rifle—while General Hampton waited! Why did the general's staff seem unconcerned? Jake couldn't bear it. "Shouldn't we ride out and help?"

Wade Hampton, Jr. snorted. "Not as long as the fight is one-on-one. Pa, uh, the general will take him down. You wait and see."

Finished with his cleaning job, the man in blue climbed back into position and the long-range duel resumed. This time the rifleman's aim was better; his bullet nicked a piece off Hampton's uniform.

As the adversaries took aim for the third round, a Yankee cavalryman burst from cover off to the side of the action. Apparently, Hampton didn't see the new threat.

Jake rose up on one knee, cupped his hands, and yelled to his commander. The warning was lost in the ensuing gunfire. Jake felt so helpless, but with two hundred yards separating them and his rifle not at hand, there was little he could do but watch.

The reports echoed from the hillside, the puffs of smoke cleared, and the onlookers saw the Union rifleman clutch his bloodied wrist and retreat into the bushes. A moment later, the charging Yankee cavalryman blindsided Hampton with his sabre. Jake cringed as the shiny blade arced toward the unsuspecting general.

The sabre ripped through Hampton's hat and glanced off the back of his head. A mist of blood flew from his scalp. He reined his horse around, raised his revolver, and fired.

Jake braced in anticipation of the death of the Yankee assailant. But nothing happened. Was Hampton out of ammo or was it a misfire?

The man in blue spurred his horse and took off for the thicket. Hampton charged in pursuit. His arm moved as if firing the revolver, but no sound followed. The fleeing Yankee jumped his horse over the downed tree and vanished into the underbrush. Hampton broke off the attack. Apparently just becoming aware the back of his head was bleeding, the general turned his mount and galloped to rejoin his staff.

The brigade surgeon, Dr. Benjamin Taylor, helped Hampton from the saddle. "Let me tend to that wound, sir."

Hampton's eyes burned with fury. "Did you see what that dastardly coward did? May he rot in hell!" Blood flowed steadily down the left side of his neck.

Dr. Taylor reached for the general's hat. "Please, sir. I must—"

"Yes, yes, yes. I know." Hampton eased to the ground and charily lifted the ruined hat from his head. The back brim was sliced clean away, along with a small patch of his thick, wavy hair. An ugly, four-inch cut ran along the back of his skull.

The doctor opened his bag and pulled out a clean strip of cloth and a jar of lint. He cleaned the wound, packed it with lint, and stepped back as if to admire his work.

"Here, now, what is this?" Dr. Taylor leaned down and inspected Hampton's chest. A small splotch of blood marked the area just above the heart. "You better let me have a look at that, sir."

Without waiting for a reply, the medic unbuttoned Hampton's shirt and revealed a shallow chest wound. "You were blessed, sir. A glancing blow off the breastbone. Another quarter of an inch . . ." he said ominously. He dressed the wound and rebuttoned the commander's shirt.

Hampton took a long, slow breath, then let it out. "That feels much better. Thank you, doctor. Now, if you'll just give me something for a headache, we'd best get back to the rest of the column. No telling how many more Yanks are out there."

In the distance behind them, the cannons at Gettysburg rumbled like a brewing thunderhead.

-6-

David awoke to find Sergeant Fosnaugh's face six inches from his.

"Sorry, Becker, didn't mean to startle you."

As Fosnaugh stood, David groaned and sat up. He'd gotten just enough sleep to know he needed a whole lot more. "What time is it?"

"Around two."

Fosnaugh handed David a blue flannel blouse to put on. "Sorry that it's been, um, *used* as you might say. But it ain't got no holes or stains, and we don't have a lot of shirts as tall as you." He handed David a dark blue kepi cap.

David eyed the cap suspiciously. No signs of previous use. He snugged it over the crown of his head and it fit tolerably well.

"And here's a Sharps for you. Ever use one before?"

"No, sir." The carbine, about the weight of a gallon bucket of water, felt lighter than his rifle. The weapon's shorter barrel was a little over three feet long. Fosnaugh showed David how to load the paper cartridge containing ball and powder into the breech. When the action snapped shut, the "falling block" clipped the paper from the rear of the cartridge. A brass percussion cap furnished the spark to ignite the powder.

David dry-fired a few rounds and grinned broadly. "Not bad, not bad at all."

"Here's a cartridge box you can wear on your belt. You've got forty rounds, that's your daily ration. Course, you kill forty Rebs, we'll be glad to give you more."

While the sergeant unsheathed a sabre, David fastened the cartridge box to the right side of his belt.

"Now this here blade's been sharpened, so be careful where you end your swing," Fosnaugh said. "You don't want to cut your own leg."

"You mean some sabres aren't sharpened?"

"Used to be none of them were, just the tips. Regular cavalry were trained to use sabres to knock the other man off his horse, but last year a Georgia outfit told the 7th Pennsylvania that they had sharpened their blades, 'to show Federal cavalry what sabres were intended for.' Now most of us sharpen our blades. Makes for a nasty business, it does."

David took hold of the sabre. Twisted wire bound the black leather cover on the handle. The brass handguard felt cool against his flesh.

Fosnaugh showed David how to wrap the leather loop around his wrist to prevent dropping the weapon if he lost his grip.

After a brief lesson in sabre wielding, the sergeant helped David mount the scabbard on his left side. "You need to reach across your body to draw the blade. Now come look at the McClellan I put on your horse."

The McClellan saddle looked like the drawings David had once seen of a medieval torture device. And his body already ached from several hours of riding. He didn't look forward to sitting atop this saddle with its metal-reinforced wooden tree. Thankfully, his bottom had gained a few extra pounds of cushion in recent years.

Fosnaugh pointed to one of the small saddlebags. "You'll find a curry comb, picket pin, and nose bag in there. There's a housewife in the bag on the other side."

David shook his head. "A what?"

"A 'housewife' is a sewing kit. And that," Fosnaugh pointed to the black leather rigging on the saddle, "is the boot for your carbine." He reached into the pouch on his belt, pulled out a manual, and handed it to David. "Read through this as quick as you can, then study it."

David only read the top line of the long title, *Cavalry Tactics*. He flipped through the book's two hundred-odd pages, then turned back to the page with an illustration of a sabre held curved side up. The manual went into great detail about how to execute the *Moulinet*.

"I wouldn't worry too much about all that right now," Fosnaugh said. "The lessons starting on page seventy-three are a good place to begin. In the meantime, just be quick about imitating whatever the men next to you do."

David wondered if he was getting in over his head, especially since the "men next to you" all looked to be half his age, yet infinitely more experienced.

"Oh, and I guess we better get you sworn in," Fosnaugh said. "Raise your right hand and repeat after me."

David gulped and did as instructed.

"I, state your na—"

A volley of rifle shots erupted from the ridge off to the west, followed by a barrage of cannon fire. The sergeant abruptly lowered his hand. "I guess we'll have plenty of time for that later. Better start getting used to your new gear. I don't think we're going to be in reserve much longer."

-7-

Jake and the younger Hampton rode ahead of the general's staff to report the encounter with the Yankees. They spotted the oncoming Confederate column about a mile west of Hunterstown. Wade spurred his horse and galloped ahead, leaving Jake and Cat in a wake of dust. Cat needed no encouragement to catch up. She snorted, tossed her head, and broke into a gallop. Her hooves seemed to skim the ground as she quickly overtook the young lieutenant. Cat could have easily won the race, but Jake reined her in, thinking it was unwise to show up the general's son in such a way. Cat shook her head, chafing at the restraint. Jake scratched her neck, leaned over, and spoke in her ear. "Sorry, Cat. Another day, girl."

Wade delivered the message to Colonel Baker, a thirtyish man with mournful eyes and a prodigious moustache-beard combination that covered the bottom third of his face. Baker grew animated at the news of an encounter with the Yankees. "Very good." His Carolina drawl rose with excitement. "We can use some action after all this riding about." He turned in the saddle and shouted, "Forward, double-quick!"

Jake and Wade merged with the rest of Baker's staff. As the column approached the turn-off toward Gettysburg, Lieutenant Kelly stepped into the middle of the road and held up both hands. The dust-covered lieutenant looked up from beneath his low-pulled brim. "Colonel, a squad from Cobb's Legion is on patrol east of Hunterstown. They have been informed of your orders to join General Hampton. The General awaits your arrival at the top of the hill a mile out that way." He lifted his arm and pointed down the southbound road.

The Tate Farm Road, pen and ink, Lewis Francisco, artist

"Thank you, Lieutenant." The men exchanged salutes, and the column turned onto the Hunterstown-Gettysburg Road.

Jake paused at the corner and looked down the main street of Hunterstown. Last year he and Pa had spent the night at the Grass Hotel on their way back from a carriage delivery outside Mummasburg. When Pa left the dining room to use the privy, the doe-eyed serving girl flirted openly with Jake, causing him no end of embarrassment. Later, when the buxom redhead served his food, she leaned over his shoulder and whispered, "Come up to my room in the garret later. I'll introduce you to my *friends*." She pressed her ample assets into his back and rubbed against him, leaving no doubt as to the identity of her "friends."

He hadn't gone, of course. Not only was he in love with Eliza, it would have involved making up a lie in order to leave the room, and he'd never lie to his father. Nevertheless, he remembered having a very difficult time falling asleep that night.

Jake's thoughts turned to Eliza. What was she doing? Did she miss him? His body stirred with memories of their kiss on the porch and the way her tongue had touched his. And those amazing brown eyes! How he longed to get lost in them again, to take her hand in his and—

Colonel Baker raised his hand and the column slowed to a walk. "Lieutenant Hampton, you and your partner may ride ahead and inform the general we are near."

The Felty Farm, oil on canvas, Edwin L. Green, artist

Jake glanced nervously at the top of the wooded hill a half-mile distant. If General Hampton were there, the approaching column would already be in plain sight. Was this the colonel's way of making sure there was no Yankee ambush lying in wait behind the trees?

Wade spurred his horse and galloped off. Once again, Cat was more than up to the chase. This time Jake gave her free rein, and she easily overtook Hampton, Jr. But then it occurred to Jake that Cat was not *his* horse, and if the general's son got it in his mind that she was a better mount than his own, Jake might very well have to give her up. He bit his lip, swallowed his pride, and pulled back gently on the reins, allowing his competitor to reach the top of the hill first.

"She looks like a good sprinter," Wade admitted grudgingly. "But I'd rather have a distance-runner any day."

A vidette of Confederate troopers emerged from the woods. Jake and Wade reined their horses to a halt in front of the sentinels.

"No sign of Yankees, sir," a burly sergeant reported with a snappy salute. "General Hampton has sent out scouts and patrols to screen the way for the column."

"Thank you, Sergeant," Wade replied, returning the salute in kind. "And where will I find General Hampton?"

"About two miles on, sir," the sergeant said, pointing over his shoulder with his thumb.

They soon rejoined the general and his staff at the meadow where the duel had taken place. All lay quiet and serene, so Jake and Cat took a welcome respite in the shade of a gnarled oak.

About an hour later, the column finally drew near. Suddenly, a spatter of gunshots erupted from the vicinity of Hunterstown. General Hampton cupped a hand to his ear. The rate and volume of fire increased.

"Well, gentlemen," Hampton said, "we may have ridden past our foes. Captain Barker, order another countermarch. Staff, with me!" Jake and the rest of the men raced to keep up with their commander.

Though the afternoon spent in backtracking had proved more interesting than the plodding pace of the previous two days, Jake couldn't help but feel sorry for Cat as they covered the next two miles in less than ten minutes. He could sense her fatigue, yet she never balked.

From the hill overlooking the flats south of town, Jake saw a band of about forty Confederates fleeing down the far ridge and past the first of two farmhouses. A much larger contingent of Union cavalry followed, pistols blazing, sabres waving.

Meanwhile, the men of Cobb's Legion took position just past the closer farmhouse. Phillip's Legion moved up along the wood line to the left, while one of their companies dismounted and worked their way through the field of half-grown wheat. Off to the right, a company of South Carolinians dismounted and disappeared into the cornfield.

The retreating Confederates turned to face their attackers. An officer in gray spurred his horse and continued to race toward Cobb's Legion, but as he drew near them, his mount's legs buckled and he tumbled to the ground. He scrambled to his feet, shouting orders. Two of the Legion's companies charged up the road to join the melee.

The South Carolinians sprang from hiding in the cornfield and opened fire on the Yankees. Outnumbered, the Union men called off their pursuit and retreated to the woods on the opposite hill.

Hampton ordered more troops to dismount and deploy into the fields on either side of the narrow, fence-lined road. Then he motioned for his adjutant, Captain Baker, to come nearer.

"If that was the advance party of a large Union force, we may be in for a fight." Hampton pointed to the area between the two farms. The ground looked as if it had just recently been cleared of trees. "They could command the field with artillery from the other hill, and our guns have been sent on ahead."

A column of about fifty Union cavalrymen walked into view at the top of the far ridge. They proceeded down the sloping road in ranks of four, disappeared behind the distant barn, and emerged alongside the large brick farmhouse about a half-mile away. An officer in the front rank waved his sabre and the column moved out at a trot. When the riders were within a few hundred yards of the waiting Confederates, they spurred their horses to a gallop. Jake stared in wonder at the leader of the Union charge: a man with long blonde hair and a bright red bandana tied around his neck. Was it the same officer who had led the Union attack from the Forney farm in Hanover? Or perhaps the Yankees were trying a bizarre tactic, hoping the outlandish appearance of their commanders might distract their enemies.

Hemmed in by fences on either side of the country lane, the Union column charged in tight formation. Moments before the blue tide smashed into the gray wall, the staunch Confederates fired a volley from their pistols and carbines, with little apparent effect.

Union Cavalry Charge

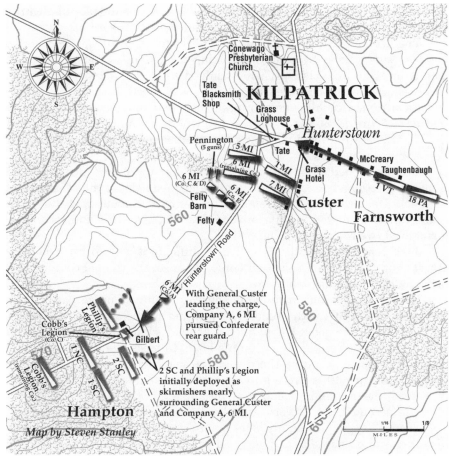

Battle of Hunterstown, 4:15-4:45

The Confederate line wavered and then broke under the force of the massed attack. They retreated past the farmhouse. Skirmishers in the fields again arose and blasted away at the attackers.

The hailstorm of bullets tore into the Union ranks. Three of the leading officers went down: a lieutenant, thrown from his rearing horse; a captain, blood spurting from his chest; and the longhaired general, when his horse took the brunt of the volley. The general hit the ground hard and appeared to be trapped under his dead mount. A Confederate cavalryman aimed a pistol at the nattily dressed Yankee.

Jake braced himself for the imminent *coup de grace*, but it never came. Did his comrade mean to take the general prisoner?

A Union cavalryman galloped up from the rear of the column, raised his pistol, and shot the man in gray. The fallen general rose to his feet, locked arms with his unexpected savior, and swung onto the horse. The two men fled north to safety, crouching in the saddle to minimize the odds of being hit by the ensuing volley of shots. A second rider hauled the bleeding captain onto his horse, and the pair joined the retreat.

The downed Union lieutenant struggled to calm his spooked horse, but was surrounded by counterattacking Confederates before he could mount up. The blue-clad prisoner trudged toward the rear, his bloody fingers clutching his left forearm.

Cavalrymen in blue and gray slashed and parried on the narrow confines of the farm road. At the head of the counterattack, Colonel Deloney's horse fell dead, trapping his master beneath him. The rest of the chargers raced past.

Deloney managed to extricate himself, but not before three Yankee troopers bore down on him. Two men brandished sabres, the other aimed a pistol. Deloney drew his blade and with an astounding flurry of counterstrokes fended off his adversaries' slashes. The man with the pistol fired two rounds. Both missed.

Jake remembered all too well how difficult it was to hit a moving target from the back of a skittish horse. Even so, the colonel couldn't last much longer in the uneven fight.

Help arrived from an unlikely source. A young Confederate bugler charged his mount up the road. The intrepid musician drew his sabre, reached back, and loosed a mighty overhead swing at the first Union swordsman. The Yankee threw up his blade to block the blow. The clang of steel on steel rang over the din of the maelstrom. The bugler deftly recoiled and thrust his sabre into his opponent's side. As sword and flesh separated, the man in blue buckled over and fell to the ground.

The second Union swordsman landed a blow to Deloney's temple. The colonel flopped across his dead horse's neck. The third Yankee drew his sabre and prepared to deliver the deathblow, but the dauntless bugler spurred his horse, lunged, and blocked the stroke.

The second Union man again thrust at the bugler, but only managed to tear a vent through the lad's gray coat. His follow-up swing clanked harmlessly against the bugle.

Looking dazed, Deloney regained his footing. While the bugler dueled the Union horsemen, Deloney slashed at his assailants. The first stroke opened a slice on one foe's leg, the second attempt cut into the other man's boot. The bleeding Yankees broke off the attack and fled for the far hill.

The rout was on. Jake's spirit soared with pride at the sight of Yankee troopers fleeing the field. In the distance, a blue-clad soldier lay crumpled in the road. Jake cringed. Any moment, the retreating Union cavalrymen would be upon the prostrate form. Was there enough space on the fence-lined lane for the riders to avoid the fallen man? The leading horsemen skirted the man, but those following had no room to do likewise. The hapless soldier flopped like a rag doll under the thundering hooves. Jake turned away, stifling the urge to retch.

Whooping and hollering, the Confederates drove the Yankees past the large brick farmhouse and its long gray barn. But then it was their turn for a rude surprise. Union soldiers rose from hiding in the fields and opened fire. The men in blue cocked their carbines and fired several times without reloading.

Someone down the line from Jake exclaimed, "Danged repeater rifles! Does the whole Union Army have them now?"

The trees quivered from the concussion of two mighty cannon shots. Puffs of smoke rose from behind the barn. The leaders of the Confederate counterattack went down in a heap. Another dozen men fell victim to the Union carbines.

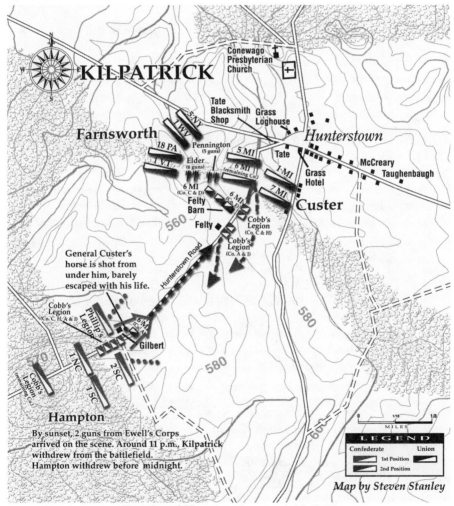

Battle of Hunterstown, 4:45-5:15

General Hampton muttered something terse, then turned to his adjutant. "Looks like that foolish Yankee charge was a trap. We must not allow them to turn our flank."

Captain Baker nodded. "We're going to need artillery, aren't we?"

"Exactly. The problem is, Captain Breathed's in Gettysburg by now, getting re-supplied. Write a request for General Stuart to send us a couple of batteries."

Glancing over his shoulder, Hampton shouted, "Becker!"

"Here, sir." Jake walked Cat to the General's side. Was he to be the one to carry the urgent message?

Hampton took the paper from his adjutant. Instead of giving it to Jake, he handed it to Wade Hampton, Jr. "Go with Private Becker. He knows these roads. Find General Stuart and deliver this message. I want you to lead the artillery back here as quickly as you can. It'll be dark in a few hours. We must have those guns!"

Jake and Cat sprang into action, leading the way south toward Gettysburg. This time, they didn't wait for Wade to keep up.

-8-

At the first sounds of battle, the sixty-five men of Company H mounted and formed up with the rest of Colonel McIntosh's brigade. Word came down the line that Rebel skirmishers were trying to dislodge the Union soldiers from a ridge about a mile west of the crossroads. General Gregg sent a couple of squadrons of New York cavalry to strengthen the Federal position. Moments later, two guns from a unit of horse artillery rumbled past.

The order came for Company H to dismount, but every man stayed close to his horse. While some men caught another nap, others ate or played cards. David finished the rest of the biscuits and salted pork he had brought from home, then stretched out and dozed fitfully.

Around four o'clock a bugle call rang out, and before it was finished, all the men were in their saddles. The short towheaded man next to David flashed a bucktoothed grin. "That bugle call was 'To Horse,' just in case you couldn't guess, and I'm Elias Eyster, but all my friends call me Eli."

The men shook hands and the column began to move out in ranks of four. David urged Streak to a trot and caught up with the rest of the company. He kept most of his weight on the stirrups while his body adjusted to the unfamiliar saddle.

The troopers of the 1st Brigade returned to the main road and turned west toward Gettysburg. Other cavalrymen and horses lolled in the clover fields around the intersection, as if nothing unusual was going on. The brigade cantered a few hundred yards up the road and halted behind a busy artillery unit.

David surveyed the rolling farmland. Brinkerhoff Ridge stood about three-quarters of a mile away. He remembered the ridge as the next to last significant obstacle for a wagon to surmount on its way to Gettysburg. Several Confederate cavalrymen clustered at the top of the distant rise, while a line of gray-clad foot soldiers advanced down the hill toward a grove of trees on the right.

Along the ridge to the left of the Rebels, a horseman in blue burst from cover and raced toward the Union line. A band of Confederate cavalry took chase. They fired their pistols and whooped and hollered as if pursuing a fleeing fox. David held his breath as the gap started to close. What chance did the poor man have to make good his escape?

Movement in the foreground caught David's eye. About a hundred yards away, a white-haired woman with a cane emerged from the Cress farmhouse. She hobbled up the hill toward the Union artillery. Two cannonballs whizzed over her head and landed in the midst of the pursuing Rebel troopers. The cavalrymen turned and fled while the old woman hit the ground as if shot. The escaping Union man spurred his horse for the safety of the Federal line.

In an instant, the old woman was on her feet. Shrieking at the top of her lungs, she ran across the field with all the agility of a teenager. While some of the soldiers cheered their hard-riding comrade, others jeered at the decrepit woman, miraculously cured by fright.

Someone shouted an order and Union skirmishers fanned out across the farmland between the woods and the ridge. A line of Confederate infantrymen charged down the hill toward them. Outnumbered, the men in blue broke and ran. Several men took bullets and fell, but most made it safely back across the Hanover Road. David watched helplessly while a few of the men were captured behind their rocky hiding places. Expecting an order for Company H to rush to the aid, he tightened the grip on Streak's reins. Why were they just standing around?

The Union skirmishers regrouped along Hanover Road and fired at the Rebels from behind a rail fence. David braced himself as Federal artillery poured shell after shell into the enemy troops, finally forcing their withdrawal.

David wondered why no one had ordered all of the Union cavalry into action to take the high ground. Was there a larger Confederate force on the other side?

The sun had sunk, almost to the level of the treetops. All along the ridge, a new line of Confederate infantry started down the rolling hill.

The bugler blew "To Horse!" and the men of Company H followed the column down the slope toward the Cress farm. David reined Streak close to Eli as the squadron veered off to the right and into the orchard behind the farmhouse.

Captain Miller raised his hand and shouted, "Dismount!" One man in each rank of four tended the horses, while Miller gathered the rest of the troopers together.

His heart racing, David slipped the carbine from the saddle's boot, pulled a cartridge from the box on his belt, and loaded the Sharps. After putting the percussion cap in place, he checked to make sure Jake's Colt was easily at hand. With no holster, David wanted to be able to draw the revolver from his belt without difficulty; but if it was too loose, he feared he might drop it while on the move.

Miller called, "We're on the right flank. Guide left on me."

David picked a spot near the middle of the line. Another captain aligned his men on the left side of Company H.

Miller walked down the line, pausing between the two companies. "Hold your fire until my command." He turned, lifted his sabre, and shouted, "To the tree line, forward march!" The rank wavered when the men maneuvered to avoid some trees and underbrush, but then reformed on the far edge of the field.

Miller pointed his sabre at the stone and rail fence a hundred yards away. "We are to occupy that fence line. Forward!"

The rolling ground blocked the view of any Confederate soldiers who might be hiding in the field. Fearing his height would make him a likely target, David walked in a crouch.

Eli said grimly, "I wouldn't worry too much about that 'til we're under fire. Besides, if it's your time, there'll be no place to hide."

David didn't much like the sound of that.

About a third of the way to the fence, they came upon a marshy brook. Wading across posed no difficulty, but the waterlogged shoes and squishy socks added to David's growing discomfort.

A line of Confederates emerged from the woods atop the rise.

Miller yelled, "Double quick!" The men in blue raced for the fence, reaching it about twenty paces ahead of the onrushing Rebels.

"Fire! Fire at will!" Miller's words disappeared beneath the deafening blast of Union carbines.

The Confederates paused to fire a volley, then charged the wall. Minie balls whistled through the air. Ricocheting bullets sent up showers of stone chips and splintered wood. Willing himself to ignore the rush of fear, David tried to think like a hunter. He lifted the Sharps to his shoulder, held his breath, and aimed down the barrel. Not fifteen feet away, a boyish-looking man with red hair and a scraggly beard raced toward him. David squeezed the trigger. A plume of red spurted from the redhead's left shoulder, and the man fell to his knees.

Another man with a bayonet on the end of his musket bore down on David. David dropped the spent carbine, pulled out the Colt, thumbed back the hammer, and fired off a round. The shot missed.

The Rebel reached the fence and lunged with his bayonet. David jumped back. The point of the bayonet ripped a button from his shirt. The Rebel regained his balance and coiled for another thrust. David cocked the revolver and fired from the hip. Another miss.

"Fall back!" someone called from the other side of the fence. The Rebel turned and ran for cover with the rest of the attackers.

Shaking, David decided not to waste any more shots with the pistol. He put the revolver back in his belt, then reached for the carbine and reloaded as quickly as his trembling hands would allow. While fumbling with the percussion cap, he felt a trickling sensation around his navel. He dropped the little brass cap and put his hand on his stomach. The shirt felt wet. In disbelief, David stared at his fingertips, lit by the soft golden glow of the setting sun.

Blood.

Fight at Brinkerhoff's Ridge

-9-

Jake and Wade encountered pickets from General Ewell's Corps about three miles down the road. One of the pickets led the way to Corps Headquarters on the Carlisle Pike. A colonel quickly issued orders for a pair of ten-pound Parrott guns to assist General Hampton, but it was dusk by the time Artillery Captain Green and the few dozen members of his crew arrived on the wooded ridge south of Hunterstown.

With darkness near, both cavalries seemed content to stay behind their lines on the edges of the open farmland. Green's men unlimbered the cannons and prepared to fire. Jake watched in fascination as the well-practiced crew went through their paces.

The crew commander shouted, "Load!" One man pushed a cloth-tipped ramrod down the big gun while another man pressed his leather-covered thumb over a small hole near the base of the barrel. A third man lifted a shell from the caisson and pushed a fuse into place. He passed the projectile to a fourth man, who relayed it to a fifth man waiting at the left of the cannon. That man slid the shell into the bore, and the first man rammed it down. The man with the leathered thumb stepped to the rear of the gun carriage and adjusted the aim according to the commander's directions. Finally, the commander bellowed, "Ready!"

A sixth man poked something into the little hole at the base of the barrel and took hold of a lanyard. The commander shouted, "Fire!" The sixth man yanked the lanyard and, with a spine-rattling blast, the shell was on its way. A spout of orange flames shot a good twenty feet from the end of the barrel as the cannon rolled backward a few yards. Four of the men quickly shoved the big gun back into position. In less than thirty seconds the crew repeated the well-choreographed process, as if in a macabre ballet.

The ensuing hour-long artillery battle did not bode well for the next day's action. Clearly outnumbered, the Confederate cannon crew lost almost half of their men: two dead, fourteen wounded. Finally, Hampton ordered a withdrawal for the night.

Jake had curried Cat and was about to bed down when Wade came looking for him. "Private Becker! The general would like to see you. Bring your horse and gear."

"Great," Jake muttered. "More messages, no doubt. Sorry, girl." He quickly saddled Cat and followed the lieutenant.

"Ah, Becker, there you are." The elder Hampton sat with his bandaged head resting against the trunk of an ancient birch. "I need you to take a report to General Stuart. General Ewell's men should be able to tell you where to find him."

Wade, Jr. handed Jake a dispatch bag. "Die before you give this up." His tone implied he'd just as soon Jake died in any case.

Jake stood at attention and gave a snappy salute. "Yes—*sir.*" It was only a small victory, but the look of annoyance in Wade's eyes was worth the risk of further offending his superior.

Fortunately, it took little more than an hour to find Stuart's headquarters. Sleep was only moments away!

General Stuart flashed a big smile. "Thank you, Private Becker, well done. Now I have another job for you."

Jake stifled a groan. Would this be his third sleepless night in a row?

"Since you know the area, I'd like you to guide Captain Blackford to a small stone farmhouse on the Chambersburg Pike. He will give my report to General Lee."

Eyes aglow, Jake couldn't help asking, "General Robert E. Lee?"

Stuart's blue eyes sparkled. "Oh, so you've heard of him?"

-10-

David stared at his belly, where a dark spot the size of a silver dollar circled a small slit on his blue flannel shirt. He leaned the carbine against the wall, yanked the Colt from his belt, and tore the shirt open with his free hand. Blood oozed from a narrow cut just above his navel.

Squatting behind the wall, Eli said, "Looks like you got lucky."

"Yeah, guess so." David slumped to the ground next to his carbine.

"I got my first wound back in February, down in Virginny near Hartwood Church. Took a Minie ball in the left arm." Eli rubbed the spot just below the joint. "I got lucky, too. Only lost a little chunk of flesh. Another inch to the right and I'd'a lost my whole arm. A couple more inches and I'd be dead—same as you if that bayonet went another few inches. Ain't no way the surgeons can save a gut wound."

"Thanks, I'll try to remember that." David dabbed at the cut with the edge of the shirt.

A few hundred yards away, the Rebels loosed their famous yell and again charged down the hill. Eli poked his head over the wall and aimed his carbine. "Here we go . . ."

David knelt, set the revolver down within easy reach, and steadied the rifle's aim on the wall. When the line of Confederates got to within a hundred yards, Miller shouted, "Fire!"

David sighted down the barrel at the man directly ahead of him and squeezed the trigger. Another miss. The Union artillery opened up and broke the Confederate charge before it reached the wall.

Both sides exchanged sporadic fire as darkness enveloped the field. David reloaded the carbine, then checked to make sure he could find the spot where he had laid the Colt, just in case he needed to grab for it without looking.

Once more the hideous Rebel yell rent the air, this time from somewhere to the right. A strong force of Confederates burst from cover behind a grove of trees halfway down the ridge and charged the far end of the wall. Their gray uniforms looked ghostly in the dim light.

Outflanked, the men in blue cursed and fell back. David and Eli held their fire for fear of shooting their own men. Miller's voice soared over the din of battle, "Rally on me! Rally on me!"

David grabbed the Colt in his right hand and held it at arm's length, looking for an enemy target. He shuffled two quick steps to his right, got a clear view of the onrushing Rebels, and fired at a cluster of men twenty feet away. One of them screamed and clutched his leg, then went down.

"Charge!" Miller roared.

Several dozen Union men surged forward and flung themselves at the attackers. Pistols blazed and sabres glinted as the fight became hand-to-hand. Reminding himself he had three shots left, David shifted the revolver to his left hand and drew his sabre. A Confederate stumbled and fell at his feet. David's gun barrel was within inches of the Rebel's head, but he couldn't bring himself to blow the hapless man's brains out. Instead, he swung his right hand with all his might and bashed his foe's skull with the sabre's brass handguard. The man crumpled to the ground.

The gray wraiths disappeared as quickly as they had come. A few final pistol shots cracked like embers in a dying fire.

Miller's voice sounded husky. "Well done, men!" He gestured along the ground with his sabre. "Now form up here on an angle with the wall. I doubt we'll be seeing any more of the Johnnies tonight, but since we hold the flank, I don't want to take any chances."

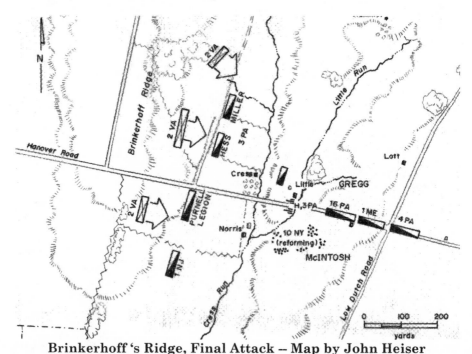

Brinkerhoff 's Ridge, Final Attack -- Map by John Heiser

The men of Company H took their new position. Miller called, "Sergeant Whaler, tell Captain Hess to spread Company M over this way, so he can cover the gap. Now then, Lieutenant Caufmann, I'll have the casualty report."

Miraculously, no one in the company had been killed or wounded in the action. There was an assortment of scrapes and bruises common to such a melee, but nothing serious enough to warrant medical attention. Even David's belly had stopped bleeding.

Besides the man David had coshed, two other Rebels lay too injured to escape. Captain Miller took a cursory look at their wounds. "Sergeant McCullough, search these men for weapons, then put them under guard. I'll not spare any men to carry them to the rear."

David poked his sabre at the unconscious man at his feet. "I've got a Confederate out cold here."

Miller turned and peered through the dim light. "Who said that?"

"That was Private Becker, sir," Eli replied. "I saw him put that man down with one blow to the head."

"Well done, Becker. Glad to see you know how to handle yourself in a brawl. Stay near me next time, hear?"

A few of the men chuckled. Several others pretended to feel slighted, but the banter ended when a sniper shot rang out from the woods.

While the rest of Company H turned their attention to defending the tenuous line, David and Eli dragged the senseless Confederate over to his fellow prisoners, then joined the rest of the Company on their bellies, facing the woods from whence the most recent attack had issued.

Moonlight filtered through the clouds and cast a warm glow on the line of trees a few hundred yards away. An eerie calm descended on the scene. David's eyelids grew heavy.

His grogginess vanished at the sound of someone approaching from the rear. David rolled onto his side. Using his peripheral vision, he was able to distinguish a crouching figure about twenty yards away. Before David could decide what to do, the newcomer called out in a loud whisper.

"Captain Miller. Orders, sir."

"Advance," Miller replied tersely.

David rolled back onto his stomach and resumed the watch.

A few moments later Miller whispered, "Naugle, Eyster, and Heffifinger. Pick a partner and stand picket. The rest of you, quiet as field mice, fall back to the crossroads."

It felt as though someone had lifted a boulder off David's back. He rubbed his bleary eyes as if to wipe the fatigue away. He couldn't wait to curl up in that clover field and sleep. A hand touched his shoulder.

"Hey, David," Eli whispered. "Watch with me?"

How could he say no? As exhausted as he was, at least he had gotten a full night's sleep in his own bed just two nights ago. The rest of the company had been in the saddle for four days. "Sure, Eli. Just tell me what to do."

Eli leaned in close. "We're gonna be about ten yards apart. Every five minutes or so we gotta check and make sure we're both awake, so don't let yourself get too comfortable."

"Right." David yawned, then blinked his eyes rapidly to fend off a surge of drowsiness.

"It's not likely the Rebs will try anything in the dark. If they do, our job is to make a lot of noise and slow them down."

David wondered how long pickets were expected to stay in place in order to "slow them down."

"In a few hours, they'll send some men to relieve us," Eli whispered. "That's why I like first watch. It's the best chance to get some uninterrupted sleep later on. Oh, and if you have to piss, don't. It's the best way I know to stay awake."

"Right." While Eli moved to his position, David rose to one knee, planted the butt of the carbine on the ground, and leaned on the barrel.

After a couple dozen furtive exchanges to check on each other's state of alertness, someone approached from the rear, whispering, "Corporal Naugle . . . Corporal Naugle . . ."

"Here."

"All fall back."

David and the other pickets crept away from the front and worked their way back to the orchard near the Cress farmhouse. Once on the main road, the courier spoke in a low tone.

"We're all pulling farther back. Rumor has it that more than seventy thousand Johnnies are on the other side of Gettysburg, itching to have at us in the morning. Who knows where we'll wind up tomorrow?"

David couldn't help feeling annoyed. The men of Companies H and M had risked their lives for possession of that stone wall and hay field, now they were ordered to abandon it as if it was just a worthless piece of dirt. How many men had bled and died over that land? What was the sense of it? But then again, no one ever said war made sense.

-11-

Jake found the small, stone farmhouse without difficulty. He felt certain Captain Blackford could have easily managed the same, but at least now he might get to see the famous Robert E. Lee. Even though it was well past dark, the headquarters of the Army of Northern Virginia bustled with activity. Couriers came and went, seemingly in all directions. Not even the smoke from several campfires could cover the odor of their hard-ridden horses. Three rows of tents lined the Chambersburg Pike. Lanterns in the larger tents cast flickering shadows on the white canvas. Somewhere, a mediocre fiddler scratched out a melancholy tune.

Widow Thompson's house, R. E. Lee's Headquarters (1863)

Blackford groaned as he stepped down from the saddle. He held Magic's reins out to Jake. "You can wait for me here."

Swallowing his disappointment, Jake slid off Cat, took Magic's reins, and led the two horses to the water trough. He worked the pump handle up and down, but the water only trickled out. The thirsty horses lapped it up as fast as they could. After two or three quarts, the water stopped completely.

"Sorry, girls. The well's drawn down. Have to try again later." Cat nuzzled Jake when he tried to lead her away from the water source, then pulled free, poked her head back into the trough, and licked the wood.

Jake grasped the side of her bridle and pulled gently. "Come on, Cat." She shook her head and snorted, spraying Jake with slobber.

He wiped his face on his dusty sleeve. "Thanks a lot! I love you, too, Cat." His heart seemed to skip a beat at the sound of those words.

Blackford returned, looking peevish. "General Lee is not available to take my report." He lowered his voice. "I wonder if something is amiss. He has always seen me on previous occasions."

The farmhouse door opened and Major Venable came out to join them. "It is such a beautiful evening, Captain, why don't we sit out here and I will hear your report."

Blackford readily agreed, and the officers sat on a small bench against the wall. Jake took advantage of the break to give the horses a good brushing. Luxuriating in the attention, Cat nickered softly.

A few minutes into the grooming session, an elderly gentleman emerged from the nearest tent. He wore a plain white shirt and gray dress uniform pants. The light from the campfire glowed on his shiny black cavalry boots. Walking gingerly as if weak or nursing a pain, the old man made his way past Jake toward a cluster of outbuildings between the house and the barn. His destination soon became obvious: the tiny shed with the half-moon cut into the door.

Jake turned his attention to Magic, who was skittish at his unaccustomed touch. By the time he had brushed, combed, picked, and re-saddled both mounts, Blackford returned—and the old man had made a second trip from the tent to the privy.

Blackford ran his hand down Magic's neck and along the side of her flank and belly. He gave Jake an appreciative nod. "Thank you for doing such a fine job of tending her for me."

"You're welcome, sir. Thank you for bringing me along. I'd hoped for a chance to meet General Lee, but maybe some other time."

"Didn't you see him? He walked right past you a couple of times."

Jake felt almost too stunned to speak. "You mean that old, um—"

Blackford leaned in and whispered, "I'm told the general is suffering with a bout of diarrhea, but you best keep that information to yourself."

Jake stared thoughtfully at the tent. The shadow indicated Lee was seated at a small writing desk. Perhaps the next time he went to the privy, Jake could at least say "good evening" or wish him well. No telling if there would be another chance to speak with the great leader.

But Blackford had other plans. "Well, Magic, now that you're all gussied up, how about we go find us a few old friends to visit?" He swung up into the saddle and looked at Jake expectantly.

Jake climbed onto Cat's back. The mare tossed her head, lifted her tail, and pranced after Magic as if showing off her groomed coat.

Blackford led the way out the Chambersburg Pike and turned south, along the rear of the Confederate lines. They spent the next hour weaving their way through the bivouacs in search of Blackford's friends.

They learned that Blackford's brother, Eugene, was posted along Baltimore Street with a battalion from General Rodes' division. Of course, the captain insisted on searching him out. Jake led the way through the moonlit night.

Dark forms huddled on the ground behind the two- and three-story brick houses. The dozing infantrymen seemed oblivious to the scattered sounds of gunfire. Not even the occasional cannon shell interrupted their hard-earned repose.

Jake peeked around the corner of a house and glanced nervously down the street, where relatives of both the Forneys and Shrivers lived. Was he fated to be the harbinger of war to all of his family and friends?

Blackford made a few inquiries and was directed to a rowhouse near the edge of town. He walked Magic over to a spot that looked relatively safe from the intermittent fire. "I don't want to leave my horse unattended, so you can wait for me here." Blackford handed Magic's reins to Jake, dismounted, brushed the worst of the dust from his uniform, and climbed the stairs to the back entrance of the elevated first floor. He stepped through the open door and disappeared inside.

Jake decided to try to catch a nap. He slid off Cat, tied one set of reins around each wrist, and curled up on the ground. The earth vibrated with each cannon shot. From inside the building, Confederate snipers exchanged fire with their Union counterparts in the cemetery on the ridge. It seemed only moments later when Blackford shook him awake. Feeling utterly wretched, Jake struggled to his feet.

The captain chattered the whole way back to Stuart's headquarters. "Quite a remarkable way to fight, I must say. Never saw the like of it."

Jake grunted in reply. Where did Blackford get his energy?

"The houses in that block were built flush together, so Eugene's men cut passageways in the walls, enabling them to walk under cover from one end of the houses to the other."

Jake was glad the Shrivers and Forneys lived on the other side of the street. As did Eliza and Kathleen's vivacious friend, Tillie Pierce, whose father ran a butcher shop on the corner next to the Shrivers.

"They covered the rear windows with mattresses and bedding, then fired from 'cover,' if you'll pardon my pun."

Jake gave the expected snicker, but felt sorry for the homeowners.

"Imagine, while some of Eugene's men took their turn sniping, their fellows reclined in luxury upon divans, or lounged in comfy chairs, quaffing wine and eating delicacies around a marble-topped table. Now that's the way to fight a war!" Blackford slapped his thigh and chortled.

Jake turned away to hide his scowl. "You both must be very proud."

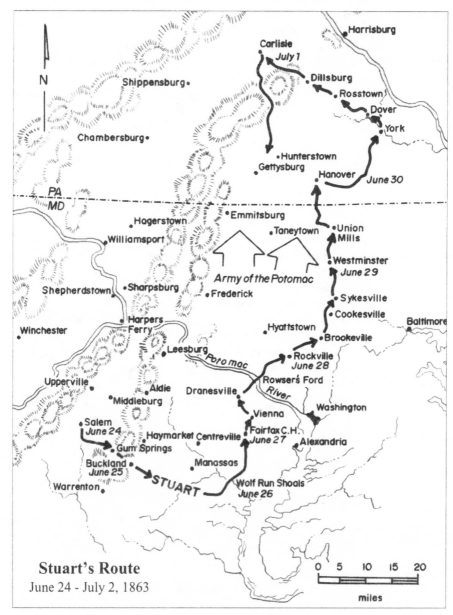

Stuart's Route
June 24 - July 2, 1863

Map by John Heiser

Friday, July 3, 1863

The first cannon blast wrenched David from his slumber. He was on his feet with carbine in hand by the time two more big guns joined the bombardment. The ground trembled, though the cannons sounded as if they were some distance away. Judging from the general lack of concern around him, he figured the volley must be from Union artillery. David cocked his head. Would the Confederates return the sunrise salute? The fleeting moment of quietude vanished when a murder of crows suddenly took flight from the treetops. Their frantic squawks faded eerily as they retreated eastward toward the reddish-orange horizon.

"As long as you're up," Elias Eyster called from his bedroll, "you can make the coffee."

"Glad to," David said through a yawn. "But where do I get it, and who has a pot?"

Sergeant Fosnaugh sat up and shouted over the din of the cannons. "You should find the supply wagons near the artillery park, this side of the Baltimore Pike."

Still groggy from the midnight ride to the rear of the Union lines, David looked through bleary eyes at the rows of sleeping men in blue. How long had they served before they learned to doze through such a ruckus?

Captain Miller called from his nearby tent, "Hey, Fosnaugh, two weeks as quartermaster and already shirking your duty?"

Fosnaugh untangled himself from the bedroll and scrambled to his feet. "Uh, no, sir. I'm going to have Private Becker assist me with the morning rations, sir."

"Very good." Miller came out, saluted with his cup, and went back inside his tent.

Fosnaugh led the way down Low Dutch Road to the brigade's supply wagons, where the battalion Commissary Sergeant, George Ewing, oversaw the morning distribution of rations. One of his men pried open a barrel marked SALTED PORK. The packing nails squealed as he worked the lid free and the stench of rotten meat permeated the air.

Ewing spit his chaw of tobacco on the ground. "Damned government contractors, stinting on the salt again!" He tried in vain to wave the foul aroma away from his nose. "At least the worms are still good. Maybe I'll give it to the infantry."

A freshly-shaven corporal offered a better idea. "Maybe we can send it to old Bobby Lee's headquarters—with our compliments, of course."

Someone farther back in line called, "How 'bout we build us a catapult like in olden days and lob it on top of them there Johnnies?"

"Nah, that's no good," the corporal scoffed. "They'd just think it was manna from heaven."

Ewing waved his hand at the reeking barrel. "Enough chatter. Get rid of that disgusting filth!" Two of his men rolled the barrel of rancid meat across the road and into the underbrush.

Fosnaugh peered into the supply wagon. "Any oats today?"

"No," Ewing said, grumbling. "We had expected a supply train of 150 wagons from Washington City, but Stuart's men captured it earlier this week. So if you want a well-fed horse, you'll have to steal a Rebel nag."

Fosnaugh nudged David and pointed to a pile of empty crates marked HARDTACK. David grabbed one of the wooden boxes and set it on the tailgate of the supply wagon. The corporal loaded the crate with hardtack and unspoiled pork from another barrel. Fosnaugh took the bag of coffee just before the corporal set it on top of a slab of meat. "Don't need no porky-smelling coffee."

By the time they got the rations back to the Company H bivouac, two of the men had a fire going. A large coffee pot sat on a rock at the edge of the flames.

"You hand out the rations, Becker, and I'll introduce you to the men," Fosnaugh said.

David shook each man's hand in turn, trying his best to find a way to remember which name went with which face. Though old enough to be father to most of the men, David saw that their eyes bespoke experience well beyond their years.

Eli waited until last and invited David to join him for breakfast. "Have you ever had hardtack before?" David's bemused expression was answer enough. "Try dipping it in your coffee first," Eli explained. He held the corner of the rigid bread in the coffee for several seconds before setting to work on it with his teeth.

David wasn't sure which was worse, the coffee or the hardtack, but at least the coffee's aroma purged his nose of the rancid meat smell and the hardtack quieted the growling in his empty stomach. He inspected the salted pork very carefully before devouring it.

The sun cleared the horizon and golden rays of light peeked through the break in the clouds. David smiled at the memory of six-year-old Jake, exclaiming at a similar sight, "Look, Papa! Are those guardian angels looking for their people?"

David stared into his tin cup and swirled the dark coffee, wishing he could read the future in the dregs. But reading the present would be even better. How was Jake, and where was he? David refused to consider the possibility his son was injured—or worse. If 70,000 Confederates had gathered around Gettysburg, how long would it be before General Stuart added his forces to the fray?

Eli spoke softly over the distant sounds of battle. "Homesick already?

You'll get over it quick. In a couple of days we'll be all the family you need. For now, anyway."

David sighed. "My son, Jake, joined the Confederate Army a few days ago, and I got word he's with Jeb Stuart."

"Now if that don't beat all!"

"It gets worse." David pulled the Colt revolver from his belt. "This was Jake's. One of my friends found it in his hayfield after the battle in Hanover two days ago. A Union officer did some checking for me. There was no sign of Jake among the prisoners or casualties, so I'm going to presume he's all right."

"Well, if I see any Johnnies that look like you, I'll be sure to aim low," Eli said.

Though he appreciated the sentiment, David's stomach churned at such a thought. Even with his very limited experience he knew that in the chaos of battle, there was no time to scan enemy faces.

The sound of cannon fire gradually died away in the west, and a deathly silence fell over the encampment. The trees stood mute, empty of birds. Several horses whinnied nervously. Up and down the line, men spoke in hushed tones as if at a wake.

An odd sound echoed faintly in the north. Was it the patter of rain on leaves? David studied the sky. There were certainly enough dark, patchy clouds to deliver an isolated shower, but as the noise deepened and spread, the randomness of the rhythm took on a recognizable character. It was the sound of horses on a macadam road. Thousands of horses. And the nearest road with a macadam surface was the York Pike. Less than two miles away, the highway ran parallel with the Hanover Road. Low Dutch Road, where the company camped, ran perpendicularly between the two highways.

David stood and called, "Captain Miller! Do you know if we have any troops up on the York Pike?"

"I doubt it. Why?"

"If that sound is cavalry on the move, then there is only one road in the area with a hard enough surface to make that much noise, and that's the York Pike. That's where this road ends, a couple of miles from here."

Miller's eyes lit up. "Which means we may be in for some company. Come with me, Becker. I want you to report this to Colonel McIntosh."

-2-

Still drowsy after five hours of fitful sleep, Jake and Herb rode in silence, but for the low rumble of several thousand trotting horses. The days of torturous travel on dirt roads and rutted lanes were finally over. Better yet, the cumbersome wagon train was finally in the hands of General Robert E. Lee's quartermaster. Riding on the York Pike's hard-packed gravel seemed like a cavalryman's dream come true. Even so, Jake sensed his comrades' contemplative mood. No one talked, no one sang. Now that the sun shone through the cloud cover, the air grew thick and warm. Jake's eyes felt dry and heavy. He shook his arms and twisted his torso to ease the morning stiffness.

A couple of miles east of Gettysburg, the column met up with General Hampton's men at Hunterstown Road. Jake's heart beat faster. If the veterans' expressions were any indication, today would not end without a battle. But where would they find their foe? Evidently, the Union troops around Hunterstown had managed to slip away in the night and join the rest of the Union Army just south of Gettysburg. Was Stuart planning to skirt around their flank and hit them from the rear?

Sure enough, a short distance further Stuart's advance party turned south onto a narrow farm lane. The column followed, tension brewing like water about to boil. Another half-mile and they emerged from a dense woods bordering on a series of cultivated fields.

Stuart led the way to the high ground on the right. The ridge angled off to the southwest, revealing a panoramic view over the lush fields and copses. Waves of gentle breezes flowed through half-grown stalks of wheat and corn. A large white dairy barn and fieldstone farmhouse lay a couple hundred yards below the ridge. The crump of distant cannon fire punctuated the chatter of birds hiding in the trees.

Once atop the ridge, Stuart issued a flurry of orders to his adjutant. "Send Colonel Witcher's battalion to occupy that barn and hold the fence line to the right. I want Colonel Ferguson's men to split up on either side of that position, and have Colonel Chambliss secure the right flank." McClellan scribbled down the commands.

Stuart's bright blue eyes surveyed the field. "Have the artillery unlimber along this line. Order Captain Griffin to fire a salvo in different directions, and then keep a sharp ear for the Yankee reply. Blackford, use your glasses to look for the smoke." Blackford pulled the binoculars from his saddlebag.

"Now, I must have General Hampton's men here," Stuart said grimly. "I want them hidden in those woods off to the left. Courier!"

Jake nudged Cat's flanks and moved forward. "Here, sir."

Stuart grinned at Jake. "Ah, Becker, I see you are becoming my personal telegraph line to General Hampton. Yes indeed, we shall have to see about your commission."

Was this to be the important work Jake had always imagined he would some day do? His face flushed with excitement.

McClellan thrust the written order into Jake's hand. "Do you know where to find General Hampton?"

"Yes, sir!" Jake gave the major a snappy salute.

Setting off at a canter, Cat and Jake wove their way past two artillery crews unlimbering their guns. A few moments later, a cannon blast shattered the midday air. Jake slowed Cat to a walk and glanced over his shoulder. Under a canopy of slowly dissipating smoke, the cannon crew rotated its big gun forty-five degrees. One man swabbed the barrel, a second man pushed a bag of powder into the muzzle, and a third rammed the powder home, but no one added a shell or ball. A sergeant pushed something coppery into the breech, then gave the lanyard a yank. Jake lurched at the concussion. Flames shot thirty yards from the end of the barrel. As the crew rotated the cannon and repeated the process, Jake put his heels to Cat's flanks and raced to find General Hampton.

-3-

After reporting their suspicions to Colonel McIntosh, David and Captain Miller returned to Company H to await orders. Over the next hour, a few Union patrols trotted north out Low Dutch Road. General Custer followed with a brigade of 1,900 Michigan troopers. David counted ten artillery pieces in the impressive parade of Federal strength. A half-hour later, the bugler sounded the clarion and McIntosh's 1,400-man brigade took to their horses. David slowly lifted his stiff, aching leg into the stirrup. He pulled himself into the saddle and groaned; every muscle seemed to beg for mercy. Streak swished his tail and danced a few side steps as if he, too, would have enjoyed a day to recuperate from the rigors of cavalry life.

Miller shouted, "Column of fours!"

The men of Company H took their position in the road. David joined a rank with Eli on his right, John Murray and Melchior Ziegler on his left. His new "family" looked grim with purpose.

After General Gregg and his staff rode past, the 3rd Pennsylvania Cavalry started north, with Company H as the vanguard. McIntosh halted the brigade a quarter-mile south of the intersection with Hanover Road. Fifteen minutes later, the order came down the line to dismount.

Eli turned to David and handed him the reins. "Your turn. Every fourth man watches the rank's horses when we dismount."

John and Melchior handed over their reins. Leading two horses with each hand, David walked the mounts into the hay field to graze.

The sound of horses tearing grass reminded him of last week when he had come upon Myrtle pulling weeds in Rose's garden. At first glance, Myrtle looked exactly like her mother, from her posture to her hair. David's throat tightened and a tear formed in each eye. His daughters had probably read his letter by now. How had they taken the news? He hated to cause them worry, but far better they fret over their father's safety than someday face the anguish of sending their own sons off to war. Surely a "Dis-united States" could never co-exist in peace. Human nature simply wouldn't allow it.

He studied the long line of soldiers lounging along the road. There had to be a thousand men and horses within sight. He tried to imagine 150 times again as many men—according to rumor, that was how many soldiers surrounded Gettysburg—but he couldn't fathom the idea. Reportedly, several thousand men had died here in the past two days. How many more thousands would breathe their last today?

The heat rose with the sun. Despite the solace of an occasional cloud shadow, the troopers languished in the stifling air. Across the road someone carped, "The Devil's stoking the fires of Hell again."

David prayed, *Lord, please keep Jake far from this place.*

Rather than consider his own immediate safety, David's thoughts turned to his eternal destiny. He felt secure enough in his faith that he did not fear dying, yet he dreaded the thought of what his death might mean to his family, especially Myrtle. *But I must see my duty through. I'll just have to make sure I keep my head down whenever possible. I can't miss Myrtle's wedding day.*

Fatigue soon overcame the horses' hunger. They stopped grazing and stood still, eyes closed. David chose an unfouled patch of grass in the horses' shade and curled up for a nap. He drew his cap down across his face, but a pesky fly bumped and buzzed against it as if desperate to find shelter inside. Already irritable from shortage of sleep, David swatted savagely at the insect, spooking the horses in the process.

"Need a break?" Eli called. "I've got the next watch anyway, so I may as well take my turn now so you can get some rest."

"Thank you, much obliged." David handed over the reins and scanned the vicinity for a shady place to snooze.

Deciding to empty his bladder first, he headed for a row of brush twenty yards up the road. As he turned to rejoin the Company, a rider galloped from the south. The man rode past David and met with a small group of officers coming from the north.

"General Gregg, sir, important news!" The dust-covered courier pulled a piece of paper from his dingy uniform blouse and announced the contents of the message. "General Howard reports from Cemetery Hill that a large force of Rebel cavalry is traveling east out the York Pike. And you are ordered to relieve General Custer's men on the right flank so they may report to General Kilpatrick on the left flank."

General Gregg did not looked pleased. "Thank you. You will find General Custer at the farmhouse on the other side of the crossroads up ahead." The courier galloped off to complete his mission.

Gregg continued in a disgruntled voice. "I do not see the sense in it, Colonel McIntosh. If there is indeed a large force threatening our flank, why move anyone away, let alone replace Custer's 1,900 men with your 1,400? Besides, what will old 'Kill-cavalry' do to Custer's men that he can't do to his own?"

A cannon blast rumbled from the ridge to the north. David counted three more shots in succession, though none was as loud as the first.

"Colonel McIntosh, I want you to take this brigade to the crossroads and await orders there," Gregg said. "I am not favorably disposed to turn

Custer's men over to General Kilpatrick. If our line is turned, it could mean disaster for the entire Army of the Potomac!"

David hustled back to Company H. His heart pounded at the thought of impending battle. Perhaps today he would see action on horseback. Part of him was intrigued at the thought, but his rational side argued for combat on foot, where his inexperience might be less of a disadvantage.

The bugler blew "To Horse!" and the road filled with mounted men in blue. McIntosh's staff rode past, then Miller raised his hand and bellowed, "Forward!"

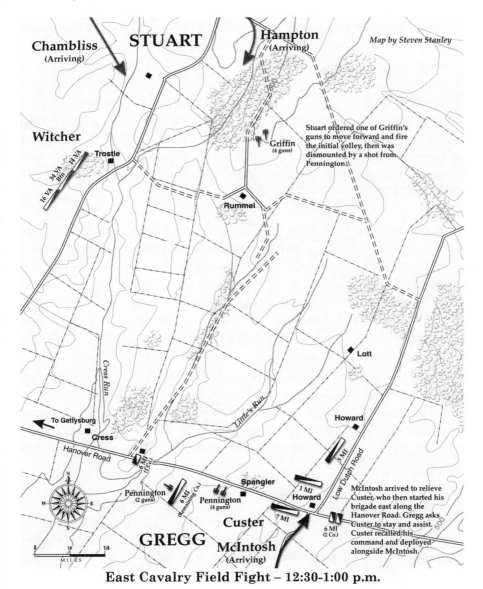

East Cavalry Field Fight – 12:30-1:00 p.m.

Company H followed McIntosh to the crossroads, where the lead elements of Custer's troops had already started back along Low Dutch Road. Custer and several other officers stood in deep discussion nearby.

A major rode up and shouted for all to hear. "The Johnnies are up on that ridge, sir. And there are lots of them!"

Custer looked pleased at the news, but before he could speak, cannons boomed in the distance and several shells poured down on the Union position. He turned to an aide. "Tell Lieutenant Pennington he may commence showering that ridge. And get my men back here at once!"

McIntosh ordered his column forward at a canter. David's heart raced in rhythm with Streak's hooves. From behind them came the blasts of Union artillery firing on the wooded ridge northwest of the crossroads.

The column halted next to a farmhouse several hundred yards up Low Dutch Road. McIntosh dismounted and entered the house with his staff in tow. The rest of the column remained in the saddle and out of sight of the enemy guns as the cannon duel continued.

The sun chose that moment to break through a bank of passing clouds. In a matter of moments, sweat rolled down David's brow and dripped onto his woolen uniform. He took a swig from his new canteen and winced at the oaky flavor. Streak shifted his feet and swished his tail. Unfortunately, there was no place to water the horses.

The barrage continued for the better part of an hour. Ready to spring into action at a moment's notice, the Union troopers chafed at the delay as they waited astride their horses in the baking sun. The bombardment finally ended, but a ripple of distant rifle fire quickly took its place.

McIntosh emerged from the house and shouted for an orderly. A young lieutenant rushed to obey.

"Tell Major Beaumont to bring his regiment up," McIntosh said. "They are to dismount and relieve General Custer's men."

Meanwhile, the rest of the waiting troopers continued to roast in the sun. Off to the west, the crackle of small arms fire intensified.

The stalking colonel's patience wore thin. "Where is the First New Jersey? Is Beaumont 'sick' again? Damn him." He turned to an aide. "Bring them up at a gallop!"

A few minutes later the troopers raced up, a cloud of dust trailing behind them. Through the haze, David heard McIntosh bellow, "Well, I am heartened to see a brave man has answered the call at last. Thank you, Major Janeway."

The dust cleared and David stared in astonishment at the man leading the New Jersey troopers. The lantern-jawed Janeway sported a sparse beard and looked to be even younger than Jake.

McIntosh ordered, "Major Janeway and Captain Boyd, dismount your regiment and relieve that position along the fence line." He pointed to the spot several hundred yards to the west, below the big white barn.

As they advanced, the regiment drew some long-range fire, but they

managed to splash across the marshy brook and reach the fence in good
order. Rebels rushed to secure a parallel fence. Gun smoke roiled above
the two opposing lines. When more Union troops charged across the fields
to aid their beleaguered comrades, the Confederates responded with a
hailstorm of bullets.

From his position on Low Dutch Road, David watched in horror as
many of the men in blue broke and ran. One officer turned and shouted,
"Rally, boys! Rally for the fence!" But a Minie ball put an end to the
exhortation when it turned the officer's forehead into a pulpy mass.

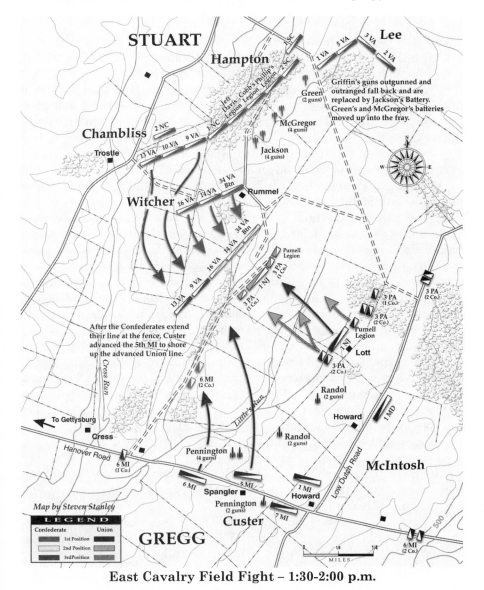

East Cavalry Field Fight – 1:30-2:00 p.m.

Colonel McIntosh quickly ordered more troops into action. "Treichel! Rogers! Purnell! To the front, double-quick!" The captains hustled their companies into the action.

The colonel, eyes ablaze with determination, surveyed his remaining men. "Miller! Hess! Walsh! Move into those woods." He pointed to the grove a quarter-mile north along Low Dutch Road. "You will be the right flank of the entire Army of the Potomac. You must hold that position *against all hazards*. If the Rebels get behind us, all may be lost."

-4-

Jake found General Hampton and his staff on the York Pike, just west of the farm lane leading to Stuart's position. Hampton was in the midst of delivering an order to an agitated Lieutenant Robertson.

"You must find him and tell him we have captured a man belonging to the Sixth Army Corps, who says his corps has just arrived and gone into the Gettysburg breastworks. It is most important that General Stuart know this."

Jake waved for Hampton's attention. "I just came from General Stuart, sir. He sent me with this message for you."

"Excellent." Hampton took the paper from Jake. "Now ride back to him with Lieutenant Robertson. Hurry!"

They galloped the mile back to the ridge and found Stuart leaning against a tree, arms folded, as he surveyed the rolling landscape. Hundreds of blue-clad cavalrymen covered the fields less than two miles away. The proof of Robertson's news?

Stuart listened to Robertson's report without taking his eyes off the enemy's deployment. "Thank you, Lieutenant. Now ride back to General Hampton. Tell him to get here as quickly as he can, and to keep his men out of sight in the woods. I do not want him to engage yet."

The lieutenant saluted and galloped off.

The cannons along the ridge opened a steady fire on the fields to the south. An answering shell screamed in their direction and found its mark directly in the muzzle of a Confederate cannon! The barrel shattered. Shrapnel knifed through the crew, bloodying several men. Both cannon wheels collapsed as the weapon turned into a heap of scrap metal.

Shocked at the sight, the other artillery crews paused for a moment, then returned to their labor with renewed intensity. Another shell headed for the ridge. This one hit a wheel on the next cannon in line. Two of the crew were dead before they hit the ground. The rest of the crew fell, writhing and screaming in agony.

The Confederates feverishly moved their guns to a new location. During the brief lull, a roar rumbled in from the west like an out-of-control freight train. Jake figured there had to be hundreds of artillery pieces to produce such a din. The trees quivered as if trembling in fear.

Cat swished her tail, lifted her head, and sniffed the air while prancing a couple of steps backward. Jake wanted to speak soothing words to her, but he didn't trust his voice to hide his own fear.

He scanned the fields below and recognized Hanover Road. And that must be Low Dutch Road on the left. The undulating landscape made it difficult to know for certain exactly where the enemy lay in wait. He expected at any moment to see thousands of Union troops charge the ridge. Instead, a couple hundred Yankees dismounted and marched in a line toward the stone fence facing the dairy farm. Other Federals turned their horses and cantered north toward the grove on Low Dutch Road.

The Confederate cannons resumed their barrage.

A short while later, Jake spied some movement at the edge of the trees below. The Yankees had taken up position in the grove.

-5-

An eerie aura emanated from the ancient trees. Thick, gnarled branches stretched across the road. Tendrils of creeping vines clutched the trees' twisted trunks and floated from their misshapen limbs like threads from an abandoned web. David's exhausted brain conjured the image of a giant spider out of the base of an uprooted tree. And were those hundreds of baby spiders crawling up his back?

Bleary-eye, he blinked and reached for his canteen. Even though the water had warmed in the midday heat, the liquid soothed his parched throat and calmed his jittery nerves.

Captain Miller led his sixty-four-man squad into the woods. Captain Hess' squadron joined them on the left. The horses carefully picked their way through brambles and boulders and fallen limbs. Dozens of chipmunks darted for hiding while a cloud of gnats descended on the riders. Perhaps being posted in the shade was not going to turn out to be the plum duty it had first appeared it might be.

Fortunately, the grove ran only a hundred yards deep. Even so, it took the troopers a good fifteen minutes to traverse the labyrinth. When they neared the other side, Miller gave the order to halt. His lieutenants went with him to the tree line to survey the fields to the west and north.

Returning a few minutes later, Miller stopped his dappled gray horse and surveyed the line of men. Although he raised his voice, the thick woods muffled the sound. "I suspect there will be action in the open fields around us. Our orders are to hold this position. Dismount, but keep your horses close. I want every man out of sight just inside the tree line."

David climbed off Streak and tied him to a sturdy, low-hanging branch. He pulled his Sharps from the saddle, trudged to the edge of the woods, and sprawled in the space between Eli and Melchior.

What sounded at first like a few thunderclaps swiftly grew into a torrent of cannon blasts, and David instinctively ducked his head. The ground rumbled as if it were about to spew forth all the demons of hell. Shell after shell screamed past, their wails dropping in pitch before they exploded near the crossroads. The Union cannons roared in reply.

Realizing the woods were not in the line of fire, David lifted his head and looked out across the pastoral landscape. Wheat stalks danced in the gentle breeze. Sunlight on the trees turned the leaves a lively shade of green. Though half-covered with patchy clouds, the sky was the clearest it had been in days, perfect for cloud watching. So why were thousands of men apparently willing to die in the midst of such beauty and serenity?

David glanced down the line. Melchior dozed. Eli stood and stared worriedly at the horizon. David turned to see the cause of concern.

Puffs of smoke floated over the ridge less than a mile to the northwest. A few mounted men in gray watched the cannoneers at their deadly task. From this distance, the enemy cavalrymen looked relaxed and unconcerned. David wished he had some binoculars to read their faces. Did they have any idea of the desecration to human flesh the artillerymen's labors wrought? Visions of Manassas filled his mind: the mounds of mutilated and disjointed bodies rotting in the sun, horses rent in two, the ground stained with blood and entrails, and that reek of sulphur and decay—Satan's incense.

After a mind-numbing hour the barrage slowed to a stop, but the ground continued to tremble from what must have been hundreds of artillery pieces blasting away on the far side of Gettysburg. David shook his head with the deepest of sorrows. *How many cannons does it take to assault the earth in such a manner? What must the poor men be suffering who lay at the receiving end of such a bombardment?* He prayed for mercy. Mercy for the men under attack, and mercy for humankind for failing to live together in peace.

-6-

The shelling finally stopped, but Jake heard the incessant crackle of small arms fire from the area south and east of the dairy farm.

McClellan called, "Becker, deliver these orders to General Hampton."

Jake raced along the ridge toward Hampton's position and delivered the message. Two squadrons of South Carolinians trotted off to strengthen the Confederate line in the fields below. Jake watched in fascination as the experienced troopers deployed. From the ridge it was difficult to discern exactly what was happening since the rolling terrain sometimes obscured the battle lines.

The Union artillery zeroed in on the area surrounding the big white barn. The soldiers in gray slowly withdrew from their positions around the farm, firing as they went. When a couple of shells dropped amongst them, they ran for the safety of the ridge. Jake bit his lip. Was this the harbinger of defeat? Why did General Stuart allow his men to retreat when there were still a few thousand cavalrymen waiting in the woods?

More Confederate artillery batteries arrived and unlimbered. In less than three minutes' time, six more big guns boomed from the ridge.

General Fitzhugh Lee's regiments emerged from cover behind the trees on the left. Were they about to sweep down across the wheat field and hit the stubborn Yankees on their flank? Jake hoped so. He had the perfect spot from which to view the charge.

Two Union shells burst in the field just ahead of Lee's line, and a third explosion sent dirt spraying over the men in gray. The riders turned their mounts and retreated to the safety of the woods. Jake spotted Herb over near Blackford, and the two young men exchanged grim looks. What could any cavalry do in the face of such accurate cannon fire?

-7-

David's consternation dissipated as the Rebel cavalry fled back into the trees. The men of Company H doffed their caps and raised cheer after cheer for the skillful artillerymen. David hoped the accuracy of the cannons might put an end to the Confederate probe of the Union flank.

But why were so many Federal soldiers withdrawing from the fence line off to the west? And now the Confederate artillery renewed its fire from the ridge. The fleeing Union foot soldiers scrambled for cover.

Captain Miller called over his shoulder, "Where's that new man, the one that's from around here? Becker!"

"Here, sir." Stifling a gulp, David hurried to Miller's side.

Miller held out a torn piece of paper. "Find Colonel McIntosh and deliver this message. He's probably still at the Lott farmhouse, north of the crossroads. Hurry back here with any reply."

"Yes, sir." David's heart steadied under Miller's determined visage. He took the proffered half-sheet of paper, folded it, and tucked it under the band inside his cap.

The longest part of the trip came in picking his way through the woods, Streak in tow. Once on the road, the pair galloped to the farmhouse—and into the teeth of the roaring Union cannons. Streak tossed his head at each horrifying concussion. "Steady, boy, you're doing fine. That's not meant for us."

David reined up by the Lotts' front porch, dismounted, and tied his nervous stallion to the hitching post. "I'll be right back, Streak."

A frazzled lieutenant emerged from the farmhouse, eyes darting from side to side. "Have you seen Colonel McIntosh?"

David snapped to attention and offered a quick salute. "No, sir. I need to find him, too. I have a message for him from—"

Muttering under his breath, the lieutenant ignored David and dashed around the north side of the house. A flurry of activity down by the crossroads caught David's eye. Was McIntosh there?

Though several junior officers milled about in Custer's wake, there was no sign of McIntosh. Custer shouted a series of orders from the back of his bay mare. Several companies of troopers dismounted, formed up, and marched at the double-quick toward the front line.

The Confederate fire intensified, driving the reinforcements to take cover behind a stone and rail fence near the middle of the open fields. Now the Federal position formed an ell—and just in time—the Rebel cavalry renewed their attack, pouring from the ridge in an all-out assault.

McIntosh barreled around the corner on the south of the house. "First Maryland! Where in hell is the First Maryland!" He swore a blue streak, as if to make the devil blush. And were those tears streaming down his cheeks?

David stared in dismay at the apoplectic commander. Dare he try to deliver Captain Miller's message when the colonel was in the midst of such a tirade?

The harried lieutenant hurried from behind the house. "There you are, Colonel. I have a message for you from General Gregg, sir."

McIntosh rounded on the courier. "Well, what is it? Speak up man, there's a war going on!"

"Um, sir, yessir!" His hasty salute nearly knocked his cap off. "The general ordered the First Maryland to guard our rear, sir."

"Hell and damnation! Now I have no one left to send in!"

David took a step back, half-expecting McIntosh to turn and pummel the first man in his path.

A great shout arose from the crossroads. With banners bravely flapping, rank after rank of fresh Union cavalrymen trotted up the road from the south. David recognized the Michigan regimental flag from earlier in the week in Hanover. General Custer rode to meet them. After a hurried exchange with their commander, Custer drew his sabre and bellowed, "Come on, you Wolverines!"

David's heart pounded in rhythm with the sound of hundreds of galloping hooves. Determination burned in the eyes of every man. Only their rosy cheeks and smooth skin gave away their youth. Was any one of those brave lads out of his teens?

The chargers slashed their way through the first disjointed Rebel line with little resistance, but faltered under the concentrated volley from oncoming Confederate reinforcements. Custer veered to the left, toward the Union line facing the dairy barn and the ridge beyond; but not all of the Wolverines were able to follow his lead. Most of the riders butted up against the stone and rail fence as the wild charge disintegrated into a discombobulated mass of horses and men. Some of the cavalrymen wound up crushed against the barrier, trapping the Union foot soldiers. Guns blazed on both sides of the fence. Men screamed and swore—and died. A thick fog of gun smoke quickly enveloped the battlefield.

David tore his eyes from the carnage to see if Custer had managed to turn his wayward troops back toward the center of the fierce melee, but the general and his remnant continued to gallop toward the dairy barn and the strong Confederate position on the ridge. Was the man mad? Perhaps he was unaware that most of his troops were no longer with him. Or was he suicidal? The Confederate cannons were only a few hundred yards away!

A distant bugle called retreat. Custer's men turned their mounts and dashed back toward the crossroads.

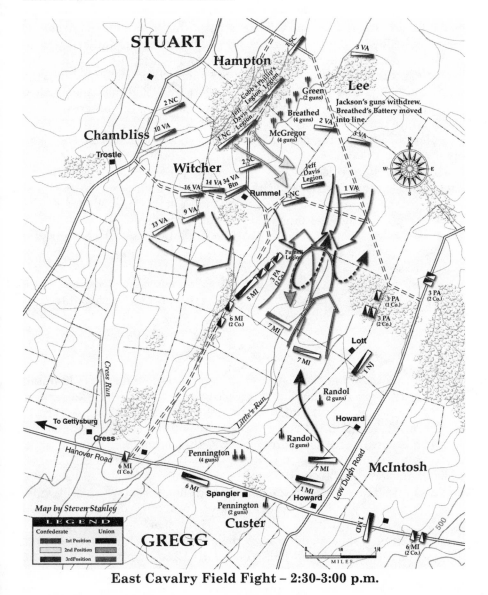

East Cavalry Field Fight – 2:30-3:00 p.m.

More Confederate reinforcements burst from cover on the ridge. The Union soldiers at the fence broke and ran. The Rebels at the fence took to their mounts and chased after the fleeing men in blue.

As the surviving Wolverines streamed past, McIntosh balled his fists and screamed, "For God's sake, men, if you are ever going to stand, stand now, for you are on your own free soil!" But panic had taken root, and there was no stopping the headlong flight for safety.

Frantic to help, David wondered if he should volunteer to go fetch Captain Miller and the men waiting in Lott's woods. The message! How could he let it slip his mind? He steeled his nerves and strode to McIntosh's side. "Colonel, a message for you from Captain Miller."

The colonel reached for the paper without taking his eyes from the battlefield. From the west, a squadron of Union troopers charged into the flank of the pursuing Rebel cavalrymen. More blue-clad horsemen rallied and quickly followed. A new melee broke out, slowing the progress of the Confederate pursuit.

McIntosh waved the note in the air and shouted, "Huzzah! There are my brave boys! God bless you all!"

But the battle looked far from over. The Confederates clearly outnumbered the Federals, and they still held the high ground.

McIntosh regained his composure and stole a quick glance at the message. "No, no, no," he muttered. He turned his steely eyes on David. "You skedaddle back to Captain Miller and tell him my orders are unchanged. I don't know what other surprises that wily Stuart has in store for us."

"Yes, sir!" David gulped. *If those are Stuart's men, does that mean Jake is up on that ridge, too?* His heart faltered at the thought. *Dear God . . .*

-8-

Jake's spirits soared at the sight of Union troopers fleeing the field in full stampede. All around him the reserve cavalrymen cheered and hooted. Jake glanced at General Hampton to gauge his reaction to the turn of events. Would he allow the rest of his men to join the pursuit?

The general's face looked grave. "No, that is too far," he muttered. His voice rose with anxiety. "Pull back. You are overextending." Then he spurred his horse and took off down the ridge, yelling, "No! Pull back! Too far!" His voice faded beneath the gunfire and shouts.

Hampton's adjutant, Captain Barker, drew his sabre and shouted over his shoulder. "Our time is here, men. Draw sabres!"

Hundreds of sabres zinged from their scabbards with a glorious ring. Jake studied the shiny length of steel in his hand and hefted the blade. He felt an irresistible urge to swing the weapon in broad strokes, to mow through his foes like a scythe through grass.

Barker walked his horse a few paces forward and turned to face the regiment. "For Virginia!" The men echoed, "For Virginia!" at the top of their lungs. Barker reined his horse to face the enemy and raised his sabre high. "Forward!"

Each company emerged from the woods in its own column of four, forming a wide front. Jake joined the middle of the third rank in Barker's column. Every man held his sabre perpendicular to the ground. The mid-afternoon sun glinted malevolently off the row of blades. Jake squinted against the glare.

At first, Barker kept the pace at a walk. All along the line, horses snorted and pranced, eager to race down the open field. To their left and right, more Confederate squadrons joined the advancing gray line.

Up ahead, General Hampton reined to a stop. A sizeable force of Union men appeared near the farmhouse along Low Dutch Road. Hampton's overzealous pursuers must have recognized their danger, for they broke off the chase and galloped west toward the Confederate line by the dairy barn. Hampton turned his horse around and started back up the ridge, then halted, gaping at the sight of his approaching troops.

The line increased its gait to a trot and Jake stood in the stirrups to get a clearer look at the field ahead. In the distance, several Union officers dashed from cover, waving their arms for their lingering men to flee the impending charge.

Hampton cantered up the slope, turned his mount, and took his place next to his color bearer. With a wave of his broadsword, the line broke into a canter.

The Union cannons spouted flame. The sound of the blasts followed a second later. A few seconds after that, several shells burst overhead and hot shards of metal ripped through the Confederate ranks. Clusters of horses and riders cried out as they tumbled to the ground. Cavalrymen from the rear ranks quickly moved up to fill the gaps.

Jake's heart pounded in his ears. The men around him raised their voices in the Rebel yell. With a rush of exhilaration, Jake joined in the long, trilling shriek.

A rush of activity south of the farmhouse drew Jake's eyes. Five hundred yards away, a long row of Union cavalry stood ready to meet the challenge. And could it be? A Yankee officer sporting long blond hair and a red bandana around his neck moved front and center.

Hampton's forces broke into a gallop. More cannon shots. More shattered men in gray. The ranks reformed on the move. The Yankee cavalry burst into action. With only a hundred yards of open field until the waves met, the Confederate cavalrymen brandished their sabres and renewed their fiendish yells.

Fifty yards. Twenty. Hampton hollered, "Keep to your sabres, men. Keep to your sabres!"

Jake searched the throng of onrushing Yankees and selected his first target. He squeezed Cat with his thighs, tightened his grip on the sabre, and braced for his first attack.

-9-

"Would you look at that," Captain Miller said, awestruck.

Out of breath from his frantic scramble through the woods, David followed Miller's gaze to the top of the distant ridge on their right. Hundreds upon hundreds of Confederate cavalryman calmly walked their horses from the woods. Their sabres shone like quicksilver. Battle flags and guidons fluttered in the breeze. Down the slope the Rebels came, as stately as if on dress parade. Murmurs of admiration rippled through the Union soldiers in the woods, and David finally understood why some men thought war a glorious thing.

The sounds of battle dissipated while the stragglers in the field rushed for cover. Meanwhile, on the other side of Gettysburg, the horrific cannonading finally came to an end.

"Carbines!" Miller ordered tersely. "We *must* hold this position!"

Union cannons opened fire from the left. David followed the path of the deadly shells. Every hole in the long gray line quickly filled, and the Rebel advance never wavered. They broke into a trot. A canter. A gallop. The thumping of thousands of hooves reverberated through the woods. Then David realized that what he heard was more than just an echo. From his left, General Custer and a new contingent of Union cavalry raced to meet the enemy head on, but they looked to be outnumbered at least three to one! David slowly shook his head. What would happen if they failed to hold off the superior force?

The head of the Confederate line drew even with the woods. Miller shouted, "Fire at will!"

David took aim with his Sharps and squeezed the trigger, hitting his target in the leg. Several other Rebels fell from the flanking fire, but the gray wave rolled on at top speed. Now only a few yards separated them from the counterattacking men in blue. David winced in anticipation of the impact. The horses slammed into each other with sickening thuds. Many of the lead mounts flipped end over end, flinging some of the riders into the air, while crushing those whose feet got tangled in the stirrups. Sabres clanged, men shouted, pistols cracked, and still the Rebels charged down the slope.

Shouting to be heard over the din, Miller leaned in his saddle and conferred with the lieutenant next to him. "I have been ordered to hold this position, but if you will back me up in case I am court-martialed for disobedience, I will order a charge."

The lieutenant nodded vigorously. "I shall not desert you, Captain. My squadron will be right beside you."

Miller's eyes glowed. "Draw sabres!"

David rammed the carbine back into the saddle's boot and drew his sabre. The blade zinged from the scabbard, vibrating as if eager to spring into action.

"Forward, men!" Company H emerged from the woods. "Charge!"

David kicked Streak's flanks and raced toward the passing Confederates. They hit the Rebel column about two-thirds of the way from the front. Confederates swarmed around them like angry gray hornets, but these hornets carried a far more deadly stinger.

A lanky Rebel bore down on David, reached back with his sabre, and slashed with all his might, rising in the stirrups with the effort. David dug his knee into Streak's left flank, pulled back on the reins, and lifted his sabre to block the blow. As the Rebel's blade swooped toward David's head, Streak slowed and veered to the left. It proved to be the difference between life and death. The extra space allowed David to deflect the stroke, but the clanging impact stung his hand. A flash of pain gripped his arm and his fingers lost their grip on the hilt. He leaned forward in the saddle and let the blade fall sideways across Streak's back. Without prompting, Streak bolted away from the encounter and sprinted to catch up with the rest of the troopers from Company H. Strength returned to David's hand and he regained his grip on the sabre.

Should he use his pistol instead? Maybe with the revolver he could avoid another sabre duel. No matter. He didn't have time to switch weapons. The charge carried them into the middle of the Confederate ranks. Everywhere he looked, David saw men in gray, their blades whirling and slashing as if to reap a human harvest.

-10-

Moments before the blue and gray waves collided, General Hampton yelled one final exhortation. "Charge them, my brave boys, charge them!"

Jake focused his attention on the Yankees directly in front him. The horses in both lines tried to shy away at the last instant, but there was no room to maneuver, the riders were packed too close together. The thumps of crashing bodies and the cracks of breaking bones mingled with angry shouts and shrieks of pain, both human and animal. Several horses hit the ground nose first; their momentum flipped them end over end. The hind hooves of one Union steed slashed the flank of a Confederate horse, and a bloody mist sprayed the air as if to baptize Jake and Cat.

The lines merged and the fight was on. Against the background of booming cannons, the random crackle of gunfire punctuated the frenetic rhythm of sabre on sabre.

A Yankee officer headed straight for Jake, first parrying a slash from a Confederate on the right, then blocking another blow from the left. Jake gritted his teeth and braced himself to meet the attack. The man came in on the right side, coiling for an overhead stroke. Jake reined Cat to the left and lifted his blade at an angle in front of his head. Every nerve in his body tingled with energy. He had never felt so alive!

The oncoming trooper swung his sabre, but instead of bringing it straight down, the crafty Yankee bent his elbow and delivered a slanting stroke in the effort to elude Jake's defense.

Jake's eyes narrowed. He dropped his elbow and turned his wrist to bring the sabre to an upright position, absorbing the brunt of the attack just in time. The force of the blow pushed Jake's sabre away from his body and into the perfect position from which to launch a counterattack. As the Yankee regained his balance, Jake slashed sideways. The end of his blade sliced across the man's forearm. Blood squirted from the gash. The officer yowled, dropped his weapon, and drew the damaged arm to his mid-section. Doubled over in pain, he turned his horse and fled.

Expecting to feel an enemy blade in his back at any moment, Jake looked for a new foe. Several feet to the left, a Union man leveled a pistol at him. Jake swung his sabre up as if to block the bullet. Realizing his folly, he kicked Cat's flanks and reined to the right. The bullet whizzed past. By the way Cat's ears perked up, Jake figured the projectile narrowly missed her head.

He glimpsed a flash of red out of the corner of his eye. It was that silly bandana on the Yankee with the long blonde hair! Suddenly, the officer fell from his wounded horse and landed in an inglorious heap amidst the maelstrom. Jake turned Cat and urged her forward. Might he be the one to finish off Hampton's nemesis?

The officer regained his feet and deftly swung into the saddle of a riderless horse. A dueling pair of cavalrymen swerved in front of Jake, blocking the way.

Suddenly, a new threat appeared on the right. Two dozen Union men charged into the chaos. Their target appeared to be the regimental color bearer—and General Hampton.

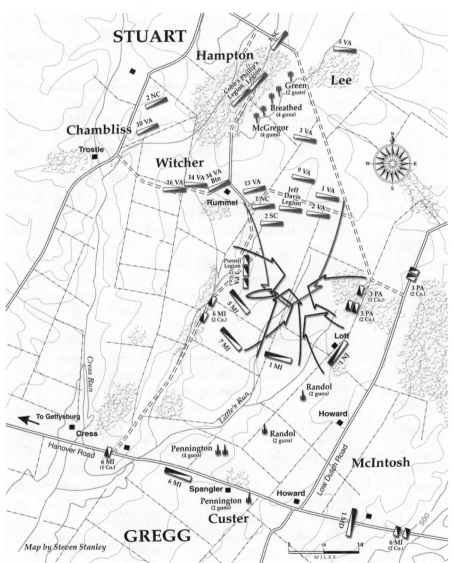

East Cavalry Field Fight – 4:15-4:45 p.m.

Map by Steven Stanley

-11-

The overwhelming rumble of thousands of galloping horses assaulted David's ears. He realized he had never truly understood the word "chaos" until that moment. He blinked hard, trying to make sense of the swirling mass of flesh and steel. Riders in blue and gray intermingled as if they were tin soldiers shaken up and spilled from a bag. And it was every man for himself.

Captain Miller's bellow cut through the din. "Charge!" His sabre hacked and slashed in great sweeping motions, left and right, left and right. The Rebels veered away from the madman.

Heartened, David followed his commander's example. With Eli on his left and Melchior on his right, the trio made a formidable threshing machine.

The few Confederates who chose to stand and fight were quickly dispatched. Most turned their mounts and fled; some fell back toward the ridge on the north, others retreated toward the dairy farm. Company H pressed westward after them, cutting a swath through the tail of the charging Rebel column.

A dismounted man in gray trained his pistol on Captain Miller. David rode up from behind, swung his sabre, and clapped the Rebel on the side of the head. The soldier's knees sagged, and then David and Streak were past him. From behind them came a strangled cry as Melchior's horse rode the man down.

Ten yards to David's left, Eli aimed his carbine at a dismounted Confederate, and shouted, "Drop your weapons, you are my prisoner!"

David reined Streak to a halt. Did Eli need any help?

The Rebel slowly reached for his pistol to comply, but then a bullet whizzed past Eli's head, causing him to flinch and duck. The Rebel drew his gun and fired. Eli's horse collapsed in a heap on the ground. Though Eli managed to scramble free, he was now the captive. David raised his revolver, then lowered it. If he missed, the Rebel might shoot Eli.

Help came from the opposite direction. Sergeant Thomas Gregg galloped up from behind the man in gray and nearly decapitated him with his sabre. A spray of blood splattered Eli and his fallen mount. The sergeant reined his horse to a stop, grinning from ear to ear.

David spotted a new danger. "Behind you!" He thrust the revolver out and fired at the approaching Rebels, thumbed back the hammer and fired again, but to no avail.

Several Confederate horsemen burst upon them. The lead rider stood in the stirrups and slashed sideways at Sergeant Gregg. The sergeant's hat flew through the air, along with the top of his scalp.

Hopelessly outnumbered and unable to do anything more for his comrades, David reluctantly turned Streak and galloped after Captain Miller and the rest of the company. He stole a glance over his shoulder.

No one pursued him. The Confederates seemed content with two prisoners. Sergeant Gregg sat astride his mount in obvious pain, hands covering his bloody, closely shaven pate. Eli stood scowling with his hands in the air. David prayed his brothers-in-arms would not be mistreated.

Turning his attention back to the battle, David spotted Miller dueling with a Rebel officer. Miller parried a mighty blow, but his blade split in two. The larger section whirled away end over end, finally coming to rest near a wagon shed.

David and Streak hurried to join the combat. Too late. Miller threw the hilt of his sabre at the assailant, thereby freeing his weapon hand to draw his pistol. With David closing in, the Rebel dropped his sabre and surrendered. The blade bounced off the torso of a blue-clad cavalryman, his face twisted in death. At his feet lay a man in gray, eyes staring vacantly. Both dead men gripped their sabres as if clinging to life.

From the direction of the farm, Confederate footmen laid down a steady fire in support of the withdrawing troops. And their artillery stood only a couple hundred yards away. Miller rose in the stirrups and shouted, "Company H!" A few dozen troopers quickly gathered around their dauntless commander. "We must return to the woods. Follow me!"

Streak stumbled over the bodies of another pair of fallen antagonists. David only caught a glimpse of the corpses, but the image burned in his mind. The men's heads and shoulders were covered with slash marks. Their frozen fingers dug into one another as if to squeeze the last ounce of blood from the other's flesh.

Trying in vain to blink the horrific tableau from his memory, David turned his eyes toward the woods. A quarter mile of open terrain lay littered with fallen horses and bodies too numerous to count. The main fight still raged to the south, but scores of straggling and retreating Confederates blocked the company's route to the woods.

The gunfire from the dairy barn intensified. Rebel cavalrymen regrouped nearby. Miller yelled, "Forward!" and the troopers of Company H cantered away.

A Minie ball whistled past David and took off the tip of Streak's ear. The stallion neighed and reared. Caught off balance, David's feet slipped from the stirrups. He tumbled from the saddle and fell flat on his back in the trampled wheat. Through dazed eyes he saw Streak bolt toward the Hanover Road.

Good boy, David thought groggily. *Maybe one of us will make it home safe and sound.*

-12-

The Union officer leading the charge against General Hampton's colors extended his arm to grab the regimental flag. A member of the color guard intervened with his sabre, but the attacker deftly countered the blow. The color-bearer lowered the banner like a medieval lance and drove the spiked flagpole through the Yankee's scrawny goatee. Even before the dead man hit the ground, a bullet found its mark in his arm and a sabre slashed his face.

Jake arrived in time to help fight off the rest of the small band of attackers. This time he swung his sabre on the offensive and sent two foes running. Though he was unable to inflict any damage, neither man came close to landing a blow on him. With a surge of confidence he cast an appreciative look at his blade. Next time it would draw blood. No one could stop him!

A riderless Morgan galloped past. Jake blinked in astonishment; the chestnut stallion looked so much like Streak! His feeling of invincibility vanished with the memory of what had happened to Skipper on the road to Union Mills.

From the left, another squad of Yankees cut a swath toward Hampton. With a rail fence protecting his right side, Hampton took on two men at once. The broadsword in his right hand dispatched one attacker, the pistol in his left felled the other. But more Union men quickly took their place. Jake and Cat joined the rush to defend the beloved commander. Two Confederates quickly fell victim to Yankee sabres. Hampton's pistol wreaked vengeance on one of the swordsmen, but the other man managed to land a blow on the general's head, reopening the wound from the previous day.

Jake barely fended off his more experienced Yankee foe. Fortunately, a stray bullet ended the duel and the man in blue toppled to the ground. Jake reined Cat to the right and found Hampton, skillfully fending off two enemy sabres. His blade flashed tirelessly despite the blood oozing from the back of his bandaged head.

Jake and Cat swept down on the scene. His slashing sabre disabled one of the attackers. To Jake's horror, a Union man came up behind Hampton and fired his pistol, hitting the general in the thigh.

Eyes flashing with anger, Hampton roared, "You dastardly coward! Shoot a man from the rear?" He raised his sword at the gunman, who turned and fled for his life.

The remaining Yankee turned his attention on Jake, raining blow after blow on the inexperienced young man. Now Jake's sabre felt so heavy, he knew he couldn't hold out much longer. A part of his mind dispassionately wondered what death would be like.

The next slash knocked Jake's fingers loose from the hilt. He lowered his eyes and fumbled to regain control of the sabre dangling from the cord around his wrist. His skin crawled, expecting to feel the cut of the Yankee blade at any moment.

But by then the man in blue had to fend off Hampton's attack. The weakened Hampton managed to parry two slashes, but the third slipped past his sword and opened another gash on his head.

Meanwhile, Jake slipped his hand through the guard and lifted his sabre, but before he could join the melee, Hampton rose in the stirrups and delivered a great overhand stroke, cleaving the Yankee's skull to the chin. The dead man's horse whinnied and reared, sending the corpse toppling to the ground.

More Union troopers closed in. Jake sighed in despair. Was there no end to them? Even though several Confederates rallied to their general's aid, there were far more blue uniforms than gray. Now Hampton was trapped against the rail fence.

A Confederate sergeant arrived just in time to shoot a Yankee swordsman whose blade was about to blindside Hampton. The sergeant pleaded with his commander. "General, General, they are too many for us. For God's sake, leap your horse over the fence and withdraw. I'll die before they have you!"

Hampton spurred his horse and the steed soared majestically over the railing. The sergeant shot the closest pursuer, urged his mount over the fence, and then hurried to cover the general's retreat.

Jake tried to follow, but a Yankee officer galloped past, blocking the path. When the Union man's horse refused to jump the obstacle, the officer angrily turned in search of a new target. His dark eyes fixed on Jake. He raised his sabre at arm's length, pointed its tip at Jake's face, and charged.

Having no idea how to defend against such a thrust, Jake frantically tried to rein Cat out of the way. But there was not enough time. He threw up his sabre arm in a last ditch effort to save himself.

The Yankee's blade rattled along Jake's sword, deflected off the handguard, and sliced through flesh. Jake felt a warm, wet sensation from the right corner of his mouth to the middle of his ear. Just as the pain set in, a pistol fired on his left. Cat whinnied and reared.

Jake felt a wave of dizziness. The ground rushed up to meet him; his head and right shoulder hit first. Something in his shoulder cracked. Lightning flashed in his brain. Pain shot through every nerve. Something massive crushed his legs. Bones cracked. Agony. Darkness.

-13-

Two horses trotted up and halted next to David's prostrate body. He struggled to a sitting position and raised his hands in surrender.

"Hurry up, we gotta get outta here!" It was Melchior, and he led an extra horse!

Ignoring the bolts of pain shooting up his spine, David retrieved his sabre and climbed onto the large roan. The horse's previous rider must have been several inches shorter. When David slipped his feet into the stirrups, his knees bent at an awkward angle, which made it difficult to hold his seat as he galloped after Melchior. David felt like a child gripping the pommel, but this was no time for adjustments.

They caught up with the rest of the squadron in the middle of the field, where a cluster of Rebels looked ready for a stout fight. The men in blue would have to force their way through.

Miller raised his arm. "Rally on me, boys!"

Having fought together for two years, the troopers quickly formed their battle line. Fearing his inexperience might be more of a hindrance than a help, David decided to lag behind the chargers, where he hoped he might be able to lend a hand if one of his comrades got into trouble.

Miller waved with his pistol and bellowed, "Charge!"

A Rebel carbine blazed in front of them. The bullet pierced Miller's arm and his revolver fell to the ground. Heedless of the pain, the weaponless captain spurred his horse and led the assault. David brandished his sabre threateningly as the Company bore down on the Confederates.

An enemy officer cantered toward David from the right. Blood streamed from the back of the man's head and thigh. His face was as gray as his uniform.

For one brief moment, David considered turning and giving battle, but then they locked eyes. Judging from the officer's fierce countenance, David realized such a move would probably be as foolhardy as taking on a wounded she-bear protecting her cubs.

Suddenly, a shell exploded above them. A piece of shrapnel cut a hole through the brim of David's cap and buried itself in the saddle's pommel.

Apparently wounded yet again, the Rebel officer lurched to the side and clutched his hip. Blood seeped between his red-stained fingers. He slumped forward while his horse raced for the ridge.

Shaken by another close call, David hurried after the remnant of Company H. He easily dodged a half-hearted swipe from a passing Confederate before finally making it to the safety of the woods.

Miller gave the orders to dismount and fire from cover. David cautiously slid from the saddle, but when his feet met the ground it felt like a knife was thrusting up his spine. He bent in two, crying out in agony. When he tried to straighten, the pain only worsened. He hobbled over to a big maple tree to lie down.

The clash of sabres slowly dissipated, the gunfire abated, and the pounding of horses' hooves faded into the distance. Was it finally over?

David eased onto his side and bent his knees, searching for a more comfortable position. He groaned with each little movement.

A distant scream answered his groans: another wounded man, crying out? The scream grew louder and closer. Someone at the tree line yelled, "That shell is coming our way! Heads down!"

David curled into a ball as the projectile exploded in the tree above him. Shards of metal and splinters of wood knifed through the foliage. A large branch crackled and split from the maple's trunk. David glanced up. The fractured limb was coming directly at him! He closed his eyes against the pain in his back and tried to roll to safety. *Oh, Lord*—

-14-

A man in a gray uniform grabbed Jake's left boot and twisted it round and round. A Yankee gripped the other boot and wrung Jake's leg as if it were a waterlogged towel. Great drops of blood oozed from his legs and fell through the air, splattering Myrtle's new carriage until it was fire-wagon red.

Jake's legs, shoulder, and cheek burst into flame. He tried to swat out the fire, but none of his muscles obeyed. He couldn't even open his mouth to vent the screams billowing up inside. Who would douse the flames?

All four of his sisters came and stood over his helpless burning body. Tears streamed down their faces and landed on the flames with a sizzle, but it was not enough to quell the blaze.

Ma and Pa emerged from a cloud and added their tears to the effort, but to no avail. The flames raged on.

Eliza and Kathleen appeared. Not even their heartrending tears could satisfy the fire's demands.

With nowhere else to turn for salvation, Jake cried out, *Oh, Lord, save me from this hellfire!* The heavens parted and a pure white stallion galloped out of the clouds. The white-robed rider's long brown hair flowed in the wind. He calmly dismounted and held Jake in his arms.

Jake whispered, "Oh, Lord, please, please save me."

The man in white turned his scarred palms to the heavens and shouted, "It is finished!" He wept. At long last, the fire fled those tears.

The vision vanished, but the agony remained.

Jake's muscles slowly returned to life. Pain slashed from his toes to his head. He swallowed, tasting blood and dirt. His eyes opened to a world in darkness. Where was he?

The sound of men's voices drew near. "Here's another one. Open that lantern up a little more, will ya?"

A faint beam of light revealed trampled wheat and a mangled blue-clad corpse. Jake's memory returned, piling anguish on top of his agony. No wonder he couldn't move. Cat's body pinned his leg.

A rough pair of hands tugged on Jake's shoulders, trying to turn him onto his back. He screamed from the pain, then screamed again when the hands let go and his face hit the turf. He nearly passed out.

A voice hissed furtively, "He's still alive!"

"Yeah, but he's not going anywheres, not with his horse riding *him*," the first man quipped. He reached under Jake's chest and emptied the shirt pocket.

"So what's he got?"

The thief spat. "Just a Bible. Hold on, what's this? Bring that light closer and let's have us a look."

"Is that a picture? Lemme see. Say, she's a purty one!"

The first man spat a stream of tobacco juice near Jake's cheek. "I'll say. Shame that other girl's all fuzzy. I bet she's a looker, too. Well, he ain't gonna be needing this no more."

Jake tried to turn over, but when he began to push up on his arms an unbearable pain pierced his right shoulder. He gasped and held his breath while the agony slowly subsided.

The second man sounded agitated. "Didja check his pants?"

"If you can get at them under that horse, be my guest," the first thief snorted.

"Is there any money in that there Bible?"

"Nah, just locks of hair."

Jake groaned. "Stop . . . mine!"

Someone shouted in the distance. "Hey, what are you men doing over there?"

"Outen the light," the first thief hissed. The glow from the lantern vanished and the robbers retreated into the darkness. The sound of boots swishing through wheat faded beneath the throbbing in Jake's ears.

A few moments later a wagon creaked up. An old man's voice called, "Gosh danged looters, you better run!"

A swath of lantern light lit the scene, but Jake didn't dare move for fear of the pain. His fingers clutched the earth as if letting go would mean the surrender of his life.

The old man with the lantern sighed. "You'd better bring the saw, Lenny, his leg's pinned. We'll have to bury him in pieces."

Jake lifted his head to speak, but it was his agonized scream that announced he was not yet dead. He lost consciousness before his head hit the ground.

When he came to, he found himself lying flat on his back on a hard surface. Moving only his eyes, he determined he was in the back of a cart, and it felt like a bandage circled his chin and head. He tried to move his legs. Pain swept over his body in waves. Each breath was an excruciating ordeal. *Oh, Lord, please let me die. Take me home, Lord, please?*

Someone climbed onto the back of the cart and set a lantern near his head. A woman's voice said, "I have something for the pain."

Her voice sounded so soft and gentle, Jake wanted to curl up on it and slip into eternal sleep. In the background, he heard the musical clink of glass on glass.

"Open your mouth, just a little. This dropper's got laudanum in it."

Jake nearly gagged on the liquid. He wished it would drown him, anything to end the agony. The wagon started to move, groaning and creaking like an old set of stairs. He cried out with each jolt.

A few minutes into the ride, the woman spoke to the driver of the cart. "Look there, Adam! Can you believe that? How can those soldiers sit on that blanket and have a picnic amidst all this death?"

"Just the smell of dead horses is enough to put me off my feed," Adam said.

Jake started to smile at Adam's dark sense of humor, but shuddered when a streak of pain shot through the right side of his face. It felt as if the sabre sliced through his flesh all over again.

A distant cannon boomed. A shell screamed their way. The woman leaned over to shield Jake with her body, and the bomb burst overhead off to their left. Raining shrapnel broke the picnickers' crockery and sent the swearing soldiers scrambling for cover.

Jake began to feel woozy as the pain finally lessened. His eyes grew heavy. The last thing he remembered was the Smiling Man, his skin now the color of coffee, beckoning with his finger. "Your time draws ever nearer. Will you join us?"

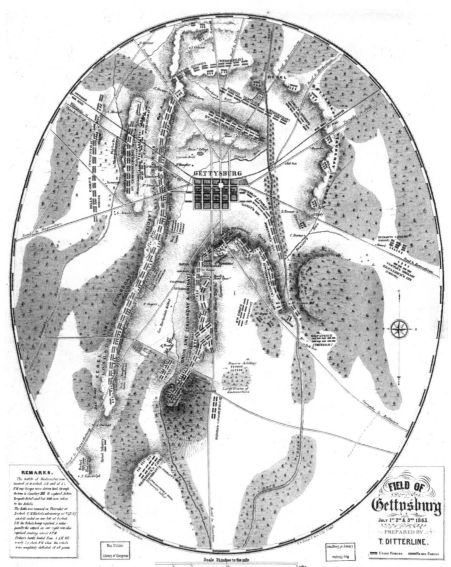

Field of Gettysburg, July 1st, 2nd, & 3rd, 1863, T. Ditterline (1863)
East Cavalry Field is in the clearing, east of Gettysburg

Part Three: Weeks of Healing

Saturday, Independence Day, 1863

Was it the sizzle or the smell that woke him? Jake groaned and opened his eyes upon a world in flames. Great tongues of fire licked at a vast column of soldiers clad in blue and gray. The men's skin smoldered, shriveled, and peeled, then floated on the hot breeze like remnants of burnt paper. Though some of the soldiers tried to swat out the flames, most paraded along as if oblivious to their impending doom. Jake cried out to warn them, but his single voice had little hope of being heard over the roar of the conflagration. Who would douse the flames?

Jake turned his eyes toward heaven. "Oh, Lord, how long must your people suffer?"

The disembodied reply resonated in his head. *Ask instead,* why *do they suffer?*

Why indeed? Calling on his religious instruction, Jake considered the possibilities. "Do they suffer for what they have done?"

These men suffer for what was left undone.

Left undone? Whatever could that mean? Jake peered into the faces of the marching men. The raging fire glistened in guileless eyes, determined eyes, frightened eyes; proud, anxious, and happy eyes. But only the eyes of those men swatting the flames held any inkling of guilt. Was there no hope for the soldiers?

"Oh, Lord, what if they acknowledge their guilt? Will you then save them from their suffering?"

The answer came in the form of a Bible verse Jake had memorized in childhood. "If we confess our sins, He is faithful and just to forgive us our sins, and to cleanse us from all unrighteousness."

And then the voice asked, *Whom should I send to tell them?*

Should he volunteer? The column continued to march in lockstep. Blue uniform or gray, they headed for the same destination, their fates intertwined.

Jake felt a tap on his shoulder. Startled, he spun around and found himself staring into the face of the Smiling Man. The now dark-faced apparition implored, "Will you join the fight? There is so much left to do."

Jake covered his ears and clenched his eyes shut. "What fight? What is it that was left undone? What do you want of me?"

"Ouch!" Eliza gritted her teeth, stifling a profanity. What was it with sharp objects and her fingers? At least this time it was only a sewing needle. She sucked the droplets of blood from the fleshy part of her thumb, then flung the sock against the bedroom wall. "Gosh darned darning!"

"Eliza! I should wash your mouth out!" her mother shouted from across the hall. Footsteps sounded in the hallway and Mama appeared at the bedroom door. "What in Heaven's name has gotten into you?"

Eliza folded her arms, flopped back onto the bed, and stared at the ceiling. "You know I'm no good with a needle, Mama. Why couldn't the mending wait for Kathleen? It's not fair that she gets to skip out on her chores to go play nursemaid to some Yankees with bloody noses."

"Well, are we feeling a bit green with envy today?" Mama entered the room and sat on the edge of the bed next to Eliza. "You know she's also tending our brave Southern boys. Why don't you go, too?"

"You want to see green? Take one look at my face if you ever catch me among the wounded again." Eliza's stomach heaved with the memories of what she had witnessed after the battle in Manassas: the mutilated bodies, the gut-wrenching shrieks, the reek of decay, and, worst of all, the God-forsaken look in those wretched men's eyes. Even now, their cries haunted her.

Oh, God, let me die. . . . Somebody shoot me. . . . Mama . . .

Mama patted her arm. "I understand, darlin', but the worst is over now. You can write letters for them and read to them while they're recovering. Isn't that what your sister does most of the time? Think of how lonely those poor boys must be, so far from home. God forbid Jake ever got hurt, wouldn't you want someone to do the same for him?"

Eliza inspected her fingernails and considered the idea. Maybe they had a separate room for the men who didn't stink any more. Surely she could stomach helping a Southern boy—just so long as he wasn't missing any body parts. She shuddered at the thought. Besides, she hadn't been into town since Wednesday. Maybe the Winebrenners or the Forneys had gotten word from Mr. Becker or, dare she hope, Jake.

"All right, Mama, I'll do it. For Jake."

"That's my girl. Now hand me that darning basket, I'll tend to it." She tucked a strand of gray hair back into her snood.

Eliza looked up into her mother's face. Where had all those lines come from, radiating from the corners of those puffy eyes? And those dark circles? Eliza had never thought of her mother as "old," but now that the seeds of aging had sprouted, she found the image of an "elderly" mother disturbing.

"What's the matter, darlin'?" Mama asked. "Why so fretful?"

The tenderness in her mother's eyes released a torrent of emotion in

Eliza. The world was changing so fast, and she wasn't ready for it. Though she was happy to be a woman, she'd forgotten that everyone else aged at the same time. Once she and Jake got married, babies would soon come along, and that would make her Mama a grandmother! Eliza sat up and hugged her mother tight. "I love you, Mama."

"I love you, too, sweetheart." Mama sighed. "Everything will be fine, you'll see. With good men like Jake fighting for the cause, we'll all be able to go back home soon."

Eliza reveled in the encouragement in Mama's words. Why had it taken so many years and so much turmoil to break down the wall that had separated them for so long? Eliza vowed she would never let that happen with her own children. And Jake would be a much better father than she'd had. What a difference that would make! She smiled at the image of little Jake, Jr., toddling toward her outstretched arms.

"There, didn't I tell you?" Mama stood and held out her hand. "Now show that beautiful smile to our poor injured boys in town. Go and brighten up their day."

Eliza took her mother's hand, eased off the bed, and caught a glimpse of her visage in the mirror. "Oh, Mama, I look a fright!" She raked her fingers through her hair. "Just look at this rat's nest! Help me with it?" She bit her lip, waiting for the reply. Mama hadn't helped her with her hair since she was a little girl.

"What a splendid idea! Do you know how many years I've waited for you to ask me that?"

Eliza's jaw dropped. "What do you mean?" Could it be? Had Mama been willing all this time, but waiting for an invitation?

"Don't you remember?" Sadness filled Mama's eyes. "You were ten years old the last time I did your hair, but you didn't like the way it looked. You threw the brush on the floor and told me that you didn't need my help any more, and if you changed your mind, you'd let me know."

It felt like the bottom fell out of Eliza's stomach. Now she remembered, all too well. She even recalled the part of the tirade Mama had omitted, "But don't hold your breath!" What an intolerable brat she had been! Why, if she ever had a daughter who spoke in such an impudent manner, she'd slap her face.

"Oh, Mama, can you ever forgive me? I'm so sorry. I was such a foolish child. I can't believe I was so selfish." In a flash of self-awareness, the word hit her like the slap she had so richly deserved. Selfish. Was there a better way to summarize her existence thus far?

Tears rolled down Mama's wrinkled cheeks. "Of course, darlin'. We've all made mistakes."

Eliza stepped over to the dresser, picked up her brush, and held it out. "Mama, would you please do my hair? It would mean a lot to me."

It was as if each stroke of the brush unsnarled a tangle that had encumbered their lives for years.

-3-

A clap of thunder shook the house. Eliza went to the kitchen window and glumly stared out at the sheets of rain drenching the barnyard. Huge raindrops bounced like glassy marbles on the hardened turf. Uncle Henry emerged from the carriage barn and sloshed his way around the deepest of the puddles. When he made it to the porch, he stomped the worst of the mud from his boots, then scraped the remaining muck on the bootjack.

Eliza stepped behind the door as she opened it for her uncle. She had to lean on the door to shut it against the wind.

"Sorry, Eliza, we'll have to wait to go into town until this blows over, what with the lightning and the danger of tree limbs coming down." Uncle Henry removed his slouch hat and oil-cloth slicker, shook them out, and hung them on the pegs next to the door.

Aunt Ida looked up from peeling potatoes at the dry sink. "Is there any sign of clearing?"

"Not that I could see." Uncle Henry sat on the chair next to the door and pulled off his boots. "I'm thinking they'll have to cancel the Independence Day concert. Can't very well move it into Albright Hall with all the wounded men in there."

Lydia thumped the bread dough on the table. "What about one of the churches, or would that be too crowded?"

Aunt Ida rubbed her nose with her wrist. "Better too crowded than cancel the whole thing."

"I doubt many folks will come out in this weather." Uncle Henry sighed. "I'll go fetch Kathleen when this lets up." He pulled a towel from a peg and rubbed his hair.

Irene Bigler came in from the parlor and set the darning basket on the counter. "Thank you, Henry. I don't want her to have spend another night in town."

Another night in town. Eliza felt a flash of jealousy, remembering Kathleen's last night in town and the close relationship she had forged with Mr. Becker. At least he was off fighting in the war now. Kathleen would just have to find another shoulder to lean on instead of selfishly—

Eliza cringed. There was that word again. Selfish. But was Kathleen the selfish one? Eliza shook her head slowly. How insufferable she must have been! Perhaps today would be the day she cast off selfishness once and for all.

Someone tromped onto the porch. Eliza flung the door open and a sopping wet Kathleen hurried into the kitchen. Outside, the rain slowed to a downpour. The driver of the buggy flipped the reins and the horse splashed toward the carriage barn.

Mama gasped. "Poor Kathleen, you got caught in this deluge. You'll catch your death!" She flung open a drawer under the counter and grabbed a handful of towels. Uncle Henry stepped aside and Kathleen sank onto the chair, shivering.

Eliza held out a hand for a towel and wrapped it around her sister's shoulders. "You poor dear. Let me help you."

Pushing the soggy strands of hair from her face, Kathleen looked up at Eliza. "Wouldn't you rather help Jonas when he comes in?"

The implication stung Eliza. "Help Jonas? What do you mean?"

Lydia's look of shock echoed the question.

Instead of answering, Kathleen took a towel from her mother and pressed it to her face.

Lydia hurried to the window. "Did Jonas bring you home?"

"Yes," came Kathleen's muffled reply.

While Mama dried Kathleen's arms, Eliza stood in a daze. Why would Kathleen think she would rather help Lydia's beau? So she was friendly. It wasn't her fault the boys seemed to like her so much. Besides, only a shameless flirt would stoop so low as . . .

Eliza slumped against the door. Had she really been so self-absorbed all this time? So completely unaware of what others thought of her?

Lydia moved from the window and stood expectantly in front of Eliza. Catching the hint, Eliza turned and opened the door as Jonas arrived on the porch. Lydia beamed and welcomed him inside.

In the midst of the hubbub, Kathleen removed the towel from her face and stood. "Thank you, Mama. I better go upstairs and get out of these wet clothes now." Mama nodded and turned to hand the unused towels to Jonas.

Eliza was startled at the disturbed look in her sister's eyes. Kathleen loved getting wet, especially in the rain. Something must have happened to upset her. Had she heard news of Jake? Or his father? "Mama, I'm going to go help Kathleen."

Without waiting for anyone's approval, Eliza plucked a dry towel from Jonas' hand, put an arm around Kathleen's waist, and ushered her up to their bedroom. She didn't even mind when her dress got wet. Kathleen wordlessly accepted the assistance.

Once the bedroom door closed, Eliza eased the dress over Kathleen's arms and hung the sodden garment on a bedpost. While Kathleen peeled off the rest of her clothing and toweled dry, Eliza opened the top dresser drawer for a fresh set of under garments. Kathleen wriggled into her clean clothes, then sat on the edge of the bed.

In all the times Eliza had seen Kathleen look bedraggled, she had never seen her look this forlorn. What could she do to help? She knew just the thing. The comb.

Surprised at the offer, Kathleen shifted on the bed and allowed her sister to begin the pampering. Eliza carefully drew the comb through the long tawny hair, stroke after loving stroke. Kathleen sighed softly.

Judging the time to be right, Eliza rested a hand on her sister's shoulder, leaned close, and whispered, "Now then, what has gotten my baby sister so upset?'"

Kathleen stiffened.

Eliza waited, but her sister said nothing. "Did you hear any news about Jake or his father?"

She sniffled and shook her head no.

Eliza wondered if one of Kathleen's patients had died. Maybe she just felt sick—God forbid she had caught some disease! Or had one of those filthy Yankees attempted to take liberties with her? "Please tell me what's bothering you, Sis. Did someone hurt you? Tell me, and I'll wring his neck."

Kathleen looked shocked at the thought. "No, no, nothing like that." She sighed. "It's something I've been reading."

"Reading?" Though Kathleen had been a regular bookworm back home in Manassas, the only reading material the Wertzes owned were the Bible and the current Farmers' Almanac, and it was hard to tell which of the two received more attention.

"Today one of the wounded men asked me to read to him. Someone had brought him a book, you see, and he asked for me in particular."

Eliza's suspicions deepened. "And why you?"

Kathleen blushed. "He told me it was because I was a Southern belle, a daughter of slave-holders, and he picked the book because he wanted to remind himself why he was fighting."

"You don't mean—"

"Yes. *Uncle Tom's Cabin.*"

Eliza pursed her lips and shook her head. "But you know what poisonous claptrap that book is, don't you?" At the sight of Kathleen's thoughtful expression, her disgust subsided somewhat.

"Yes, I know there are a lot of exaggerations in it, but did you know one of the slave women is named Eliza?"

"No . . ." She wasn't sure she wanted to hear any more, but she had to know what was behind all of this.

"I only read several chapters, but that was more than enough." Kathleen gulped as if struggling to stifle her emotions. "Once I read her name, all I could think about was what if that was happening to *you.*" Her voice grew tight. "What if you were the Eliza whose husband was owned by another man and you could only see him now and again? And what if it was your precious little boy who was sold to a slaver?"

Eliza tried to imagine the horror, but her mind shrunk from such painful thoughts.

"The Eliza in the story is as much white as black. Like Abby." Kathleen's voice grew soft. "So much like Abby and her dear little ones." Her eyes narrowed and her voice turned cold. "And Papa *sold* them— apart from each other." Resolve burned in Kathleen's eyes. "I won't go back there. I can't live in a place where it's legal to own someone and do things like that."

Eliza nodded slowly. "I see what you mean."

"There's more." Kathleen fingered her locket and looked out the window at the raging storm. "I want to do something to stop slavery."

"How? What can you do?" Eliza reached over and took her sister's hand. "What can anyone do?"

Kathleen bit her lip. "Maybe I've been hoping for the wrong people's independence." Suddenly, she looked and sounded twice her fifteen years. "I can't fight, but all this fighting hasn't solved anything anyway. When this war is finally over, there will be a lot of Negroes who need help. Maybe that's a fight I can join."

Eliza patted her sister's hand. Poor girl, so easily persuaded to the abolitionist point of view. And what would those abolitionists do if they got their way? Eliza doubted they'd ever show their faces in the South and spend money to help all those darkies get started on their own. If it ever came to that, what could Kathleen possibly do that would be of any use to four million freed slaves? It would be well and good if she wanted to take on some charity work after the war; lots of society women were much admired for such kindness. Just so long as she didn't become one of those fanatics. No one wanted a fanatic in the family.

Gen. Thomas Addressing Negroes on the Duties of Freedom

-4-

"Jacob."

The sound echoed as if from a distance. Was that an angel's voice?

"Jacob."

Jake opened his eyes and blinked away the fog. He lay flat on his back on a lumpy mattress. A lantern glowed atop a shabby dresser at the foot of the bed. A buxom woman with sweet brown eyes leaned over him. His heart pounded. "Eliza?"

"No, Leah. Don't you remember? I guess not. Laudanum does that to a body, but it is the Lord's own mercy against the pain."

When Jake tried to turn his head for a better look, a bolt of pain shot through his right cheek. He clenched his jaw to keep from crying out, but that only made his cheek feel as if it might rip asunder. "Yee-ouch!" He shuddered. His right leg throbbed as if a blacksmith was pounding it into shape on an anvil.

"You'd do well to remain still, Jacob," Leah said softly. Her light brown skin gleamed in the lantern light. "It's too soon to be giving you more laudanum, but you can have some white willow bark. I'll be right back. You hold still now, hear?"

"No worry there," Jake mumbled without moving his lips.

He racked his brain trying to recall what had happened. He remembered the battle, the sabre slicing his face, the fall. The next thing he knew, two men were robbing him in the dark. An old man chased them away but wanted to saw his legs off. Then this woman rescued him and took him away in an oxcart. Or was all of that just another nightmare? No, this pain was all too real.

Now that he was more awake, he could tell that the woman only resembled Eliza in the vaguest of ways. She looked old, probably in her thirties. Besides, she was mulatto. An educated freed woman? Must be, since slavery had been outlawed in Pennsylvania for decades. And who was that man who had been on the cart with her? Perhaps he was the one who had bandaged the sabre cut on his face and put this splint on his right leg.

Careful not to move his head, Jake took a moment to scan his surroundings. The tiny room barely fit the narrow bed and plainly built dresser. There was no table or set of shelves. On his left, three pegs protruded from the wall next to the door. A calico work dress hung from one peg; a white, collarless nightgown hung from the middle peg; and a burgundy shawl draped over the third. From his right, the dim light of dawn crept through the room's only window.

Jake turned his eyes to the door as the woman returned. In order to avoid aggravating his wound, he barely moved his lips when he spoke. "Leah, is it?"

She smiled and nodded.

"How do you know my name, Leah?"

"You told me your name last night, but for some reason you kept calling me Eliza. Is she your wife?"

Jake started to smile at the thought but froze at the streak of pain. "No. Maybe someday, I hope."

Leah nodded knowingly, then held up a small piece of candy. "I'm going to slip this pastille in your mouth. It'll help numb the hurt. Don't chew on it or swallow it, just let it melt away. It's bitter, but I added a touch of lemon and a lot of sugar to help against that."

Jake slowly parted his lips and allowed Leah to deposit the lozenge. It was a curious combination of bitter and sweet, soothing his parched throat. "Thanks," he mumbled.

Outside, the wind picked up and heavy rain splattered against the windowpane. Jake closed his eyes and sighed. Though the deluge might wash the blood from the fields, he doubted it could purge the stain. Would the land ever be the same? Would he?

Overwhelmed with questions, Jake turned his eyes to Leah. The pastille clicked against his teeth as he spoke. "Where am I? Is it over? Who won the battle?"

Leah smiled and gently placed a hand on his left forearm. "Now don't go fretting. You're in my house near the Hanover Road. No fighting today, too much rain." Her voice grew bitter. "Ain't nobody gonna win this war, far as I can see, least of all the people they're supposed to be fighting over."

Surprised at the fire in her eyes, Jake figured he'd best avoid the topic of slavery. Perhaps she was only recently freed, or maybe she still had family in the South. Yet she had rescued him in his Confederate gray? He had to know more, but this might not be a good time to broach the subject.

Thunder rumbled in the distance. At least Jake hoped it was thunder and not a renewal of the battle. His stomach grumbled in reply, but he felt too nauseous to eat. He couldn't imagine how painful it would be to vomit.

"Sounds like your belly wants tending," Leah said. "I've got a pot of chicken broth on the Franklin."

Jake opened his mouth to decline, but closed it to ease the flash of pain in his cheek. His stomach growled again. He reconsidered the offer of food, but how would he manage to eat anything in this condition?

As if reading his mind, Leah called over her shoulder, "Adam, would you heat up the broth and cut a reed for this young'un to slurp with?"

Using only his eyes, Jake smiled. "Thanks. I can use some breakfast."

"Breakfast? You eat breakfast at sunset where you come from?"

"You mean . . ."

Leah nodded. Her playful grin reminded him of Kathleen.

If it was sunset, then he must have been unconscious all day. After the severity of the previous night's pain, he wouldn't have wanted it any other way. Deciding it was time he knew, Jake screwed his courage to the sticking-place and asked, "So, how bad off am I?"

"Not so bad as to die over. I set your right leg. Good thing it broke clean. If you're good to it, you'll be getting around just fine in a couple of months." She pointed an index finger upward. "And it'll even ache to tell you when there's a storm a-brewing."

Jake gulped. Two months to heal. No telling what things would be like come September. He'd hate to be a burden on Pa, but at least now he should be able to make it to Myrtle's wedding.

"As for your left leg, well, nothing's busted, but that knee is swollen like a gourd. It kind of looks like one, too. And with that nasty bruise on your right hip, you're gonna be one colorful feller."

Though Jake appreciated her humor, he felt apprehensive. Why did he sense she was avoiding bad news?

As if she were describing something mundane, Leah said matter-of-factly, "You probably got a couple of cracked ribs on your right side, and I had to pop your right shoulder back into its socket. Even so, I think your collar bone might be broken."

Jake didn't like the way she averted her eyes as her voice trailed off. He braced himself for the worst. "And my face?"

She *tsked*. "Oh, that's another good reason I brought you here rather than take you to one of them field hospitals. To think those butchers have the nerve to call themselves surgeons! I swear, the more education those men get, the dumber they be. They can probably set a bone as good as me, but ain't none of them can sew as good as me."

Jake cringed at the image of an embroidery hoop clamped to his face while Leah pulled the needle and thread through his flesh.

"Besides, they'd want it to fester and turn to pus, thinking then they'd saved you. But I know better than that. I always pour dandelion wine onto a deep cut. Chases away the bad humor, it does. So, my way leaves you a rascally scar, but their way would leave you with half a face. And the ladies don't go much for a man with half a face." She leaned closer and winked. "Not even with the size of what you've got dangling between your legs." Snickering, she sat back in her chair.

Jake cringed. It was bad enough she had seen him unclothed while treating his wounds—at least he'd been unconscious during that—but to comment on his private region to his face?

His face. He tried to imagine how he would look when the bandages came off. What would Eliza and Kathleen think? Would they look upon his scar as a badge of honor, or turn away in horror?

Sunday, July 5, 1863

resh air wafted across Jake's face. He blinked his eyes and tuned his ears to the sounds of dawn. No cannons. No gunfire. Rain dripped from the eaves and trees. A few birds warbled miserably. Somewhere in the house, dishes rattled and pewter utensils clinked. Jake sniffed the air. Foul odors from his body, what a way to start the day.

Taking inventory of his injuries, Jake discovered that as long as he didn't budge, his wounds merely throbbed painfully. He resolved to keep his breathing shallow, and he knew he must not sneeze, no matter what.

Then his stomach rumbled.

After the ordeal he had gone through last night just to sit up, Jake tried to convince himself he wasn't hungry enough to go through all that agony again. Leah and Adam had been most kind and gentle with him, even so, the slightest jostle had caused excruciating pain. When they finally got him into a sitting position, it felt like the right side of his face was sliding off his head. He'd nearly fainted. *All of that for a cup of chicken broth? No thank you. I'd rather starve to death.*

Jake let his eyes wander across the rough log ceiling. What had he been thinking when he'd joined that charge; hadn't he learned anything from losing his revolver in Hanover? Sure, he wanted to do his duty in battle, but it was foolhardy for someone with no training and no experience to throw himself into the front ranks of a cavalry attack. Only luck had saved him from being amongst the men blown from their saddles by the Yankee cannons. Even so great a warrior as General Hampton had taken a thrashing. *Next time, I'll . . .*

Jake's spirit sagged. Would there be a next time? Perhaps more importantly, should there be a next time?

A growing heaviness in his bladder added another discomfort to his list of woes. How was he going to manage that task? He closed his eyes and stopped breathing. Better to die than wet himself, especially in a stranger's bed.

"Good morning, soldier boy." Leah entered the room and beamed down at Jake. "How are you feeling after all that sleep?"

Only his parents' good upbringing kept him from snarling. Manners won out over irritation, but just barely. At least his slashed face gave him a good excuse for mumbling. "Fine, thank you, ma'am."

"I brought you a towel."

Did she expect him to wash up in this condition? Surely, she didn't have in mind to do the washing. "Um, I don't think I can manage a bath."

"Oh, not for that." Leah leaned over and lowered her voice. "We can put it between your legs so you can, you know, relieve yourself." Without waiting for his approval, she peeled back the sheet and lifted the nightshirt until it barely covered his privates. She tucked the towel between his thighs. "Let me know when you're done. I'll fetch it up and wash it for the next time." She turned and left the room.

Next time? Jake snorted. He didn't even want there to be a *this* time! If he'd had any inkling he would wind up like this, would he have gone off to war? Somehow, political convictions didn't seem very important in the face of all this pain and indignity.

Now that the possibility of relief was near, Jake's bladder felt as if it might burst. Swallowing his pride, he used the towel. Now for the difficult part.

"Um, Miss Leah? I'm finished."

Leah poked her head around the corner of the door and took on an exaggerated Negro accent. "Now ain't dat bettah? Tol' ya so!" Chamber pot in hand, she sauntered over to the bed, plucked up the soggy towel, and dropped it into the pot.

Averting her eyes, Leah pulled the nightshirt down, then draped the sheet back into place. In her normal voice, she said, "You done well, the bed's still dry." She glanced at the towel. "And between the sun and the piss, this old towel will be whiter than ever."

Jake wrinkled his nose. "What?"

"You know, like in the Roman days, when they collected piss to bleach all their togas white."

"Really." Jake took a sideways glance at the bedclothes. Is that how she whitened all her laundry? She must be joking. "How do you know that?"

Leah struck a pose with one hand on her hip and resumed her exaggerated drawl. "What, you think I gots me no eddication just cuz I is a woman? Well, I got better larnin' than you if you don't know nuttin' 'bout dem Roman days. I ain't no dumb nigger."

Face reddening, Jake exclaimed, "Oh, but I didn't mean—"

She burst into laughter. "I got you good, boy. Wait'l Adam hears, he'll have a good hoot."

"Huh?" Jake felt even more ridiculous than when he had peed into the towel.

Leah flashed a wide grin. "My Mama was a white lady, and my Papa worked the cotton fields on her plantation back in Loo-easy-anna."

While Jake had heard plenty about men fornicating with their slaves, he had never imagined a woman would so much as think about doing likewise.

"Good thing for me my Mama's a strong-willed woman. She made her hubby raise me as his own, she did. And made him sell off his half-nigger son, too. When I was old enough, she even got me my own tutor to teach me my three R's. My Mama taught me my three H's."

At the risk of revealing his inferior education, Jake asked, "Three H's?"

"Herbs, History, and—How to Make Your Man Obey!" Leah threw back her head and guffawed.

Bemused, Jake could only mutter the obvious. "She's a remarkable woman."

Adam appeared in the doorway holding a breakfast tray. "You don't know the half of it. But give her a chance and she'll tell it."

Leah huffed as if insulted. "You saying I'm a chatterbox? Well, the more fool you, then, for marrying a chatterbox."

Jake's eyes darted from the mulatto woman to the white man and back again. They were married?

Leah slipped her arm around her husband's waist and arched her eyebrows at Jake. "What, did you think he was my slave?"

"No! I mean, that is, um . . ."

"Well, he is." Leah giggled and nuzzled Adam's neck. "Here, boy, give me that breakfast and you take care of this nasty old pee pot."

Adam winked at Jake, then exchanged the tray for the pot. "Yes'm, right away, mum." He shuffled off to do his wife's bidding.

Leah walked around the bed and set the tray on the dresser. "Now it's time for you to start doing for yourself, young man. There's nothing wrong with your left arm, so you can use that to set yourself up. I'll put the pillows behind your back."

Gritting his teeth against the pain, Jake carefully rolled onto his left elbow. "Argh!" Groaning, he eased back onto the bed.

"What's the matter, soldier boy, afraid of a little hurting? You've got the courage to ride against an army, but not enough to take on the consequences?"

Jake barely suppressed a glare. Bracing for the agony to come, he again rolled onto his elbow and pushed himself upright. The blood drained from his face as wave after wave of pain racked his battered body. Leah stuffed two pillows behind his back and helped him settle in.

"Now, let's see what we have here for you." Leah put the tray across Jake's lap. "Yum, yum, yum. Milk, applesauce, and scrambled eggs." She moved the fork, spoon, and hollow reed to the left side of the tray. "You eat up whilst I keep you company."

He discovered that tilting his head to the left helped alleviate the sensation of his cheek sliding off his face. It also made it a bit easier to get the food into the good side of his mouth.

Leah went back around the bed and sat on the stool. "So as I was saying, when I was all grown up, my Mama made her hubby set me up with my own herb shop in Nawlins. Women can do such like in Nawlins, you know."

No, he'd never heard of such a thing. It was particularly inconceivable, considering her mixed race. What kind of a place was this

Nawlins? "Where's this?"

She reached over and poked a wiggling pinky into his ear. "Better clean them ears, boy. You got enough dirt in there to start a tater patch. I said Nawlins. New-ah-lins."

"Oh, New Orleans. So how did you wind up in Gettysburg?"

"That's Adam's doing. He'd been on his way out west in the gold rush, but he fell in love with the Mississippi steamers instead."

Adam returned with the clean pot and picked up the story. "Then one day I happened into her shop looking for something for heartburn— crazy hot food in New Orleans. Well, she cured my heartburn, only to make my heart ache." He gave Leah an adoring smile. "I just had to make her my wife. Then, things being the way they are in the South, I figured we'd be better off living up here, near my family."

Leah rubbed her husband's arm. "It's best to let folks think I'm his maid."

Pausing in mid-swallow, Jake shook his head sadly. He knew that even in the North few people would tolerate the couple as man and wife; yet folks were perfectly willing to accept them living under the same roof as master and servant, all the while secretly presuming the couple engaged in illicit relations. Where was the sense in that?

Jake swallowed and stared out the window. It just wasn't fair. Someone ought to do something to change that.

-2-

". . . *denn wir sind sein Werk, geschaffen in Christus Jesus zu guten Werken, die Gott zuvor bereitet hat, daß wir darin wandeln sollen . . .*"

The jumble of German syllables seemed to drone on and on. Eliza recognized several of the words—work, Christ Jesus, good, God—but any semblance of meaning was lost in the monotonous rendering of the reader. She knew that most of Hanover's residents were of German heritage, but St. Matthew's had been around for 120 years already. Couldn't they do *any* part of the service in English?

". . . *denn Er ist unser Friede, der aus beiden eines gemacht hat und den Zaun abgebrochen hat . . .*"

Hopelessly bored, Eliza twirled a strand of hair around an index finger and allowed her eyes to wander among the congregation. Only a few of the elderly folks looked as if they were paying much attention, and she suspected that was because they had mastered the skill of sleeping with their eyes open. One old farmer's head lolled to the side, his mouth agape. He was either sound asleep or dead. She almost hoped for the latter, simply to see if the congregation would spring to life.

The back door creaked open and the sound of slow footsteps rustled in the narthex. Eliza casually turned her head to see who had entered. Jonas Serff crept up the far aisle and took the empty seat in the second row from the back.

As she turned to face front, she let her elbow brush against Lydia's arm. Lydia turned and Eliza motioned with her eyes toward Jonas. On the pretext of adjusting her bonnet, Lydia managed to scan the rear of the church. After finally spotting her beau, she sighed in relief and resumed proper church posture.

At least now Eliza had something to occupy her mind for the rest of the service. Lydia had grown distraught when Jonas failed to appear for church, especially since he had been invited to dinner afterward. He'd better have a good excuse for his tardiness. He couldn't very well ask Uncle Henry for Lydia's hand on the same day he was late for church.

Eliza settled back to imagine a fantastical misadventure that might account for Jonas' absence. Her eyes glazed over. By the time the organ intoned the introduction to the closing hymn, she had entertained herself with scenarios for Jonas ranging from fending off a bear to fighting a squad of Yankee deserters who had come to kidnap Lydia.

St. Matthew's Church (1878)

It was time for a hymn. Eliza stood with the rest of the congregation and opened the hymnal at random. On her right, Kathleen's voice rang with conviction, soaring over the throng.

"Ein feste Burg ist unser Gott . . ."

When the last word of the benediction faded, Eliza felt free at last. Anxious to hear what had kept Jonas, she followed Lydia outside to meet him.

Jonas doffed his hat. "Good morning, Lydia. I am sorry I was unable to greet you before church today."

Worry lined Lydia's face. "Is everything all right? You're never late for anything."

Eliza's heart quickened. Which of her imagined excuses was closest to the truth?

"Oh, I'm fine, thank you. On the way here I met up with three wagons full of men wounded during the battle at Gettysburg. The surgeons asked for my help moving them into Marion Hall."

From behind the two young ladies, Irene Bigler boomed in a haughty tone, "It is bad enough the Union Army does not observe the Sabbath, now they impress civilians to do the same."

Jonas' eyes turned steely. "It is pain and suffering that do not observe the Sabbath, Mrs. Bigler. It was my Christian duty to assist in any way possible."

Irene sniffed, turned on her heel, and stalked away.

Jonas offered his arm to Lydia and smiled. "Will you walk with me, my dearest?"

She slipped her arm into his, and the couple strolled off toward the row of carriages parked along Chestnut Street.

Eliza trailed along, curious. "Jonas?"

The couple turned as one.

"Is there any news from Gettysburg? Any word of Mr. Becker, or anyone else from Hanover?"

"No word of anyone we know, but the battle is over. The Confederates retreated south in the middle of the night." His face darkened. "There are thousands and thousands of dead and wounded. They say all the fields are strewn with bodies, and that this is far worse than what happened in Manassas."

From behind Eliza, Kathleen gasped. "Was Jeb Stuart's cavalry there?"

"I'm sorry, Miss Kathleen, I have no idea."

Eliza wrung her hands. "Did you help move any Confederate boys? Maybe one of them would know more about the whereabouts of Stuart's cavalry."

"No." Jonas frowned. "They were all Union men."

Kathleen put her arm around Eliza's waist "Any men from General Gregg's cavalry? You know, the ones who went through Hanover a few days ago."

"Sorry, I didn't think to ask."

"Well, Eliza and I will just have to go and find out." Kathleen withdrew her arm and grabbed her sister by the hand.

"Kathleen, Mother won't approve, you know that."

Kathleen looked even more determined. "It is our Christian duty to assist the suffering."

Eliza wriggled her hand free. She didn't mind if her sister wanted to go, and she was just as eager to discover news of the whereabouts of Jake and his father as Kathleen, but it wasn't likely the answers would be found at Marion Hall. Besides, she was so hungry, even the hog maw Lydia had prepared for Jonas sounded appetizing. "You better ask Mama first."

"I will." Kathleen spun on her heel and headed back toward the church.

Eliza fumed. *What plagued that girl? It's nice to be kindhearted, but this is carrying things a bit too far. Those Yankees don't deserve any compassion. They've sown the seeds of this war; let them choke on the harvest.*

-3-

Jake felt odd missing church on Sunday. Maybe it was just as well. Was it only a week ago he had felt so certain God had told him to go off to war? Look at what had happened since. Unless God had some sadistic and obscure purpose behind this mess, Jake figured he must have gotten it all wrong. Still, he'd never missed a Sunday in his life, not even on the few occasions when he and Pa were on the road delivering carriages. There had been no shortage of churches to visit. He had even looked forward to seeing how non-Methodist worship services differed.

He wondered what Adam and Leah did about church. It wasn't very likely a mixed-race couple would find a welcome in any of the churches around here. He recalled the Sunday a few years ago when he and Pa had passed a Negro church outside Baltimore. At first, Jake wondered if there was a terrible argument, what with all the screaming and hollering, but when they got closer, he realized the people were shouting amen, hallelujah, and the like. Then the choir sang. Jake begged Pa to stop and listen. Such music!

With the refrain still vivid in his mind, Jake hummed the tune to the words. *Every time I feel the Spirit, moving in my heart, I will pray. Yes, every time—*

From the next room Adam and Leah joined in, singing, ". . . I feel the Spirit, moving in my heart, I will pray."

Leah called out, "That ain't bad—for a white boy. Where did you learn that song?"

Jake recounted the experience as Leah and Adam entered the room. Leah nudged her husband. "See, even before we went to fetch him, I told you he was a God-fearing boy."

"Before you found me?" Jake couldn't fathom it. "What are you talking about?"

She took a seat on the stool. Adam stood behind her and rested his hands on her shoulders while Leah looked pensively into Jake's eyes. "Adam and I were busy praying for all you fellers during the fighting. Once the battle was over, I went out to the springhouse to fetch some water." Her eyes sparkled. "I heard a voice, and it says, 'Leah, there's a boy out in those fields that needs your help.' Well, I says, 'Sure, Lord, probably hundreds of them. How will I know which one You mean?' And He says right back, 'He'll be the one they think is dead, and if you don't help him, he will surely die.' So I says, 'You notice it's dark out here, Lord?' And don't you know, He says to me, 'Trust and obey.'"

Leah chuckled. "'O-bey,' that's what He says, 'Trust and o-bey.' So I says, 'Lord, I will o-bey.' Now, Adam was like to pitch a fit when I told him to hitch up the ox, but when I told him the why of it, he stepped right to work. We were only on Lott's field a few minutes when we heard the corpse pickers talking about sawing the legs off a man trapped under a horse. Then you screamed. We figured that was sign enough for a deaf man to o-bey."

Jake sat in stunned silence. A sly voice in the back of his mind prompted, *That's quite a coincidence. Be glad you were the first one they stumbled upon. You were mighty lucky, that's all.*

Massaging Leah's shoulders, Adam added, "The Lord's not finished with you yet, Jacob. He must have some mighty work waiting for you to do."

Jake closed his eyes. *Right. Well, Lord, You have an odd way of showing it. If that's true, then why did You let me get hurt so bad? What kind of work can I do like* this?

Not wishing to offend his rescuers, Jake opened his eyes and spoke with as much conviction as he could muster. "That's a wonderful story. I can never thank you enough for all you've done for me. God bless you both."

Leah patted his arm and dabbed a tear from her eye.

"If you don't mind, I want to sleep now," Jake said sadly.

Adam and Leah blessed him, then left the room.

Jake closed his eyes. Part of him wished he would never wake up.

Friday, July 10, 1863

Gasping in pain, Jake gritted his teeth and eased his broken leg into place across the divan's cushions. Cold sweat beaded on his forehead. His cheek throbbed and itched beneath the bandage encircling his chin and head. He shifted his weight to ease the stress on the broken collarbone and ribs. Had it been only a week since the battle?

Leah leaned over and studied his face. "Do you want I should tighten the binding?"

He paused a moment for a wave of dizziness to pass. "No, ma'am. I think it's tight enough." She had put a sling around his right arm, then bound it to his chest, explaining it would be good for both the shoulder and the cracked ribs. Since he couldn't put any weight on his broken leg and it was too painful to hop, Leah had cradled the splinted limb when Adam carried Jake to the divan.

"You done good," Adam said. "A lesser man would've cried out with the pain."

Leah reached into her apron pocket and pulled out a small brown bottle and dropper. "Here's that laudanum I promised." She filled the dropper, then squeezed some liquid back into the bottle until the proper dosage was left in the tube. "Open wide," she said playfully.

Jake rolled his eyes at the suggestion. He parted his lips just enough for the dropper to fit through, then swallowed the painkiller. "Now, what about that news you promised? Did Pa get the letter you wrote for me? Did he send a reply?"

Leah looked up from adjusting her apron. "Your family is coming to fetch you tomorrow."

"My *family*?" Was Myrtle back home already?

Leah acted as if puzzled. "What, you don't know you have a family?"

"Of course I do. I mean who exactly is coming?"

"Mr. Mummert didn't say. He just told me he got word to your family on Thursday, and that they'll send a carriage to fetch you on Saturday."

Why not today? As eager as he was to get home, he felt more than a little dread at the thought. How would Pa react? What would Myrtle think? And the townsfolk? He didn't dare consider how the Biglers would take the news.

Adam clucked his tongue. "Well, Leah, judging from the look on his face, I guess he likes your broth so much he'd rather stay here."

As if overburdened, Leah sighed, "Lord knows we can always use another pair of hands in the herb garden."

"I'm sorry." Jake's face softened. "I'm worried about how everyone will act towards me. And not only because I'm all banged up."

"I wouldn't fret yourself about that," Leah soothed. "Any family worth its name will love you back to health. As for the rest, well, what better way to find out who your real friends are?"

True enough, but how would he learn to deal with his enemies? And how would those people treat the rest of his family? Exhausted and beginning to feel the effects of the drug, Jake stifled the urge to yawn.

Adam crossed to the spittoon and spat out the remnants of his chaw. "We best let the lad sleep. I'll help you in the garden." He offered Leah his arm and led her out the door.

Glad for the solitude, Jake cautiously laid his stitched cheek against the back of the divan. At least the pain stopped the itching. He scanned his surroundings. Half of the one-story cabin had been sectioned off to form the two bedrooms. He had already figured out that the smaller bedroom he occupied was there for show, so guests would presume Leah slept apart from her "employer." The other half of the house was the common room: sitting area and fireplace at one end, dining area at the other. A kitchen stood in what appeared to be a small wood-frame addition on the other side of the dining area. Drying herbs hung from lines strung along the walls. The simple pine furniture and both of the corded area rugs had seen better days, but the cozy confines exuded an aura of love and security. It was enough to make anyone long for the home hearth.

As Jake closed his eyes and drifted toward sleep, he decided it would be good to get home after all. It didn't matter what anyone thought of him; he had done what he believed to be right.

The Smiling Man winked at him. *Good! That's the kind of spirit we're going to need in this fight.*

Jake felt too drained to care.

Saturday, July 11, 1863

Jake again sat on Adam and Leah's divan, his right leg carefully propped on the cushions. As long as he took shallow breaths, sitting up didn't bother his cracked ribs, and the swelling had nearly disappeared from his hip. The right corner of his mouth felt like it went up in a lopsided smile. He knew he was not exactly the picture of "the conquering hero"; still, it would be good to get back home. From outside, he heard the clippity-clop of horses' hooves and the creak of an approaching carriage.

Adam called from the front stoop. "You must be the Beckers."

"We're so glad you could come," Leah added.

A muffled female voice answered. Jake strained to hear, but all he could make out was garbled conversation. A long minute later, he heard the sound of light footsteps rushing up the path, and then his sister burst into the common room.

"Myrtle! Thank God you're here!" Jake held out his good arm, inviting her embrace.

"Oh, Jake!" Her eyes filled with tears as she rushed to his side. She knelt and gave him a gentle hug. "Are you all right?" She began to reach toward his bandaged head, but pulled her hand away to cover a soft gasp.

How to answer her? He could tell his body was on the mend, but his spirit was an entirely different matter. Seeing Myrtle was a bittersweet tonic. Not wishing to disappoint her, he mustered up a cheerful voice. "I'll be fine." He wiped a tear from her cheek with the tip of his finger. "Don't worry on my account."

Jake nodded toward Leah as she and Adam entered. "Miss Leah's herbs work wonders."

Myrtle stood and turned to face Jake's rescuers. "I know we can never repay you for all you have done." She fumbled to untie the drawstring to her reticule. "But I brought—"

"No, no, no!" Leah held up a hand. "You keep your money, Miss Myrtle. I was just doing the Lord's work."

"I must at least pay you for your remedies."

"No, ma'am. You help Jacob get his strength back. The Lord has work for him to do. I just did my part, and that is more than enough payment for me."

Frowning, Jake only half-listened. Why was Myrtle handling the money instead of Pa? And what was taking him so long to come inside? "Myrtle, isn't that Pa tending the carriage?"

Her face went blank. "No, Jake. Sam brought me."

Why was she behaving so oddly? "Is Pa all right?"

Myrtle smoothed her dress and took a deep breath before answering. "Pa isn't able to come right now." Her eyes begged Jake not to inquire any further.

His stomach churned. Pa never got sick, so what other reason could there be for his absence? Surely he wasn't angry. Had he been injured during the battle in Hanover?

Sam called from the front stoop. "Hello?"

Adam led Sam into the common room. Jake made the proper introductions, finishing with, "Sam and Myrtle are to be wed in September."

"How lovely for you both," Leah gushed. "May the Lord richly bless your union."

Myrtle and Sam exchanged loving glances.

"Won't you please sit down?" Adam said. He grabbed two rail-back chairs from the dining area and set them near Jake.

Sam winced. "I'm sorry to say we can't stay. My family needs the carriage this afternoon, so I need to return as soon as possible."

"And Jake is to have a very special caller this afternoon." Myrtle beamed at her brother.

Leah wagged a finger at Jake. "Did you hear that, Jacob? I'll bet Miss Eliza is coming to call."

"So," Myrtle said with a lilt in her voice, "you've heard about Eliza."

"Not nearly as much as I'd like." Leah folded her arms and tapped her foot. "Well, Jacob? Not much time left to tell me all about your young lady."

Lost in thought, Jake wrestled with his concern for Pa while trying to decide how he felt about Eliza seeing him in his current condition. Then he realized the room had grown silent. All eyes were upon him. What should he say?

Myrtle broke the silence. "Eliza's mother and sister are coming, too."

That's just great. What a fine impression I'll make, Jake fretted.

As if reading his thoughts, Myrtle's eyes saddened. "I'm sorry, Jake. I thought it would cheer you to see Eliza, and she couldn't very well come calling without her mother."

His heart sank at the sad look on his sister's face. "No, that's all right, really. I'm, uh . . ." He remembered the last time he saw Eliza and the feel of her body pressed against his during their goodbye kiss. "It's just, um . . ." Kathleen's visage flashed in his mind. Her crooked smile. The wistful look in her eyes just before she laid her head on his chest. The tenderness with which her lips touched his.

Jake blinked and found the words to finish his sentence. "It will be good to see them again. Thank you for inviting her."

An impish voice in his head inquired, *Which "her" do you mean?*

-2-

The days had dragged on with no news from Jake. Eliza continually moped around the house, even though she knew it might well be a matter of weeks before anyone heard from him.

Kathleen had offered a word of comfort. "Jake is probably on his way to Virginia with General Stuart. Besides, what harm is likely to befall a wagon driver?"

Eliza had bristled at first, thinking Kathleen scorned Jake's lowly position. But the look of admiration on Kathleen's face soothed the irritation.

Two days ago, Sam Forney had stopped by to tell them he was on his way to fetch Myrtle home from Lancaster. He'd gotten word Jake was wounded in the battle at Gettysburg. "The man said Jake was hurt bad, but that he'll get over it in due time. Myrtle and I should make it back to Hanover late in the day on Friday, and then we'll fetch Jake first thing Saturday morning."

Kathleen had tugged on Sam's sleeve and blurted, "Oh, please let us come see him Saturday afternoon. We'll already be in town with Mother. I'm sure no matter how badly he feels, it'll cheer him to see us, um, to see Eliza."

Eliza had held her breath while Sam considered. Finally, a grin spread over his face. "Well, I know if it was me who was suffering, your visit would surely brighten my day. I'll discuss it with Myrtle to make certain she doesn't mind. On second thought, I feel certain that she won't, so why don't you just plan on calling at two o'clock?"

So here it is Saturday, I am going to see Jake in another hour and fifty-eight minutes, and I've still not decided what to wear!

Donning her inner petticoat, Eliza tried to picture poor, wounded Jake. *Will he have a bandage around his head like in the painting of those Revolutionary War soldiers? Or a sling on his arm? Crutches? Crutches might be nice, that way I can truly be a shoulder for him to lean on.*

Bundled in a soggy towel, Kathleen burst into the room. She crossed to the window, parted the curtains slightly, and yelled, "We're finished with the tub in the kitchen, Uncle Henry!"

Eliza adjusted her hair in the mirror. "Can you hurry up and dry off so you can hand me my pink dress from the closet? Better yet, be a dear and help me with my stockings."

Kathleen turned and arched one eyebrow. "May I get dressed first, your majesty? Besides, you can put your own stockings on. I'm not going to touch those stinky old feet."

In the time it took Eliza to put on her stockings, hoopskirt, and outer petticoat, Kathleen had toweled off, slipped into all of her undergarments, and retrieved two dresses from the closet: her calico and Eliza's pink. Eliza wriggled into the pink dress. But there was a problem.

On the verge of despair, Eliza tromped across the bedroom and stood in front of the full-length mirror. Her eyes confirmed the bad news. In spite of the corset, she had finally outgrown her favorite dress, and the seams had already been let out as far as they could go. Her bosom bulged from the bodice. She had taken pride in her beautiful cleavage, but now the dress made her feel like a woman of ill repute. And when had her waistline ballooned past twenty-two inches? No matter. She couldn't let her future husband see her in such an ill-fitting dress.

"Don't feel bad, Eliza," Kathleen commiserated. "How about your pretty new white dress? Besides, Jake will be so happy to see you it won't matter what you wear."

"Oh, all right." Eliza tore her eyes from the mirror and walked dejectedly to the middle of the room. Kathleen brought the white dress from the closet and helped Eliza change.

"This *is* a pretty dress." Heartened, Eliza returned to the mirror and admired her figure in profile. The dress, with its lacy trim and blue ribbons, looked adorable on her.

Now the only question was what to do with her hair. "Do you think I should leave it in a bun or add a ringlet to each side?"

No answer.

Irritated at being ignored, Eliza spun to see why her sister wasn't paying attention. Kathleen stood by the window. One hand held the pink dress under her chin, the other hand smoothed the fabric against her hoops. Eliza remembered doing the same thing the day she had gotten the dress. Touched by Kathleen's longing look, she suggested, "Why don't you try it on?"

"Really?" Kathleen's eyes lit up. "You don't mind?"

"I guess not. In fact, if it fits, why don't you go ahead and wear it today?"

Kathleen squealed with delight. She put on the dress, stood tall, and clasped her hands at her waist. "Well, what do you think?"

When had her little sister developed such a comely figure? "You look most fetching!" Eliza wondered if it was too late to take back her offer.

"Oh, thank-you-thank-you-thank-you! Do you have any idea how wonderful I feel?"

Eliza had a pretty good idea. And she wasn't sure she liked it.

"Now I truly feel like a woman," Kathleen said, beaming.

Suppressing a flare of jealousy, Eliza smiled weakly. "And what a lovely woman you have become, Kathleen." *And if Jake knows what's good for him, he'd better not notice.*

-3-

The carriage bounced over a rut. Jake winced. When the surge of pain subsided, he turned to Myrtle on the seat opposite him. "Now tell me why Pa isn't here. Is he all right?"

Her eyes tearing, Myrtle reached over and grasped Jake's hand. "I don't know how Papa's doing." Her voice grew strained. "Oh, Jake, I don't even know where he is."

"He's missing? How long? Since the battle in Hanover? Oh, dear God, was he hurt in the battle?"

Myrtle reached for her reticule and pulled out a folded piece of paper. "Here. It's a letter from Pa."

"A letter? Why—"

"Please, just read it."

Jake's eyes raced over Pa's familiar hand. "Oh, no, not . . . poor John Hoffacker." Jake tensed at the news of the shell striking the Winebrenner house. Had a similar fate befallen Pa in their house? Jake shook his head. Pa must be well. After all, he had written the letter.

Reading on, Jake paused at the words "leaving quite a mess around the cemetery." Was that a fact or just rumor? Surely, no one would desecrate a cemetery.

He skimmed over the part about his enlistment; he'd have plenty of time to discuss that with Myrtle later. When he came to the words "your sons and their sons and their sons will have to fight in a never-ending series of wars," he slowly lowered the letter to his lap. He hadn't thought about the effects this war might have on their descendants.

Myrtle's face was etched with anxiety. "All I've been able to find out is that shortly after Pa wrote this, he went with a large number of Union cavalrymen. I believe they were headed for Littlestown."

Jake pictured the area around Gettysburg. Littlestown lay to the south. At least Pa wouldn't have encountered any of Stuart's forces there.

"The Confederate Army left Pennsylvania a week ago, so perhaps Papa will be home any day now." Myrtle's voice sounded frightened and small, reminding Jake of the times when they were kids and she crawled into his bed in the middle of the night for protection from the "booger man."

"You're probably right," Jake said, forcing himself to sound calm. "Don't worry. It may be a bit longer until he's free to return, especially if he signed on as a ninety-day volunteer. Besides, he can't very well up and leave at the first opportunity, else he'd look like a coward. They probably want to make sure General Lee doesn't turn around and come back."

Though Jake meant what he said, part of him wished Lee would do exactly that and finish this horrible war as soon as possible—one way or the other.

-4-

Situated on his bed with two pillows propped behind his back and a well-stocked nightstand within reach of his left hand, Jake leaned back and let his eyes take in the rest of the parlor, which had become his sickroom. Sam and Myrtle had brought his bed down and set it lengthwise against the windowless outside wall. The coffee table and divan had been moved to the opposite side of the room. One side chair remained, but it now stood in front of the fireplace. A red vase overflowing with fresh-cut tiger lilies perched on the mantel next to Ma's picture. The melodeon occupied its usual place between the front windows, and his tenor horn stood on its bell in the corner to the right.

Jake stared sadly at the instruments. How many weeks would it be before he could lift his arm to the keyboard? Before his right leg could pump the pedal for the bellows? And would his lips ever play the tenor horn again?

A voice in his head tried to cheer him. *You still have your voice. You can sing.*

Jake scowled, then winced from the stress on his healing cheek. *Sing. Right. Pirate songs, maybe. That's all a face like this will ever be good for.*

Before the voice in his head could reply, Myrtle called from the rocker on the porch. "Here they come!"

The rhythmic cadence of approaching hoof beats floated through the window. A buggy creaked to a stop. A horse snorted. Myrtle greeted Eliza and her family. "Good afternoon, I'm so happy you have come to call."

Heart pounding, Jake smoothed his hair around the bandage circling his head. He sat up as straight as he could without aggravating his ribs and shoulder. The women entered the hallway. He gulped. Was he ready for this?

"May I take your bonnets?" Myrtle asked. Jake heard Mrs. Bigler and Kathleen conversing with their hostess in the hallway, but where was—

Eliza appeared in the parlor doorway.

Jake couldn't breathe, she looked so beautiful! Her eyes sparkled. Her lips parted in a loving smile. A delicate ringlet framed each perfect cheek. *Perfect cheek.*

What was I thinking? How can I ever go strolling with Eliza when small children will shrink from me in horror? "Beauty and the Beast" is only true in French fairy tales. He groaned softly.

Eliza gasped and hurried to his side. "You poor dear!"

Heartened at her words, Jake searched his beloved's face. Eliza's worried eyes moved from his splinted leg to his bound arm to his bandaged head. She leaned down and tenderly placed her lips on his forehead in a long kiss. His spirit soared! Could it be? Did she truly—

Kathleen spoke loudly from the doorway. "Why don't you sit with me on the divan, Eliza?"

Eliza stood and smiled adoringly at Jake, but then her eyes clouded and she quickly turned to face the others in the room. "Thank you, I shall," she replied, her voice sounding strained.

Jake's forehead tingled from the kiss. His eyes followed Eliza as she glided to the divan and eased onto the seat between her mother and Kathleen. Then he noticed Mrs. Bigler's appraising stare.

Myrtle announced from the doorway, "I'll hang up your bonnets and be right back with some tea and pastries."

Remembering his manners, Jake said, "I must tell you how good it feels to see you all again."

"It does our hearts good to come," Mrs. Bigler replied warmly. "You have been in our thoughts and prayers these past days, doubly so since you have spilled your blood in defense of our cause." She reached over and put her hand atop Eliza's. "Perhaps my daughter may aid you in your return to health. She has my blessing to call on you, as you are able."

Eliza bit her lip and looked out the window. A tear glistened in the corner of her eye.

Could it be? Have I just received permission to court Eliza?

Myrtle returned with a tray and set it on the coffee table. "The tea needs to steep just a bit longer. I'll be right back with the pastries."

"I'll help." Eliza quickly rose to her feet.

"There's no need—"

"I insist." Eliza's eyes begged for permission.

Myrtle smiled. "That would be very nice, thank you." In a mock whisper, she added, "It will give me a chance to get to know you better."

Jake's heart warmed as the future sisters-in-law left for the kitchen. But then Kathleen stood. He'd been too preoccupied with Eliza to notice that Kathleen wore Eliza's pink dress. And she looked *beautiful.*

Kathleen's entrancing green eyes held his for a long moment. "I've been helping with the wounded in the hospitals in town. May I see your wounds?" Without waiting for a reply, she crossed the room and stood at the side of the bed.

"Um." Jake cast a nervous glance at Mrs. Bigler. She didn't seem the least bit disturbed by Kathleen's offer. "I suppose so."

He pointed to his leg. "As you can see, I broke my leg when I fell from Ca—" He turned the name Cat into a series of shallow coughs. How would Kathleen feel if she thought he had named his horse after her? "Um, when I fell from my horse. I also bruised my hip, cracked a couple of ribs, dislocated my shoulder, and broke my collar bone."

"Your leg looks nice and straight." Kathleen's tone turned to a delightful mix of chiding and playfulness. "We'll have to make sure you keep it that way while it heals. Did you hurt your chin in the fall?"

Lost in the depth of her incredible green eyes, Jake mumbled slowly,

"No, I took a nasty sabre cut."

Before he knew it, Kathleen untied the bandage, gently turned his head to the left, and leaned in for a closer look at the damaged cheek. Jake averted his eyes to avoid peeking down her dress. His eyes met Mrs. Bigler's approving smile.

Kathleen's lips were inches from his ear as she spoke. "This is a wonderful job of stitching. You were blessed to have such a fine surgeon."

Could it be she was unfazed by the sight of his ruined face? Jake's heart beat faster.

She kissed the tip of her finger and ran it lightly along his cheek below the stitches. Reaching the end of the wound, Kathleen paused, then gave his ear lobe a gentle tug. "Happy birthday," she giggled.

"Hey, it's not my birthday for another month," Jake protested.

"I know. It's the day after mine. Just consider that an early present."

Jake feigned indignation. "And since when does someone give ear tugs for birthday presents?"

Eliza's voice rang from the doorway. "Presents?"

Kathleen stepped back. Jake felt his face flush.

Eliza gaped at Jake's cheek. Her hand covered her mouth. She gathered her skirt and hurried out the front door. Then came the sound of retching. Irene Bigler, red-faced, rose to her feet and went to her daughter's aid. Myrtle hurried from the kitchen and joined them on the front porch.

Jake's heart withered. He was only vaguely aware of Kathleen's soothing tones; her words were drowned out by the voice screaming in his head: *You are a hideous freak! Your face is revolting. Eliza will never have anything to do with you now. See what your foolishness has wrought?*

". . . everything will be fine, Jacob, you'll see," Kathleen insisted, her voice finally penetrating Jake's self-deprecation.

But he didn't dare look into Kathleen's eyes. How could she stand to be near him? He fought back tears but wondered whether anything, even crying, could make things worse than they were.

Outside, he heard Eliza say in a low voice, "I'm sorry, Mama, I can't go back in there. I can't stand to see him like—"

As if to cover her sister's words, Kathleen interjected, "Jake, I have a list of wounded soldiers I've been visiting every day. May I add your name to it?" She picked up the bandage and started to rewrap his face. "It's really no trouble at all, since I'll be just down the street anyway. If you like, I can read to you. And if you don't mind, I could even sing for you, or *with* you, as soon as you feel up to it. Maybe you can show me how to play the melodeon. I'd love to learn."

Myrtle returned, looking flustered. "I'm sorry, Jake, Eliza has taken ill. She wants me to tell you how dreadfully sorry she is to be unable to say goodbye for herself. Mrs. Bigler is helping her into the buggy now." She smiled sadly at Kathleen. "I'll be right back with the bonnets."

Jake stared at his feet. Despair tightened its grip on his soul.

"So may I come after church tomorrow?" Kathleen asked quietly.

His dying heart fluttered. "What? Tomorrow?"

Kathleen leaned over and put her face in front of his. "Yes. I will see you tomorrow afternoon."

He started to tell her not to waste her time, but she silenced him with a sudden, brief kiss on the lips. As she drew back, they exchanged looks of surprise at her impulsiveness.

Myrtle called, "Here are—"

Kathleen snapped to attention.

"—your bonnets." Myrtle stood in the doorway, a mystified look on her face.

"Thank you, Myrtle." Kathleen smoothed her dress, then turned back to Jake. "Thank you for your kind invitation to call again tomorrow." She kissed the tip of her finger and placed it on Jake's good cheek. "God bless you, Jacob."

She went to the doorway and accepted the bonnets from Myrtle's outstretched hand. "I'm sorry our visit had to end so abruptly, but I look forward to seeing you tomorrow after church."

"You're very welcome, I'm sure. Tell Eliza we shall pray for her."

"Thank you, I will." Kathleen flashed Jake a smile, and then she was gone.

Looking dazed, Myrtle walked over and sat on the edge of the bed. "When did Kat turn into such a stunning young woman?"

Adrift in a sea of emotions, Jake sat speechless.

"And what was it in your eye she had to help remove?" Myrtle asked, grinning.

Jake sighed as deeply as his broken ribs would tolerate. "I'm *really* going to need your help figuring something out."

Myrtle nodded sagely. "You most certainly are."

-5-

Once the buggy moved away from the house, Eliza took a few deep breaths and her stomach began to settle. Unfortunately, the turmoil in her mind only worsened. Maybe she had been foolish to think Jake, though bandaged, would seem virile and heroic, but who would have ever imagined he would look so pale and emaciated? She barely recognized his sunken eyes, and that horrendous gash across his face was the stuff of nightmares. She remembered the battlefield at Manassas: the dead and dying, and that awful stench! Her stomach roiled yet again. Heaving, she leaned over the side of the buggy and spewed what little remained in her stomach.

Mama steered the buggy off the road and onto the Methodist Church lot. She stepped down from the vehicle, pulled a hanky from her sleeve, and rushed to Eliza's side. "Here, darlin', let me help you." She tenderly wiped her daughter's face.

"Oh, what am I to do?" Eliza whimpered.

"*What?*" Mama's eyes narrowed. "Don't expect to be mollycoddled. You stiffen your backbone and you love your man all the more for what he's done for you. For all of us."

Eliza folded her arms across her chest and glared off into the distance. It was easy for Mama to say such things, she wasn't the one who'd have to spend the rest of her life looking at that hideous face. Maybe Kathleen would understand.

"How do you do it, Kathleen? How can you stand to be around all those mutilated soldiers every day?"

Kathleen looked flabbergasted. "Eliza, Jake isn't just any soldier. He's your beau!"

"Not any more he isn't," Eliza retorted. "He's changed. Surely he doesn't expect—"

"Eliza!" Mama's eyes had never looked so fiery. "Do you truly think any man can go off to war and not be forever changed by it? Imagine the horrors that fine young man must have gone through *in defense of our freedom*. And now, when he needs his loved ones the most, you dare to turn your back on him? Lord help you, girl, if you don't come to your senses, and right quick!"

Eliza cast a glance at Kathleen, who quickly averted her troubled eyes. Why didn't anyone understand? "Mama, that's all well and good, but I'm afraid I just don't have the constitution for it. And you'll have to blame the good Lord for that, for He's the one who made me."

Mama stiffened, but didn't immediately respond to the challenge.

Prompted by a twinge of conscience, Eliza thought, *Do I really love Jake? Well . . . yes, I do. But do I love him enough to be able to ignore his face the rest of my life? Perhaps it won't always look this horrible.* "Maybe after he heals, we can try again," she said aloud.

Mama shook her head and said haughtily, "He deserves far better than that!"

"Don't we all?" Eliza countered.

"Well!" Mama spun on her heel, gathered up her skirt, and returned to her seat. The trio rode in icy silence the rest of the way home.

While Eliza sat brooding in the buggy, Kathleen went into the house, changed into her work dress, and returned to tend to the horse. Harness in hand, Kathleen leaned over to catch Eliza's sulking eyes. "Can I ask you something?"

"You just did," Eliza snapped.

Kathleen ignored the sarcasm. "So, you don't mind, then, if I visit Jake every day and help him with his recovery?"

Jealousy pricked Eliza's pride, but she felt too drained to lash out. Besides, her sister looked genuinely concerned for Jake's well-being. "I guess not." She smiled wanly. "If I can't be the one to see him through this, then there's no one I'd rather have tend him than you." *And that way no one else will catch his fancy, just in case his face turns out all right and I change my mind.*

Kathleen's face lit up. "Thanks. I'll take good care of him."

"I'm sure you will." *Just don't be too good to him.*

-6-

That night, Mr. Winebrenner, Mr. Forney, and his son Sam came to call on Jake and Myrtle. They expressed their compassion and assured their immediate assistance with any needs.

As comforting as that was, Jake sensed from their uneasiness that something else was on their minds. "Come on, Sam, out with it. What haven't you told us?"

The three men exchanged sad glances. Henry Winebrenner cleared his throat and spoke as if choosing his words carefully. "Well, Jake, after what the town went through during the battle here, and with all the wounded men they brought in from Gettysburg, there's a lot of ill will toward any soldier in gray."

Karle Forney nodded. "We were thinking you might want to consider letting folks presume you got hurt fighting for the Union cause. The few of us who know your true alliance will keep it to ourselves." He hastened to add, "We don't fault you none. We just don't want you to face any trouble for following your convictions."

Sam added tersely, "There are some folks who'd applaud you for your service and sacrifice, Jake, but there's a lot more who'd look for any opportunity to cut you down."

Jake winced at Sam's choice of words. Worse, something in Sam's eyes and tone of voice hinted he agreed with the latter view. Had Jake lost a friend? How would this affect Myrtle? He already knew she was consumed with worry for Pa's safety. Though Jake bristled at the suggested deception, he certainly didn't want to add the town's hostility to her burdens. Pennsylvania Dutchmen could hold a grudge as long as anyone. So for Myrtle's sake, he reluctantly agreed to the plan.

He realized now that it had been childish to hope to return from the war a hero, but he never imagined that following the call of duty would bring him shame. He couldn't wait for Pa to get home. Surely, Pa would understand.

BATTLE OF HANOVER, (PA.) JUNE 30, 1863

LOSSES— UNION: 200 Killed, Wounded, Captured. CONFEDERATE: 100 Killed-W'd-Captured. Battle Flag

KILPATRICK   CUSTER   FARNSWORTH   VS.   JEB. STUART   WADE HAMPTON   FITZHUGH LEE

"GOD BLESS THE LADIES OF HANOVER"

HOSPITAL DEPARTMENT, HANOVER, PA., JULY 11, 1863.

Editor Hanover Citizen—Sir:—At the request of the sick and wounded, I have undertaken to perform a labor which Napoleon "never thought of" when he said that there was "no such thing as impossibility," and that is to render thanks in a suitable manner to the citizens of Hanover for their generous and patriotic care of our patients. Do the Ladies (I think it always proper to write Ladies, in speaking of Hanover, with a capital) know to what an extent their generosity has carried them. We have connected with the Hospital not less than 150 men. Independent of other things, the rations of these for the number of days we have been here, at Government rates of 40 cents per day, amounts to $700. To speak of or estimate the amount of clothing, bedding, bandages, lint, delicacies, and above all, the value of their constant presence and sweet smiles—in me would be simply preposterous. I am not scholar enough to make the estimate—and as long as such problems are placed before me, I foreswear mathematics and stoicism and become an admirer of the "fair sex" and an epicurean of the deepest color. It would be impossible for me to individualize, notwithstanding many have been brought into editorial notice by acts of unprecedented kindness. All have seemed to make it their first care to ascertain, not only what we needed but what we could make use of. "God bless the Ladies of Hanover," will be heard through the land—uttered by mothers and relatives from Michigan to Maine, and from Maine to Carolina. It may not be placed in flowing hand bills on the New York bulletins, but it will be felt in the warm, earnest hearts of the soldier and his mother. This must be your reward, noble Ladies and kind gentlemen. It is not enough, but it is all we have to offer. Expressing my thanks for personal favors, I subscribe myself,   A. McKIMM, Ward Master.

NOTE:—Confederate General Stuart left his dead and wounded lay on the field at Hanover. His wounded received the same kind treatment at this hospital as the Union soldiers. His dead were buried in trenches along the Hanover road between Hanover and Buttstown (Pennville.)

HOSPITAL DEPARTMENT, HANOVER, PA. JULY 11, 1863

Editor Hanover Citizen—Sir:—At the request of the sick and wounded, I have undertaken to perform a labor which Napoleon "never thought of" when he said that there was "no such thing as impossibility," and that is to render thanks in a suitable manner to the citizens of Hanover for their generous and patriotic care of our patients. Do the Ladies (I think it always proper to write Ladies, in speaking of Hanover, with a capital) know to what an extent their generosity has carried them? We have connected with the hospital not less than 150 men. Independent of other things, the rations of these for the number of days we have been here, at Government rates of 40 cents per day, amounts to $700. To speak of or estimate the amount of clothing, bedding, bandages, lint, delicacies, and above all, the value of their constant presence and sweet smiles—in me would be simply preposterous. I am not scholar enough to make the estimate—and as long as such problems are placed before me, I foreswear mathematics and stoicism and become and admirer of the "fair sex" and epicurean of the deepest color. It would be impossible for me to individualize, notwithstanding many have been brought into editorial notice by acts of unprecedented kindness. All have seemed to make it their first care to ascertain not only what we needed but what we could make use of. "God bless the Ladies of Hanover," will be heard through the land—uttered by mothers and relatives from Michigan to Maine and from Maine to Carolina. It may not be placed on flowing hand bills on the New York bulletins, but it will be felt in the warm, earnest hearts of the soldier and his mother. This must be your reward, noble Ladies and kind gentlemen. It is not enough, but it is all we have to offer. Expressing my thanks for personal favors, I subscribe myself,

A. McKIMM, Ward Master

NOTE:—Confederate General Stuart left his dead and wounded lay on the field at Hanover. His wounded received the same kind treatment at this hospital as the Union soldiers. His dead were buried in trenches along the Hanover road between Hanover and Buttstown (Pennville.)

Sunday, August 9, 1863

Standing in the parlor doorway, Kathleen smiled brightly at Jake. Her voice took on a very proper British accent. "Are we ready for our 'lesson,' milord?"

Jake's heart skipped a beat. Kathleen again wore Eliza's pink dress, and she looked absolutely radiant. "Uh, 'lesson,' milady? Um, yes, I are. I mean, we am!" He gave up trying to get it right and basked in the musical lilt of Kathleen's laughter.

She entered the parlor. The ringlets cascading down the back of her head bobbed gently. Loose ringlets framed her sweet face.

"Happy sixteenth birthday, Kathleen! You—" He was about to say she didn't need to get all dressed up for him, but from the glow on her face, he realized he *was* the reason for the fancy dress and elegantly styled hair, "—look, well, more beautiful than ever."

Blushing, she reverted to her soft Virginia drawl. "Why, thank you, Jacob. You are most kind."

Myrtle appeared in the doorway. "Good afternoon, Kathleen. My, don't you look pretty! Here, let me take your parasol and gloves." She looked Kathleen up and down, her eyes pausing on the full hoop skirt. "Will you be able to sit at the melodeon with that thing on?"

Giggling, Kathleen replied, "If I may borrow your room later, I have a change of clothing out in the buggy." She handed the gloves and parasol to Myrtle.

"Certainly, dear. And will Eliza be joining us today?"

"No, I'm afraid not. Her constitution still won't allow." Kathleen's frown gave away the little white lie.

Jake bit his lip. Eliza's "constitution" had been weak for an entire month now, ever since she had seen his injured face. Outside of her occasional bouts of ill humor, Jake hadn't seen Eliza sick once in the two years he had known her. He couldn't help feeling hurt. After all, Kathleen didn't seem to mind the gash on his face. Besides, the wound didn't look nearly as hideous now that the stitches were out. He tried hard not to feel abandoned or angry. It wasn't Eliza's fault she had such a delicate constitution.

Myrtle stared thoughtfully at Jake. "Shall we start with some tea and blueberry muffins?"

Jake's eyes met Kathleen's and his mood brightened. "Maybe I should have my 'lesson' first?"

Kathleen smiled and nodded her agreement.

Puzzled, Myrtle looked back and forth between the two. "Lesson?"

"He means the exercises to keep his leg from withering," Kathleen explained in an airy tone.

"Oh, of course. That will give me time to warm the muffins and heat water for tea. If someone should come to the door, let me answer it. We wouldn't want anyone to know I left you two unattended, Kathleen."

"That's fine with me. Thank you, Miss Myrtle."

During her daily visits, Kathleen worked with Jake to keep the muscles in his arms and legs from weakening, then she helped him over to the melodeon so he could give her a music lesson. Reading and singing together rounded out each session. Myrtle was present for the entire visit the first couple of weeks, but, as time passed, she showed no hesitation in leaving the couple alone while she worked upstairs or in the kitchen.

Jake eased himself to a standing position, supporting all his weight on his left leg. Kathleen seemed to float across the parlor to join him. His eyes feasted on her graceful movements and the sensuous lines of her neck and bare shoulders in the décolleté gown. A heart-shaped locket dangled from a fine gold chain looped around her neck. It took all his will power to keep from focusing on the area below the locket. Kathleen stopped barely a foot away. Their eyes met.

Jake wondered. Did she love him? With each new day, his feelings for her had deepened. He knew he loved her, but what of his fading feelings for Eliza? And why did his love for Kathleen feel different? And stronger?

He swallowed hard, willing his voice to remain steady. "Kathleen, I made you a little present for your birthday. It's nothing much, really, but after all you've done for me, it seemed the least I could do." And he wanted to do so much more.

Jake pulled the gift from his pocket. He reached for her hand and placed a beautifully crafted wooden cross on her palm. "I carved this out of one of the splints. I thought—"

"Oh, Jacob, this is perfect, thank you!" She stood on tiptoe and kissed him on the cheek—his healing cheek. "This means more to me than you can imagine."

His face tingled where the warmth of her kiss lingered. "Without your help, no telling what shape I'd be in now." He decided to lighten the mood, lest he reveal his deepest feelings. "Why, in another month I'll be able to kick down a barn door."

"I once said you were stubborn," she said with a crooked grin, "but I never called you a mule."

She set the cross next to her reticule on the coffee table. "Now then, Mr. Becker, we better get to work if you expect to be ready for your bout with that barn door."

Kathleen motioned for Jake to hop clear of the divan and took her position facing him. She placed his left hand on her shoulder, looked into his eyes, and lowered her voice. "All right, soldier boy, swing that leg!"

Jake began the routine of swinging his injured right leg in a slow arc from the hip. His hand felt clammy against the smooth skin of Kathleen's shoulder. As her eyes followed the progress of his leg, a ringlet of her tawny hair bounced teasingly against the back of his hand. His leg slowed to a stop. Again, their eyes met.

"Kathleen." He took his hand from her shoulder and eased her into his embrace. Their lips met in a tender kiss. After a long moment, he started to pull away, but she pressed her lips tighter against his. Her hands caressed his back. Was that his heart pounding, or hers? Her bosom felt warm against his chest. It was all more than he could bear. Reluctantly, he drew back. "Kathleen?"

In response, she gazed up at him, her deep green eyes filled with emotion. And, in that moment, Jake knew it was love.

"Jacob?" Her eyes took on a mischievous glint.

What was she thinking now? He loved how he never quite knew for sure. Maybe this time he could surprise her. "Care to dance?"

Her eyes brightened. "Dance? Yes . . . but—"

Jake took her hands in his and struck a waltz pose. "You must have a birthday waltz. You'll have to lead for now because I have to keep my weight on my left leg. Think you can manage it?"

"Watch me!" She sang the opening strain. "Dum-ta-da-da dum-ta-da-da dum."

"Ta-da dum," he responded with the finishing bass notes.

Kathleen sang an improvised waltz melody and circled elegantly around Jake while he pivoted on his good leg. He felt like a mechanical toy, but he didn't care, he'd never felt so happy.

"My gracious," Myrtle exclaimed from the doorway. "Now if that doesn't heal a body, I don't know what will!"

The swirling couple slowed to a halt. Kathleen beamed up at Jake and curtseyed. "Thank you, milord. You dance wonderfully."

He bowed and kissed her hand. "The pleasure is all mine, milady. You are grace and beauty personified."

Myrtle clucked her tongue and set the tray with tea and muffins on the coffee table. "Well, do I have to be more careful about my chaperoning duties?"

Jake feared his blush might give him away. "I was just giving Kathleen a birthday waltz. It wouldn't do for her to turn sixteen without one." Kathleen gave him a glance, as if to say she also appreciated the special birthday kiss. His blush deepened.

"I see," Myrtle replied thoughtfully. Her eyes shifted from Jake to Kathleen and back again. "I see."

-2-

Jake barely slept that night; he could not stop wrestling with his feelings for Kathleen and Eliza. After the way Eliza had acted since his return, what possible relationship could he have with her now? Barely suppressed, his anger and resentment over her abandonment nearly devoured his love for her, yet his sense of duty and commitment lingered. After all, he had announced his intentions to Mrs. Bigler. Then again, she had not accepted; therefore, he was free to love whomever he would. Realistically, however, he was smart enough to know the perils of falling in love with his former beloved's sister.

No one had ever done more to earn a man's love, of that he felt absolutely certain. Kathleen had not only accepted him and his disfigurement, she had worked tirelessly to speed his recovery, in body and spirit. He knew his bond with her had grown beyond mere feelings. She had come to mean so much to him, he couldn't imagine life without her. He couldn't possibly marry another, not even Eliza. Every day in such a marriage would be a betrayal—of both Kathleen and himself.

As twittering birds announced the dawn, Jake came to the inevitable conclusion. He loved Kathleen and, from the loving look in her eyes and her attentive healing touch, he firmly believed that she loved him as well. Though he still harbored some feelings for Eliza, he must tell her that things had irrevocably changed. If he was lucky, she already felt the same way. And judging from the way she had ignored him this past month . . .

Suddenly, worry for Pa's safety and whereabouts flooded Jake's mind. It had been more than three weeks since the Confederate Army had crossed the Potomac back into Virginia. Surely, Pa should have been able to get some word to his family in the five weeks since he'd been gone. Jake could think of no good reason for the lack of news, other than the reasons he shuddered to visualize, but he refused to give up hope for Pa's imminent return.

To fend off further anxiety, Jake turned his thoughts back to Kathleen. Perhaps with a few years' hard work he could establish himself in life and then ask for Kathleen's hand in marriage.

Sleep finally overtook him

Monday, August 10, 1863

Jake could barely wait for Kathleen to arrive. Why was she late? Should he tell her how he felt right away or wait until just before she had to leave?

Myrtle called from the kitchen, "Ooh, the blueberry pie looks perfect!"

But Jake was too preoccupied to respond; he heard a buggy approaching from the direction of the Square. It stopped in front of the house. It had to be Kathleen! But why were there *two* sets of footsteps on the porch?

Myrtle hurried to the door. "Good afternoon, Kathleen. And Eliza! It is so good to see you again, especially looking so well."

Jake froze. *Eliza is here! Now what?* His stomach churned. His mind raced. What could this mean?

With a sheepish look on her face, Eliza entered the parlor. "Hello, Jake. Happy birthday."

"Um, thank you, Eliza." He struggled to keep any emotion from his voice. "It is nice of you to come."

Finally, Kathleen entered slowly. Jake couldn't help noticing her bloodshot eyes; she had clearly been crying. The thought of what must have occurred before the two sisters left the Wertz house made his heart ache. He wanted to hold Kathleen in his arms and assure her everything would be all right, but with this new situation shaking his resolve, he wasn't certain he would be able to make good on such a promise.

Eliza untied her bonnet and handed it to Myrtle. "I'm sorry I was unable to come see you this past month, Jake dear. Kathleen tells me your recovery is going well."

Jake noticed Eliza avoided looking at the right side of his face. "Yes, she has been a Godsend. I don't know where I'd be without her."

A look of jealousy flashed across Eliza's face. She shot a glare at her sister, but then quickly changed her expression to one of relief. "I'm so glad she's been of help to you in my absence, but now that I'm feeling better, I can take my proper place at your side."

Too stunned to speak, Jake felt as if he stood on the edge of an abyss—and he was losing his balance. Any moment now he would tumble into oblivion.

Myrtle spoke in the awkward silence. "May I take your bonnet, Kathleen?"

"Yes, ma'am," came the lifeless reply. Kathleen pulled the bow loose with one hand, slid the bonnet off, and held it out like a limp dishrag.

"Please have a seat and I'll be right back." Myrtle took the bonnets to the hallway. Jake tried to catch Kathleen's eye to invite her to sit next to him on the divan, but Eliza staked her claim first.

"I'll sit next to you Jake. Kathleen, why don't you be a dear and come sit here?" Eliza ushered Kathleen to the seat on the left side of the couch, then took her own place in the middle. Jake sank into the divan, very much aware of the fact that Eliza had arranged things so the right side of his face was away from her. Myrtle sat in the wing chair and eyed the trio thoughtfully.

He could not let this tension continue, but he didn't know how to confront Eliza about her absence over the past month. And he was eager to tell Kathleen how he felt about her, but how, and when?

Eliza patted Jake's left knee sympathetically. "I'm sorry to hear there has been no word from your father."

Surprisingly, the touch of her hand and the sound of her voice awakened old feelings. The remnant of his love for her cried out for another chance, but how could he even consider such a thing? He closed his eyes and thought of Kathleen. His heart ached for her; he loved her more than ever. So *why* did he have this lingering desire for Eliza? And how dare she bring up Pa's absence!

Myrtle again broke the awkward silence. "We have written letters to Washington City and to General Gregg to see if someone can find out anything about Papa. Jake even sent letters to President Davis and General Stuart, hoping they might be able to learn if our father was taken prisoner."

Thoughts of Pa only compounded Jake's burden. He knew his father often said, "Don't start what you can't finish." Too bad Pa hadn't warned him about the pitfalls of starting a new relationship before the old one was finished.

Well, I had every reason to believe my relationship with Eliza was over. She hadn't so much as sent me a note in response to any of my letters. The nerve of her to march in here like this, so casually, as if to pick up where she wants Kathleen to leave off!

Myrtle's "hostess voice" interrupted his angry thoughts. "Eliza, I have a pie warming on the stove. Would you like to help me bring it out?" Myrtle stood, looking as if she would not accept "no" for an answer.

"Yes, I would." Eliza rose and smiled down at Jake, but when he turned his full face toward her, she stiffened and quickly looked away. "We'll be right back, dear one." She followed Myrtle to the kitchen.

Kathleen stared at the floor. Her hands fidgeted with her skirt.

"Kathleen," Jake said quietly.

She didn't respond.

He eased himself next to her. "Kathleen, please look at me."

She slowly raised her head and met his eyes. She looked so forlorn, so full of despair.

Jake took her hand in his. "Kathleen, I love you. I—"

Her lips trembling, she swallowed hard and looked down again. "No, please don't say that. Not now." She stifled a sob. "I can't . . . because

Eliza . . . oh, what am I to do?" Her eyes fixed on him. She whispered in a rush, "I love you, too, Jacob, but how can we love each other when Eliza still loves you. At least she says she does. How could I get in the way of her love? I didn't mean for this to happen. I started loving you that day before you left, but then Eliza convinced me I just loved you like you were my brother, but I really knew better, and now after all that we've been through this past month, I know I could never love anyone but you." She sighed heavily. "Oh, what am I to do?"

Jake took her face in his hands and kissed her. Her lips met his, but then she suddenly pulled away.

"Oh, Jacob, I can't. Not while Eliza is in love with you. I just can't get away from feeling like I'm betraying my sister."

"But our love can overcome that, can't it?" He knew the folly of such words, even as he whispered them.

Kathleen shook her head slowly. "I think we know better than that. How could you love someone who would stoop so low as to steal from her sister? In any case, I am not that person."

But what was the alternative? He couldn't possibly marry Eliza knowing how he and Kathleen loved each other. Not even the highest sense of duty could demand such a sham.

"Well, wasn't that a pretty little speech." Eliza glared at the couple from the doorway. Myrtle stood behind her, looking shocked.

Eliza carried the pie into the parlor and set it on the coffee table. She turned to Jake, seated next to Kathleen on the divan. "I see my place is taken." She started for the empty spot on Jake's right side, then changed her course and sat in the wing chair.

Myrtle took the seat next to Jake. She leaned forward to cut the pie, but sat back when Eliza spoke her mind.

"So, I see you two have grown 'attached' to one another while I was sick."

Kathleen flinched. "Sick? Don't you mean sickened? Sickened by—"

Eliza held up her hand. "I admit I do not have the stomach for misery that you do, Kat, but that doesn't mean my love for Jake is any the less for it." She turned her eyes on Jake and met his dubious stare. "I'm sorry I have been unable to attend you myself." Her eyes moved to his scar. She quickly looked away. "I, uh, love you more than ever, Jake. I missed you terribly while you were gone to war. I've spoken with Mama, and she told me she would not object if you asked permission to court me. She very much appreciates the sacrifice you have made for our cause."

Jake didn't know which hurt the worst: Eliza's aversion to his face, his "sacrifice" that had caused such hurt to his family, or the mess he had made by falling in love with Kathleen before knowing for certain about Eliza's feelings. And now that he had gotten Mrs. Bigler's approval, how could he ever ask for Kathleen's hand *instead?*

A flash of fury coursed through him. He steadied himself, then said coldly, "I had no idea you still cared, Eliza. You never even *wrote* to me. What was I supposed to think?"

In an apparent attempt to break the tension, Myrtle cleared her throat. "How about some pie?"

"Not now, Sis," Jake said tersely. "We need to settle this. I'm in love with Kathleen and she loves me. I'm sorry, Eliza, but the way you have acted since I've been back has—"

"Stop. Please." Eliza's sullen eyes pleaded with him. "I do love you, Jake. I never stopped loving you this whole time. I am very sorry it took me so long to overcome my weakness. Can't you forgive me?"

Jake felt bad for her, but his mind was made up. He reached for Kathleen's hand and squeezed it, but when she didn't squeeze back, he looked at her questioningly.

"Look at me, Jake," Eliza said sadly.

He slowly turned back to her.

"Look me in the eye and tell me you do not love me. If you can do that, I will let you go."

Finally, a way out of the dilemma! Surely he could tell her it was over between them. Jake opened his mouth to speak, but the words died on his lips. The longing in Eliza's eyes gave new hope to that last glimmer of love he felt. He remembered his passion for her over the past two years. For so long he had desired no one but Eliza, could he honestly say those feelings were dead? "Eliza . . . I . . . I do care for you, but it is not the same. Not any more." He was about to add, "Not like I love Kathleen," but he couldn't bring himself to add to the pain he saw in Eliza's eyes. He felt himself sinking inexorably into the quagmire.

Eliza pursed her lips, then said, "But you love Kathleen more."

"Yes." Somehow, he took no joy in the confession. Kathleen squirmed. Her dress brushed against him, sending a surge of warmth through his body.

"I suspected as much when I saw the way Kathleen acted when she returned home yesterday." Eliza clutched the arms of the chair. "We got into an argu—, um, we had a discussion with Mother about this, and she had an idea."

"What do you mean?" Jake asked warily.

"Perhaps you should give me the same chance you gave Kathleen. If the two of you go without seeing each other for a month, like you and I did, perhaps you will discover whether it is true love or 'calf-love' you feel for each other. Give me that month to prove my love for you. If you find you no longer care for me, then I will release you. Kathleen will no longer have to feel like she is stealing you from me, and I will have to learn to love you as a brother, for I shall not waste my love on a man who loves another woman."

Only the ticking of the mantel clock broke the silence. In all the time he had known Eliza, she had never sounded so determined. He hated to admit it, but the proposal made some sense. At least, his mind accepted the idea; his heart was an entirely different matter.

"On one condition," Kathleen interjected. "I think after that month, we should go another month without either of us seeing Jacob while he decides."

Jake cringed at the thought of going a day without spending time with Kathleen. How would he last two months? Still, he couldn't help being curious to see if Eliza was right. What if he and Kathleen were besotted due to his dire circumstances? He had loved Eliza for two years, Kathleen for two fortnights. He'd better know for certain before things grew even more complicated.

Kathleen grasped Jake's hand and he turned to her. "Jacob, it sounds like the only way to resolve this." Her eyes brimmed with tears. "I love you, Jacob, and I will be waiting for you, but if you find that you still—"

He stopped her with a kiss. Ignoring Eliza's gasp, he whispered, "I love you, Kathleen. You have become part of me—"

She put her hand to his lips. "No, not now. We'll talk again in two months." She caressed his injured cheek, gave him a quick parting kiss on the lips, and then stood.

"I'll trade seats with you, Eliza. After we have some birthday pie, I'll go visit the soldiers at the hospital for an hour or two while you visit with Jake."

They ate the pie in silence. His stomach and soul in turmoil, Jake had no appetite.

When Kathleen stood to leave, Eliza announced, "Maybe it is better that I go, too. We can start again tomorrow. May I come in the afternoon?"

Much relieved, Jake nodded. "That sounds like a good idea." His injuries began to throb.

Kathleen avoided looking at him as she mumbled, "I almost forgot. I have something for you out in the buggy." She hurried outside and came back in with a long, rolled-up piece of paper in her hand.

"I made this for you. Happy birthday, Jacob." She handed Jake the gift and smiled fleetingly. Turning to Myrtle, she added, "And thank you for having me here. I'll look forward to seeing you again in October." She gave Jake a quick peck on the cheek. "Good bye, my love." And then she was gone.

Jake felt as if his heart had left with her.

Eliza thanked Myrtle and gave Jake a gentle hug. He noticed she put her face against his good cheek.

"Happy birthday, Jake." She kissed him on the lips, gently at first, then with growing passion.

Jake pulled away. "Thank you, Eliza." His heart pounded and his mind raced. What had he gotten himself into? Why did part of him want to return her ardor? What was wrong with him? He wanted to dash outside and beg Kathleen's forgiveness.

"I'll see you tomorrow, darlin'." Eliza collected the bonnets from Myrtle at the door and departed.

Jake sagged onto the divan as Myrtle eased into the wing chair. "Well, brother dear, you're in a fine mess." She grinned. "Perhaps you should move out west and take up Mormonism so you can marry both of them."

"Now there's an idea," Jake said, rolling his eyes. How could any man marry more than one woman? As he had learned in Sunday school, having more than one wife was only an excuse to indulge one's lust. The lessons on love versus lust lurked in the back of his mind. He tapped the rolled paper against his palm.

"So, what did your sweetheart make for you?" Myrtle asked, joining Jake on the divan.

He sighed wearily. "Already made your pick, huh? Well, I can only hope it will be that easy." Jake untied the shiny pink ribbon and unrolled the paper across his lap. It was a remarkable likeness in charcoal of Kathleen and him at the melodeon, gazing into one another's eyes. Love-filled eyes.

Thursday, September 10, 1863

The first several days without seeing Kathleen had been agony for Jake. Initially, he resented Eliza for coming between them, but after a week of anguish he concluded there really was no better way to resolve the situation. His sense of duty and fairness demanded that he do his best to see the proposition through.

Now that there was no further need for "nursing," Eliza and Jake spent the daily visits conversing, singing, and playing the melodeon. Eliza was so talented at the keyboard that she was the one who gave the lessons, though she often pumped one of the pedals so Jake could avoid putting too much stress on his mending leg. He noticed she always sat to his left on the bench, apparently so that she only saw his "good" side.

Now her elbow rubbed against him as she pumped. "Eliza, please don't sit so close. You're, um, making my leg feel bad."

"But what about your promise to give me a chance to earn your affections?" She smiled coyly. "This is my last day with you for a month while you decide."

Jake felt his resolve weaken. Her pouty lips poised only inches away from his. Fearing his lips might find their way to hers, he didn't dare move his mouth to answer.

Her voice grew husky. "Besides, I'll wager you didn't mind when Kathleen sat close beside you."

"Uh . . . actually, we never sat next to each other on the bench." If deception was a lie, then he'd just spun a whopper. He had sat on a stool next to the bench. Often times, Kathleen rested her head on his shoulder while they chatted, or he laid his head on her shoulder as she lifted her mellifluous voice in song. How he longed to see her again, to rejoice in her mere presence.

Tears filled Eliza's eyes. "You really don't love me any more."

Jake blurted, "That's not true. I do love you, Eliza." He immediately wished he could take the words back—but realized part of him meant it.

Eliza squealed and threw her arms around him. "Oh, you have no idea how happy you've just made me!"

Myrtle hurried down the hall from the kitchen and poked her head around the door. "Is everything all right?"

"Yes, Miss Myrtle." Eliza scooted over a few inches on the bench.

"I need to go out to the pump for some more water. You don't mind, do you, Eliza?"

"No, Miss Myrtle, not a bit." Eliza's tone implied Myrtle could take all the time in the world.

As soon as the back door closed, Eliza leaned over and gave Jake a kiss. After a few moments he started to pull away, but she put her hand on the back of his neck, parted her lips, and slid her tongue into his mouth. His initial shock gave way to waves of pleasure—followed by a flood of guilt.

"No!" Jake pushed her away. "I can't. Believe me, I want to, but it's not fair. Kathleen never—"

"Well, if she didn't, that's her fault." Eliza folded her arms under her bosom. "I'll bet you wanted to do the same with her."

Jake flushed with embarrassment. "Wanting to is one thing, doing is quite another."

"Maybe you should keep this in mind while you decide whom shall have your undivided love." Eliza turned up the heat with her smile. "I know you love me, and you *know* how much I love you." She put her arm around his waist and whispered in his ear. "Would you like to hear some of the things I want to share with you while we await our wedding night?" She took a deep breath, allowing her breast to brush against his arm.

Jake had already had more than enough fantasies of his own. "Eliza, you have no idea how much I'd like to share *everything* with you, but—"

"Don't tell me, show me." She pressed her lips to his.

Part of him wanted to give in and enjoy whatever she offered, but the mere thought of sadness in Kathleen's eyes squelched that desire. He freed himself from Eliza's arms and stood. "Eliza, I can't. This is wrong."

He stared out the window to avoid her penetrating look. "Eliza, you're incredibly beautiful. Even so, that mustn't enter into my decision on whom to ask to share my life."

"But—"

Jake held up his hand, then limped to the wing chair. "Eliza, I do feel love for you, but I have to ask myself, what kind of love is it? If it is little more than love of your body, then I'd be making a big mistake to marry you."

Eliza looked unconvinced.

Before she could raise any further objection, he added, "So if you truly want to marry me some day, then you'll show me the beauty inside of you." His voice softened. "I already know how beautiful you are on the outside."

Myrtle bustled through the front door. "Whew! Sorry I took so long. I hope you don't mind, Eliza." She set two buckets on the hallway floor. "Can you stay for dinner? Mrs. Winebrenner just gave me a ham hock that's good and ready." She pointed to one of the buckets.

Eliza sighed. "I'd like to, but Mama is expecting me home. Lydia said Jonas is going to discuss a wedding date with her Pa tonight after dinner."

Jake couldn't resist the setup. "Oh, they'd make an interesting couple, but isn't Lydia's Pa already married?" For once, Eliza seemed to understand his joke. She giggled and flashed an appreciative smile. He found himself aching with desire for her. But how could he still harbor such feelings when he loved Kathleen?

Eliza stood and walked slowly toward the wing chair, holding Jake with her sparkling brown eyes. "I shall think only of you these next thirty days, my darlin'." She held out her hand and he rose to take it. With her other hand, Eliza gently stroked his good cheek, sending a tingle through his body.

"I love you, Jake." She closed her eyes, leaned over, and kissed his scarred cheek. "I'll be waiting for you, darlin'," she murmured in a sultry voice.

Finally, she seemed to have grown accustomed to his disfigured face! Why did that seem to make such a difference now? Head spinning, Jake hobbled to the door to see Eliza off. All the old feelings came rushing back. He had dreamed of marrying her for so long, he wanted to beg her to stay and never leave.

But what about my love for Kathleen? Now what do I do?

-2-

It was a good tonic to be back in the carriage workshop, even though it felt odd to be there without Pa. Jake imagined his father, humming at the opposite bench while they worked. But there was still no word of his whereabouts.

Jake glanced at the three letters he had squirreled away on the shelf over his bench. The first letter, no return address, had come from Major McClellan on behalf of General Stuart. After expressing condolences for Jake's wounds and offering best wishes for a full recovery, McClellan wrote that he had found no record of a David Becker taken prisoner by the Army of Northern Virginia. At least he had been able to give Jake the good news that General Hampton was recovering from his injuries.

The second letter contained the reply from President Jefferson Davis' aide, postmarked in Washington City, no less! Jake grinned and shook his head. How had they managed that? The aide thanked Jake for his sacrifice for the Confederate cause, then went on to explain the difficulty in obtaining accurate information on specific prisoners unless they were officers. He assured the Beckers that prisoner lists were constantly updated. If their father had indeed been taken captive, the information would eventually make its way to the Federal government.

The third letter had arrived last week. General Gregg's adjutant said the general remembered meeting a brave middle-aged man who had volunteered in the early morning hours as the Union troops left Hanover. The man had been assigned to one of the Pennsylvania cavalry companies, and he had served well in the battles east of Gettysburg on

July 2nd and 3rd. No one knew what happened to him after that.

Jake was horrified at the thought that he and Pa might have been on the same battlefield. He immediately sent a telegram to Leah and Adam, who made exhaustive searches among the makeshift hospitals and burial sites around Gettysburg, to no avail. It was as if Pa had vanished.

So Myrtle and Sam postponed the wedding indefinitely. She insisted Jake finish her carriage and sell it. They needed the income, as the number of money jars buried in the garden continued to dwindle. Jake reluctantly agreed, vowing to build her an even better carriage in time for her eventual wedding.

Sunlight streamed through the window and gleamed on the carriage's polished oak panels. Jake shook his head. He had poured so much love into every inch of that landau. With one final coat of lacquer, it would be ready to sell. And that stuck in his craw. In his mind, the carriage would always belong to Myrtle. Where was the joy in finishing it now? Gone forever. Just like Pa?

Loneliness engulfed him, together with guilt for his part in ruining Myrtle's wedding plans. He knew in his heart that, had he not enlisted, Pa would likely still be there, working with him in the carriage shop. Despair welled up within him. He expected the Smiling Man to come for him at any moment. And this time, he might just as well go along.

Monday, September 21, 1863

To give his aching right shoulder a break, Jake shifted the rag to his left hand and continued to polish the trim. In spite of all that had happened in the past two and a half months, Pa could at least be proud of him for finishing the carriage—that is, if he ever came back home.

Rebelling at the thought Pa may no longer be alive, Jake turned his mind to a different topic: how to decide between Eliza and Kathleen. On the one hand, he was in a "no lose" situation; he could imagine himself happily married to either of the beautiful young women. On the other hand, he felt there was no way he could win, since the woman he "rejected" would no doubt feel very hurt, and he cared too much for both of them to want to cause such pain. A tiny voice in his head chided, *Maybe it would have been better if* you *were the one who never returned home from the war.*

"No!" Jake closed his eyes and clutched the sides of his head. "Pa is alive. We'll hear from him any day now." Hope. He had to keep hope alive. Perhaps Pa lay in a hospital somewhere, struggling for life. That must be it. Jake didn't want to imagine life without . . .

Imagine life without. Jake pondered the words and realized they were the key to his decision. Pa's adage rang in his mind. "A man will meet several women he imagines he'd like to spend his life with, but he should marry the woman he can't imagine spending his life without." Unfortunately, this case still left the problem of his relationship with the woman who would someday become his sister-in-law.

Jake dabbed the rag in the can of pungent polish and went to work on the running board, rubbing the cloth along the grain. He'd already seen how Eliza acted when cross, how did Kathleen react in such circumstances? Did she turn as icy as Eliza when her feelings were hurt?

Perhaps women's feelings are like day old ice, he mused. *If a man treads heavily, he'll break through the thin surface and face the frigid consequences. Lack of attention will lead to a nasty spill and bruises, followed by a chilly dowsing. But . . . the successful negotiation of such a perilous path will lead to a garden of Eden on the other side.*

Jake shook his head ruefully. What a silly metaphor! What was it about working alone that turned a man into a self-styled philosopher? Or was he merely suffering the effects of the polish fumes? He turned back to his work. The Eerdmans, prospective buyers, were due to arrive soon.

The sound of voices drifted through the window on the invigorating autumn breeze. Was that the Eerdmans already? Jake limped to the window for a better look. Sam and Myrtle stood deep in discussion at the front of the house and, judging from the frown on Myrtle's face, she didn't like what she heard.

"Ohio? Not again with Ohio, Sam, I've told you how I feel about that. I will not leave Hanover while Jake needs me, and I'm not going anywhere until I know what happened to Papa."

"Well, I am going to Ohio," Sam said in a steely tone. "If you need to stay here to tend your *brother,* so be it."

Myrtle took Sam's hand and placed something in it. Sam glared at her, then stalked away.

Jake turned and sagged against the wall. He had never heard "brother" uttered with such contempt, the antithesis of everything the name should mean. Poor Myrtle! Now his misfortunes had ruined her life, too. "No! Pa is alive and will come home any day now," Jake shouted.

Fighting back the swell of despair, Jake limped for the door. He must comfort Myrtle. The voice in his head chided, *Or is it your own comfort you seek?*

"Go to hell!" Jake snarled, leaning on the door. He'd had enough of inner demons. He was going to open this door and leave such thoughts behind, once and for all.

Jake flung the door open and found Myrtle standing on the other side. He could tell from her tentative smile that she was trying to hide something from him. "No use pretending. I heard what that lout said."

Myrtle's lips quivered as she fought back tears. "Then you agree? There will be no wedding?"

"What? I didn't hear anything about that. What did he say?"

"It's really all for the best, Jake," Myrtle said, sniffling. "I can see that now."

Jake's anger flared. This was so unfair. Why did Myrtle have to suffer the consequences of his decision to fight for the Confederacy? She had nothing to do with it, so why did Sam turn on her? Maybe a good thrashing would straighten the scoundrel out.

Myrtle studied her brother's face. "I know you, Jake. Don't get the wrong idea. This was my decision, I'm the one who called off the marriage. These past couple of months have shown me sides of Sam I never saw before. I will not marry a man like that."

When Jake started to object, she lifted her hand for silence. "Don't fret on my account. Remember what Papa used to say, 'The River of Life flows ever onward.'"

With a flash of insight, Jake realized how important it was to know he could count on his future wife to paddle in the same direction when the River of Life turned turbulent. He shook his head slowly and muttered, "I gotta get away from these polish fumes."

"Are you all right?" Myrtle asked, clearly worried.

Finally knowing with certainty whom he should marry, Jake smiled. "I will be."

A buggy trailing a pair of tethered horses pulled up to the front of the workshop. Two men wearing fashionable brown suits and derbies alit and stretched their legs. The older man doffed his hat, and said, "Is this Becker and Son Carriages?"

"Yes, sir, it is," Jake said proudly. I'm Jacob Becker, and this is my sister, Myrtle. Our father is not here at present."

"I'm William Eerdman, and this is my son, Will. We're pleased to, um," the man's eyes flitted back and forth between Jake's eyes and the scar on his cheek, "meet you."

Hoping his disfigured face wouldn't put the man off, Jake hurriedly replied, "Thank you, sir. It's a pleasure to meet you, too."

Myrtle slipped her arm around Jake's waist. "My brother was wounded in the war."

"Ah, I see," Mr. Eerdman replied. "You have our thanks and admiration, Mr. Becker. Perhaps you shall have our business, as well. We've heard wonderful things about your workmanship."

"I trust you will be pleased, Mr. Eerdman." Jake gestured toward the workshop, and Myrtle swung open the big double doors. The landau's polished wooden panels seemed to glow in the mid-afternoon sun.

Both men whistled. The younger Eerdman spoke in a hushed tone. "She's a beauty, all right."

While the senior Eerdman eyed the carriage, Will cast furtive glances at Myrtle. Jake caught her attention and arched one eyebrow. She rolled her eyes, folded her arms, and looked away.

The Eerdmans entered the workshop for a closer inspection of the landau. Rather than hover over their guests, the Beckers waited outside.

Mr. Eerdman emerged a few minutes later, looking very satisfied. "It's everything I've hoped for and more. I am quite taken with the design of the doors and the cut of the hood. I'll be the envy of York."

"Thank you, sir." His first sale!

Myrtle beamed. "It's my brother's modification of the landau design."

Will strolled from the workshop. "Congratulations, my father is not an easy man to please. We both have an eye for the highest quality." He glanced at Myrtle, then turned to Jake. "Tell me, Mr. Becker, can you make another one of these for me by Christmas?"

"Yes, sir." Their financial troubles were over! "What color?"

"Blue," Will said, smiling warmly at Myrtle. "The same shade as Miss Becker's eyes."

Myrtle shifted her feet and looked away.

It took all of Jake's self-control to stifle a smirk. "Certainly. 'Myrtle Blue' it shall be."

"I'll be in Hanover at least twice a month on business," Will continued. "Do you mind if I call upon you to watch your progress?"

"You're welcome to call at your leisure," Jake replied, hoping Myrtle didn't mind the sudden attention.

"Then I will plan on it," Will said, flashing Myrtle an engaging smile.

Thursday, October 8, 1863

Jake sat on the bench outside the carriage shop and sanded a running board for Will Eerdman's landau. A cool breeze danced through the sunlit autumn foliage. The smell of pumpkin pie drifted from the kitchen window and Jake's stomach rumbled. Good thing he had only one more edge to smooth before he could wash up for dinner.

At the sound of an approaching wagon, Jake leaned back and massaged his sore shoulder. A bay Clydesdale pulling a hay wagon rounded the bend on Frederick Street. The vehicle creaked closer. A solitary coffin rested on the wagon bed.

Many of the thousands who had died in the battle at Gettysburg were later taken home for reburial. This poor soul was probably another in the dismal parade of men on their way to their final resting places. Jake bowed his head and prayed for the poor, unfortunate family awaiting their hero's arrival.

He renewed his efforts on the edge of the running board. Finally satisfied the work would pass even his father's inspection, Jake put the finished piece in the shop, then went to the rain barrel to wash up.

Entering the house through the kitchen door, Jake was met with the sumptuous aroma of fresh-baked pumpkin pie with lots of cinnamon. "Yum! Are we expecting company?"

"Not unless you invited 'a certain someone' to come a day early," Myrtle said, donning a pair of oven mitts.

She opened the side door of the ten-plate stove and pulled out a pan of apple dumplings. She nodded toward the dish atop the warming plate on the front of the stove. "Jake, can you put the succotash on the table? I've got to get the pie out of the stove, yet."

He grabbed a pair of potholders from the hooks on the wall and picked up the dish. As expected, three places had been set for dinner; the one at the head of the table was in anticipation of Pa's eventual return. Jake had suggested Pa's place be set at every meal, and Myrtle happily agreed.

Someone knocked on the front door. Was that Eliza or Kathleen? He hadn't planned to meet with the Biglers until tomorrow. His heart beat faster with anticipation.

"Now who could that be?" Myrtle said with a bemused look on her face. "You don't suppose . . ."

"I was just thinking the same thing. But I don't know if I'm ready for this! Tonight I was going to ask you to help me figure out how to tell—"

The knocking resumed, louder.

"Well, you'd better go let them in before they break the door down," Myrtle said, shooing him on his way.

Jake set the dish on the table and started for the door.

"Oh, and you might want to leave the potholders here. Or were you wanting to impress them with what a fine wife you'll make?"

He tossed the potholders at her, but she ducked out of the way.

"You throw like a woman!" Myrtle said, chuckling.

Too preoccupied to respond, Jake headed for the front door, hoping he'd find the right words to relate his decision. But instead of two beautiful young women, he found a man in farm clothes standing on the porch. Jake recognized him as the driver of the hay wagon. The pungent aroma of dairy barn wafted through the door. The grim-faced farmer doffed his straw hat and fidgeted with the wide brim. "Excuse me, sir, but is this the home of David Becker?"

Joy lit Jake's face. Word from Pa at last! "Yes, it surely is. Please come in." Jake held the door open and shouted toward the kitchen. "Myrtle, come quick! Someone is here with word from Pa!" Wiping her hands on her apron and eyes filled with hope, Myrtle rushed down the hall.

Jake put his arm around his sister's shoulder and turned to the farmer. "I'm sorry, where are my manners? We are David Becker's children. This is Myrtle, I am Jacob." The men shook hands.

"My name is Lott. I own a farm this side of Gettysburg. On Low Dutch Road."

Jake gulped. His blood had stained this man's field! His voice rasped as he said, "Glad to make your acquaintance, Mr. Lott."

Impatient as ever, Myrtle blurted, "Do you have news from our father, Mr. Lott?"

Jake felt her body tremble. Or was it his?

Mr. Lott stared at the floor. "Um, yes, news. Um, I'm afraid I bear bad news."

Myrtle gasped and buried her head against Jake's chest. Jake asked eagerly, "Will it be much longer before our father will return home?"

The farmer coughed, then finally looked Jake in the eye. "I, uh, must tell you, God has called your father to his heavenly home."

Myrtle's knees buckled. Jake held her tight, straining his sore shoulder in the process. He ignored the stabbing pain. "How do you know that?"

Mr. Lott gestured over his shoulder to the hay wagon outside—and the coffin. "Me and my boys was out cutting firewood in the north grove when we, um, come across a Union soldier, all covered up by a big limb that must've come down during the battle."

Jake shook his head. "That can't be our father." Could it? His heart quailed at the possibility. "What makes you think it is?"

The farmer reached into a frayed pants pocket, pulled out a familiar looking gold pocket watch, and handed it to Jake. Jake's fingers trembled as he opened the lid. Sure enough, the inscription read:

Rose and David Becker
One for Eternity
June 30, 1837

The watch had been Ma's wedding gift to Pa. It was his only prized possession. How many times had Jake seen his father open the watch to check the time, then seek out Ma for a kiss and hug?

"Someone must have stolen this. Pa would never have been so careless as to lose it." Jake glared at Mr. Lott. "There must be some mistake. Let me look in that coffin and I'll show you it is some other man." He started for the door, but Mr. Lott blocked the way.

"Uh, I don't think you want to do that," the farmer said tersely. "He's been more than three months in the woods. Besides, there's one more thing." He drew a folded piece of paper from his shirt pocket. "This here has his name and town onto it. And a few words he writ, uh, just in case."

Myrtle caught her breath and reached tentatively for the paper. Her quivering fingers unfolded the note. "Oh, Lord, help us." She burst into tears.

Feeling dizzy, Jake took the paper from Myrtle's hand and without so much as a glance, he stuffed the note into his pocket. To read it would mean the death of hope—and give life anew to the nagging guilt: if he hadn't gone off to war, Pa would never have joined the Union Army, and they would be preparing for a wedding instead of a funeral.

Monday, October 12, 1863

A misty drizzle drifted aimlessly in the autumn air. There were a few black umbrellas in the crowd, but most of the mourners just pulled up their collars and stoically hunched against the miserable elements.

While Rev. Guyer intoned the funeral service, Jake stared sullenly at Pa's casket. The beading moisture looked like drops of blood oozing through the cherry wood. Blinking away the macabre image, Jake stole a sidewise glance at Myrtle. She bit her lower lip and gave his hand a tender squeeze.

Jake scanned the familiar faces across the open grave. Grace's family huddled next to Faith's. His young nieces fidgeted and whispered amongst themselves.

Five-year-old Susie gaped at him and tugged on her mother's sleeve. "Mama, why is Uncle Jake smiling so big? Is he happy Papaw is dead?"

Looking mortified, Grace stooped down and whispered in her daughter's ear.

Jake heard the word "scar" and turned his face away. Bad enough that some of the children in town pointed and gawked at him, now his own kin thought him glad to see his father dead, all because of that smile-like scar. Jake fought back tears. *Pa would've never been under that tree if I hadn't gone off to fight.*

A voice in his head asked, *So why did you go?*

Jake's eyes drifted heavenward, remembering that fateful Sunday morning in church. True, he had wanted to impress the Biglers, but every Bible passage had seemed to point the way so clearly. *Was that a message from God, or just me looking to justify my own plans?*

The voice chided, *Wrong question! Did your father die from an act of war, or an act of God? Tree branches are not weapons of war.*

No, God would never— I had to go! The Federal government can't be allowed to impose— When they invaded Virginia and drove Eliza and Kathleen from their home— It was my duty to go! My duty!

For God and country, the voice mocked. *And how does God repay such devotion?*

". . . ashes to ashes, dust to dust. Let us pray." Rev. Guyer's prayer went on and on.

The incessant drizzle intensified, wetting the back of Jake's bowed head. Droplets formed and ran down his neck. His wounds ached and throbbed in the cool, damp air, but he no longer cared about such aggravations. On his left, Eliza and Kathleen sniffled, while Myrtle wept quietly on his right. Faith and Grace huddled in tears on the other side of the grave, their somber husbands at their sides. Jake never imagined following his duty would cause all of this suffering.

Mr. Stonesifer, Mr. Stremmel, Mr. Frank, and Mr. Gobrecht each manned a strap and lowered the casket into the ground, then each family member took a turn dropping a shovel full of wet dirt into the grave. Jake flinched with every hollow thud. When it came time for him to handle the spade, he took a heaping mound of dirt and slowly tipped it into the pit. His heart breaking, Jake drove the shovel back into the pile, scooped it full, and spilled the dirt on top of his father. He did it again. And again. And again.

Myrtle put her hand on his arm. "Jake, that's enough."

He pulled his arm free. "No. I'm the reason he's dead. I—"

"Stop it, Jake! It is *not* your fault!"

The anguish in Myrtle's voice cut him.

She eased the shovel from his grip as she continued, "Jake, you know Papa. You should know better than any of us how he felt about risking his life for our country. He chose to join the fight. Honor Papa with your grief, not your guilt." Her voice caught. "Please, Jake. He'd weep to see you like this."

He narrowed his eyes and considered her words. She was right. The shovel fell from his grasp, and as the guilt melted away, grief came rushing in. Jake buried his head in his hands and let the tears flow. Sobs racked his battered body.

Eliza and Kathleen rushed to his side. Rev. Guyer laid his hand on Jake's head and offered up a prayer for peace.

Jake scoffed inwardly. Based on his experiences over these past few months, he had come to question just how much the Creator really cared about the daily goings-on of His creatures, even when it involved something as catastrophic as war. Jake figured part of the problem was that people on both sides of the conflict prayed to the same God, and what good had come of all those prayers? But he had to admit, he felt a welcomed sense of calm after the pastor's prayer.

Myrtle patted his arm. "We'll get through this, Jake."

"I know, but it's going to take a long time."

"Shall we head back to the house now? People will be stopping by."

"I'd like to spend a little time here alone. Would you mind going on ahead without me?" Jake turned to Eliza and Kathleen. "Could Myrtle please ride in the carriage with you and your mother?"

"I'm sure that will be fine," Eliza replied. She dabbed her eyes with a handkerchief and Kathleen nodded somberly.

Myrtle looked doubtful. "Are you sure you're all right, Jake?"

"Yes, I just feel like I have a little unfinished business to tend to. I'll be along in the buggy soon."

Several minutes later, the mourners had all departed and Jake stood alone at the foot of Pa's grave. He felt like he should say something, but he didn't know where to begin. His eyes wandered to the neighboring gravestone. Mama. Overwhelmed with a torrent of emotions, he whispered, "So, together forever at last. You must be so happy!"

Tears streaming anew, he closed his eyes and thanked God for his parents' love for one another. Thoughts of their marital bliss stirred something deep within him. Oh, how he longed for that kind of love and relationship! He asked the Almighty to prepare him for the day when he would have his own wife and children.

Perhaps he should consider moving to Manassas? Surely, his future father-in-law would appreciate help after the war, and with Will Eerdman calling on Myrtle twice a week, she might well be married and settled in her own home by the time Jake was ready for a marriage partner.

Feeling a renewed sense of purpose, he wiped his tear-stained face and started for the buggy. On the way, he stopped to pay his respects at John Hoffacker's grave, but when he read the headstone's inscription, his heart faltered.

Remember me as you pass by
as you are now so once was I
as I am now so you must be
prepare for death and follow me.

Jake recalled John's happy-go-lucky grin and boundless energy. Something inside him snapped.

It's so unfair! Why do so many good people have to die? There's little hope the states will peacefully reunite, and the slaves are no better off now than they were before the war. Who started this foolish, bloody mess, anyway?

The answer burned in Jake's mind. *Abraham Lincoln.*

"The Great Emancipator," Jake muttered sarcastically. "More like the Great Eviscerator, ripping the heart out of the country!"

His anger spawned hatred. Because of that one man, hundreds of thousands of men had died, and millions of lives would never be the same. How many more men would perish? How many lives would be forever changed, all because of that one man?

Wednesday, November 18, 1863

As in any small town, exciting news flew through the streets and alleyways of Hanover: President Lincoln's train was scheduled to stop in town on the way to Gettysburg for the dedication of the soldiers' cemetery. The stories varied as to the length and intent of the impending visit, but whatever the case might be, the Great Emancipator's train was due to arrive at 5:00 PM. The only question in Jake's mind was whether he would join the gathering. He had come to hold Lincoln ultimately responsible for Pa's death.

Tying her bonnet, Myrtle entered the parlor. "Do you want to take a cane along in case your leg tires?"

"No, thank you," Jake snapped. To use a crutch of any kind would seem unmanly on such an occasion. He would not appear as a cripple in front of the man most responsible for this awful war.

Jake noticed Myrtle's chastened expression. "I'm sorry, Sis. I didn't mean to sound grumpy." He rose from the wing chair and gave her a hug.

"I understand, Jake," she murmured.

He stepped back and looked into her eyes. She couldn't possibly understand, but he loved her all the more for trying. "You have done so much for me, sacrificed so much, and I have done nothing to make it all worthwhile. And with Pa gone, how can—"

Myrtle put a finger up to her lips. "No more of that kind of talk. We are in God's hands. He will always reveal our paths in His time. You know . . ."

He stopped listening. Yes, he knew what their faith taught, but spiritual platitudes were the last thing he needed. Not now. Not when he felt like he was lost in the desert, and the oasis of happiness was naught but a shimmering mirage.

"Myrtle, I'll be fine." But he knew his words rang hollow. "Let's go."

By the time they got to the station, several hundred people crowded the area around the tracks. A little boy next to Jake whined, "I don't want to eat that apple, it's all mealy by now." The child pulled free from his father's hand, lost his balance, and stumbled against Jake's right leg.

Expecting a flash of pain, Jake buckled at the impact. Thankfully, all he felt was a dull ache.

The boy's father scolded, "Jackie Melsheimer, you apologize!"

Jake's hand flew to cover the scar on his face. Yesterday, in a jarring and hurtful coincidence, a boy on the street had called him "The Smiling Man." Jake was in no mood to deal with another reminder of that specter.

Jackie looked the picture of innocence as he stared up at Jake, who was nearly twice his height. "I'm sorry, sir." A glint formed in the little tyke's eyes. "May I offer you this apple, sir?"

Stifling a chuckle, Jake shook his head. "No, thank you." That could have been him a dozen years ago.

An excited buzz ran through the crowd as the distant rumble of the approaching train grew louder. Several men shooed the onlookers from the track so the engine could ease its way into the depot. The engineer tugged on a lanyard, and at the sound of the clanging bell, the last of the gawkers hustled out of the way. The smoking engine chugged to a halt seventy feet past Jake and Myrtle. The rear of the train stood directly in front of them.

Someone started a cheer. "Hip, hip! Hurrah! Hip, hip, HURRAH!"

Jake's wary eyes spotted several other people who remained silent during the outburst. Perhaps he wasn't the only one who had come more for curiosity's sake than in a display of Unionist patriotism.

The crowd pressed closer. Jake stayed on Myrtle's left, allowing her to shield his vulnerable right side.

Rev. Alleman raised his stentorian voice. "Father Abraham, come out! Your children want to see you!"

Jake snorted in disgust. If that wasn't blasphemous, it should be.

Another round of cheers rent the air. A giant figure in black ducked through the doorway and stepped onto the rear platform of the train car. Joyful shouts and applause greeted the President. Smiling broadly, Lincoln raised his massive hands for silence, but the din only increased.

At the edge of the platform someone hoisted a small boy above the sea of bobbing heads. The little fellow held out an apple. Jackie Melsheimer! The President reached down, took the apple, and tousled Jackie's hair. Waving, Lincoln appeared to be saying, "Thank you," but the noisy throng drowned out his words.

The train bell clanged and the crowd quieted. The bell usually rang only for arrivals and departures. Was the President leaving so soon?

Taking advantage of the lull, Mr. Lincoln finally spoke. "Well, you had the Rebels here last summer." A chorus of boos and catcalls filled the air. "Did you fight them any?" Cheers and huzzahs. "I trust when the enemy was here the citizens of Hanover were loyal to our country and the Stars and Stripes."

Jake flushed, wondering if anyone gave him a sideways glance. He relaxed when he remembered that no one else had learned of his all too brief service with General Stuart.

The President's deep-set eyes took in the scene. "If you are not all true patriots in support of the Union, you should be." More cheers.

As Lincoln's gaze came to rest on him, Jake flinched. In that fleeting moment, the men took stock of one another. Jake could sense a crushing heaviness behind those eyes, a sadness beyond measure. Was it possible? Did this man suffer, too?

The Smiling Man poked his dark face from behind Lincoln's head and grinned at Jake. *Is today the day? Will you join our fight?*

Jake blinked hard and the apparition vanished. What did he mean by "our fight?"

The President waved the apple in his hand and the people quieted. "Well, you have seen me and, according to general experience, you have seen less than you expected to see."

Laughter rippled through the crowd. A few young women stepped forward to present bouquets, and a barrel-chested man hung a thirty-four star flag from the back railing of the train.

Though Lincoln smiled, Jake saw past the veneer. He sensed the man's emotional exhaustion, yet somehow, Lincoln seemed to have found the strength to continue as if nothing bothered him. Jake stood silently, pondering Lincoln's last words. *"You have seen less than you expected to see." Not true.*

The engine rumbled to life and the whistle blasted. The track quickly cleared, and the train slowly backed away from the station. Jake stared blankly at the scene. His mind and emotions churned, trying to make sense of what he had just witnessed. He couldn't quite grasp it, but something stirred deep within him. Lincoln. Something about the man made Jake want to hear more.

"Are you all right, Jake? Should I go home and get the buggy?"

"Thanks, Myrtle, but no need for that. I'll be fine." This time he actually meant it. He felt as if his burdens had already grown lighter.

As they strolled for home, Jake gazed at the sky, streaked red and purple from the setting sun. "I'm thinking of going to hear the speeches in Gettysburg tomorrow."

Myrtle's face brightened. "We'll have to leave first thing in the morning. The parade to the cemetery starts at eleven, with the dedication service following that."

Jake had wanted to go alone, but Myrtle's enthusiasm put an end to that idea. He realized he hadn't seen her look this happy in days. How could he have been so blind to the way his depression had affected her?

"That sounds like a good idea, Sis."

She grinned impishly. "Shall we invite the Biglers?"

Jake bit his lip. The journey would take them past that fateful field east of Gettysburg. "I think this is something you and I should do ourselves. For Pa."

Myrtle nodded. "But we should stop by and see Leah and Adam."

"Only if you make a pumpkin pie."

"Consider it done!"

"You better make two pies." He gave her a nudge and winked. "I suppose we ought to take one along for Leah and Adam."

"There's the old Jake!" Myrtle leaned over and kissed his scarred cheek. "It's so good to have you back."

He grimaced. *The old Jake. Who's that?*

Thursday, November 19, 1863

Since Adam and Leah had also planned to attend the dedication ceremonies, they were delighted at the opportunity to ride along with the Beckers. Adam offered to drive the carriage so that Jake could sit in the back and bring Leah up to date on his recovery. Jake took the backward-facing seat, opposite the women.

From the driver's bench, Adam said, "With all the people who've flocked into Gettysburg, there's no way we'll get through town. I'll take the Low Dutch Road over to the Baltimore Pike."

Jake's skin crawled at the mention of Low Dutch Road. He had known they would have to pass the Lott farm today, but now that the time drew nigh, his stomach knotted.

"Are you all right, Jake?" Myrtle studied his expression intently.

"Yes, I guess so." He decided he might as well tell her. "We'll pass near where Pa died."

She slumped back in her seat. "Someday I'd like to go there, but not yet. Do you mind?"

"Not at all. I feel the same way."

As the carriage headed up the rise near the Lott farm, Leah changed the conversation to a more cheerful subject. "You still haven't told me about that young lady of yours. Eliza, is it?"

Jake related the tangled story behind his relationships with Eliza and Kathleen. "So you can imagine what a hopeless mess I'd gotten myself into."

Leah chortled. "Is there a bigger fool than a man who comes between sisters?"

"I'm the living proof," Jake said ruefully. "That whole situation has been in limbo for the past five weeks, but I believe I'm finally ready to deal with it."

"I'm telling you, Jake, the Lord has his eye on you for something special, and that young lady of yours is probably part of it, too. You tell her Leah says so." She reached over and patted his knee. "Never mind, you bring her around sometime so I can tell her myself."

Jake laughed. "I'll do just that!" *Now that will be a meeting I won't want to miss!*

-2-

Wagons and carts and carriages of every size and description lined the long hill leading up to the cemetery. Several hundred people had already gathered near the bunting-draped speaker's platform. A white tent for the dignitaries stood nearby.

Adam turned in the seat. "We'd better leave the carriage here. Not likely we'll find any place closer."

Jake alit and gave the ladies his hand as they stepped down. Adam set the brake and tied the reins around a small tree. By the time they neared the gathering, Jake's leg throbbed with pain. "If you don't mind, maybe I'll wait here."

"Leg giving you problems?" Myrtle asked.

"I think it's just sore muscles."

Leah clucked her tongue. "You'll have to get that young lady of yours to rub out the aches when you get home."

"Thanks for the suggestion. Shall I tell her Leah says so?"

Myrtle narrowed her eyes. "She'd better not lay hands on you in that manner, young man. Not while I'm responsible for you."

Leah guffawed.

"Thanks for getting me into trouble, Leah," Jake muttered.

"Me?" Her big brown eyes gleamed. "From what I've heard, you do a fine enough job of that all by yourself."

The low rumble of drums echoed in the distance. The faint strains of a brass band floated on the Indian summer breeze. Jake motioned toward town and said, "You'd better hurry if you want to see the parade." The head of the procession crested the rise near the Shriver house, a quarter mile away.

Procession, viewing north along the Baltimore Pike (1863)

Dedication Ceremony (1863)

"Where should we look for you when we get back?" Myrtle asked.

Jake scanned the hilltop. "Before it gets more crowded, I'll work my way closer to the platform. If you can't find me, we can meet in front of the arch after the ceremony is over." He nodded toward the two-story brick gate.

Myrtle kissed her brother on the cheek, then hurried off with Adam and Leah. Jake shielded his eyes and peered toward the town, where he spied the row of houses from which Confederate sharpshooters had fired on Cemetery Hill the night he rode with Captain Blackford. No wonder the riflemen had chosen that spot: it afforded a great line of fire on the boulder-strewn hill.

And how were his former comrades? He'd heard that Herb had emerged from the battle unscathed and later enrolled at Virginia Military Institute. Had General Hampton returned to duty yet?

Onward came the brass band, now playing a spirited rendition of "Tramp! Tramp! Tramp!" A large crowd followed alongside. Jake noticed an unoccupied boulder nearby and took a seat to rest his leg.

Some of the thousands of Union dead had already been reinterred in the newly designated National Cemetery, but the Confederates were "not invited." *So much for unity*, he scoffed.

Those people waiting in the cemetery craned their necks to catch a glimpse of the President, then thronged to the entrance as the head of the procession drew near. Figuring it was a good time to stake out a spot near the speakers' platform, Jake went in the opposite direction. Since he was taller than most of the folks in front of him, he selected a place twenty feet away from the center of the flag-draped dais.

A squad of soldiers cleared the way for the President to approach the platform. Jake thought Lincoln looked ridiculous with his gangly frame astride a medium-sized gray horse. The man's legs nearly reached the ground! Even so, the crowd cheered and applauded. *As if for a great hero*, Jake thought wryly.

When President Lincoln mounted the stage, silence fell upon the gathering. Men removed their hats and mothers hushed their children. The two dozen dignitaries found their seats while the four bands that had taken part in the parade took up position in front of the platform. Fortunately, the bombardon players rested their elongated horns on the ground so as not to block anyone's view. One of the bands struck up the somber tune, "Tenting Tonight," and some recuperating Union soldiers displayed banners in tribute to their fallen friends. Another band followed with the dirge, "*Homage d'un Hero.*"

A minister opened the ceremony with a lengthy invocation, finishing with the Lord's Prayer. When Jake sneaked a curious glance to see if the President prayed along with everyone else, he was surprised to see tears rolling down Lincoln's face.

The Marine Band played the "Old Hundredth" tune. Jake wondered what the text, "Praise God from whom all blessings flow," had to do with dedicating the final resting place of thousands of slaughtered men.

The Master of Ceremonies read some boring regrets from bigwigs who were unable to attend. Jake smiled when the speaker read General Meade's note. At least "old Bobby Lee" was keeping his Gettysburg nemesis too busy to attend the ceremony.

Finally, the main speaker was introduced. Former Secretary of State Edward Everett had earned great acclaim for his speeches in support of the war. His oration would no doubt last at least an hour. Rumor had it that the President had been invited to follow with "a few brief remarks."

The crowd fell silent as the white-haired Everett strode to the center of the platform. Heavy folds of flesh hung beneath his piercing black eyes. He held the audience in his gaze for several moments, like a self-possessed thespian making certain no one missed a word of his eloquent soliloquy. His stentorian voice boomed in the stillness.

"Standing beneath this serene sky, overlooking these broad fields now reposing from the labors of the waning year, the mighty Alleghenies dimly towering before us, the graves of our brethren beneath our feet, it is with hesitation that I raise my poor voice to break the eloquent silence of God and Nature. But the duty to which you have called me must be performed; grant me, I pray you, your indulgence and your sympathy."

Jake groaned. The man's opening words were so pompously self-indulgent, what need had he to ask for the crowd's indulgence, too? Jake grew restless as Mr. Everett proceeded to spend the next several minutes teaching a history lesson on Greek burial practices. Honestly, did anyone care one whit?

At the words, "It is sweet and becoming to die for one's country," Jake's anger flared. What did this "great orator" know of such things? How many men had *he* watched die in agony? How many shattered bodies had *he* buried?

Then Everett finally said something interesting. "For consider, my friends, what would have been the consequences to the country, to yourselves, and to all you hold dear, if those who sleep beneath our feet, and their gallant comrades who survive to serve their country on other fields of danger, had failed in their duty on those memorable days."

Duty. Yes, that was the crux of the matter. Men were willing to die for their sense of duty, and rightly so. It was proper for Everett to ask his listeners to consider the consequences had the outcome of the battle been different, to imagine the chaos and terror in Baltimore, Washington, and Philadelphia if Lee's troops had won free rein in the North.

Everett spent many tedious minutes recapping the course of the war from its beginning. When he finally got to the days surrounding the battle at Gettysburg, Jake was surprised to hear him give 105,000 as the number of Confederate troops that had carried the fight into Pennsylvania. Now Jake hung on every word.

"Thus at nightfall on the 30th of June, the greater part of the Rebel force was concentrated in the immediate vicinity of two corps of the Union Army, the former refreshed by two days passed in comparative repose and deliberate preparation for the encounter."

Refreshed? Jake remembered all too well how he had spent that June night. And the next. Two grueling night marches with only a few hours' rest in Dover. What if General Stuart's cavalry had waited one more hour before leaving Union Mills that fateful morning? If they had not made contact with the enemy at Hanover and gone directly to Gettysburg, would the Confederacy have won the battle—and the war?

Everett droned on with a partisan recounting of the first two days of the battle. His description of the action on the disastrous third day lacked even a single word about the great cavalry battle east of town. Jake seethed. Was Everett ignorant of the facts, or did he deem unworthy the life-and-death struggles of those several thousand men? It was an insult to the brave soldiers on both sides who had given their blood and their lives. It was an affront to Pa's memory.

And had the South truly lost 37,000 men in the conflict, leaving 7,500 wounded men behind? Jake snorted when Everett broke down the Union losses into several smaller numbers, but being quick in arithmetic, Jake arrived at an even larger number of casualties for the North. Subtracting the numbers of prisoners and men who had gone missing, that left a total of 45,000 Union dead and wounded in three days.

Try as he might, Jake couldn't form a mental picture of 82,000 men. That was 27,000 per day, or 1,800 dead and wounded every daylight hour. Jake closed his eyes and did some more calculating. One man shot every two seconds for three full days! If Everett had seen even a minute of that horror, would he have dared to say how sweet it was to die for one's country?

Of course, the man lay all the blame on those who had rebelled. He even had the gall to say the "rebellion" was in no way comparable to the first American Revolution, and used such words as "crime" and "invasion" to disparage the men who served the cause of freedom from the oppressive Federal government. And who had first invaded whom?

Jake could take no more. He ignored Everett's long harangue against the Southern cause and scanned the crowd in search of Myrtle, Leah, and Adam. A considerable number of people had drifted away. Children ran and played on the fringes of the throng. He spotted fellow Hanoverian Mary Leader, who had probably come to report on the events for the *Hanover Spectator,* the newspaper she and her mother had continued to publish after her father's death two years ago.

Turning back toward the platform, Jake's eyes came to rest on President Lincoln, who nervously fidgeted with his eyeglasses. He donned the glasses, pulled a sheet of paper from the side pocket of his coat, and started to read. The spectacles magnified his heavy-lidded eyes, accentuating his simian appearance.

Applause announced the end of Everett's oration at last. Jake flipped open Pa's watch. Two hours. Would Lincoln make the wait worthwhile?

The Baltimore Glee Club sang a tune composed for the occasion by their director, who conducted using a small American flag as his baton. After a round of polite applause, a dignitary finally introduced President Abraham Lincoln, and the crowd cheered with great enthusiasm.

Still wearing his glasses and gripping the sheet of paper in his huge hands, Lincoln walked grimly to the flag-draped rail. An expectant hush fell over the scene. His reedy Kentucky accent pierced the silence.

"Four score and seven years ago, our fathers brought forth on this continent a new nation, conceived in Liberty, and dedicated to the proposition that *all men* are created equal."

Jake groaned and rolled his eyes. *Does he think to deliver a diatribe against slavery* now?

"Now we are engaged in a great civil war, testing whether that nation, or any nation, so conceived and so dedicated, can long endure. We are met on a great battlefield of that war. We have come to dedicate a portion of that field, as a final resting place for those who here gave their lives that that nation might live. It is altogether fitting and proper that we should do this."

Jake relaxed. *This is more like it.*

"But, in a larger sense, we can not dedicate—we can not consecrate— we can not hallow—this ground. The brave men, living and dead, who struggled here, have consecrated it, far above our poor power to add or detract."

Swallowing the lump in his throat, Jake vividly remembered the tragic events of those tumultuous days in July. His right leg throbbed in rhythm with the pounding in his heart.

"The world will little note, nor long remember what we say here, but it can never forget what they did here."

Tell that to Edward Everett! He's already forgotten about the cavalry battle that took Pa's life—and would probably have taken mine, if it hadn't been for Leah. Thank God, Lincoln understands. The surge of anger subsided with that thought. Jake blinked, surprised to feel his heart thaw toward the man.

"It is for us the living, rather, to be dedicated here to the *unfinished work* which they who fought here have thus far so nobly advanced."

As the crowd applauded, something deep within Jake stirred. Lincoln's words echoed in his mind—"the unfinished work"—and what he had said earlier, "*all men* are created equal." In a flash of insight, Jake realized that if the Founding Fathers had been able to come up with a plan to end slavery at the country's beginning, there probably would have been no need for secession. *Hundreds of thousands of men have bled and died because of that "unfinished work," and things will probably get worse, even if the Union wins. Most Northerners don't seem to care much for Negroes, and folks in the South have treated the slaves like property for so long, how will they ever get along as equals?*

"It is rather for us to be here dedicated to the great task remaining before us—that from these honored dead, we take increased devotion to that cause for which they gave the last full measure of devotion."

More applause.

Jake's mind raced as Lincoln's roving eyes paused on him. *Dedicated to the great task remaining . . . increased devotion to that cause.* He sensed that Lincoln had touched on the heart of the matter. It may well take the devotion of nearly every citizen before all men would be equal in fact, as well as in principle.

"That we here highly resolve that these dead shall not have died in vain. That this nation, under God, shall have a new birth of freedom." Gesturing with the paper to emphasize each key word, Lincoln concluded, "And that government *of* the people, *by* the people, *for* the people, *shall not perish* from the earth."

Suddenly, Jake felt as if the clouds Pa had talked about had finally vanished and the moon shone bright and full, revealing the path he was destined to take. Leah was right. And that was what the Smiling Man had meant: God was calling him—to "the unfinished work." It seemed so clear now. *To achieve this new birth of freedom, the Union must be preserved. But before the Negroes will be free and equal, an awful lot of people will have to change their way of thinking. That will surely be an uphill battle!*

Jake burned with desire to do his part. He bowed his head to pray, and the Smiling Man's face appeared. "Will you join the fight?"

Jake lifted his tear-filled eyes toward heaven. "I will."

Epilogue: The Unfinished Work

Monday, June 30, 1913

How about it, Old Jack?" Mrs. Becker asked, peering over her spectacles. "Go with me to pick some flowers to take to the cemetery?"

The sixteen-year-old beagle shifted his rheumy eyes but didn't budge from his favorite spot between the gas stove and the icebox. Mrs. Becker fetched a pair of pruning scissors from the utility drawer, then went outside. Old Jack followed her to Rose's Garden and curled up in the shade of a rhododendron bush.

"What do you think, Jack, tiger lilies or anemones?" But he was already sound asleep. "Tiger lilies, then." She cut the blooms and took them into the house to make five bouquets.

Taking yesterday's *Evening Herald* from the burn pile, she spread the newspaper across the kitchen table, laid out the flowers, then froze. "Well, for goodness sake!" She reread the advertisement to let the words sink in.

Mrs. Eerdman called from the parlor, "What is it, dear?"

Mrs. Becker left her work and went to join her sister-in-law on the divan. "You know I never read the personals, Myrtle—"

"The personals!" Myrtle dropped her needlework onto her lap.

"Well, my eyes just happened to fall on one, and I think it might actually be intended for me."

"Truly?" Myrtle asked, obviously flummoxed.

"It may be someone I met briefly fifty years ago, during the war. The ad says he would like to meet me today at 5:00 by The Picket Monument."

"How odd, and after all these years! Would you like some company?" Myrtle reached for the canvas bag to put away her needlework.

"No, I don't think that will be necessary. We'll be in public, and you have your grandchildren coming soon."

Mrs. Becker finished making the bouquets, then went to the barn and hitched the chestnut Morgan to the buggy her husband had made for her. The trusty vehicle had been reupholstered twice, but the frame was still as good as new—and better made and more reliable than those horseless carriages sold by Mr. Olds and Mr. Ford!

The ride out to Mt. Olivet Cemetery seemed to take no time at all. Time passed much too quickly these days. Too many friends and acquaintances had already been called to their eternal rest.

Mrs. Becker laid the first two bouquets on her in-laws' graves. The third went to Hope, the sister-in-law she had never known. Her eyes filled with tears of anguish as she stood at the foot of the next marker: her precious son, Joseph Robert, forever eight years old. She closed her eyes, but that only intensified the image of the rambunctious little boy playing on the train platform, ignoring his parents' warnings, falling beneath the passing cars. No child should ever perish, especially right in front of his parents. The pain was still fresh, even after all those years.

Her grief deepened as she stooped to lay the last of the tiger lilies next to her husband's stone. "Every day I thank God for the life we shared. I miss you so much, my eternal sweetheart." She told him the latest news about their four children and nineteen grandchildren, including the latest addition: Elwood Jacob Becker.

As the buggy carried her back down the Baltimore Pike, her eyes narrowed at the hideous sight of the poles and electrical wires marring the beauty of the small, oval memorial park in Center Square. With the trolley tracks circling the park and wires overhead, the soldiers returning for the fiftieth anniversary of the Battle of Hanover would hardly recognize the place. The Market Shed had been removed more than forty years ago in favor of a traffic circle with an ornate fountain. Eight years ago, the town replaced the fountain with a monument of a Union cavalryman, "The Picket," which stood on a tall plinth facing out Frederick Street. Two cannons completed the memorial. Now strings of bare light bulbs draped the tree-lined park. Flags and bunting hung from every window of the two- and three-story buildings facing the Square.

Mrs. Becker drew up the buggy in the corner by the Peoples' Bank, taking care to keep the back wheels far enough away from the trolley lines to avoid mishap. Several older men loitered in small groups in the park. Was her long lost acquaintance among them? She pulled Jake's pocket watch from her reticule and checked the time: 4:58.

As always, her heart warmed at the sight of the watch's inscription.

Rose and David Becker
One for Eternity
June 30, 1837

"Happy anniversary," she whispered. Today also marked forty-six years since she and Jake had married. Where had the years gone? She took a deep breath and trudged toward the park, searching for the face from the past.

She needn't have worried about recognizing him. Though he probably weighed twice as much now and stood a few inches taller, his ruddy face and blue eyes gave him away. She stopped several feet in front of him. "Hello, Mr. Caitlin." Would he recognize her?

His blue eyes brightened. "Jesus, Mary, and Joseph, it's you! How are you?" He rushed up, grabbed her hand, and gave it a firm kiss.

She smiled. "I am very well, thank you. And it is good to see that you are looking well. It's so kind of you to look for me after all these years. I must say, I was surprised you remembered me."

"Lord forbid a man ever forgets the most beautiful lass he ever did see." Johnnie Caitlin's Irish brogue took on a dreamy tone. "Look at you. Just as beautiful as when the rose first bloomed. And those eyes!"

In an exaggerated Virginia drawl, she replied, "Still the charmer, I see, Mr. Caitlin. Thank you for putting that advertisement in the paper so I might know you were seeking me."

"My pleasure. I see by the ring on your finger that you are married. Drat, I knew I should have come back sooner." He flashed a winsome grin. "You wouldn't happen to have an eligible sister now, would you?"

"I'm afraid not. My sister is happily married and lives in Manassas. But I must tell you that, sadly, my husband, Jacob Becker, went to be with the Lord eighteen months ago."

"Oh dear, I'm so sorry to hear that, Mrs. Becker," Johnnie said sympathetically. "Would you like to take a stroll and tell me about him?"

Blinking back tears, she replied, "Yes, I would, but why don't you tell me a little bit about you first?"

As they traversed the brick walkway around the perimeter of the park, Johnnie told her that after the war he had spent another twenty-five years in the army, some of that time fighting Indians with George Armstrong Custer. "Fortunately for me, I missed the Little Big Horn campaign," Johnnie said grimly.

He had served all over the West, South, and in Mexico. He had been left for dead several times, and he had numerous bullet and arrow scars to prove his bravery. "And not one of them is on my back," he boasted. In his "retirement," Johnnie was a sheriff and U.S. Marshal out in Oregon. He had made a special trip back east for the fiftieth anniversary commemoration of the battles of Hanover and Gettysburg.

Mrs. Becker told of how her husband had also fought in the war and been dreadfully wounded at Gettysburg. "Several months later, Jake felt a calling to the ministry and went to seminary."

"You don't say!"

"The Lord called him to help former slaves struggling to find their place in life. We went to churches, Christian societies, and mission organizations for aid, but many of them seemed more willing to help the Negroes in Africa than in our own country. Since he was a carriage and wagon builder by trade, he combined his work and ministry to travel all over the South, serving as an itinerant preacher."

She smiled fondly and her eyes grew misty. "We had a beautiful melodeon that we took along. We both played and sang, so the music helped draw folks in. We'd always pitch our tent and do the first services in the Negro section of town. Over the years, we were able to help many Negro families buy land or get a start in business."

Johnnie paused by one of the cannons and slowly ran his hand along the barrel. "How did you know which people to help?"

"When Jake was wounded, a sabre left a scar along one side of his face. It made him look like he had a lopsided smile. Everywhere we went, some child inevitably called him 'The Smiling Man,' and invariably, that was the family we wound up helping. You know, I believe that 'smile' opened many doors for our ministry over the years, especially in places where carpetbaggers had taken advantage of people."

They resumed strolling. "Didn't you run into any trouble with the white folks once they found out what you were doing?"

"Oh, we got occasional threats, but nothing ever came of it. The Lord took good care of us."

"As always!"

"Jake always felt strongly that his ministry was part of our country's 'unfinished work,' as he called it—fixing the slavery problem. It wasn't enough for him that slavery was abolished; there had to be a way for the former slaves to take an equal place in society. Unfortunately, far too many people still think Negroes are inferior beings."

"Now there's a thorny issue to untangle. At least they are doing better than the Indians."

She sighed wearily. "Even so, he always looked forward to the day when whites and Negroes would not only get along, but would also esteem each other as equals."

"I doubt any of us will live so long," Johnnie said sympathetically.

"I'm afraid I know what you mean. It weighed so heavily on Jake, I think he died from a broken heart." *Heart. Oh, how I wish I could once again rest my head on your chest and hear the soothing rhythm of your heartbeat, Jacob my love.* She tugged the handkerchief from her sleeve and dabbed the tears from her eyes.

After taking a deep breath to collect herself, she gestured toward the buggy and gave Johnnie an apologetic look. "I really should be getting on home now. I live with my sister-in-law, and I don't want her to worry."

"I understand. But before I leave town, perhaps we can meet again and revisit the place we met fifty years ago?"

Her face took on a youthful grin. "Shall I bring some apple pie and a bowl of milk?"

"That sounds perfect. Shall I bring my bugle? Hopefully, no one will attack the town this time." He chuckled, then his face grew serious. "But before you go, Mrs. Becker, you never mentioned your first name."

She told him.

His blue Irish eyes twinkled. "Is there a more glorrrious name for such a beeauutiful young lass?"

Remembering Jake's voice when he had uttered those very same words, Kathleen smiled, rejoicing in the warmth of his abiding spirit deep within her.

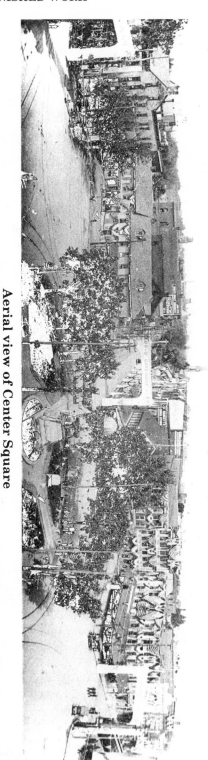

Aerial view of Center Square

The Central Hotel is on the left, Memorial Park is in the center, Schmidt's was on the right. Frederick Street exists on the left, Carlisle Street to the north, Broadway on the right.

In the photo on the opposite page: Center Square decorated for a celebration (1915)

APPENDIX: Fact and Fiction

Regrettably, the Beckers and Biglers are fictional families. That said, David Becker is based on the anonymous middle-aged man who did in fact volunteer as David did in the early morning hours of July 2nd. He was last noticed entering the fight at Brinkerhoff Ridge later in the day. Since there were few Union casualties in that battle, I presume he lived to take part in the historic action on July 3rd.

Jake Becker is based on the anonymous teen-ager who was reported to have served as guide to some of the Confederate troops. (This may have been the historical Herb Shriver.) The idea of having these two men as father and son spawned the premise of the book. The Beckers' first names are the same as my two best friends in high school: Jay Wertz (known as Jake back then), who is a noted film editor, author, and Civil War historian; and Dave Richards, whose family home overlooked the field where Jeb Stuart made his famous leap to safety on June 30, 1863.

The character of Kathleen Bigler proved to be wonderfully serendipitous. In the original outline she was merely Eliza's little sister and a bit of a comic foil, but during the writing process she seemed to continually clamor for a major role. She all but literally took on a life of her own. This provided the opportunity to explore another area in which men find themselves in conflict: love versus lust.

A special note on the character John Hoffacker: it had been widely held as fact that Hoffacker and his family were residents of West Mannheim, and thus a local boy died in the Battle of Hanover. However, John T. Krepps in "A Strong and Sudden Onslaught" (2008) proved otherwise. The Hoffackers actually lived in Maryland. Since this story was written adhering to the "history" of John as a local boy, I decided not to rewrite it. Please consider the fictional aspects of the Beckers' relationship with the Hoffackers to be representative of the tragedy all too many people experienced in reality.

Except for the three horse thieves, all military personnel and clergymen mentioned by name are historical, as are many of their words and actions. The battles basically unfolded as described, although there are some differing accounts in various historical records. I contrived to have David and Jake witness and experience things beyond what any single man would have seen in reality, and I took a few liberties with lines of sight. I trust history purists will forgive these literary devices.

The Shriver families are historical. Great care was taken to portray accurately the events at Union Mills. Many details and direct quotes are taken from various family memoirs. Among the numerous Shriver descendants are Sargent Shriver, first director of the Peace Corps, and Maria Shriver Schwarzenegger, current first lady of the state of California.

The Wertz, Forney, and Winebrenner families are historical. Adam and Leah are fictional. In an 1872 map of Hanover, the house occupied by the Beckers in this story was owned by the Eerdmans, thus Myrtle's eventual marriage to a fictional Eerdman.

Corrections and additional interesting facts are always welcome. You may e-mail the author at: TheUnfinishedWork@earthlink.net

Saturday, June 27

p. 4: The book *Life at the South, W.L.G. Smith, 1852,* is described from a first edition copy. The other two books were selected to give an indication of the wide variety of literature Jake enjoyed.

p. 5: Sam Forney and his family are historical. The Beckers and Biglers are fictional.

p. 7: Peter Frank, the smithy, is historical, as is the upcoming encounter at his blacksmith shop. The other two men are fictional, though Harvey Stremmel is named after my elderly Pennsylvania Dutch neighbor from my boyhood. The church foundation was indeed being dug at this time. Today, Spring Forge is named Spring Grove.

p. 8: Many panicky refugees fled east in fear of the approaching Rebels.

p. 10: William Bigler is historical, but he is not related to the Wertzes. Lydia Wertz is historical.

p. 11: All buildings in Hanover were as described with the exception of my addition of a clock on the tower of St. Matthew's Church. The famous British architect, Christopher Wren, designed the original spire. Rev. Alleman is historical.

p. 12+: The entrance of the Confederate troops and the dialogue between the soldiers and the townsfolk are as recorded in Rev. Zieber's memoirs. Today, McSherryville is named McSherrystown.

p. 13: The Winebrenners are historical.

p. 17: Joseph Dellone is historical. Hanover, being only six miles north of the Mason-Dixon line, had more than a few "Copperheads" in town. York County had a strong element of anti-Lincoln sentiment.

pp. 18+: Captain Myers is historical, but his activities in the apothecary are based on the actions of an anonymous soldier, who remained in the store drinking until the troops left town.

pp. 20+: There are few reports of Confederate soldiers "misbehaving" during this incursion. Most complaints involved payment in Confederate currency. Myers was one of three captains in Hanover with Col. White's battalion, one of whom had this encounter and dialogue, as reported by smithy Peter Frank.

pp. 22-23: The events surrounding the telegrapher, Daniel Trone, are factual, as is the encounter described by Abdiel Gitt. Saying Gitt might "stretch a tale to his liking" is fictional, to add color to the story.

p. 26: The Wertz family and Pennsylvania Dutch syntax are historical.

p. 27: *Smierkase* is cottage cheese.

p. 30: George Scott and the telegraph lines incident are historical. Robert is fictional, named for my brother who resides in Dover.

p. 32: Property taxes were based on the number of rooms in a house, and closets counted as rooms—an indication of Mr. Wertz's financial success.

pp. 37+: Memorization and recitations used to be considered part of a good education. Conversation and music making were cherished family past-times. For today's tech savvy generation, parlors were the original "chat rooms."

Sunday, June 28

p. 44: A melodeon is a small reed organ with a four-octave keyboard. The bellows are operated by a foot pedal. Gov. Curtin's order is historical, as is Rev. Guyer.

p. 46: *Schnitz* is made from sliced, dried apples.

p. 46: The Forney family is historical, as is the Albright family, though Deborah is named for my sister—and a childhood friend I once had a crush on, named Debbie Albright. In the sixth grade I said something typically adolescent about Debbie in her presence, hoping to gain her favorable attention. Instead, I received a slap on the face. If you ever read this, Debbie, here is my long overdue apology!

pp. 47-50: The theft of the horses and the three soldiers named are fictional. Several drunken Confederate stragglers did remain behind in Hanover. They were arrested by Rev. Alleman and held in the jail under the Market Shed until they could be turned over to the Union Army. All of the townsfolk named are ancestors of people I went to school with in Hanover. These characters and my depictions are completely fictional, as are my depictions of Joseph Dellone and Mr. and Mrs. Scott.

p. 51: Oh, for the days of 3% income taxes!

p. 52: Jonas Serff is historical. He later married Lydia Wertz.

p. 61: In one of the great ironies of the Civil War, the opening shots of the first battle were fired around the McLean farm in Manassas, so the family moved to Appomattox, where their new home eventually became the site where Grant met Lee to receive the surrender of the Army of Northern Virginia in April, 1865.

Monday, June 29

p. 62: The details about the Shrivers are historical.

p. 64: The glow in the sky and fear that it was York burning is historical.

pp. 65-66: The details of the .44 Colt are factual.

pp. 67-69: The encounter with the deserter is fictional.

pp. 70+: The details of the Confederate entrance into York are historical, and the dialogues between the soldiers and citizens are quoted from historical sources, primarily the letters of eyewitness Cassandra Small.

p. 71: When the girl presented the bouquet of flowers to General Gordon, the piece of paper within it contained a detailed map of the area.

p. 72: The situation in Wrightsville was as described.

p. 73: The Winebrenner/Shriver relationships are historical.

pp. 74+: The Shriver children are historical, depictions are fictional.

pp. 75+: William and Andrew Shriver were brothers. Andrew lived in the family homestead, was Catholic, a Union supporter, and owned slaves (slave ownership still legal in Maryland.) William was Protestant, a Confederate supporter, and did not own any slaves. Both families sent sons to fight in the Civil War, all of whom survived. The Shriver brothers ran several essential businesses, including a feed mill and the local post office. Many dignitaries, such as Thomas Jefferson, used the balcony of the family homestead to address large gatherings. James Audubon drew his picture of the Baltimore Oriole while a guest in Andrew's home. The Homestead and Mill are now open as a marvelous museum.

pp. 82+: The dialogue between Andrew Shriver and the Confederates is quoted nearly verbatim from various Shriver memoirs. Ruth and Paul were Andrew's slaves. The dialogues between William's family and Fitzhugh Lee are fictional.

Tuesday, June 30, 1863

p. 86: Jeb Stuart was so impressed with Herb Shriver's horsemanship that he invited the teen to accompany him, as related in this story.

pp. 88-90: Sam Sweeney's older brother, Joel, was a legendary banjoist and blackface minstrel musician. Sam died of smallpox on Jan. 13, 1864. The music making in the parlor is historical. What if Stuart had lingered one hour longer and therefore had no battle with Kilpatrick in Hanover? If Stuart had connected with the Confederate troops near Gettysburg on June 30, how might history have been different? Coincidentally, Union troops arrived in Union Mills a couple of hours after the Confederates left. A similar song session took place in the Andrew Shriver home. Mrs.

Heard is historical. The map session and dialogue between Stuart and Mrs. Shriver are quoted verbatim from Shriver memoirs.

pp. 90+: The Union Army arrival and the account of the girls' chorus are historical. The name Josiah Daniels is fictional, derived from the names of one of my sons and one of my brothers, both of whom are outstanding high school choir directors.

p. 91: This was George Armstrong Custer's first day as a general, yet he had the rank's accoutrements already on hand. Any skepticism at his attire was quickly dispelled by his actions over the next four days. A recently discovered letter indicates that Custer and some of his men passed through Hanover in the early morning hours and were in Abbottstown by the time Kilpatrick arrived. Since all other sources (including eyewitness civilian accounts) indicate otherwise, I chose to use this version of Custer's whereabouts.

p. 92: The events and dialogue at the Wirt house are quoted from Rev. Zieber's memoirs. The actions of the townsfolk are historical, including the distribution of beer and pretzels. Hanover has been called "The Snack Food Capital," as it is home to Snyder's Pretzels and Utz Potato Chips.

p. 93: This captured wagon train would later become a source of controversy since it greatly impeded the progress of Stuart's troops. All military personnel are historical, but their depictions, especially Wade Hampton, Jr., are my own creations.

p. 95: "Robinson and Palmer" is a fictional company, named in honor of Baltimore Oriole greats Brooks and Frank Robinson, and Jim Palmer.

p. 96: The oath of enlistment is historical.

p. 97: The encounter with the Federal patrol is historical. John Hoffacker, his last words, and how he met his fate are historical, but he did not live in West Mannheim, as was widely believed until John Krepps' research proved otherwise in 2008. (See note in the introduction to the Appendix and the page 131 footnote.) He enlisted in September of 1862. All of the other events are as described.

pp. 98+: Workers were busy digging the foundation of the new Methodist church when the Confederates made their attack. All of the grim details of the fighting are historical. Mrs. Wolf and this encounter are historical.

p. 101: Col. Chambliss had taken ill and was replaced by Col. Payne.

pp. 103+: Eliza and her cousins are fictional.

pp. 104+: Pvt. James Moran's mishap with the caisson is historical. It took place near the George Wertz farm and a corn shed burned. This account of him being taken in at the Wertz's is fictional.

pp. 107+: Col. Payne and this exchange with Stuart are historical.

pp. 108+: The encounter between Stuart and the Union squad (and the exciting escape) is historical, as found in Blackford's memoirs. Today, Stuart Avenue at this location is named in commemoration.

p. 109: The looting of Hoffacker's body is fictional, though not untypical.

p. 110: The Metzgers are historical.

pp. 111+: The scene with the injured Sgt. Isaac Peale is historical, as found in Rev. Zieber's memoirs. The dialogue is verbatim. David and Kathleen play the parts of the unnamed fellow citizens.

p. 112: Kilpatrick's words and actions are historical. His horse either died or was put down several hours later. It did not drop dead in the Square, as legend states. It was later buried on Bunker Hill, the location of Union artillery during the battle. Kilpatrick's words are historical.

p. 112: A bronze medallion marks the spot of the maple tree (no longer living) where Custer tied his horse. The "colored man" was his servant.

p. 113: The capture of the stained Confederate officer, Colonel Payne, is historical, though there are conflicting accounts detailing the capture. Payne was the source of much derision amongst the Union hierarchy. He told Kilpatrick that Stuart had over 12,000 men in the hills south of town (a gross exaggeration.) This may have contributed to the reluctance of the Union commander to press the attack on the higher position.

p. 113: *Ferhoodled* is one of those PA Dutch words still in frequent use in the area, meaning "confused" or "mixed up."

p. 113: Henry Winebrenner and the unexploded shell are historical.

p. 117: The cherry tree incident is true, but it occurred later in the day.

p. 117: According to the Hanover Chamber of Commerce, in 1963 Hanover had 35,795 residents, an amazing 97% of them native born. Many of my schoolmates were direct descendants of the Hanoverians mentioned in this book. As of the 2000 census, 42% of Hanoverians still listed their ancestry as German. With all of the changes our society has seen in the last fifty years, I can only wonder how small the percentage of native-born Hanoverians will be on the 150th Anniversary in 2013.

p. 118: Lee's tongue-in-cheek letter to Stuart is fictional, though representative of both men's love of humor.

p. 118: According to Blackford's memoirs, his strong field glasses were often used to great advantage throughout Stuart's various campaigns.

p. 119: This precaution with the wagons is historical.

p. 119: I took some liberty in having Custer within sight. If this were factual, he may have been within range of Confederate sharpshooters and might well have suffered the same ignominious fate as Union Gen. John

Sedgwick, who was quoted as saying, "They couldn't hit an elephant at this distance," shortly before he was cut down by a sharpshooter's bullet.

p. 119: Stuart calling Custer a "lost circus rider" is derived from Union Col. Theodore Lyman's comment: "This officer is one of the funniest-looking beings you ever saw and looks like a circus rider gone mad!"

p. 122: Sweitzer is the only civilian reported to have been injured in the battle. Historians are skeptical, since the first evidence appears 35 years later when Sweitzer applied to Congress for a pension based on her resulting disability. Congress granted the pension, so I accept her story.

pp. 122+: The details of the cannon shell hitting the Winebrenner house are historical. An historical marker, complete with photos, stands in front of the house. (One of many outstanding markers in Hanover.) The Winebrenner children are factual, but their ages have been altered to fit the fictional part of the story.

p. 125: Legend has it that Stuart got a copy of that day's *York Gazette*. This is unlikely since General Early left York on the 30th, after the most recent edition of that weekly paper was published.

p. 125: This was indeed the first use of Spencer repeating rifles in the Civil War. The standard joke was that a man could load his weapon on Sunday and fire all week without reloading.

p. 126: Signal flags were not likely used at this battle, but this scene provided the opportunity to show this critical, seldom described activity.

p. 126: The numbers of prisoners and confiscated horses are factual.

pp. 128+: The events in Carrickshook, Ireland are factual. This account is included to show other reasons fellow countrymen were willing to take up arms against one another. It also reveals how Eliza's father's past has affected her character.

p. 129: These events and locations are historical, the dialogue is fictional. The Knights of the Golden Circle were Southern sympathizers who duped many area farmers with this money-making scheme. Jacob Leppo took his complaint to Stuart, to no avail.

pp. 130-131: The encounter with the German-speaking farmer, his son, and the skirmish are all factual.

p. 131: Recent evidence proves Hoffacker never lived in West Mannheim. His family lived in Parkton, MD, and he worked near Shrewsbury, PA, 21 miles east of Hanover. His parents were too poor to reinter his body and later buried his brother, also a Civil War fatality, next to him in Hanover.

p. 134: The Klinefelters are historical, but the Hoffackers actually lived in Maryland.

p. 135: My stepmother was born in this hamlet of Sinsheim, named after a town in Germany.

p. 135: The overall events and storeowners in Jefferson are historical. Kroft's store was raided, but this account is fictional. Fitzhugh Lee's comments on what Robert E. Lee would have said is fictional.

p. 137: Sadly, there are those who still believe this "theology" of the "cursedness" of those with dark skin.

pp. 139+: Though such a meeting took place at this time in Ziegler's farmhouse, the details are fictional, as are the two spies. Ziegler later filed a claim for his losses: 6 horses, 6 tons of hay, 35 bushels of oats, and 500 bushels of corn.

Wednesday, July 1, 1863

pp. 142+: The details of the night-long march are accurate.

pp. 143+: FitzHugh's anecdotes are historical.

p. 144: The details about Charles Diehl and his capture are historical, but this setting is fictional and the timing is later by a matter of hours.

pp. 145+: The relationship between David and Kathleen shows one way in which a man deals with the inner conflicts experienced when a family man is confronted with an "empty nest."

p. 145: Omelettes did indeed exist at this time, and they fit perfectly with the Pennsylvania Dutch attitude of "waste not, want not."

pp. 149-150: The ransom demand levied on the city of York is factual, though this scene is fictional. Shoes were identical, left and right, thus 2,000 shoes = 1,000 pairs. This account of when Stuart received the information is fictional.

pp. 150-151: The use of the hotel is historical.

p. 152: Jake's cousin Richard is fictional, though he is prototypical of one brand of abolitionist at that time.

pp. 152-153: Sam and John Forney are historical, as is their account of what they heard and saw this day.

pp. 153+: The details of Samuel Reddick are historical, as are his words. The Forneys also had three wounded Federal troopers in their parlor on the 30th, but I presume they were taken to a hospital later that day.

p. 155: The details of Wade Hampton's wealth are true. He was reputed to have owned more slaves than anyone else in the country, and he paid for the outfitting and maintenance of his own troops.

p. 155: Very few Confederate soldiers would have stated that their reason for fighting was to preserve the institution of slavery. About 80% did not even own slaves.

p. 157: Moran was later reinterred at Paradise Catholic Cemetery.

p. 157: Lydia Wertz was home alone when the wounded Corporal Darcy crawled up onto the porch. She took him in and tended his wounds.

p. 160: The quote attributed to Pastor Cook is factual, though it is from the twentieth-century Pastor Robert A. Cook, former President of The King's College and my spiritual mentor.

p. 160: The details of the aftermath are factual.

pp. 161+: Dabney is historical, as are his biographical details and the account of his encounter at Brandy Station.

p. 161: The Confederate column rode past the editor's home in Wellsville.

pp. 162+: The events at Carlisle are true, and they did have gas works.

p. 166: The anecdote related by the old woman actually took place in northern York County.

Thursday, July 2, 1863

p. 167: The biographical details about FitzHugh and Robertson are true.

p. 168: I do not know that these defective cannon fuses were used at Carlisle, but they were used during the great cannon bombardment preceding Pickett's ill-fated charge in Gettysburg on July 3rd. That three-hour bombardment was meant to have softened up the fortified Union position prior to the infantry attack, but the vast majority of Confederate shells went too far before exploding. Though they wreaked havoc on the Union rear, they did nothing to weaken the Federal defenses. Even so, Pickett's Charge nearly succeeded in breaking through the Union line. (For alternate history buffs: what if they had known about the fuses and made the necessary adjustments, thus leading to a CSA victory?)

pp. 170-171: An anonymous middle-aged man did indeed volunteer his services to General Gregg in the early morning hours. Gregg said that the man took part in the action later that day with the 3rd PA, and he reportedly fought well. This book was inspired in part by that man. The song mentioned is one of several sung by the troops that night.

p. 172: The doctors are historical, as was the desirability of seeing "laudable pus" in a wound. Unfortunately, this was actually a sign of infection. Some physicians noticed that maggot-infested wounds actually seemed to heal faster than those with pus, and they sought out maggots (which, unbeknownst to the doctors, ate the diseased flesh) to help with the healing process. Bacterial infections were not yet common knowledge.

pp. 172+: The shooting of the deserter is factual, this setting is fictional. Cowell actually passed away in the hospital after he was shot.

pp. 174+: Details of the ride to Gettysburg are factual.

pp. 174+: Miller, McIntosh, and the soldiers in Company H are historical.

pp. 177+: The details of Hampton's duel are taken from the historical record, though a question has been raised as to whether this did occur.

p. 179: The reason for this new tactic of sharpening sabres is factual.

p. 180: West Point trained its officers following Napoleonic tactics and procedures. They used the manual mentioned here.

pp. 180+: Three of Hampton's sons served on his staff. Tragically, at Petersburg in October 1864, Hampton witnessed the death of his son Preston and the wounding of Wade, Jr. (Wade Hampton IV.)

pp. 183+: The details of Custer's charge and his young savior, Norvell Churchill, are accurate. A monument commemorating the Battle of North Cavalry Field was unveiled in Hunterstown on July 2, 2008, with many descendants of Norvell Churchill in attendance. Visit this book's website, www.TheUnfinishedWork.com, to see photographs of the ceremonies, Churchill's sabre, and his two surviving grandchildren.

p. 186: Colonel Deloney's personal battle is factual.

p. 187: Unfortunately, the Felty barn, which served as cover for the Union artillery, was torn down unannounced by a developer in June of 2006. On July 2, 2008 I heard the developer say he had offered the barn to various organizations, but that no one stepped forward to assume the cost of preserving or moving the structure. Visit the book's website, www.TheUnfinishedWork.com, for photos I took in April 2006.

pp. 188+: Details of the fight near Brinkerhoff Ridge are historical.

p. 188: Eli Eyster is historical, his words and actions are fictional.

p. 189: The account of the crippled old woman's flight is factual.

p. 192: Wade Hampton, Jr.'s attitude and rivalry with Jake are fictional.

pp. 193+: The battle scene is historical; the dialogue, etc., are fictional.

p. 198: Blackford admits that his is the sole account of Robert E. Lee's apparent bout with diarrhea. He speculates that this ailment may have adversely affected the great general's decisions during the battle.

pp. 198+: The details of the midnight ride and the Confederate position within the row houses are taken from Blackford's memoirs.

p. 199: Tillie Pierce, age fifteen, wrote a wonderful account of her experiences during the Battle of Gettysburg, "At Gettysburg, or What a Girl Saw and Heard of the Battle: A True Narrative." Rather than contrive a way to incorporate her story, I strongly encourage you to read her delightful account. It is available from Savannah Books, Inc. as part of an anthology of "all things Tillie." The Pierce House is now open as a Bed and Breakfast. Next door, the Shriver House opened as a wonderful museum in April 2006. (It even has a melodeon.) Both are highly recommended.

Friday, July 3, 1863

p. 201: Officers were required to provide their own meals; thus, many of them included servants in their entourage.

p. 203: Macadam (hard-packed gravel) on major roads was a boon to travel and a cavalryman's dream.

p. 204: The details and deployments are factual.

p. 205: McClellan later wrote that there were four cannon shots, one to each compass point. J.D. Petruzzi points out in *The Complete Gettysburg Guide* that this would have been illogical, only a few shots along the arc to their front would have made any sense. Some people have wondered if this was a signal to let Robert E. Lee know that Stuart was in position so that Pickett's Charge could take place simultaneously, but there is no evidence of such a coordinated assault.

pp. 207+: Gregg's decision to countermand Kilpatrick's order is another one of the many "what ifs" that surround this pivotal battle. If Custer had vacated the area, Stuart's men might well have succeeded in getting into the rear of the Union lines during the critical time of Pickett's Charge. (There is no evidence that this was Lee's specific plan.)

p. 208: Weather described throughout the book is accurate, as reported by Rev. Dr. Michael Jacobs, a teacher at Gettysburg College and an amateur meteorologist of the time.

p. 208: The actions of Major Janeway are factual.

p. 211: The importance of Miller and Hess anchoring the right flank is not overstated.

p. 210: These two incredibly accurate cannon shots are not only factual, they were the first shots fired in combat by that Union crew!

p. 211: This grove still stands intact. The description is taken from personal experience when as teenagers we used to take our girlfriends to the "haunted house" in the woods along Frogtown Road.

p. 214: Custer's famous rallying cry, "Come on, you Wolverines!" is factual. There is a theory afloat that Custer's amazing acts of bravery during this campaign may have resulted from suicidal impulses due to his romantic situation at the time.

p. 215: McIntosh's quote, "For God's sake, men, if ever you are going to stand . . ." is historical.

pp. 216+: These details are historical.

p. 218: The cannonading west of Gettysburg ended and Pickett's Charge began during this battle.

pp. 219-220: Miller's decision to disobey orders is factual and turned out to be a pivotal moment in the Battle of Gettysburg. The exchange with Hess is quoted verbatim from Miller's memoirs. (See note for pp. 222+.)

p. 221: Custer was again knocked from his mount, as depicted here.

pp. 221+: Everything "witnessed" by David is factual. Captain Miller's decision to disobey orders is one of the most under-reported "what ifs" in American history. His actions are credited with perhaps being the decisive factor in the outcome of the Battle of East Cavalry Field. If Stuart's cavalry had succeeded in raising havoc behind the Union lines just prior to Pickett's famous charge, the South may have won a decisive victory in the Battle of Gettysburg, and thus placed unbearable pressure on the Lincoln administration to sue for peace. Miller later earned the Congressional Medal of Honor for this decision.

pp. 223+: The details of the fight surrounding Hampton are factual.

pp. 227-228: Looters of the dead are an appalling fact in any war.

p. 228: The Union soldiers' nighttime picnic and the shell are historical.

Saturday, Independence Day, 1863

With Grant's capture of Vicksburg and Lee's defeat and retreat from Union soil, this date marked the beginning of the inevitable end to the Confederacy's attempt to win their Second War of Independence.

p. 231: Willow bark is a source of what we know as aspirin. "Laudable pus" was actually a sign of infection and should have been avoided.

p. 232: The heavy rain precluded any further action in the Battle of Gettysburg. The Union commander, Gen. George Meade, has been excoriated throughout history for allowing the Army of Northern Virginia to make good their escape in the following days. (Another "what if:" how many lives might have been saved had Meade succeeded in crushing Lee's army at this time?)

p. 238: Leah and Adam are fictional. According to the 1860 census, 186 African-Americans lived in Gettysburg; only 74 remained after the war. Many had fled in fear of being captured and enslaved by Rebels.

Sunday, July 5, 1863

pp. 244+: Here are more reminders that when it came to attitudes toward the Negro race, many Northerners and Southerners held the same views.

p. 244: Because of the large number of German descendants in Hanover, services at St. Matthew's continued to be held entirely in German until the 1930's. Even as late as the early 1940's, German was heard as often as English in Center Square.

p. 244: The Bible verse in German is Ephesians 2:8-10, the same as Jake read on the night of June 29. The hymn is Martin Luther's well known, "A Mighty Fortress is Our God."

p. 244: Lydia eventually married Jonas Serff. This scene is fictional.

Friday, July 10, 1863

p. 249: It is a widely held belief that laudanum addiction was prevalent during the Civil War. However, there appears to be little real evidence to support the theory of rampant abuse.

Saturday, July 11, 1863

p. 251: Parlors often became sickrooms. Cookbooks of the day included home remedies.

p. 251: A reticule is a drawstring purse.

Sunday, August 9, 1863

p. 264: Many soldiers wrote letters praising the outstanding care they received from the women of Hanover.

Monday, August 10, 1863

pp. 267+: The concept of marrying for love was still relatively new, especially in an area as conservative and traditional as Hanover. Parental approval was still of paramount concern.

p. 272: In 1890 the Mormon Church abandoned the practice of polygamy, under great pressure from society and the Federal government.

Thursday, September 10, 1863

p. 275: This information provided by General Gregg was actually related during the 50th Anniversary reunion in Hanover.

p. 276: The landau carriage design was very popular in Europe.

Monday, September 21, 1863

p. 278: Sam Forney did in fact move to Ohio. His romance with Myrtle is, of course, fictional.

p. 279: The Eerdmans are fictional. According to an 1872 map, an Eerdman owned the house I have the Beckers living in; thus, my contrivance to have Myrtle meet an "engaging" young Eerdman.

Monday, October 12, 1863

p. 285: The inscription on John Hoffacker's tombstone is factual. On a similar old tombstone in Indiana, someone scratched this added refrain: *To follow you I am not content, Until I know which way you went.*

Wednesday, November 18, 1863

pp. 286+: Jackie Melsheimer is historical, as is his offering of an apple to President Lincoln. His interaction with Jake is fictional.

pp. 287+: The description of Lincoln's visit to Hanover is factual, including verbatim quotes of Lincoln's and Rev. Alleman's words.

Thursday, November 19, 1863

pp. 291+: The details and descriptions of this historic event are factual.

p. 291: The tree in the background, right of center, still stands today. The Shriver and Pierce houses are on the left near the crest of the hill.

pp. 293-295: Few people today are familiar with the content of Everett's address. This provided the perfect opportunity to relate some of that content, juxtaposed with Jake's reactions.

p. 295: An article about the Address "from The Inquirer" appeared in the Nov. 27, 1863 issue of the *Hanover Spectator*. There is no direct evidence it was written by Mary Leader Shaw. A beautiful monument telling the account of her reporting the story stands by her gravesite in Hanover.

Monday, June 30, 1913

p. 298: An 1872 map of Hanover shows the location of "the Becker House" as in reality being owned by the Eerdman family. Therefore, the eventual marriage of Myrtle to Will Erdman. Thus, the carriage Jake had originally made for Myrtle turned out to be for her wedding after all.

pp. 298+: My great-great-grandfather, Joseph Robert Meredith, Sr., served as a private in the Union cavalry (13th PA, Company L) during the Civil War and saw limited action while on patrols in Virginia. Following the war, he went to seminary and became an itinerant preacher. The 1855 melodeon that his son, Marcus, used in similar services has been passed down through our family. Joseph's young son, Joseph Robert, Jr., met the tragic death described in the epilogue. My father, brother, and grandson are named Robert Joseph after these ancestors.

p. 299: The descriptions of the Square are factual, as per the photographs on pages 302-303, which are from a celebration in 1915.

pp. 299+: Johnnie Caitlin, former Union bugle boy, is historical, as is his encounter with an anonymous young lady from whom he received apple pie and milk as the battle began. His biographical details are also factual. In June of 1913 he returned to Hanover and placed an advertisement in the paper, hoping to meet the young lady from his past. He reports having met with her and, since she was married, he did not reveal her name publicly.

The Picket Monument
Hanover Center Square
Erected September 25, 1905

Union Veterans' Reunion (1899)

Original stereoscopic images of three photos used in the book.

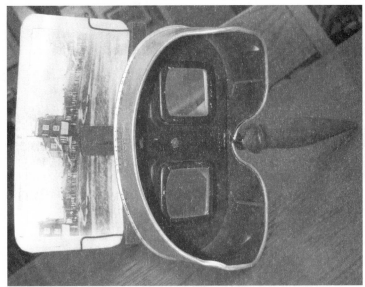

Stereoscopic 3D photograph viewer

Lincoln's train at Hanover Junction, east of Hanover,
4:00 PM, November 18, 1863.
Some people believe Lincoln is the man in the top hat, to the
right of the engine, standing off the platform.

Credits

From the Library of Congress, Prints & Photographs Division:
Gen. Judson Kilpatrick -- LC-DIG-cwpb-04870 DLC
Gen. George Custer -- LC-DIG-cwpbh-03216
Going into Action, W.H. Shelton -- LC-DIG-pga-02746
Gen. JEB Stuart -- LC-DIG-cwpb-07546
Gen. Wade Hampton -- LC-DIG-cwpb-07541
Widow White's House, Lee's Headquarters -- LC-DIG-cwpb-0165
Lincoln's Train at Hanover Junction -- LC-DIG-cwpb-01535 DLC

Public domain photograph courtesy of GettysburgDaily.com:
Procession viewing north along the Baltimore Pike

From the Smithsonian Libraries:
Dedication Ceremony -- (OCoLC)ocm04547223

Public domain photographs, Barbara Huston, Poist Studio, Hanover, PA:
Market Shed and Central Hotel, 1863
One of the earliest photographs in Hanover, 1845
Carlisle Street, c. 1870
Broadway and Center Square, viewing west, c. 1870
Abbottstown Road and the Reformed Church, c. 1870
Market Shed and Central Hotel, 1850's
From Center Square, viewing east onto Broadway, c. 19870
St. Mattthew's Church
Center Square, 1915
Aerial View of Center Square
Veterans' Reunion, 1899
Picket Monument
Original stereoscopic images of three photographs, (c. 1870)
Union cavalry counterattack, 100th Anniversary reenactment, 1963

Public Domain images from original items in author's collection:
Harper's Weekly, Aug. 17, 1861, p. 525 -- Bayoneting the Wounded
Harper's Weekly, Nov. 1, 1862, p. 698-699 – Stuart's Raid
Harper's Weekly, July 4, 1863, p. 417 -- Execution of Spies
Harper's Weekly, July 25, 1863, p. 477 – Rebels Shelling NY Militia
Harper's Weekly, Oct. 31, 1863, p. 692 -- Cavalry Charge
Harper's Weekly, Nov. 14, 1863, p. 721 – Thomas Addressing Negroes
Ladies of Hanover penny postcard
Stereoscopic 3D photograph viewer
Reenactment of fight at East Cavalry Field (2008)
Young women on cover and on p. 272: anonymous CDVs, date unknown

Public Domain Photograph from "A Photographic History Of the Civil War," Vol. 4, p. 282 (1911)
Gen. Fitzhugh Lee

Artwork by living artists:
The Tate Farm Road, by Lewis Francisco
The Felty Farm, by Edwin L. Green

Maps by Steven Stanley:
Battle of Hunterstown: 4:15-4:45 p.m.
Battle of Hunterstown: 4:45-5:15 p.m
Fight at Brinkerhoff's Ridge
East Cavalry Field Fight – 12:30-1:00 p.m.
East Cavalry Field Fight – 1:30-2:00 p.m.
East Cavalry Field Fight – 2:30-3:00 p.m.
East Cavalry Field Fight – 4:15-4:45 p.m.

Maps by John Heiser used by permission of Eric J. Wittenberg and J. David Petruzzi:
Battle of Hanover, Meeting Engagement
Battle of Hanover, Phase Two
Brinkerhoff's Ridge, Final Attack
Stuart's Ride

From the collection of the York County Heritage Trust, York, PA:
Map of Hanover from the 1860 Shearer & Lake Atlas

From the Library of Congress, Geography and Maps Division:
Field of Gettysburg map, T. Ditterline -- g3824g cw0331000

The Union cavalry counterattack at the 100th Anniversary
reenactment in 1963. The Central Hotel is on the right.
The author is in the crowd near the infantrymen on the right.

145th Anniversary reenactment of the fight at
East Cavalry Field, Gettysburg, PA (2008)

Acknowledgments

I would like to thank my wife, Betsy, for her patience, support, and endurance during the research and writing of this book. My wonderful sons, Christopher, Jonathan, and Nathan, each appear in small ways in various characters throughout the book.

A BIG THANK YOU to the following people:

Dianne E. Dusman, for her superb editorial insight and skill, for inspiration with characters and their development, for her ideas for improving the final edition, and for encouragement to produce a screenplay and audio edition.

Meg Irish, for her amazing eye for details and proofreading talents. Who ever thought a red pen could provide such polish? Thank you!

Sharon Cole, first draft editor, for her unflinching eye for historical detail, anachronisms, and mediocre writing. Ultimately, I followed her final words of advice and wrote the kind of novel I like to read.

Jennie Cole, for assistance editing the first draft and for exploring the plausibility of various actions described in the book.

All the "critters" in the Working Writers' Critique Group. Each one of you has left your mark in this work. I have learned so much from you all.

Lorae French, Andre French, and Betsy Meredith, for proofreading and critiquing the first draft.

As the bass trombone player with the Glimmerglass Opera, Catskill Symphony, and Utica Symphony, I often have extended passages in the music during which I do not play. Much of this book was written during those lulls. Thank you to maestro Charles Schneider and my fellow musicians for creating such a stimulating environment in which to work! A special word of thanks to fellow trombonist Dan Martin, whose timely nudges saved me from many late entrances.

Lea Holmes at Celestial Massage, for her healing touch which set off the four-month flurry of writing that culminated in the first draft. I had dealt with recurring health problems over the period of a few years, and her treatments made it possible to complete this book while continuing with my day job, appearing on stage in community theater, and performing with three orchestras and a brass quintet.

Tim Goard, for enhancing the illustrations from *Harper's Weekly* and *Frank Leslie's Illustrated*, and for retouching the "aerial" photo of Market Square. To contact him for freelance work: tgoard@nycap.rr.com

Poist Studios in Hanover, for their nice collection of nineteenth-century photos of downtown Hanover, and their work in producing the digital files for reproduction. Many more may be viewed on the book's website: www.TheUnfinishedWork.com

The Guthrie Public Library in Hanover, PA, and the volunteers who staff their outstanding resource, the Pennsylvania Room.

Eric Wittenberg and J.D. Petruzzi, for permission to use the maps created by John Heiser for their outstanding books, *Protecting the Flanks: The Battles for Brinkerhoff Ridge and East Cavalry Field, Battle of Gettysburg, July 2-3, 1863* and *Plenty of Blame to Go Around: Jeb Stuart's Controversial Ride to Gettysburg.*

Steven Stanley, cartographer, for permission to use his superb and enlightening maps. See his full color maps in *The Complete Gettysburg Guide* by J.D. Petruzzi and Steven Stanley, the definitive guide with driving tours of the Gettysburg Battlefield and surrounding area. His work is also widely distributed through the Civil War Preservation Trust.

Scott Mingus, author of several outstanding Civil War histories and host of Cannonball Blog, for feedback and corrections.

John T. Krepps, for his important research and book, *A Strong and Sudden Onslaught: The Cavalry Action at Hanover, Pennsylvania.*

My grandfather, C. Homer Meredith, for his work on the seminal resource for this book, *Prelude to Gettysburg: Encounter at Hanover.*

Please visit the book's website for an annotated bibliography of other key references. I am very grateful to build on the work of these authors.

P. Hobbs Allison and Bryan Carroll at Greenleaf Book group, for their help and guidance through the production process.

Lisa Woods, cover designer at Greenleaf Book Group, for the seminal concept and finished production of our design for this outstanding and evocative book cover.

Alyse French, for her photographic talents and the author's photo.

Christopher Meredith, for website hosting and design assistance.

Jonathan Meredith, for processing the first edition rear cover photo.

Nathan Meredith, for website content assistance.

My father, Robert Meredith, for proofreading and his unwavering love and support.

My stepmother, Florine Meredith, for input on the various aspects of the Pennsylvania Dutch way of doing things.

And my mother, Rosemary Neail Meredith (1934-68), who taught me to read and love books.

Visit the book's website at:
www.TheUnfinishedWork.com
for historical and contemporary photos,
reviews, links, selected bibliography,
and to order autographed copies.